Forbidden Blood

Felicity Heaton

CHAPTER 1

She shouldn't have looked.

Amber hurried through the dark side streets of central London, heading for the nearest Underground station. She glanced back over her shoulder. The man from the courtyard of the redbrick factory building stood on the other side of a busy road. The hood of his black coat obscured his face but Amber could feel his eyes on her—intent and cold.

She turned away, huddled up into her thin black suit jacket, and carried on walking. She could feel the man still staring at her.

The courtyard flashed across her mind. Two men with sacks and another sweeping disinfectant out into the street. She had never seen the wooden gates open before, but there was always a puddle of disinfectant outside in the mornings. What did they have in those bags? What were they trying to wash away?

Car headlights snapped her out of her thoughts. A white Audi sports car purred past her, rear lights flashing bright crimson in the darkness as it stopped at the junction ahead and then turned and roared away.

Amber undid the button on her jacket and one on her white shirt, hot from her leaving party and panic. She had to get a grip. She glanced back again, shifting her handbag on her shoulder. No one was there save a few Londoners making their way home from the pubs or going to nightclubs. She hated walking around the city so late at night. It always got her jittery and the few drinks she'd had with her work colleagues at the pub weren't helping.

It wasn't far to the Underground station. If she focused on thinking about good things, she would be there before she knew it and then she would feel foolish for being so nervous. She smiled when she thought about her leaving party. She had worked for the company for years, but it was time for a change and she couldn't wait to start her new life. In only a few weeks, she would be working in Paris. She would be able to see her brother more often and would be able to soak up a different culture. It seemed like a dream and she was so caught up in it that she didn't care about all the work she still had to do—the crash course in French, even though it was a British firm she was going to work for and there would be English speakers there, all the packing and things she had to arrange.

Amber turned down a narrow one-way street. A light on the wall of a building above her blinked on and off. Footsteps rang out behind her, echoing along the road. Pleasant daydreams about her future life in Paris disappeared. She walked faster, her heart beating quicker now as fearful thoughts crowded her mind.

She had almost reached the other end of the road when two men appeared, walking towards her. She went to cross the road to avoid them but they split up and motioned to each other. Her hazel eyes shot wide when she recognised them from the courtyard. She turned to go back the other way.

The hooded man stood at the other end of the street.

Amber searched for a way to get past him. Why had he followed her? Her heart beat harder. Long heavy black sacks. Pink disinfectant.

Bodies?

Blood?

A hand around her wrist sent a jolt through her and she tried to pull free. One man twisted her right arm behind her back and the other grabbed her left wrist. They pulled her backwards into the shadows.

Amber kicked her legs and opened her mouth to scream. A heavy gloved hand covered it. The smell of leather filled her nostrils and she breathed hard through her nose, staring wild-eyed at the man in front of her. The hood obscured his face but she could see his jaw, see the hint of a smile on his lips.

He nodded to the two men behind her and their grip increased. Amber flailed, desperate to escape. It was impossible. She stamped on their feet, kicked their legs, wriggled with all of her strength, but they wouldn't let her go.

The man motioned to one of the others holding her. The moment he removed his hand from her mouth, another covered it, keeping her silent. She tried to call out anyway, her eyes darting between her attackers and the street. The hooded man smiled at her, as though amused by the muffled sound and her panic.

Amber stilled when he reached inside his long black coat and pulled out a knife. Her eyes went round and her heart raced, fear thundering in her veins.

He was going to kill her.

She shook her head and didn't stop, not when the man took another step back and not even when he raised his left hand and drew the knife down the palm of his leather glove, cutting into his flesh beneath. Not a trace of pain showed on what she could see of his face. Was he trying to frighten her by showing how strong he was? She was already petrified. He stepped towards her and she redoubled her fight against the men, kicking with all of her might.

"Hurry," the man to her right said in a low voice as her heel connected with his shin. "Get to it already."

Tears rolled down her cheeks and a chill swept in constant waves over her skin, stealing her strength. She shook her head again and begged the man not to hurt her, but the other man's hand over her mouth turned her words into nothing more than a frightened murmur. Futile.

The hooded man stepped up to her, balled his cut hand into a fist, and raised it towards her face. What was he going to do? She kept her eyes fixed on the knife in his other hand, afraid that he would stab her if she dared to look away from it.

She gasped when the man holding her mouth released it but didn't have time to call out for help. He pressed his fingers into her cheeks, forced her mouth open and tilted her head back. Her gaze snapped to the hooded man's hand. He held it above her and drops of blood trembled on the edge of his black glove.

He was going to make her drink his blood.

She tried to move but couldn't. The men's grip on her increased again, fingers pressing hard into her arms, bruising her. The drop fell, landing on her tongue, and another quickly followed it. The hooded man tightened his fist and more dripped into her mouth. She tried not to swallow, didn't want to taste his blood. It slid down her throat, one drop after another, until she wanted to be sick.

And then she felt strange.

A hollow feeling opened inside her and her mind emptied.

His hand hovered above her, feeding her blood, and it no longer felt repulsive or frightening. It tasted good. Thick, heavy fog rolled into her mind, weighing her head down. She closed her eyes and then struggled to open them again.

The men behind her released her arms.

Amber stood there facing the hooded man, her shoulders relaxed and her head tilted to one side. He wavered in her vision as he raised the knife and licked the blade. It didn't scare her. Her handbag slid down her right arm to the crook of her elbow as she raised her hand. She held it out to him, palm up, and blinked languidly.

He took it in his, so gently that she smiled, and ran the knife over her palm. The sting of pain was pleasurable, flooding her with hazy warmth from head to toe, awakening blissful awareness of his touch and his hungry intent.

The man lifted her hand towards his mouth and dipped his head. Was he going to kiss it better? She continued to smile, amused by his chivalry.

What a nice man.

His tongue came out. White lights flashed across him.

They blinded her and she flinched away, afraid of the bright light that drowned out the world. The man released her hand and was behind her in an instant. Her handbag dropped to the floor and she tried to blink away the white spots in her vision and they multiplied.

The sound of footsteps echoed in her mind and she cursed the other men for fleeing. They would pay for leaving her here to deal with this Venator.

Her hands tightened into fists.

She couldn't risk fighting the Venator but she had to taste the blood. She raised her hand towards her mouth. This was an unexpected twist but she could work it in her favour. First, she had to be sure she was a Source, and then she would take care of the Venator.

What was a Source?

3

She stopped with her hand mid-way to her mouth. Blood pooled on her palm, black in the low light.

What was she doing?

The door of the white car opened and Amber looked at it. It was the Audi. A man stepped out and she moved back. Damn interfering Venator.

Amber frowned at her thoughts. What was a Venator? What was going on? She tried to remember but her thoughts became tangled with others, ones she didn't understand. They didn't feel as though they were her own.

She turned towards the hooded man. The car lights shone on the lower half of his face, highlighting his jaw and mouth. A tilt of a smile touched his lips. She needed to taste the blood.

"Get in the car," a male voice said behind her, deep and intense.

She refused. She had to taste the blood and then leave. She raised her hand and poked her tongue out. A taste was all it would take. Then she would know. "Now!"

Amber jumped, startled by the volume of that word. She looked at her palm, horrified by what she had been about to do, and then at the hooded man. He continued to smile at her and she felt compelled to do as he silently wished.

"Car, now!" the man behind her said. He was right. She had to get away from the man who had cut her but she couldn't move.

Her thoughts became strange and distant again, and no matter how many times she told herself to run, her feet wouldn't cooperate. She wanted to go with the hooded man, even though she knew he would kill her.

Her head spun.

She took a step towards him, her mind heavy and thick again.

Someone grabbed her arm from behind and then a bright blue flash burst out of the corner of her eye. She stared at the silver handgun beside her head and the strange blue marks on the man's hand. They glowed. Shiny. Amber reached out to touch them.

The new man moved his arm away from her and pulled her back, so she was almost behind him. She tried to focus on his arm and the gun. The fog descended on her mind again, swamping everything, turning her numb and empty. Her gaze moved of its own accord, shifting to the man's face. Silver hair. Green eyes. Damned Venator.

She struggled against his grip, clawing at his hand.

"Calm down." He glanced at her and then back at the hooded man. "Lower the knife and come peacefully."

"Peacefully?" She yanked on her arm in an attempt to free herself, twisting her wrist in his tight grip and not caring that it hurt. She had to get away from him. The silver-haired man turned her way, his vivid green eyes bright in the car headlights and boring into hers. She sneered. "I will never come peacefully, Venator."

"Let her go," he said and she shook her head.

Amber kept shaking it, trying to clear the weird dull feeling and get her mind into order. How did she know this man? The knowledge she sought shifted and evaded her grasp, as though it was a living thing and could anticipate her. The haze in her head lifted long enough that she saw the silver-haired man clearly at last. His eyes were cold as he stared into hers, pupils narrowed and an edge of darkness about his handsome face.

"I said, let her go." He turned to the hooded man.

Amber looked there too. She couldn't see them, but she could feel his eyes on her, and could feel him inside her head and her body. She scrubbed her throat with her hand, her mouth, trying to get him out of her. The silver-haired man held her tighter. What was he waiting for? Shoot him. He had tried to kill her. He had put something inside her and now she felt strange.

The silver-haired man started to pull the trigger.

"No!" she screamed and knocked his hand away. She stared at his raised gun and her outstretched hand. What the hell was she doing? She wanted the man dead, so why had she stopped him?

The man holding her shoved her backwards and then ducked away from her. A silver streak shot past her wide eyes. The knife clattered to the floor a short distance behind her and a thin dark line flowed down the man's neck from his ear, soaking into his white shirt. He raised his gun again but she grabbed it and pulled it around to point at her.

He froze.

The hooded man laughed.

Amber's gaze shot from the barrel of the gun to him. She stared at his mouth.

Fangs.

He grinned and it felt as though he was looking straight through her. Whispered voices filled her head, clashing with each other so she couldn't make out what they were saying. She tried to focus on one of them but couldn't. The clamour in her mind rose and a deep sense that she wasn't alone washed through her. Someone else was in her head with her. The hooded man's smile widened. Him. How? One of the voices rang out above the rest and her questions fell away, leaving her docile again. He knew something about her that she didn't. Something important. She had to know too.

She took a step towards him and he was gone, leaving the street empty in front of her. Why? She went to walk after him and frowned when her arm lagged behind her, held fast by something. Her eyes drifted to her wrist and the hand tightly grasping it.

"Are you all right?" the silver-haired man said and her head suddenly felt lighter.

Her gaze ran up his left arm to his shoulder. A trail of blood stained his white shirt and she followed the drips and dashes downwards to the black holster around his shoulders. His gun was in it but not secured. If she made a lunge for it, would he reach it before her? Amber shook that thought away.

This man had saved her. Why would she do such a thing to him? Because he was dangerous. She didn't want to go with him. She wanted to find the man. The feeling ran deep in her blood, flowing through her veins, compelling her. She needed to find the man.

This Venator would be her downfall.

Amber shook her head again and the haze in her mind dissipated for long enough that she felt her normal self again. Her panic and fear returned full force, crashing over her. What was happening to her? She kept thinking about things she wasn't familiar with, like Venators and Sources, and wanted to do things that went against her nature, like injuring someone.

The man held his bleeding ear with his right hand. There were pale tribal markings on it. They wove down over his wrist and under his white shirtsleeve. Those markings had glowed ethereally earlier. She couldn't have imagined it.

"You need to come with me," he said, and before she could take in what was happening, he dragged her to the white Audi R8 and pushed her into it on the passenger side.

He closed the door, picked up the knife and her handbag from the pavement, and rounded the car. Amber sat there, thoughtless and empty, her eyes fixed on the spot where the hooded man had been. She should have gone with him.

No. She shouldn't have. She didn't know what she was thinking anymore.

The car moved and she became gradually aware of the man next to her. Her gaze slid to him. He was handsome, his green eyes fixed on the road now, shadowed by a frown of concentration, and the messy finger-length strands of his silver hair brushed back out of his face. He didn't look old enough to have such white hair. He seemed barely five years her senior.

Venator.

It echoed in her head, as though something inside her knew it applied to him even when she had never heard the word before tonight.

"What is your name?" His deep voice soothed her, easing away some of her tension even when she felt she should be on alert, or escaping.

Amber didn't reply. Her eyes dropped to the gun tucked under his left arm when he clipped the leather strap over it, securing it in place. It unnerved her but not as much as the fact that she wanted to use it against him, or the fact that his arm had glowed blue and the other man had fangs. None of that made sense, even when she felt it did.

The man looked at her and she glanced up, meeting his gaze. The streetlights flashed on his face, stealing all colour and warmth from his eyes. They were so cold that she couldn't tear hers away. She stared into them, chilled by the detached air that he emanated but fascinated by him at the same time. Was he as empty inside as his eyes? She had never met anyone who looked as hollow and emotionless as this man did. Something terrible must have happened to him to make him look this way.

She remembered the way his arm had glowed.

Inhuman.

Her head spun.

Venator.

She wanted to get away from him. Her priority was to escape, not fall under a spell.

They pulled to a halt at a set of traffic lights and her hand went straight for the door. She shoved it open and the man grabbed her, pulling her back against him. The door slammed shut without her touching it and the locks clunked into place. She elbowed the man in the ribs, struggled out of his grip and lunged for the door again, frantically tugging on the handle. It wouldn't open. Her eyes darted over the moulded leather of the door. No way of unlocking it. The Venator would stop her before she could find the button on the dashboard that would unlock the doors. She spat out a curse. Never mind. If she couldn't escape, she could at least taste her blood.

"You cannot leave. You are in too much danger out there."

Amber stared down at the cut on her right palm. It had bled all over her trousers.

She had to lick the blood and taste it.

She raised her hand but the man caught her wrist.

"What happened?" He frowned at the cut.

Amber tried to get her hand back but his grip was vice tight. Interfering Venator. She gritted her teeth and twisted her arm. He didn't let go. Her stomach turned when she saw the blood on her palm and her vision distorted. She stopped struggling and looked at the man. His expression was soft, silently reassuring, and the longer she stared at him, the calmer she felt, until the sense that she wasn't in control of herself disappeared again.

Amber tried to remember what had happened to her hand but it slipped through her fingers every time she came close, as though she didn't really want to recall it.

"He gave you his blood, didn't he?"

That memory popped to the forefront of her mind and she nodded. The man had made her drink his blood. It had been disgusting and she could feel it inside her.

"Hold on." He released her hand, put the car into gear and roared off the white line.

Amber did. She grabbed the edge of the seat with her left hand as they raced through the streets of London so fast they were a blur. She couldn't take her eyes off the road and the cars as they swerved around them, barely missing each one. Her heart lodged in her throat, her right hand trembling where she held it out in front of her. What was happening? It felt as though she had slipped into some dreadful fantasy world and she wanted out.

He turned the car around a corner so sharply that the tyres screeched and she slammed against the door, and then they were going down a slope towards an underground garage. The car spun around in the brightly lit space, coming to a halt facing the exit, and the engine cut out. A grey shutter slowly rolled down, eclipsing the world outside.

Amber stared at it, still trying to catch up.

The man had given her blood, and then he had cut her. She needed to taste her blood before the Venator stopped her. She was about to lick her palm when the door beside her opened and he pulled her out of the car.

"Damned Venator!" She kneed him in the groin and ran for the garage door.

He reached it before her and stood in her path, his eyes darker and colder than ever. He glared at her and drew his gun.

"Let her go," he whispered, voice strained.

She grinned, satisfied by the pain in his voice.

"No." Amber tried to pass him.

"You do not want to leave, woman. You do not want to do as he bids."

Amber stopped. "As who bids?"

The strange feeling inside her grew worse, something telling her to keep going and not listen to him. She had to get past the man and drink her blood. That was all that mattered now.

"Listen to my voice." He put the gun away and stepped up to her.

The moment his hands touched her shoulders, Amber felt different. She stared into his eyes and her thoughts fell into better order, enough that she could recall things clearly again.

Her heart pounded.

"The man made me drink his blood... I saw him in that place with the gates and the disinfectant and then they were after me. He cut me." She held her hand out and it trembled between them, fluttering in time with her heart. "I just want to go home. I want this nightmare to end. Please? I can't take this. Please?"

The man stepped back, his eyes still fixed intently on her face, the frown not leaving his.

"The man will come for you."

"Fangs," she whispered and her eyes widened. Her heart missed a beat and then slammed painfully against her ribs. "He had fangs. He was going to drink my blood."

"I will not hurt you. You must ignore your instincts and listen to me. I will not allow him to harm you. You will be safe here," he said, so calmly and softly that the deep waves of fear surging through her eased to gentle ripples. "He will find you if you leave. I can protect you. I will not allow the man to harm you."

Amber looked at the closed garage door and then back at him.

There was honesty in his green eyes and her options were limited. Either she stayed here with him, or she ventured outside where there were monsters.

If she did that, and the man found her, she wouldn't escape him a second time. He had fangs. He had been about to drink her blood.

Something inside her said that she would be fine outside, and that she wanted to find the hooded man again. She wanted him to taste her blood. Desired it more than anything. This man was lying to her.

No. Amber closed her eyes, battling the compulsion to leave, and then looked back into the silver-haired man's eyes.

The other man had wanted to kill her and drink her blood. This man had saved her. He said he could protect her.

"I will bandage your hand and make you feel better if you come upstairs," he said in a low voice, one that soothed her ears and quelled her fear. The desire to escape him drifted away, replaced by a need to remain.

"Will you tell me what's happening to me? I feel strange."

He held his hand out, pointing to his left. "If you come with me."

Amber looked at the dark grey metal door far to her right across the empty garage and then back at the man. His gaze held hers, cold but honest, and she ignored the voice inside her that was screaming for her to leave and taste her blood.

She nodded and went with him.

CHAPTER 2

Kearn closed the door to his apartment behind them and locked it. It wouldn't stop the man from entering if he wanted to reclaim the woman, but it would make her feel safer. He walked past her where she stood in the middle of the large white open plan room holding her black leather handbag and pointed towards the living area to his right beyond the modern fireplace that divided it from the study near the door. She followed him and stopped near the back of the long low black couch that faced the wide bank of windows, setting her bag down on the cushions. She stared out of the windows, her hazel eyes bright with fascination. He had grown bored of the view of London from his apartment a long time ago. He rarely looked out at the rooftops now.

He looked at her instead. She reached up and removed the band from her messy ponytail, freeing her long brown hair. It fell down in loose waves over her shoulders and blended into her black suit jacket. Its rich shade contrasted against her pale face. The colour was gone from her skin, the only visible sign of her ordeal. She placed the band around her wrist and then stood with her left hand clutching her right, the palm of that hand turned upwards, crimson staining it. She remained still and he frowned after a few minutes. Had she slipped into shock? He couldn't sense it in her.

She seemed incredibly calm considering everything that had happened to her and her situation. A little too docile for his liking. He studied her. It wasn't normal for a human to be so unafraid after everything she had experienced. He had expected her to put up more of a fight about remaining with him and coming up to his apartment.

The man had given his blood to her. She was under his influence. It would explain why she was so at ease and why not a trace of fear laced her scent. The man wasn't afraid, so she wasn't either.

Kearn kept his guard up and approached her. She wasn't herself and wouldn't be until her body had eradicated the man's blood from her system. She had flitted between afraid and angry during the journey here and in the garage. The man was using his blood to control her.

"Make yourself comfortable." He stripped off his holster and then his white shirt.

Her gaze moved to him. It roamed unabashed over his body. He headed back to the door and tossed the ruined white shirt onto the floor of the beech wood kitchen. When he turned around, the woman didn't take her eyes off him. She continued to stare at his torso. He touched his ear and then frowned at the blood on his fingers. Without looking at the woman, he crossed the room to the bedroom door and opened it. He dropped the holster and his gun onto the deep brown duvet covering his double bed to his right and then flicked the light on. The dark earthy walls and low lighting in his bedroom soothed his tired eyes.

Kearn touched his ear again and walked straight through the gap between the foot of his bed and the built-in wardrobe, heading for the door across the room. He flinched when he turned the light on in the en-suite bathroom. He needed to put a dimmer one in at some point but it always slipped his mind. The white tiles bounced the light around, making it too bright for him. He looked into the large black-framed rectangular mirror that occupied the wall above the wide black sink cabinet in front of him. The cut had already started to heal but he still needed to help it along, if only to stop it from bleeding down another shirt.

He washed the blood off his neck and chest, watching the red swirl down the drain of the white oval sink. The cut began to bleed again. He took a small dark brown hand towel off the side of the black cabinet, dabbed his ear to dry it, and set it back down. Before his earlobe could bleed, he spat on his index and forefinger, and rubbed the saliva into the nick. It stung. The man hadn't been aiming at the woman. He had wanted to use her distracting him as a chance to kill him.

He should have realised sooner that the woman was under his control.

Kearn stared in the mirror, through his bedroom to the main room of the large open plan apartment. The knife in his car would yield nothing. Only her blood had been on it and the man had been wearing gloves. The woman was his only clue, and the best one he'd had since he had started hunting this man three years ago.

He looked at his reflection and cursed the sight of it. It was still strange to him. Not himself staring back at him but someone else. He hadn't seen himself in the mirror for over one hundred years, and he never would again.

He crouched, opened the two doors on the sink cabinet, and took out anything that would help a human heal. There wasn't much. He could only offer bandages.

Or he could help her heal.

Kearn shoved that thought away.

It wasn't going to happen. The woman was a lead and that was all. Her wound would heal with time. He didn't need to interfere. If she were a Source Blood as he suspected, then drinking from her would be dangerous.

He grabbed a fresh black shirt from the built-in oak wardrobe in his bedroom and then walked out into the living room. The woman looked up from the couch facing the window, her hand still held in front of her. It was bleeding badly, filling his apartment with the sweet scent of blood.

Kearn stopped beside the couch that lined the wall between the living area and his bedroom.

He wasn't sure what to do with the cut or with her. He had never worked with a human before nor had this sort of contact with one. Normally they were dead by the time he met them. The thought of tending to one was disgusting, but she was the lead he had been searching for. He was sure that the man who had attacked her was part of the group he was after, if not the leader. They had been testing her in the side road, and the man had been powerful enough to control her and make her try to drink her own blood even at a great distance. He would have to be a Lesser Noble or a Noble to be able to determine through their connection alone whether she was a Source Blood.

The woman continued to look at him, a dull edge to her hazel eyes. The man's blood was still affecting her. Kearn scanned the separate areas of the room. There was nothing she would be able to reach before him and use as a weapon, and she was only human so the furniture posed no threat. She wouldn't hurt him if she used her fists, although she had done a good job with her knee back in the garage. He placed the bandages down on the large square wooden coffee table in front of her.

Her gaze followed him across the room, unmoving from his back as he went into the kitchen. He filled a clear bowl with warm water and placed it down on the black granite work surface while he unravelled a wad of paper towel from the roll. He crossed the room back to her and placed the bowl and paper towels down next to the bandages. She watched intently as he put his black shirt on, leaving it unbuttoned, and then looked at her hand when he came to sit beside her.

This close to her, the smell of blood was overwhelming.

Kearn clamped his teeth shut and held the change at bay. It had been too long since he had smelt anything like her and it pushed at his control. He had been able to subdue the effect of her scent when he had been at a distance from her, but he couldn't contain it now. His gut clenched and twisted, saliva pooling in his mouth and his fangs itching to extend as hunger to taste the blood that went with the divine scent tore through him.

"Keep still," he said from between his teeth and soaked some of the paper towel.

Kearn took her hand in his and forced himself to focus. Her skin was warm and soft, and he used his senses to see how much vampire blood was in her system. Enough to keep her under control and stop her from answering his questions. He had promised that he would make her feel better. He only had one way of doing that and he wasn't sure if he wanted to go through with it or not.

He wiped the blood from her hand. It mixed with the water and covered his, ran down his arms in beautiful rivulets, soaking into his shirtsleeves. He slowed without thinking, fascinated by how her blood blossomed on the surface of the cut and savouring the warm alluring smell. He swallowed the burning ache in his throat and focused. She inhaled sharply when he wiped the blood away again and he grabbed the bandage. He wound it around her hand as quickly as possible and pinned it on her palm. The smell of blood lessened but it was all over his hands. He licked his lips. The fiery thirst in his veins begged him to quench it. Did he really want to do this?

"Why did he make me do that?" she whispered and Kearn looked at her. There were tears in her eyes as she stared at her hand. They trembled on the brink of falling. Her feelings travelled through their joined hands, filling him with a sense of fear and confusion. He released her fingers and sat back.

"There is a reason he made you drink his blood. It will help him find you, which is why I need to keep you with me."

She didn't seem shocked by what he had said. He had expected her to react with disbelief or horror. Perhaps the blood in her veins and what she had witnessed was enough to make her believe him.

"Why did he cut me?" She raised her hand and toyed with the bandage. The blood was already soaking into the edges of it.

Kearn looked down at the scarlet ambrosia coating his hands. "Your blood may be of a type which is valuable to his kind."

He curled his fingers into fists. They shook.

"I must wash my hands." He stood and headed straight through his bedroom and into the white and black bathroom. He stared at his hands. The blood looked even redder against the white sink beneath them. They trembled uncontrollably.

Did he really want to do this?

He needed answers and to get them he needed to eradicate any control the vampire might have over her.

Kearn lifted his hand to his nose and sniffed the blood. It smelt strong and enticing. His mouth watered. He took a deep breath followed by another two, trying to prepare himself. This could be a grave mistake.

Closing his eyes, he tentatively reached out towards his fingers with his tongue. The moment the blood touched it, a jolt rocked his body. She was definitely a Source Blood. He hadn't tasted forbidden blood since becoming a Venator but he hadn't forgotten the effects.

He licked his finger and swallowed. The jolt became an intense buzz and his fangs extended. His eyes shot open and familiar red ones looked back at him from his reflection, a fragment of the real him that he didn't often see. He grasped the edge of the cabinet with his other hand to steady himself and then licked the blood off his other fingers, gaining pace. He needed more. Just a little more, so he would be sure of his ability to command her and clear her blood of interference. That was the only reason he had to suck each of his fingers clean. It had nothing to do with the delightful way her blood made him tremble, made his breath stutter and his heart beat faster, at an almost human speed.

He went to lick the blood from his palm and stopped himself. Unpeeling his fingers from the edge of the cabinet, he forced himself to turn on the tap. The water ran fast and hard down the drain but he couldn't bring himself to put his hands under it and wash the blood away. He only wanted a little more. A warm pulsing feeling relaxed every muscle in his body and his head felt light. His eyelids fell to half-mast and the warm buzz became a hot inferno in his blood, an ache to feed and give in to his animal instincts. His breath shuddered. Just a little more.

No.

Stop it.

Kearn forced his head under the water instead of his hands but it did nothing to stop the hunger gnawing his stomach and the hard ache in his trousers. He groaned under his breath and kept his head under the freezing water, begging it to clear. He didn't want to remember.

High laughter. The scent of sex. The mindless lust. The painful betrayal. The blood on his hands.

He didn't want to remember any of it.

He didn't want to feel that way again.

Kearn squeezed his eyes shut and shoved his hands under the water the moment he pulled his head out of it. The scent of blood instantly diminished and his control came creeping back. He focused on it, trying to expel the effects of her blood on him. It was difficult. Her blood was more potent than what he had experienced before. He had never had blood direct from a Source, only diluted from another's veins. He closed his eyes and kept his hands under the water, gradually clawing back a sense of calm and shutting his rampaging feelings down.

The cold water numbed his hands. He kept them there, not trusting himself. If any trace of her blood remained on his skin, he would be tempted to lick it off, and it would undo all the work he had done to regain some control over himself. He grabbed the bar of soap from the side of the basin and washed his hands with it, erasing every drop of crimson on his pale skin. When he had been washing them for nearly ten minutes, he turned off the tap.

He glanced at himself in the mirror.

His eyes were still red.

The colour of blood.

Kearn focused on thinking over everything that had happened tonight. The woman was lucky that he had been patrolling the area and had smelt the blood. It had been the vampire's blood that had caught his attention, carried on the night air in a rich vein that had been easy to detect. Unfortunately, he couldn't use its scent to recognise the man. Vampire blood all smelt the same. Heavy and strong.

Human blood was a light fragrance. He resisted the temptation to take a deep breath and see if he could smell her blood. He was almost in control again.

The knife, the vampire's blood, the man's appearance, none of it was the break he needed.

But she was.

He looked at himself in the mirror again. Green eyes welcomed him back, cold and empty, familiar in their darkness. He turned away from them, hating the sight, and walked back through the bedroom to the living room.

The woman was still fraying the ends of the bandage around her right hand. Her gaze fixed on him and she frowned. Water dripped from the jagged tips of his silver hair and soaked into his black shirt. He raked his hair back, picked up the bowl and paper towels, and walked past her to the kitchen area. Her eyes followed his every move, her focus intent on him. She could look all she wanted. She wasn't going to figure him out, not even with her blood in his veins.

"Are you feeling any better?" Kearn ignored the warm sedated buzz in the depths of his bones that constantly switched between whispering hungry words to him and making him want to smile. He felt normal. There was no reason to get ideas about her blood. He was in control and she was nothing but a lead.

Not dinner.

He couldn't kill a human.

"Just now." Her voice ran as deep in his veins as her blood, teasing his senses. The soft sound of it wrapped around him, caressing him and making him want to look at her. He ignored it too. It was just her blood affecting him. "My head feels clearer."

That was what he had wanted to hear. It was difficult to use her blood in his veins purely to control the effect of the vampire's on hers rather than controlling her, but he would keep it up for as long as he could. Soon her blood should have cleared enough that the vampire wouldn't be able to control her at any great distance.

Kearn filled a glass with water and carried it back to her. He placed it on the coffee table in front of her and then sat beside her again. The smell of her blood drifted on the air and flowed down into his lungs with each breath he drew, pushing at his restraint. He had never smelt anything as alluring and tempting.

The connection between their blood shattered.

"What was he?" she said without any hint of trepidation.

"I'm sorry?" He tried for confused while he struggled against her blood and the vampire's. The bastard was pushing for control.

The woman scratched at the bandage. Kearn kept an eye on her. If she made any move to open the bandage, he would stop her and restrain her. Until then, he would keep fighting the vampire's hold over her.

"I'm not crazy, and I know what I saw would make me sound as though I am, but I wasn't imagining it." Her hand left her other one and settled on her thigh.

He made the mistake of looking at it. There were damp spots on the black material of her trousers. Blood. Delicious, fragrant, blood. Diverting his eyes before they changed again, he stared out of the window.

She leaned forwards into view and frowned at him. "That man had fangs. They couldn't have been fake. It all felt so real. He wanted to drink my blood... I felt it inside me. Some dark hideous hunger. He had some sort of power over me. Now either tell me I'm insane and heading for a spell at the nearest asylum, or tell me the truth. He's a vampire."

Kearn's silver eyebrows rose. There was no point in lying to her if she had already figured out what she was up against and believed it.

He nodded.

She gasped and grabbed his hand. The contact sent a sharp jolt through him and pushed at his control. Her blood called to him. The same dark hideous hunger she had sensed in the man. He fought his desire to look at the smooth column of her throat, knowing that if he did he wouldn't be able to stop himself from licking it and acting out his desire to sink his fangs into the soft flesh and drink his fill of her.

Instead, he kept his eyes fixed on her face and was struck by a different sort of hunger.

She was beautiful.

He had never paid much attention to humans. They had been nothing more than a mission to him for centuries and only a meal before that, but now he had stopped to look at one and some part of him wished he hadn't because she mesmerised him.

Her wide round hazel eyes were fascinating. The overhead lights of his apartment played on them, highlighting the flecks of gold and green. Long wavy brown hair caressed her face, cascading over slender shoulders. Rosy lips spoke to him and he didn't hear a word they said. He watched the way they moved and the sensual shapes they made, and the tiny flash of soft pink tongue against straight white teeth.

"What's a Venator?"

That question broke his reverie.

"Me."

"You?" She stared blankly at him. No, through him. She was trying to remember something. "I knew that word. I wanted you to kill that man and then I wanted to stop you. I knew you. There was something else too. I wanted to taste my blood."

She sounded as confused as she felt.

"The man desired to test you to see if you were a Source Blood."

"Source. I knew that word too and that it meant something different. You said my blood is valuable."

"It is." He picked up the glass and offered it to her. The water would thin her blood and lessen the vampire's control over her, but it would weaken his too. It was a risk he had to take. "It is very valuable on the black market but also extremely illegal. My job is to find those who dare break the law by attempting to purchase, sell or harvest the blood."

No fear touched her features but he could feel an underlying sense of nerves in his veins that belonged to her.

He studied her blood and the strength flowing through it surprised him. Her blood within him, and the vampire's within her, was enough to convince her that she wasn't going insane and that everything that had happened tonight was real. She understood and accepted it, and had even found some sense of resolve to face it all. He had expected her to be more fragile and sensitive, to panic and plead him to protect her. Her calm acceptance of the situation made him reassess his earlier thoughts about her. It wasn't the vampire's blood in her veins that made her unafraid. It was her own natural strength, and it only added to her beauty.

"Why is it worth so much? Are all humans Source Bloods to vampires?" She took the glass, tilted her head back and drank some of the water.

Kearn refused to look at her throat.

"No. Source Bloods are very rare. It refers to a specific gene in your blood that affects vampires. Vampires believe that millennia ago, they branched away from humanity and evolved separately. At that time, the same gene in their blood was stronger. Over the generations, it weakened to what it is today and has remained that way."

She frowned and lowered the glass. "So I share a gene with vampires?"

He nodded. "Your bloodline did not evolve and gain the ability to use the power that gene gives you."

She swallowed and a sense of unease ran in his veins. Her blood. It was potent. He was constantly aware of it and how it mixed with his, stirred it to a frenzy of hunger and need. Kearn shifted his focus back to her, using all of his strength to keep it pinned on her and not his blood.

"I'm like a vampire?"

"No, you are human, but different. Special."

A hint of colour touched her cheeks and she dropped her gaze. He raised an eyebrow at her reaction and cocked his head to one side. Her blood whispered warm words at him, teasing him into submitting to her. She had watched him earlier when he had removed his shirt and sometimes her pupils dilated until they darkened her hazel eyes. Desire? Was she attracted to him? A human? As though he could desire such a weak creature in return.

The colour on her cheeks deepened, sending a gut-tugging jolt through his blood, and his lips parted. He swallowed when she shyly raised her eyes and looked at him through her dark lashes. His body burned with the desire to sweep her into his arms and taste her again. Kearn forced his eyes down to the floor. It was just her blood commanding him to do as she wanted. It wasn't his desire.

It couldn't be.

He cleared his throat and frowned, trying to make sense of the feelings running riot in him. Not all of them could be hers. Some of them had to be his.

"Do vampires only drink from people like me?" Her voice shook and he was tempted to touch her hand again to reassure her, but restrained himself.

If he did such a thing, he would have a hard time resisting pulling her against him and slaking his growing thirst for her. Taking her blood had been a mistake. He had less control over himself than he had anticipated. He had forgotten how potent Source Blood was.

"Vampires gain sustenance from all human blood. Source Blood is different. It is a drug to vampires. Most only drink enough to produce a natural high that makes them giddy and removes their inhibitions." He battled his need to look at her throat. "Others are seeking something more sinister. In a large enough dose, it temporarily restores the strength in the shared gene, enhancing them and reinstating the devastating power they once commanded. With enough Source Blood in their veins they would become living gods."

His gaze slid to her neck and he turned away, cursing himself for tasting her. He had needed to be sure that she was a Source Blood though and needed to calm her enough to get answers.

"That man knew I was a Source Blood and that's why he followed me?"

"No." Kearn shook his head, as much to clear it of the whispered command to feast on her as to answer her. "Source Blood is difficult to detect if the human is not bleeding. You said he gave you his blood. He was seeking to turn you compliant so he could kill you. When his blood joined with yours, he realised that you were different. Your blood saved you."

"It doesn't feel as though it saved me. I feel as though it damned me."

Would she rather be dead than in this situation? He glanced at her out of the corner of his eye. He couldn't sense any fear in her, but there was an edge to her eyes, a look that said she was desperately trying to be strong but everything was beginning to take its toll on her.

"I will protect you," he said and felt her look at him. He couldn't meet her gaze, not yet, not until the need to look at her throat and taste her blood had passed again. "If you help me, we can find the man who hurt you. I have been searching for him for three years. If we can capture him, you can go back to your life. No one else will know what your blood contains."

"What will happen to him?"

"He will be sentenced." He looked at her now, trusting himself not to change and frighten her. She wasn't likely to help him if she knew that he was also a vampire.

"Are you a cop? Is that what a Venator is?"

"No—sort of. I have to carry out the sentence on the people whose names are given to me by my... bosses." He had never needed to explain his position before. It was difficult to put it into words that didn't sound medieval or make him a murderer. He hunted those the Sovereignty deemed had broken the law. He sentenced them to eternal darkness. Usually they knew the name of the law-breaker. This time there wasn't one. There had only been a location to start looking. "Will you help me?"

He didn't really need her to answer. Either way he wasn't letting her leave. He needed her and she was going to help him, although he would prefer that she did so of her own free will. Forcing her wouldn't solve anything but he would if she left him no choice.

"He'll come after me." She looked down at her hands, playing with the bandage again. Her pulse began to pick up pace and he sensed her rising panic. Was she remembering what had happened to her? Her blood inside him whispered of fear and death. She looked up at him, blinked away her tears and nodded. "I'll help you if you promise to keep me safe."

"It is a promise." Kearn tried to think of how humans made deals. He held his hand out to her.

She slipped hers into it and shook it a single time, and then her hand lingered in his.

And his eyes fell to her neck.

"Do you remember anything else?" he whispered, those words distant to his ears as he perused the gentle sloping grace of her throat.

Her hand left his and he dragged his eyes away, forcing them up to hers. They were watching him again, giving him the impression that she was looking for a secret or trying to see past his exterior and down to his heart. It wasn't going to happen.

Kearn stood and walked around the square coffee table to the windows. He placed his hands behind his back. The rooftops of London stretched into the distance, lights twinkling in the darkness. It was barely past midnight. The night still lay before him.

"The man was in a courtyard. They're always cleaning it with disinfectant in the morning. The other two, the ones who held me, were there too, carrying black sacks over their shoulders."

Kearn frowned.

A storehouse?

He turned to face her.

"I need you to show me this place," he said and she nodded. "And we need to lure the man out. The man will want to finish what he started and test your blood. He will come looking for you. I will keep my promise and see to it that nothing happens to you. Would you be willing to act as bait?"

She didn't look so sure now. She was silent and a myriad of emotions flickered in her hazel eyes.

A sense of resolve laced his blood. Her resolve.

She nodded.

"If it will get rid of that man, I'll do anything. Just keep me safe."

Kearn nodded.

He wouldn't let anything happen to her.

A voice deep inside him said that it wasn't only because he needed her as bait. There was something else at work here too.

She really was beautiful.

But she was forbidden blood.

And he had tasted her.

CHAPTER 3

Amber kept her eyes fixed on the man. The passing streetlights flickered across his face as he drove. He was a mystery and, for some reason, she wanted to crack him. She hadn't witnessed one trace of emotion in his eyes. At least nothing that had been real. Sure, there had been feigned feelings, but she had seen straight through those. The whole time he had been talking to her about her blood and tracking the man and keeping her safe, the whole time they had been together, his green eyes had remained empty and dark. If it weren't for them, for the sense of iciness that he radiated like a barrier around him, she would have thought him sexy.

He held rank at handsome though, and she couldn't deny that he was attractive. His longish silver hair and vivid green eyes were unusual, but only added to his masculine beauty, and his body pushed the bar and threatened to break him back through into sexy territory, regardless of his detached air. It could easily grace the cover of a male fitness magazine—all compact muscle without a trace of fat. Her eyes roamed his face, over his fine dark silvery eyebrows and down his nose to the curve of his dusky lips that had tempted her more than once this evening, to the defined line of his jaw. He was definitely handsome, but the edge to him, the invisible walls that he didn't bother to hide, stole something from his looks and warned her away.

Perhaps his profession made him so cold and distant. It was difficult for her to understand his role or even the effect it might have on him. She had never known anyone in the police force or military. She looked at the gun in the holster under his left arm. How many people had he killed? Not people. Vampires. He killed vampires and protected people, and now she was playing bait so he could catch the man who wanted to kill her, and no doubt kill him. Was that the reason he seemed so heartless and distant?

Was that why he lived alone in that building?

She wasn't blind. Even with that vampire's blood sending her crazy and controlling her, she hadn't failed to notice that his car had been the only one in the garage and that there was no sense of life in his building. He was alone there.

Did he live that way in order to protect humans like her from the vampires that might come after him, or for different reasons?

Her gaze slowly fell to his chest. The black buttoned shirt didn't stop her from remembering how good his body had looked. Her eyes shifted to his right hand on the black steering wheel. Or the strange tattoo that covered his entire right arm. She hazily remembered it from when he had rescued her. It had glowed blue. Had that been real or just the effects of the vampire's blood on her?

She shuddered with the thought that the vampire's blood was still in her, crawling around in her veins, and looked down at her bandaged hand. Could he still control her? She felt normal again now, back to herself, almost. Her mind was playing catch up and computing everything that had happened, making it all seem like some surreal dream even when she knew that it was reality. She was with a vampire hunter en route to kill the demon who wanted her blood. It should frighten her, she knew it should, but whenever she looked at the man beside her, her fear faded away.

"I'm Amber," she said, not only to break the steadily turning oppressive silence but because she wanted to know his.

"Kearn."

Amber presumed that was his name.

"So... you're a Venator." She felt silly the moment she said it but she had to do something to start a conversation with him.

He sped over a crossroad and then turned left at the next. They were heading back to where he had rescued her. She felt uneasy about returning to the area and leading Kearn to the factory, but he had assured her that he would keep her safe, and she was determined to believe him, if only to stop herself from feeling scared.

"I am."

He wasn't very talkative. She had hoped that he would turn out to be a talker so she could chip away at his hard exterior and see what lurked beneath.

What could she say to get him talking? His distance wasn't going to deter her. If they were going to be working together, then they at least needed to be on talking terms. Perhaps he wasn't used to company. If his building were empty as she suspected, it would make sense that he hadn't had much practice at making idle conversation. Her apartment building was full of people of all ages, and most of them stopped in the corridors to talk about trivial things like the weather, work and where they were going to or coming from. She'd had plenty of practice at making conversation. He would just have to catch up.

"Must be a pretty lonely job." She regretted her choice of words when he looked at her out of the corner of his eye and a strange sense of hurt filled her. It wasn't in his eyes, they were dark and narrowed, but something about him gave her the impression that he was lonely. "Sounds more interesting than my job though."

"And what is your profession?" He had a very formal way of talking at times, speaking with a regal edge to his deep voice.

"I wouldn't exactly call it my profession, but I'm an analyst."

His expression turned thoughtful. "An analyst? That could be useful in finding the man who is after you."

Amber laughed and he glanced at her.

"Only if he needs his numbers crunched. I'm more like an account... not the sort of analyst you're thinking of."

"I apologise." He frowned at the road. "I do not know much of offices and such."

Amber smiled. "I got that impression."

Kearn didn't say anything. She picked at her bandage again. Her hand still hurt but the bleeding had stopped now and the pain was lessening.

"Where is the building from here?" he said and she realised they were in the side street where the men had attacked her.

Amber directed him towards the building, leading him through the maze of one-way streets. He pulled the car to a halt around the corner from the gates of the old redbrick factory and looked across at her.

"Stay here. Under no circumstances are you to leave the vehicle." The hard edge to his voice made her nod in agreement even when she wanted to say that she was coming with him and he had no right to tell her what to do.

He turned off the engine and then stepped out of the car. The moment the door clicked shut, she felt on edge. With Kearn around, she had felt safe from the vampire. He had been a talisman that had kept the dark thoughts and her fear at bay. What if the man was in the building? Would he try to control her again if he knew that she was here? She didn't want to be his pawn in whatever game he was playing with Kearn, and she didn't want to die.

Amber stared at Kearn's back as he walked away from her in the beam of the headlights, her sense of safety leaving with him. He reached across and removed his gun from the holster. It flashed in the white light. He looked menacing dressed head to toe in black, his silver hair dancing in the night breeze and his gun in his hand. A fitting look for a man who hunted vampires. At the corner, he looked back at her and then he was gone.

She went to curl up on the black leather seat and then thought the better of it. Judging by the way people had stared at it during the journey here, the car had to be worth a hundred grand at least. She couldn't go putting a dent in the leather or scuffing it with her heeled work shoes.

The empty road was too quiet, increasing the creeping chill inside her. After a few wrong choices, she found the button for the radio on the black console and it came on, illuminating the dashboard. She kept the volume low, afraid that it would attract the wrong kind of attention if it were louder, and then tried to figure out how to turn off the headlights. She couldn't find the switch for them but she did find one that locked the doors. This car was nothing like any she had driven before.

Someone walked past the end of the road ahead of her and she froze, cautiously watching them until they disappeared from view.

What was Kearn doing? Had he gone into the building to find the men who had attacked her?

Vampires. It seemed incredible that they existed and she felt as though she shouldn't believe it even when she did.

Was Kearn going to kill them?

She didn't like the thought of him killing someone because of her, but she wanted to be safe again and go back to her life, and she knew that wouldn't happen without the vampire dying. Did France have vampires too? Kearn had said that once he had captured the man, she would be safe. No one else would know about her blood. No one except Kearn at least. Would he keep her secret for her? She wanted to escape London more than ever now, wanted to go somewhere new, where no one knew her, but she wasn't sure if she would ever feel safe again. Vampires would constantly be on her mind. Maybe she could ask Kearn for some self-defence lessons in return for helping him. She would feel a whole lot safer if she knew how to kill a vampire.

Amber pushed her wavy brown hair out of her face and then tied it up into a ponytail. The building to her left was dark. Would Kearn find anyone in it? If the vampire had known he was a Venator, then surely he knew that Kearn would come after him. He wouldn't have remained in the building.

The hairs on the back of her neck rose and she swore she heard someone saying her name. She looked around the streets but no one was there. The feeling came again, a notion that someone was calling to her. Was it the vampire?

She reached over to turn the radio up in the hope of drowning out the feeling and stopped dead when a loud cracking noise echoed around the streets. She had seen enough movies to recognise the sound. A gunshot. Kearn.

Without a second thought, Amber left the car and ran to the corner. No one was in the narrow road. She hurried on, heading for the gates. Another gunshot rang out and she flinched, instinctively hunching up to make herself small in case the bullet was coming her way.

She was about to move when a man landed in front of her, close enough that she stumbled backwards and fell, jolting her coccyx. He glanced at her with red eyes and then ran off. A vampire? Where had he come from?

Amber looked up the three-storey height of the building and wished she hadn't.

Kearn was falling out of the sky.

She screwed her eyes shut, not wanting to see him die. A warm breeze washed over her and then silence. She had expected more of a commotion when someone hit a pavement from a great height.

"I told you to stay in the car." Kearn's sharp voice cut the silence and she cracked an eye open. He stood over her, not a scuff on him, looking as though he had just walked along the street to see her rather than dropped from the heavens. She glanced up at the top of the building and then back at him. It wasn't possible for someone to fall like that and survive without a scratch.

The vampire had done it.

So had Kearn.

His green eyes narrowed, darker than usual.

Amber opened her mouth to explain but fell silent when he extended his right hand to her. It was glowing blue, the marks on it shining so brightly they were dazzling. Just what was it? Just what was he?

Her hand shook as she slipped it into his. His fingers closed over hers, the glow lighting her skin and washing all colour away, and he pulled her up off the ground. He didn't release her hand. He led her back to the car at a brisk pace and opened the passenger side door.

"Get back in the car," he said and she didn't hesitate or protest.

He slammed the door and ran off.

Amber breathed hard and tried to shake the image of him falling from the sky and his arm from her mind. How could he do that? Was he like the vampire? She kicked off her shoes, locked all the doors, and huddled up on the seat, afraid of Kearn coming back.

She lost track of time as she stared at the road in front of her, trying to make sense of everything and wondering why she was suddenly frightened. Kearn had never said that he was human but he hadn't mentioned that he was anything like the vampires he hunted either. Who was she to think that made him bad? She shared a gene with vampires, making her like them too. Perhaps he had found a way to use the power in that gene as the vampires did. Perhaps he was a vampire. Why did it frighten her if he was? He was still trying to protect her.

But he was keeping things from her.

And she didn't like it.

Her eyes widened when he stepped into the path of the headlights. They threw his shadow out long behind him. He holstered his gun under his left arm and walked towards the car, all glowering darkness that reminded her of the vampire who was after her. Was Kearn one too? She wanted to ask him but was too afraid of the answer.

His eyes bore into hers and she couldn't look away. She stared straight into them, still trying to decipher what he was hiding behind their impenetrable emerald shield.

He stopped at the driver's side door and tried to open it. Twice. Amber dropped her gaze when he bent over and looked at her through the window.

"I am sorry if I was rude. I only wish to keep you safe," he said, as though he honestly thought his somewhat arrogant attitude had forced her to lock him out of the car. She made herself look at him. There was no darkness in his eyes now, only a touch of confusion that was real. He smiled and she expected to see fangs but only saw normal teeth. "Apology accepted?"

What if she let him in and he tried to drink her blood, just as the other man had? She reasoned that he was helping her, and he did genuinely want to keep her safe, even if it was only so he could use her as bait to lure out the vampire. If he was like the vampire and wanted to kill her for her blood, he probably would have done so back at his apartment.

And she was safer with him than by herself.

A sense of calm flowed through her as she stared into his eyes, chasing back the darkness and the fear. Even if he was a vampire, he was her only protection against the man. She needed him. She couldn't fight the man herself.

She unlocked the doors and Kearn opened it, slid into the seat and stared at her.

"Did you find anything?" Her voice was a tight squeak and he frowned. "You seemed quite intent on chasing that man."

Intent enough to jump off the roof of a building and survive unharmed.

"Vampire," Kearn said and started the car. "And no, there was nothing in the building besides some bloodstains on the floors. Whatever they were doing there, they have moved location now that I know about it. I only managed to catch that one vampire."

"What happened?"

Kearn didn't say anything. He pulled the white Audi R8 out into the road and drove to the junction at the end of it.

He stopped the car at the line and his grip on the black steering wheel tightened.

"The next time I tell you to remain in the car, do just that. Unless you want to get yourself killed." The hard edge was back in his voice and she saw a flicker of how he had looked in the street.

His arm had been glowing. Human arms couldn't do that sort of thing. Could a vampire's?

"What will you do now? Was this your only lead?" she said rather than asking him whether he too had fangs and hungered for blood. She stared at his eyes, wondering if they might turn red, and then told herself to stop overanalysing things. He had bandaged her cut hand without so much as a hint of wanting her blood and the vampire Kearn had been chasing had red eyes and the other had fangs. Kearn had neither of those things.

"No," Kearn said and she almost jumped. Her eyes darted away from his face when he looked at her. The dashboard of an Audi was very interesting. She stared at it, frowning at times, doing her best to look fascinated by it and not him. "There is a club where we might get some answers."

"A club?" She looked down at her neat black trouser suit. "I'm not exactly dressed for that sort of place."

"I will handle that."

Amber's eyes drifted back to him when the car pulled away, accelerating along the wide tree-lined shopping street.

She couldn't shake the feeling that there was more to Kearn than met the eye, that he hid the real him behind a mask to keep the world at a distance. Why? The bright streetlights flashed on his face.

If he was a vampire, would he hurt her like the other one wanted to?

Or was there such a thing as a good vampire?

CHAPTER 4

Kearn led the way up through his apartment building. With all of the stores closed until morning, he would have to wait to visit the club and see if he could attract attention with Amber and her blood. He had hoped to end this tonight and take her home, ridding himself of both the temptation she presented and his unending mission to capture the man, but fate had never been kind to him. For now, he would battle his lingering hunger for her and bide his time. Tomorrow, he would buy her some clothes to wear to the club, and together they would hunt down the vampire. He didn't have much experience of dressing women, but was sure someone at the shops would be happy to assist him, especially since money wasn't a factor.

Humans and vampires were very similar in that respect. Money could buy you anything and the more you had, the more people were willing the crawl on their bellies for you.

Amber's fatigue flowed through the connection between their blood. It wasn't the only feeling that he could sense in her. Her emotions were steadily turning towards fear again. Perhaps it was a good thing that they had been unable to go to the club tonight. She needed to rest. All he had done since meeting her was push her into doing things his way. The man he sought would be cautious tonight. Going to the club wouldn't have produced any results. Tomorrow was a different matter. The vampire would want to find her. He would come out hunting and Kearn would be waiting for him.

There was another reason for him to take things more slowly. Pushing her now, when she was tired and afraid, would only lead to him losing her. She had locked him out of the car tonight and she hadn't done it out of fear of the vampire. She had feared him. He needed her to remain with him. His instincts whispered that he could force her to stay, at least until her blood was completely absorbed into his. No. No good would come of it. His mission was to protect humans, not prey on them. Not anymore. If it came down to it, he would confess that her suspicions were correct.

He was a vampire.

"So did they hurt when you had them done?"

He stopped just short of the black door to his apartment and turned to face her.

She looked nervous. Her heart was racing, sending her blood to the surface. It filled the white hallway with the sweet enticing scent and caused his fangs to itch. Her blood had tasted so delicious. His stomach ached, hunger to taste her again causing it to cramp, and he struggled to hold his fangs at bay. It was just the remnants of her blood affecting him still. The effects were already wearing off. He just needed to hold it together for a few more hours and then he would be free of the haze induced by her blood and she wouldn't be such a temptation. His gaze slid to her neck and his throat burned. He closed his eyes when the hallway brightened, signalling a change in his irises, and clamped his teeth together. It was just her blood in him. It would pass. He told himself it repeatedly but it didn't ease the tight ache in his gut. He wanted her blood, and it went deeper than a craving for another high.

"Kearn?" she whispered and he drew a long, steadying breath, and then opened his eyes. The hallway was dim again. He looked up at her.

Her gaze fell to his hand.

His did too.

He raised his right hand and her eyes followed it, fixed intently on the silver marks that covered it to his fingertips.

She seemed fascinated by them. He had caught her looking at him countless times since meeting her, and several of those she had been staring at his arm, her gaze tracing the marks that flowed over it from his shoulder to his hand. He was surprised that she hadn't asked him about it before now. Twice she had seen it activated. Now she was asking him whether the marks had hurt, as though they were just a tattoo, rather than asking what they did and what he was.

Didn't she want to know?

Or was she trying to pretend that she hadn't noticed, and that he was only human?

Perhaps she wasn't as strong as he had thought and was having trouble believing everything and taking it all in after all. Kearn reminded himself that she was human. This was probably some strange dream or nightmare to her. There had been moments when her blood had conveyed that she trusted him, and wanted to remain with him. Was her denial of the truth standing before her all because she wanted to continue to trust that he would save her? If he told her that he was a vampire, would she want to leave? Would she fear him then and see him as she saw the man—a beast and a monster?

Part of him didn't want her to feel that way towards him.

He would never harm her.

He only wanted to protect her.

He opened the door to his apartment while considering what to say about his arm and whether to tell her about himself. It wasn't a good idea. The moment the door swung open, he drew his gun and aimed it at the person standing in the middle of his home.

His brother raised his hands in an act of surrender and smiled.

"What are you doing here, Kyran?" Kearn holstered his gun and walked into the apartment. Only one of the lights in the kitchen was on, leaving the rest of the large room in near-darkness.

Amber followed him. When she stepped out from behind him, Kyran's dark blue eyes were on her.

"He cried like a baby when they put those marks on him." Kyran smiled broadly, his gaze assessing Amber.

"I did not." Kearn closed the door. It was unusual for Kyran to drop by unannounced to his apartment. His brother knew how much he hated it.

"It isn't like you to bring a girl home, Kearn." Kyran's blue eyes remained locked on Amber and he inhaled deeply.

His gaze slid to Kearn. The look in his eyes and the connection they shared through a familial bond asked a question. Was she Source Blood? Kearn refused to answer. His brother didn't need to know and wouldn't be able to tell from Amber's scent alone.

"Don't tell me you are planning to go a little rogue? The old habits die hardest, don't they?" Kyran said with a wicked smile.

Amber stared at Kearn.

Kearn glared at his brother. He wasn't intending to take Amber's blood. He knew the law and he wasn't going to break it by using her blood purely to get high. He had only taken a small amount for testing purposes. That was as far as it went. This wasn't the same as back then. He hadn't known he was breaking the law. He hadn't known she was tainted.

It was typical of his brother to bring up his past. Kyran had always found it amusing to make him uncomfortable but that trait had turned vicious since Kearn had become a Venator, to the point where Kyran took intense pleasure from saying things that would get him into trouble. He was convinced that his brother did it to see him suffer, to make him pay for the things that had happened between them centuries ago, so he bore it as punishment for his sins against his own blood.

He bore it in the hope that one day they would finally move past what had happened and would be able to forgive each other.

"Why are you here?" Kearn looked hard at his older brother and then moved back to the door of his apartment. It wasn't like Kyran to hide in the dark and he could smell blood other than Amber's. The flat dull smell of vampire blood. It all smelt the same, not unique like human blood. He turned on the ceiling spotlights. "And why are you bleeding?"

Kyran touched a gash on his face. It wasn't the only cut. A myriad of thin red lines covered his face, neck and hands. He grinned.

"I was playing with Earl Huntingdon and Marchioness Montagu. You know what they can be like." Kyran's grin widened. His blue eyes shifted back to Amber. "Although if I had known you had such sweet company, I would have come here earlier."

Kearn crossed the room, grabbed Kyran's arm, and led him over to the small dining area in the far left corner of his apartment. He didn't relinquish his grip on his brother.

"She does not know what we are."

"Kinky," Kyran whispered and raised a dark eyebrow in Amber's direction. "Do you intend to reveal it during the act?"

Kearn tightened his grip on his brother's arm, bringing his attention back to him. Kyran frowned down at his hand and then into his eyes.

"She is a lead on a case. Bait." He kept his voice low so Amber didn't hear him. He wanted to tell his brother that he wasn't interested in drinking from Amber, or anything sexual, but couldn't bring himself to lie. His eyes threatened to stray to her, to take in her beauty, but he kept them fixed on Kyran.

"A Source Blood?" Kyran went to look at Amber again but Kearn stepped into his path.

"If you reveal what we are—"

Kyran slapped a hand down hard on his shoulder and smiled. Kearn could see straight through it. Whatever his brother was going to say, it was a lie. The look in Kyran's eyes screamed trouble.

"I will not say a word out of place." Kyran removed Kearn's hand from his arm and was past Kearn before he could stop him.

Amber still stood by the door, an air of hesitation about her, as though she had noticed the tension between him and his brother and didn't want to be caught in the crossfire.

"I have been unforgivably rude." Kyran stopped far too close to Amber for Kearn's liking. "Permit me to introduce myself. My name is Kyran, and I am Kearn's older brother."

"Amber," she said and then peered around Kyran to him. "Brother? You don't really look alike."

They had looked alike before he had become a Venator. His hair had once been black like Kyran's and his eyes had been an equally deep clear blue. In terms of stature and build, they had remained much the same, and he could see himself in his brother's face. His eternal torment.

"Kearn looks like our father." Kyran's tone was sharper than razor blades. Kearn could sense the hate and the hurt in him. It was never going away.

Kyran should have been Venator. It was the tradition in the Noble and Lesser Noble families. The eldest son carried on the duty of their father as Venator. He had wanted it to be that way, because Kyran had thought of nothing but becoming a Venator since they had been children. Kearn had fought the Sovereignty, had tried to convince them to give the duty to his brother, but they had given it to him regardless. Kyran had hated him ever since. A part of Kearn still hated his brother in return for his role in what had happened, but the pain of what he had gone through was nothing compared to the fact he had stolen his brother's dream.

Time had healed some of the breach between them, but sometimes Kearn got the feeling that nothing had been forgiven or forgotten. No matter how much progress they made with each other or how they tried to get along, the past would always stand between them.

The countess would always stand between them.

There was something akin to concern in Amber's eyes as she looked at him. Why? Because of his silence or because of the mix of sombre and fiery feelings that accompanied his thoughts? She would be able to sense them if she tried. The connection her blood in his veins caused between them was open and transmitting the emotions in his blood back to hers.

Kearn reached out to her through their connection and felt the concern in her. He closed off his emotions and monitored her in case the vampire tried anything.

She forced a polite smile at Kyran.

"You mentioned an earl and a marchioness. I've never met anyone who knew fancy people like that."

Kyran looked over his shoulder at him, his black eyebrows raised again. Kearn shook his head a fraction, enough that only his brother would notice the answer to his silent question. No. He hadn't told Amber about them and their family and he wasn't going to let Kyran mention it either. It was best she knew as little as possible.

"Kearn doesn't approve of Earl Huntingdon. He believes him a bad influence. Don't you, brother?"

Kearn left the dining area and came to stand near Amber in the open space between the four areas of the main room of his apartment.

"Because he is." Kearn held his hand out, indicating the living area beyond the wall of the open fireplace. "Perhaps we should sit down since Kyran seems to have no intention of leaving soon."

"Sounds like a wonderful idea." Kyran flashed a smile and held his arm out to Amber. "Shall we?"

She hesitated, looking unsure of what she was supposed to do, and then slipped her arm around his brother's one. Kearn glared at his brother's back as he led Amber to the couches, his eyes shifting to red for a moment and the world sharpening with it. Kyran would feel the threat. Hopefully, it would improve his behaviour.

Kearn turned away and went into the kitchen area, trying to clear his head. What was Kyran playing at? Of course he despised Earl Huntingdon but Amber didn't need to know that, or about anything to do with the sordid man. Earl Huntingdon was an animal. His family had always relished power and embraced the myths surrounding vampires, and had always been the most blood-soaked and violent because of it. Sometimes Lesser Noble families had no sense of breeding.

He took a fresh glass from the cupboard and filled it with water.

Kyran wouldn't talk to him about what had happened during his century of exile from their family, but he knew that Earl Huntingdon had invited him into his home and treated him like a brother. The earl was young, almost the same age as them, and had taken the role as head of his household when his parents had died around two centuries ago. He had been only one hundred and fifty at the time, the equivalent to a human fifteen year old, but he had been bloodthirsty and ruled in violence with his sister.

Kearn carried the glass with him across the room to the living area and rounded the black couch that faced the window. Kyran was sitting on the one against the wall, his legs crossed, revealing a rip in the knee of his black tailored trousers. Had Kyran been out killing tonight with the earl and marchioness? The three of them were prone to such acts of debauchery when together. He couldn't smell human blood on him, but it was difficult with Amber in the room. The heavenly scent of her blood drowned out everything else, filling his mind with the need to take more.

His gaze roamed to her where she sat on the couch that faced the window, staring out of it. Forbidden. Why did that word only make her more tempting? He placed the water down on the coffee table in front of her and she looked up at him.

"Thank you." She smiled and then it melted away into a frown. Her voice dropped to a whisper. "Does your brother know what you do?"

Kearn flinched internally at that question. He could feel Kyran's eyes on his back, boring a hole through his chest as though he wanted to rip out his heart with thought alone.

"Yes," Kearn said in a tight voice and sat beside her. She shuffled over to give him room and then sat with her hands in her lap, her body angled towards him and his brother.

He tried to think of something to talk about that wouldn't give Kyran an opening to hate him, ridicule him, or reveal anything about them and their family.

"I think Kearn has some more bandages if you need some." Amber smiled in Kyran's direction. She toyed with the cream crepe bandage around her hand.

"Did something happen to you?" Kyran sat forwards, resting his elbows on his knees. He reached a hand out to Amber.

Something inside Kearn said to knock his hand away and not let his brother touch Amber again, but he kept still. He didn't have any claim to her and his brother was behaving himself. If he stopped him, the next thing his brother said would probably be something about his penchant for blood drinking. The introduction had been bad enough. Permit me to introduce myself? He might as well have said—I'm a ridiculously portrayed vampire from a cliché low-budget movie.

Amber placed her hand into Kyran's. His brother cooed over it in a way that made Kearn want to hit him.

"This is terrible. You poor thing. What happened?"

It would have been more convincing to Kearn had his brother not been drawing a deep breath the whole time, trying to catch the scent of her blood.

"A man attacked me. A vampire, actually." She eyed Kyran closely.

"Damned vampires." He rolled his eyes.

Kearn did take her hand away from Kyran now, and gave his brother a dark look for good measure.

"I take it you know about them?" Amber put her hand back in lap and started toying with the bandage again. Kearn kept a close eye on her, concerned that the vampire's hold over her might not have faded completely. Since it was the vampire's blood in her body, and not the other way around, he would still be able to find her using the lingering connection between them until tomorrow night, or even beyond that, but Kearn had expected his ability to control her to have left her system by now.

He picked up the water and offered it to her with a smile. A delightful blush stained her cheeks. She had reacted the same way when he had smiled at her earlier tonight. Did she like it? He smiled again and she took the glass, running her fingers around the rim of it with her eyes downcast. Shy?

He could feel Kyran's eyes on him. Watching. It wasn't illegal for him to study a human and Amber fascinated him.

"I know all about vampires," Kyran said in a tone as black as an abyss. Kearn looked at him when Amber lifted the glass to her lips. Kyran blatantly ignored the silent command not to watch her by staring at her throat while she drank. Red briefly ringed his irises. "I know about them and the terrible things that Kearn does to them."

Amber choked, coughing and spluttering, her hand over her mouth. Kearn quickly took the glass from her. She stared at his brother with wide eyes. He didn't like the question he could see in them. She didn't need to know what he did.

He touched her shoulder and used the connection between them to give her feelings a slight push. Not too much influence over her thoughts. More of a suggestion than a command. He wouldn't control her as the other vampire had.

She rubbed her eyes and yawned. "I feel tired."

"It is late." Kearn placed the glass down on the square coffee table, feeling Kyran's glare on him the whole time. "Perhaps you should rest. You have had quite a night. I will stay on the couch. Please, make yourself at home in my room."

"Really? I couldn't." Her beautiful hazel eyes met his, full of warmth and honesty. They backed up the message her blood sent to his. She felt bad for taking his bed.

"I insist." He took her elbow, bringing her with him when he stood. Kyran was still staring at him. He led Amber past him and to the bedroom, and turned the light on for her. "The bathroom is just through that door. The control for the blinds is on the bedside table, as is the remote control for the television, in case you feel uncomfortable sleeping without background noise tonight. I will be here if you need anything."

She nodded and he closed the door. The moment it clicked shut, his eyes changed to red and he looked at Kyran. Scarlet eyes stared right back at him.

Without a word, Kearn walked to the door of the apartment and opened it. Kyran stood, stalked across the room, and stopped toe to toe with him.

"That was uncalled for. I was merely making conversation."

"I did not like the direction your apparently innocent conversation was heading." Kearn's red eyes locked with his brother's ones.

"Do you really believe the lie you are telling yourself when you say she only needs to know as little as possible?"

Kearn frowned.

"It is a lie, brother, and a shallow one. You do not keep her in the dark about your true self because you believe she doesn't need to know it in order to play the role you have assigned her." Kyran stepped past him but remained facing him, his back to the hall. "You do so because you are afraid of what she would think of you if she found out what you are... a vampire no different to the one who attacked her... a fiend lusting for her precious blood."

Kearn curled his fingers into a tight fist at his side and gripped the door hard with his other hand.

Kyran stepped back into the hall.

"She will find out, little brother."

He was gone.

Kearn growled under his breath at the truth in his brother's words.

It was only a matter of time before Amber saw past the façade.

For some reason, he didn't want her to see him for what he was.

He didn't want her to fear him.

Hate him.

Not even when it felt inevitable.

Kearn cursed and slammed the door.

CHAPTER 5

Amber woke slowly to an unfamiliar view. She lay on her back, staring at the ceiling, and could see the edges of the brown walls either side of her and the window behind her that formed another wall. She felt very calm, as though she had slept deeply. It surprised her. After what she had been through last night, she had expected not to sleep at all. She had drifted off waiting for the nightmares but felt as though her dreams had been pleasant, or non-existent.

Perhaps her dreams and reality had swapped places. She was living a nightmare and dreaming her old life now. The fear that had settled in her heart last night hadn't gone anywhere. It was quieter now, lessened by the steps Kearn had taken to protect her, to make her feel safe, but it wasn't going away. Deep inside her heart, a voice whispered that she should fear Kearn too, but for some reason she couldn't bring herself to feel that way, not even when a part of her knew that there was something different about him.

It didn't matter what he was. He was protecting her and she could help him. They needed each other. In order to swap her dreams and reality back around, she had to be strong and get through his, and she would, with Kearn at her side.

The quiet noise of the flat panel television built into the oak wardrobes opposite the foot of the bed filled the silence along with her breathing. She stretched. Kearn's bedroom was soothing. She wanted to sleep here forever.

The bed was soft and warm, the room peaceful and quiet, and she felt safe.

Amber rolled onto her side and took a deep breath. The brown pillows smelt like Kearn. She hadn't noticed it before. It was a warm smell. She smiled. Probably a very expensive warm smell.

There was no doubt in her mind that Kearn's job paid well. The car, the apartment, and the terribly modern décor that gave it an air of something out of a perfect homes magazine, all pointed towards money.

Another smile touched her lips when she remembered him insisting on her taking his bed. Very chivalrous.

And then there was his brother.

They looked alike in some ways and the very opposite in others. She imagined Kearn with blue eyes and black hair cut short around the sides but longer on top. They would definitely look alike then.

His brother had a different personality though. He was open, playful, and seemed to take great amusement from saying things that Kearn thought weren't suitable. If they hadn't told her that Kyran was the older brother, she would have thought him the younger.

Kearn seemed so cold in comparison, and more distant than she had first placed him. His behaviour around his brother, the flashes of anger swiftly chased by sorrow that had crossed his face at times, and the way he had ended the night so abruptly, all of them increased her feeling that Kearn was hiding something. What did he want to conceal?

Kyran had said that he knew vampires and he knew what his brother did to them. What did Kearn do to them? She had been about to ask him when she had felt incredibly sleepy. The tension in the apartment had risen the moment Kearn had closed the bedroom door on her and then the front door had slammed. Had they argued? Because of her?

Amber sat up on the double bed and pulled the brown duvet to her chest, covering her bare breasts with it.

Why would they argue because of her?

Because Kyran had been too friendly or because he had said something he shouldn't have?

Amber looked over at the bedside table.

And why were her clothes gone?

She scrambled across the double bed and peered down at the floor in case they had fallen off. They were gone. Her shoes were too. Only her black handbag remained.

Had Kearn taken them?

She blushed from head to toe at the thought of him coming into the room while she had been sleeping in his bed wearing only her knickers.

Her eyes widened.

He had even taken her bra.

Her cheeks burned now.

Amber wrapped herself in the brown duvet and shuffled carefully to the bedroom door. She opened it a crack and looked out into the main room. She couldn't see Kearn. The television in the white dividing wall above the low rectangular open fireplace was off. The apartment was silent save the noise of the television behind her.

Kearn was gone.

She hitched her duvet toga up and went back into the bedroom, crossing it to the bathroom. There was a white bathrobe on the back of the door. She dropped the duvet and put on the robe. It was too big for her but it was better than walking around Kearn's apartment in only her knickers.

She made the bed, turned off the television and then returned to the bedroom door and opened it.

There was no sign of her clothes in the living area, or in the kitchen in the right hand corner opposite it. The glasses and bowl were on the drainer, and Kearn's bloodied shirt was gone. She picked up one of the glasses, filled it with water and drank it down in one go. Her stomach growled. Food. She hadn't eaten in almost a day.

Amber checked the pale wooden cupboards. The first two being bare didn't bother her, but after the fifth, she started to find it strange. When she had checked every cupboard and found only a few glasses and some other kitchenware, but not cutlery or plates, she was disconcerted. She approached the large white refrigerator with caution, fearing what she would find in it. Vampires drank blood. What if the fridge was full of bits of people or blood bags stolen from the local hospital?

She grabbed the refrigerator door and yanked it open.

A blank white space greeted her.

Her heart pounded against her ribs.

She was going crazy.

She had to stop being so suspicious.

Vampires killed people. Maybe he didn't keep his food in the house. Maybe he ate street food of the vampire kind.

Amber shut the fridge door. She really was being stupid now.

Kearn hunted vampires.

Maybe he ate out all the time. There were people who did that. She had seen television programs where famous people had never used the expensive stove in their oversized kitchen. Kearn could be just like them.

Or he could eat blood.

She walked out of the kitchen, trying to distance herself from her thoughts as easily as she could distance herself from the refrigerator.

She stopped at the black front door of the apartment.

There was a note stuck to it, written in neat cursive script.

Do not even consider leaving. I shall return by the time you have showered and shall bring you breakfast. Kearn.

She tried the handle anyway. Locked. Some of the locks she could open from the inside, but one of them needed a key.

Well, that was considerate of him. He stole her clothes and locked her in his apartment, and then offered her a shower and said he would bring her breakfast. He was confusing her more every minute that she knew him.

Breakfast?

Amber glanced to her left, through the small study area to the bank of windows that formed the wall there. The sun was heading towards the horizon, casting a golden glow over the rooftops of London. He had a strange concept of meal times, but then he hunted vampires. It was probably a job he could only do at night.

She perused the books in the beech bookcase that lined the wall of the study opposite the open fireplace, her fingers tripping from spine to spine. There were many novels on the side nearest the front door, but closer to the wooden desk in front of the window, the books were all factual, and some of them were definitely not available in stores. Books on demons, vampires, werewolves and other creatures. All of them old and large, and leather-bound. None of them had authors or publishing houses on the spine. She took a thick, heavy tome on vampires, placed it down on the desk and opened it carefully to somewhere near the middle. Her gaze scanned the neatly hand written paragraphs on the yellowing page and stopped on a name she recognised.

She had to read it three times to make sure she wasn't imagining it.

Earl Huntingdon.

She cast a quick glance around the apartment, her heart starting to race and tremble at the thought of being caught snooping in Kearn's things, and then read the passage about the earl.

A vampire.

Kyran knew vampires. Was that why Kearn didn't like Earl Huntingdon? Perhaps there were good vampires after all and that was why Kyran was friends with him.

Or perhaps not.

Amber read the page, enthralled by the things it said about the earl and his bloodthirsty ways. He sounded dangerous, the sort of vampire that people had written tales about centuries ago, like Vlad the Impaler. He sounded like the sort that Kearn should kill.

She went to turn the page and read on but stopped herself. Reading about the horrible things vampires did to people and to other vampires would only frighten her. She closed the book and placed it back on the shelf. She was better off not knowing. They said ignorance was bliss after all. When Kearn had caught the vampire, she would be going back to her life. Kearn wouldn't be there to protect her from the scary vampires. She would be alone again and she didn't want to spend the rest of her life afraid, fearing that someone like Earl Huntingdon would somehow find her. She wanted to live life.

Dragging herself away from the study, she walked around the wide white dividing wall of the modern double-sided fireplace and stopped dead when she saw a black jacket and Kearn's gun on the end of the long black couch against the bedroom wall. The setting sun glinted off the silver gun, luring her to it.

She stopped at the window-end of the couch beside the gun and stared hard at it, memorising the weapon's exact position on the jacket so she knew where to place it so Kearn wouldn't know what she had done. With her heart in her throat, she reached a trembling hand out to the gun and closed the fingers of her left hand around the grip. Her whole arm shook as she lifted it. It was heavier than expected and felt cold against her fingers. She kept it pointed away from her, afraid it would go off, and studied it. It looked like a gun from a movie, sleek and modern, and dangerous.

What kind of bullets did it take? They had to be special to kill vampires.

Amber tried to figure out how to open it, turning it one way and then the other, and even looking closely at the bottom of the grip. In the movies, people changed the clip so quickly she never saw how they got it out. She lifted her other hand, tempted to pull the top part of the gun back and then stopped herself. She didn't know what would happen if she did that. If she blew out a window or made a hole in the white wall, Kearn would know that she had been messing around with his gun. Afraid of the consequences if that happened, Amber placed the gun back down in the precise spot and position she had found it, and stepped back from it. She didn't like it.

Turning away, she walked back to Kearn's bedroom and through it to the bathroom. Take a shower. Kearn had said he would be back when she had showered. She looked at the large white cubicle to her left. Take a shower she would.

She stripped off the bathrobe and her knickers, and closed the bathroom door. The clear shower door squeaked when she slid it open. She turned the water on and stepped under the jet, showering quickly and holding her hair up so it didn't get too wet. It would frizz if it did and she didn't want to look like a prize poodle around Kearn.

Amber shut the water off and stepped out of the shower. Her head spun. She closed her eyes and waited for it to clear. It had done that from time to time last night too. Was it the vampire trying to control her?

She shuddered at the thought. She didn't like the idea that someone could control her and make her do things against her will. She unravelled the bandage on her hand. The cut across her palm was still raw and it was bleeding in places again. She washed it in the sink and then looked for a new bandage, finding some in the cupboard in the black sink cabinet. She carefully wound it around her hand, tight enough that it would stop the bleeding, and pinned it.

The vampire had wanted her to taste her blood but she hadn't been tempted this time. Was his hold over her fading?

The sound of a door closing made her look up at herself in the mirror. Kearn.

She clawed her hair back into a neat ponytail, slipped the robe on, and tied it.

Kearn was in the kitchen when she walked out of the bedroom. He glanced over at her, his green eyes as impassive as ever. Not even the sight of her in his bathrobe fresh from the shower provoked a reaction. He crossed the room and held two large black paper bags out to her. There was a store name she didn't recognise written on the side in a white cursive font. She peered inside the first one at the clothes. The second had a cardboard shoebox in it.

"What is it?" She looked at Kearn.

"Your outfit for tonight." He dropped another similar bag on the couch facing the window and she looked in it too. Her own clothes. He had taken them to a store and, judging by the bags, it had been somewhere expensive.

Kearn held a small brown bag out to her.

"What's this?" She took it from him.

"Breakfast," he said without any trace of emotion, his eyes not leaving hers. "Coffee and pastries. I asked the woman what you might like."

Amber frowned. What she might like? As though a stranger would know such a thing. Couldn't he have judged for himself? Maybe he didn't know what food tasted like. Maybe vampires didn't eat anything other than blood.

Maybe he just didn't eat pastries. She had known men in her past that didn't touch sweet things. He could be like them.

"What about you?" She placed the clothes bags down on the couch beside the other one and eyed him closely, studying his face.

"I ate when I was out."

Amber stared at him. He stared back, colder than ever. He really wasn't very talkative. The effort of trying to make conversation with him was exhausting.

Kearn walked around her and along the length of the couch beside the wall to the far end of it. He leaned over and paused with his hand just above his gun. He kept his back to her as he picked it up.

"Do not ever touch it again," he said and went into his bedroom, closing the door.

A few minutes later the shower was running and Amber was still standing in the middle of his apartment feeling guilty for snooping and wondering how the hell he had known she had touched the gun. It had been in exactly the same place as he had left it.

He was an enigma.

He had no food, a lot of money, and treated her coldly even though she was helping him. She looked at the clothing and the food that he had bought. She couldn't figure him out at all. She had never met anyone so distant either. Was it his work? Maybe he was just unused to company. He hadn't been that at ease with his brother too.

Maybe he wasn't human.

She couldn't push that thought away. Whenever she gave it a chance, it came back.

Amber walked over to the kitchen island and placed the brown paper bag down on the granite top. She sat on one of the black and wood stools that followed the curve of the island, and opened the bag, removing the white paper cup of coffee. She took off the lid and scooped up some of the foam with her finger. Cappuccino. Just the fix she had needed.

There were a lot of different pastries in the bag. Covering his bets?

The bedroom door opened and Amber looked over her shoulder at Kearn. He rubbed a brown towel against his wet hair. Water dripped from the ends of the long silver strands and rolled down the bare strip of chest and stomach visible between the two sides of his black shirt. His body was delicious. Just what she wanted to eat for breakfast. His muscles shifted and bunched with each move he made as he dried his hair, a feast for her eyes only. She stared, unashamed of what she was doing. If he was going to put it out there, then she wasn't going to shy away.

Kearn tossed the towel back into his bedroom, ran his fingers through his hair, and then walked over to the jacket on the couch. He picked it up and placed it over the back of the couch facing the window. Amber sipped her coffee and kept watching him, or at least his body. He ruined her fun by buttoning his shirt and tucking it into his black trousers.

He came over to her and looked at the paper bag. She took another sip of her coffee and drank her fill of his face, putting to memory the curve of his lips as they parted and the way a line formed between his dark silver eyebrows when he frowned. He was undeniably good looking and was starting to creep back into sexy territory.

"Want one?" Amber offered the bag, part of her doing so out of politeness and the other part wanting to test him.

His green eyes shifted from the contents of the bag to her hand that was holding it. Blood was seeping into the bandage again.

"Take it if you want it," she said and his eyes met hers, incredulous and searching. It was the first sign of something other than cold calculation in them today. He almost looked shocked.

"No, thank you." Kearn pushed the bag back at her. "You should dress. We need to arrive at the club before everyone else so we do not look as though we are together."

She took a long leisurely sip of her cappuccino, unwilling to be rushed by him, and then slipped down off the stool.

When he had said they would go to a club, she had expected them to be together the whole time. The thought of being alone when the vampire could be stalking her was frightening but she had promised to play bait for him. She picked up the bags of clothes from the couch. What sort of bait did Kearn have in mind? The clothes would give her a hint.

She walked into his bedroom, kicked the door closed, put her coffee and pastries down on the side cupboard and dumped the bags on the bed.

Refusing to hurry, she ate a croissant and drank half of her coffee, and then devoured another pastry.

Amber pulled the large shoebox out of the first bag and opened it.

She tipped the contents of the other bag out on the bed beside it.

Her eyes widened.

"What the hell!"

CHAPTER 6

Kearn stopped putting on his shoe the moment the wave of anger washed through the apartment. Amber wasn't happy about something. He couldn't think what it would be. He had seen humans enjoying coffee and sweet things, and the woman at the boutique had assured him the clothes would suit her.

He looked at the door, shrugged it off, and finished putting on his leather shoe. He picked up his jacket, considered bringing it with him to the club, and then thought the better of it. He didn't want to look too formal.

The door to his bedroom swung open with force and Amber came out.

Kearn only meant to glance at her but it became a stare when he saw her. A strange gut wrenching jolt rocked him, and it wasn't just his desire for her blood this time.

She looked incredible.

He couldn't help himself. His gaze started at her feet, roaming up the length of the black leather knee-high heeled boots, over the sheer tights that barely hid her slender thighs, to the short black layered skirt that wouldn't have a chance at covering her backside if she bent over, and finally to the black leather corset. Her cleavage, pushed up and on display, was temptation in its most alluring form, but he forced his eyes to keep moving upwards. She stepped towards him and placed her hands on her hips.

Soft waves of brown hair caressed her shoulders.

A thick black velvet choker with a silver cross on it ringed her neck. The cross didn't bother him, or any of his kind, but he couldn't stop staring at it and the sublime curve of her throat. He resisted his desire to lick his lips and swallowed to wet his dry throat. It burned and he fought the terrible hunger that had been rising since he had awoken this afternoon. Her blood was weaker within him now, but his thirst wasn't abating as he had expected. It gnawed at him, making his insides twist and spasm, and he placed his hand on his stomach. He couldn't take it. His fangs extended behind his closed lips and his mouth watered. He kept his feet planted to the wooden floor, refusing to give in to the urge to cross the room, drag her soft body flush against his, and sink his fangs hard into her throat. The battle raged inside him and her blood spoke of her growing confusion over his silence and staring. It took every ounce of his will to force his fangs away but he managed it and clawed back control.

When his gaze finally found her face, another jolt hit him, this time in his chest and worrying.

She was beautiful.

The make-up the lady in the boutique had recommended when he had described her enhanced her natural beauty until he couldn't tear his eyes away from her. The dark brown around her hazel eyes turned them pale and mysterious, and the red lipstick tempted him to take hold of her and kiss her until she was moaning for more. Begging him to bite her.

Kearn ripped his eyes away and fixed them on the window, shaking off his desire. She was bait. That was all. This was business. His gaze crept back to her.

Amber held her arms out and glared at him. It didn't suit her.

Neither did the rage emanating from her.

"I look like a slut!"

Kearn couldn't resist the excuse to peruse her again. She looked more attractive than he had imagined she would. A perfect lure for his hunt.

"I think you look good." It wasn't a lie or at all difficult for him to say, not even when she was human.

She blushed and cast her gaze at the floor. Her teeth teased her red lips, nibbling in a way that increased the dry burning feeling in his throat.

He instinctively took a step towards her and her eyes met his, her pupils wide and dark. She had looked at him like that when he had come out of the shower. Her scent said that she wasn't here purely for protection. She was attracted to him. He looked at the windows. She shouldn't be. There was a whisper in her blood sometimes that said she knew what he was. Why hadn't she confronted him about it yet? Was she going to keep pretending that he was human?

Was it such a terrible thing that he was a vampire?

Was it such a terrible thing that she was human? She was stunning, a perfect rose in form and fragrance, and the hunger inside him wasn't all about her blood. He could deny it all he wanted, could lie to convince himself that she was human and therefore beneath him, but every fibre of his body was burning for her touch.

He took another step towards her and then got the better of himself. This was business.

"I need you to fit in tonight and women at the club often wear such clothing. It is important that the man can find you and that you attract attention," he said.

She huffed. "Do the women also wrap themselves around poles?"

His eyebrow rose. Compared to her conservative black suit, he supposed it was somewhat revealing, but he couldn't allow her to go into the club looking out of place. She needed to look as though she wanted some action, and she needed flesh on show for the vampires to smell her.

He took a discreet breath of her scent. His fangs itched and hunger tightened his stomach again. Drinking her blood had been more than a mistake. He'd had two blood packs this evening and they had done nothing to quench his growing thirst for her.

"It is not that sort of club." He pointed towards the door, eager to escape the confines of his apartment and breathe the fresh night air. "Shall we go?"

Amber was almost past him when she stopped and her gaze flicked warily to his chest.

"No gun?"

Her nerves rose, speaking to him and increasing his hunger. Nothing made a vampire thirsty like fear.

"I will not need it."

"But if that man comes—"

"I can handle him without it."

She still hesitated. Her fingers went to the bandage on her hand and she picked at it again.

"How? Doesn't the gun have special bullets?"

Kearn laughed. It had been so long since he had laughed that it sounded strange and alien to his ears. Confusion replaced the fear in Amber's eyes.

"No," he said. "The bullets are normal."

"But they kill vampires…" She trailed off when he raised his hand.

"The bullets only slow vampires down." He held his right hand out to her. The silver marks on his arm began to shine pale blue as the power activated, starting at his fingertips and slowly creeping up his arm in a cold wave that whispered dark hungry things to him. The glow lit her face, reflecting in her eyes. This was more than she needed to know, but he needed her to see it so she could no longer deny his difference to her. Not human. A beast who thirsted for her blood and had dreamt of her all day. "This kills vampires."

He closed his fist when the power urged him to feed it and the marks deactivated, leaving his vision dampened and his arm aching.

"Now, are you coming?" He walked to the door and opened it for her.

She nodded and walked past him, not waiting for him to lock the door. She walked down the hall, giving him an enticing rear view of her. Her hips swayed with each step. He raked his eyes over her, frowning when he reached her boots and their tall heels. His gut tightened again, warm hunger sparking into life and mingling with his need for blood. Lust. He was familiar enough with the feeling to recognise it when it was throwing his mind into disarray. It wouldn't do. He couldn't be distracted tonight.

Amber was bait.

Beautiful bait.

He followed her down the stairs, allowing his feelings some freedom. It was strange to feel anything positive. Had he grown so used to only negative emotions that positive ones like desire or need born of beauty rather than blood were a foreign thing?

Amber stopped by his white car in the large concrete garage.

In a ridiculous moment of unrestraint, Kearn opened the passenger door for her. His reward was a wide smile and a hint of colour on her pale cheeks. He closed the door when she was in and wished the soft click had signalled the shutting down of his emotions as he had planned, but they wouldn't go back into place. He slowly rounded the car, aware of her eyes on him, fighting his feelings the whole time. Kyran was right but a human didn't belong in his world.

Kearn got into the car and closed the door. This time his emotions did die with the click and he started the car.

He drove out of the garage and pulled onto the road. The sun was setting. By the time they had reached the club, it would be dark enough for Lesser Nobles to come out. Nobles were strong against the sun and would be out by now, but they wouldn't make an appearance at the club until nearer midnight.

Kearn managed to keep his thoughts off Amber and on work until they were half-way to the club and she moved in the seat beside him. His gaze jumped to her thighs and her bandaged hand where it rested in her lap. His throat turned dry again and he rubbed it, trying to alleviate the burn of thirst.

The collar of his black shirt felt too tight so he undid it but it didn't relieve him at all. The air in the Audi was suffocating and hot. Amber sent the temperature up another notch when she turned her hands over and he saw the blood on the bandage. The smell of it filled his senses.

Kearn opened the window and breathed in the night, using the scent to remind himself that what he was considering with Amber wasn't an option. He was a vampire. A Venator. Even if he never wanted to be one, he had to carry out his duty. Amber was only a means to an end. He would kill the vampire, part ways with her and never see her again. It was safest that way.

He didn't want her to fear him.

If she knew about him and the things he did, she would feel the same way as everyone else. She would hate him.

He pulled the car to a halt down the road from the club and got out. Amber followed, and he locked the car, crossed the quiet street with her, and walked straight towards the club. They were almost there when Amber stopped. He turned and looked back at her.

"Is something wrong?" he said.

She was staring at the building ahead of them, her eyes wide and red lips parted. "I've been here before."

Every muscle tightened in response to that and a desire to step towards her, to remain close to her, bolted through him. The thought that she had been here before, where so many vampires hunted each night, disturbed him as much as it clearly disturbed her.

"How many times?" he said and her wide hazel eyes shifted to him.

"I don't know... five or six... vampires come here?" Her blood relayed the feelings behind the tremor in her voice. Fear. Disbelief.

He nodded. He hadn't come to the club in years but Kyran kept him posted on the things that happened there. Vampires were regular patrons. Had Amber flirted with the men here? How many times had she come close to leaving with one? He searched her eyes for the answer, a burning need to know setting his blood aflame. A darker urge followed in its wake, compelling him to take her back to his place and keep her away from all of his kind. He wouldn't let another vampire touch what was his.

Kearn pushed that desire away. Amber didn't belong to him. He had no claim on her. Yet he couldn't contain his dark hunger to protect her.

"I will not allow any of them to harm you, Amber." He meant every word. If any of them touched her, he would use his power to break them from the inside out before they could defend against him.

She nodded, the nervous edge back in her eyes, and looked towards the club.

Kearn led the way, remaining close to her now, aware of his surroundings and what awaited them in the building. It would be quiet at first, but Kyran had told him how it was normally full to capacity every night, and how many of the crowd were vampires. If he felt he was losing control of the situation, or Amber was in danger, he would get her out of the club and back to his apartment. He would find another way to lure the man out of hiding.

The two large men on the door stepped aside to let them pass. He pushed the door open and turned to Amber.

"Just as we planned. Go to the bar and order a drink with the money I gave you. Wait there until either I or the vampire comes for you."

She nodded and walked past him. His gaze followed her through the low-lit black walled room. She sat on a stool further along the bar.

The music in the club was quiet but later it would be pounding so loud he would have a headache for a day. He never enjoyed coming out in company, not anymore, and he especially hated this place. The vampires who came here were usually younger Lesser Nobles and Nobles looking for a quick snack or some amusement. The humans didn't realise the danger they walked amongst. To them it was just another nightclub. He glanced at Amber, still unable to believe that she had been to this wretched place, had come close to the less refined of his kind before, and then pushed his gaze onwards. He scanned the gathered people. The crowd was light, a few humans mingling with some Lesser Nobles or grouped together in the square booths around the large black dance floor.

The only Noble in the club right now was him.

The sandy-haired well-dressed man behind the bar gave him a nod. Kearn didn't grace him with one in return. The man was a Commoner, the rank of vampire far below Lesser Noble. Nothing more than a peasant. He had worked here in all the times that Kearn had visited and was the only vampire on the staff. Kearn had often wondered if the man owned the club. The Commoner walked down the length of the black glass-topped bar towards Amber. Kearn kept a close eye on the man. There was a momentary spark of red in his eyes as he took her drink order, his gaze darted down to her bandaged hand as she gave him the money, and then he moved away. Wise decision. Kearn didn't want to have to start the evening by killing someone. The Commoner stopped at the till near Kearn and looked right into his eyes. Kearn's switched briefly to red and he glared at the man, letting him sense his intent and making it clear that Amber belonged to him. The Commoner acknowledged him with a bow of his head and then made Amber's drink.

She smiled at the man as he gave it to her, distracting Kearn from his dark thoughts. She did look beautiful tonight. Perhaps he should have told her that just to see her reaction. He could imagine the deep crimson blush that would have stained her cheeks and it stirred his blood.

Perhaps he should concentrate on his work.

Kearn sat several stools away from Amber. They were the only two at the bar but that soon changed.

The minutes ticked by and each one brought more people into the club. Another Noble showed up, a tall dark-haired man with three human women draped all over him. Lord Montagu. The man's dark eyes narrowed on Kearn in contempt and then he was walking down the steps at the end of the bar area to the dance floor. Kearn shook off the irritation of such a weak-blooded man looking down on him and watched the rest of his entourage enter. All unranked Montagu men and women. The most interesting was a doe-eyed woman who watched the lord like a hawk. She was human and going through the transition judging by the scent of her blood. She had probably thought that Lord Montagu would change his ways once she had let him bite her and her dark fairytale would be complete. Humans were so gullible.

Kearn looked along the length of the bar at Amber.

Would she ever consent to becoming a vampire?

It was a ridiculous thought that he immediately shoved aside but it crept back into his head and he found himself musing it. Pondering how sweet Amber's throat would taste under his lips as he sunk his fangs into it reignited his ardour for her, fanning it back into life until it blazed through him, hotter than the surface of the sun and equally as fierce. The deep unrelenting thirst for her constantly flowed in his blood, pleading to be sated, even though he knew it was impossible.

If Amber were a vampire, she would sense his intent as he stared at her, and would know his dark pounding lust for her. If he turned her, she wouldn't become a weak vampire as other humans did, fit only to serve his pureblood kind. She would become the most beautiful creature on this planet, surpassing even pureblood vampires. Her power would be devastating, everything he had at his command and more, amplified by the gene in her blood. She would be as vampires had been many millennia ago. She would be a goddess.

His goddess.

He had never changed a human and had never wanted to before now.

While others treated it as nothing more than a thrilling moment, uncaring of the consequences or how the human felt, Kearn treated it with the respect that such a beautiful thing deserved. That he could give a human, Amber, the gift of immortality and the powers of his species was incredible.

But it was something he couldn't do, no matter how much he thought about it and how enticing it sounded in his mind. Had he been his old self, had he not become a Venator and not walked the path of solitude, despised by his kind, he would have thought differently. He would have been able to give Amber the life as a vampire that she deserved. If he bit her now and turned her, they would only have each other. She would find herself hated by not only humankind but by the vampires too. He couldn't ask her to tread the same path as him and bear the loneliness. Only he deserved to live such a life.

Amber deserved so much more.

People lined the bar between them. She ordered another drink and fiddled with the cocktail stirrer when it arrived. A man approached her. Human. She smiled politely and waved him away. Kearn focused, wanting to hear what she was telling him, but he couldn't make it out over the noise of the music. It was louder now and using his heightened senses hurt his head.

A few minutes later, another man approached her. Human again. She excused herself and then looked around the busy club.

Someone bumped against him and Kearn growled. He hated crowds almost as much as he hated this place. How many more people were they going to let in? He could barely see Amber now through the sea of black and red clad men and women, and he needed to keep an eye on her. He leaned forwards to catch a glimpse of her.

Her eyes settled on him and she blinked slowly, a hint of a smile touching the corners of her sensual red lips. He cast his gaze downwards at the bar and touched his throat again. It ached. He wrapped his hand around it and clasped it tightly. He needed a drink but blood wouldn't satisfy his thirst. He needed Amber.

He glanced at her out of the corner of his eye. She was flicking the cocktail stirrer back and forth across her half empty glass.

If she didn't stop looking so bored, she would never catch the vampire for him.

She smiled at him again, her painted lips luring him in until his field of focus zeroed in on her. She was supposed to be attracting the other vampires in the club, not him, but he couldn't take his eyes off her, and the more he stared, the hungrier he became.

He rubbed his throat again, wishing he could get something here to quench his thirst as easily as the humans could. The Commoner that had been behind the bar earlier was gone, replaced by two human males and one female. There was no chance of getting blood now.

"You should go speak to her."

Kearn frowned at the male bartender.

He nodded towards Amber. "Go speak to her. You're clearly interested. I've not seen her here before but she looks a little lonely… like you."

Kearn's expression darkened. He looked lonely? The bartender was probably putting things together from the evidence in front of him, a man sitting alone in a bar staring at a beautiful woman, but the conclusion he had drawn was too close to the mark. He was always alone but he had grown used to it and it was better than being around company who didn't want you there.

"I am too old for her." Kearn waved the man away.

The man didn't leave. He leaned across the bar and smiled consolingly.

"Listen." He crooked a finger, signalling for Kearn to come closer. Kearn didn't. The man smelt sweaty and he had no desire to interact so closely with a human. A voice at the back of his mind said he would interact this closely with Amber given the chance. He would sink his fangs deep into her neck and drink his fill of her to slake the thirst in his heart for a connection to someone. Kearn ignored it. "You don't look a day over thirty five and she's no younger than twenty five. There's an unwritten rule with men. Halve your age and add seven. That's the youngest you can go for."

Kearn calculated it in his head. Half of his age plus seven? He smiled. Unless Amber was really one hundred and eighty seven, he was too old for her.

Another group of vampires entered. More Nobles. This time they were higher ranking. The Marquess Montagu and Marquess Pendragon sneered at him as they passed. Kearn looked over towards Amber and held his throat again when it itched. He swallowed but it didn't relieve the ache.

The smell of everyone in the club wasn't even drowning out her scent. It was a good thing because he needed the vampires to smell her blood so it would lure them into speaking to her but it constantly pushed at his restraint. Since tasting her, he hadn't stopped desiring her. His lust for her blood was strong, so much so that he had dreamed of her and nothing else. She had been in his embrace, bare breasts against his chest and her arms around him, holding him close as he kissed and licked her throat. He had drunk from her, sinking his fangs deep into her neck and marking her as eternally his. He knew that was what he had been doing. He hadn't intended to kill her. He had wanted to make her a vampire like him. He had wanted to keep her.

Which was insane.

But her blood had tasted so good even in his dreams.

Kearn struggled for control as the memory of it assaulted him, sending an echo of the buzz he had felt through his body and fogging his mind. Something deep within him cried out for more, for another taste, another fix.

The club started to heat up as people moved and the smell of her blood grew stronger. It was a divine smell—sweet and fragrant. The voice at the back of his mind whispered that it could be his, just as it had been in his dreams.

He touched his neck again, pulled at the collar of his shirt when it felt as though it was strangling him, and frowned. He couldn't remember a time when he had felt so hungry.

"Are you okay?" Amber's voice startled him. "You don't look so good."

His eyes leapt to hers and then fell to her neck. His temperature increased the moment his gaze landed on the black choker wrapped around it. Her blood was delicious. She was delicious. His throat ached at the sight of hers, his hunger rising. He tightened his hold on his neck and tried to get a grip on himself. It wasn't just her blood doing this to him. It couldn't be. There was something deeper at work.

He forced his eyes up, until they met her wide ones. She stepped closer and her scent grew stronger, overwhelming him. He stood and took a step back, trying to distance himself and keep control.

"I am a little thirsty." That was an understatement. He was parched, gasping for the smooth slide of her blood down his throat and the giddy rush of it in his veins.

Like an addict.

"Come on." She grabbed his arm.

He looked at her hand on him, slender but strong. She walked away, luring him along the length of the bar to where she had been sitting, and he followed her blindly.

Kearn's eyes stuck like glue to the back of her neck, catching teasing glimpses of the nape of it and the black velvet choker through her dark hair. He longed to part the brown waves and kiss there, to run his tongue over her skin and taste her, and feel her shiver in pleasure. He wanted to ease his fangs in deep and slow, claiming her and her blood as his and his alone. Nothing compared to biting someone, to the incredible rush from the connection and the intense intoxicating feel of their blood in your veins. It was what he had been born to do—to take life from the blood of humans like a thief.

Like a beast.

And right now, he wanted to take all of Amber. He wanted to strip away the mask and show her just what he was underneath—a creature lost in her, thirsting for her body and blood.

For her love.

He tore his eyes away from her neck, horrified by his last thought and the realisation that his hunger for her went beyond physical need to an emotional one.

She stopped by her stool and flagged down the bartender, giving him a wide smile.

Kearn stared at the man, remembering what he had said. Lonely. The hand around his throat dropped to his chest and he focused there. Did it really show? Had Amber seen it? He had been on his guard around her but there had been times when he had felt as though she had looked right down into his heart and seen the man beneath the armour.

Amber put a tall glass of icy dark liquid into Kearn's hand, bringing his attention back to her. She held a similar glass. He sniffed his. Sweet and bubbly. Some sort of soft drink. It was cold against his hand but would do nothing to satisfy his thirst.

Amber only made it worse.

She tilted her head back, her profile to him, and drank her drink. He couldn't stop himself from staring at her throat. It was unbearable to see it so exposed, so clean and soft and smooth, crying out for him to mark it. He wanted to tear off her choker and sink his teeth into her, to pull her close and feel her heart pound against his, beating as one.

Kearn clamped his mouth shut against the strong urge to bite her. His fangs extended enough to catch his lower lip. He licked the blood but it wasn't enough. It had to be her blood. Only that would satisfy his craving. The voice at the back of his mind, deep in his heart, commanded him to bite her.

She lowered the glass from her lips and looked at him with beautiful round eyes, tempting him with her innocence.

His fangs receded with only a little resistance.

"You're not drinking?" She frowned at his glass. "It's my treat."

She flicked the long dark waves of hair away from her neck and strands of it stuck to her damp skin. He narrowed his eyes on the pulse fluttering on her throat. If it was her treat, he would drink her down in one go.

It took all of his willpower to resist surrendering to the desire to give in to temptation. His blood pounded in his temples, driven to a frenzy by the unquenchable and undeniable hunger he felt for Amber. It wasn't just her blood. It was everything about her—her smile, her beauty, her body, and how she looked at him sometimes with concern. He had never experienced such need, such intense attraction and desire, for anyone in all his years.

Not even the countess.

His need for Amber, his hunger for her, was raw and uncontrollable. It thundered in his veins and ran deep in his bones. It commanded him. Ruled him.

She smiled and then frowned at his face.

"You've cut your lip." She touched it with her delicate fingertip, peering closely. The warm caress enticed him, making his lower lip tingle, and the smell of blood was too strong to fight. He couldn't take it.

His fangs began to extend again and he almost gave in to the desire to nick her finger with them. He couldn't do that. He couldn't make her like him.

Kearn stepped back and covered his mouth as his fangs fully extended, his eyes as wide as hers were.

The flames of desire burnt away the last threads of his restraint and he turned away, sensing that his eyes were about to change against his will too. He didn't want her to see him. He didn't want to be himself around her.

"Is something wrong?" Amber touched his arm.

He shirked her grip and took another step away from her.

"I am unwell. Excuse me," he said and rushed into the crowd, heading through the packed club towards the bathroom.

Humans blocked his path, bumping into him and making it hard to get through. The smell of their blood increased his hunger. He kept his hand over his mouth and pushed through, shoving them aside in his haste to reach the relative safety of the bathroom. The room began to brighten. His eyes were changing. He squinted and lowered his head, forcing his way through the hot bodies that stank of wretched blood.

And all the while, he could smell the sweet scent of hers.

His mind filled with visions of Amber. He saw himself taking her into his arms, her warm supple body moulded against the hot hard steel of his, and sinking his fangs deep into her throat. He would drink every drop of her blood without a moment's regret and it still wouldn't be enough. He would do it regardless of the fact that he would hate himself in the aftermath.

Kearn hit the bathroom door so hard it slammed into the tiled wall and wouldn't close automatically. A man standing at one of the white basins lining the left hand wall of the bright room made a quick exit. Kearn grabbed the door and forced it shut. He stumbled to the row of white sinks and ran the water in one until it was freezing, and then splashed it over his face. It didn't stop the images of Amber from dancing around his mind. He could see everything he had dreamed and swore he could feel her naked body against his.

Kearn doused himself in water again. It did nothing to cool him. He was on fire, sweat beading and running down his skin. Burning for her.

He gripped the edge of the white basin with trembling hands and stared at himself in the long bank of mirrors above the sinks. Red eyes watched him. His other side. The one he didn't want her to see. Why did he fear it all of a sudden? Being a vampire had never bothered him before. His species were above humans. They were strong and beautiful. Not beasts.

So why did Amber make him feel like an animal?

How did she make him feel so hungry?

He had never felt such thirst. Never. He had tasted forbidden blood before but it hadn't left him feeling this way—needing another fix. Needing her.

Water dripped from the ends of his silver hair. The sound of the running tap and his rough breathing filled his ears. He stared hard into his red eyes, struggling against his hunger. After a few long minutes, his irises slowly melted back to green from the pupil outwards.

He took a deep breath and sighed, regaining control.

The bathroom door opened and a human male walked in, nodding at him and then heading into the stalls behind him.

Kearn turned off the tap and left. The music in the club was loud when he opened the bathroom door and walked out into the darker main room, grating in his ears. Even more people were crammed into it now. He made his way back to where he had left Amber at the bar and stared wide-eyed at the empty stool.

She was gone.

He scanned the club for her, trying to keep his cool. Perhaps she had gone to the bathroom too.

Perhaps the vampire had found her while he had been acting like a ridiculous junkie.

No. That couldn't have happened. He wouldn't let the man have her.

Amber was his.

He headed down towards the dance floor, methodically searching and taking account of every face, marking each as either human or vampire. He was nearing the back of the club in a quieter spot favoured by Nobles when he saw her.

And he saw who she was with.

Kyran stood beside her, both of them facing away from him, with his hand against her lower back, far enough down it that his fingers were lazily resting on the bottom of her corset, close to her backside. Fire burned through Kearn's veins. How dare his brother touch her so familiarly? Kyran laughed with his friends and Amber laughed along with them. The sound of it and the sight of her smiling into Kyran's eyes fuelled the inferno inside him. He wouldn't let it happen again. His eyes changed and Kyran looked over at him.

Kearn shut his emotions down in an instant, forcing his eyes to switch back.

Kyran's dark eyebrows rose, his blue eyes cold and empty.

"There you are," he said casually, as though he hadn't felt the threat Kearn had directed at him.

Amber turned around, broke out of his brother's grasp, and came over to him.

"Are you feeling better?" Concern shone brightly in her eyes.

She reached up with her right hand and touched his face, sweeping the wet strands of hair from his face. Her actions brought the bandage around her hand too close to his nose. The smell of her blood threatened to overpower him. He caught her hand and slowly brought it away from his face, trying not to startle her by reacting as he had wanted to and throwing it aside.

"You look terrible." Kyran stopped beside Amber. His brother placed a hand on Amber's bare shoulder and looked him over. "Amber mentioned that you were unwell. Rough day?"

Kyran's gaze slid to Amber's throat.

"You seem to be struggling." Kyran smiled at him and released Amber's arm. "I thought you of all people would be used to it."

Amber's eyes met his. He didn't want to answer the question he could see coming. His brother wasn't talking about his job. He was talking about forbidden blood.

He grabbed Kyran's arm and dragged him away, leaving Amber with Kyran's friends. They wouldn't dare hurt her. A thousand things he wanted to say sprung to the tip of his tongue, all accusations and anger, but he let them go and released Kyran's arm.

"Thank you for keeping her safe." It was difficult to say those words when he knew that Kyran had probably only been friendly to Amber to irritate him.

Kyran smiled and, for once, it was genuine. "She looked lost. I approached her and she seemed so relieved to see me. She started babbling about you and how you were sick and thirsty and I knew where you had gone. Are you better now?"

Kearn nodded. He was back in control at least.

"I can get some blood sent over—"

"No." Kearn cut him off. "I do not want you on my list. The hunger will pass."

Kyran looked worried. Kearn's senses said he wasn't lying.

He forced himself to look at Kyran. A reflection of him, but not the one he had seen just now in the mirror. The dark shorter hair, the blue eyes, the wide charming smile and fine black suit. Kyran was everything he had once been, and everything he wanted to be again. His brother's face and his own were torture to him, a constant reminder that no matter what he did, he would never be the man he had once been. He couldn't change the past, and that meant he could never undo the damage to his relationship with Kyran either.

Kyran smiled. It warmed his eyes and reminded Kearn of better days when they had been young. It was unusual for vampires to be born so close together in age. Their mother had given birth to them only four human years apart, and due to a difficulty in her health, they had been her only children. To a human, they looked the same age, and would have appeared to be twins once.

But not now.

A Venator was different to a vampire, and his appearance now marked that. They were distinguished.

Hated.

None more so than him.

"You should take more care of yourself." Kyran touched his shoulder. "Especially now that there is another of you in town."

Kyran looked to his left and Kearn followed his gaze. A female Venator stood alone in the corner of the club opposite the one where Amber and Kyran's friends waited. With her long silver hair flowing over her slender shoulders and her vivid green eyes, she was unmistakable. Her appearance was enough to make every vampire around her cautious, but she was even wearing her black uniform. The silver buttons down the breast and the sky blue detailing on the collar and cuffs of the thigh-length military-style jacket caught the flashing lights of the club. She was new to the job if she was foolish enough to wear her uniform in public.

"You should introduce yourself, shouldn't you?"

Kearn nodded. The Venator was watching him, and so was Amber. He sensed her gaze on him, the remnants of her blood in his veins calling to him, and then the feeling was gone. He glanced at her to see her looking at the female Venator.

He was required to introduce himself and greet any Venator in his territory, but this wasn't a good time. His thirst for Amber's blood burned strong in his veins and Venators were trained to recognise the effects of forbidden blood on a vampire. The Venator would see what he had done. There was an allowed amount that they could take in the line of duty, but it was still taboo for a Venator to do such a thing.

It wasn't the only reason he didn't want to greet her.

Amber was glaring at the woman and he wanted to go to her instead.

"Go on," Kyran said. "I will make sure that Amber is safe here. I have teased you enough and will not reveal anything to her."

He still hesitated.

Kyran pushed him forwards.

Kearn felt Amber's gaze on him again but walked over to the female Venator. She lowered her head when he reached her.

"Lord Savernake." She pressed her right hand to her chest. The silver markings on it were different to his. She was shorter than he was, possibly even more so than Amber, and was much weaker. Females that became Venators were never as strong as their male counterparts were. The role passed from father to eldest son. Daughters were only involved when there was no son in the Venator line. He studied her. She wasn't a Noble either.

"Venator. We are above such formalities, are we not?" A remnant of his old self, buried deep inside him, said that she was below him. A Lesser Noble. She deserved to scrape and bow at his feet. Weaker blooded, poorer connected, and lower bred. She was beneath him in all ways. The only things worse than her kind were Commoners and humans.

She kept her head bowed.

"Welcome to my territory. I hope our meeting is fortuitous and not a sign of something else." He kept his tone warm, trying to tamp down his thoughts. The woman was a Venator. They were equals, and he had no right to judge her by her blood when he was an outcast of his own family.

She raised her eyes now, green irises and wide pupils betraying her shock at his words. Her expression only added to her appearance of youthful innocence. She looked as weak as he sensed her to be. Far too young to deal with their duty. He placed her at no older than two hundred. To the humans around her, she looked like a twenty year old.

"You have noticed, have you not?" he said and she glanced towards Amber.

"You are struggling against the effects of blood." Her voice was soft but he could still hear her.

The corners behind the speakers were far quieter than the rest of the club, and Lesser Noble and all Noble vampires desiring to protect their hearing favoured them. It was a good place to discuss business, and afforded them a view of the entire room so they could pick out prey at their leisure without suffering from the ear-bleeding volume of the music.

She gave him a shy look, as though she felt guilty for confirming that she knew he had recently tasted blood from a Source, and then her expression gradually changed back to awe. Had she never met another Venator? How many vampires had she killed and how long ago had she been given her duty?

"You have seen the human with those vampires." He didn't look their way but he could feel Amber's eyes on him and the female. "A vampire I have been seeking for several years attacked her and fed his blood to her. I tasted her blood to confirm her as a Source Blood and so I could maintain control of her and question her. The human is now bait in my plan to lure out the man and sentence him."

"I see." The woman peered past him. "It is forgivable then. Did your plan include her leaving?"

Kearn turned on the spot. Amber was gone.

"Excuse me," he said and crossed the dance floor to his brother.

"She wanted to go." Kyran shrugged. "We tried to make her stay and wait, but it seemed the little thing did not like seeing you with another woman."

Kearn glared at him and then hurried through the club. Had Amber really left because he had been speaking to the Venator, or was Kyran lying? The thought that she might be jealous warmed his chest but he didn't allow himself to believe it. He had given Amber no reason to feel that way and he had no reason to feel anything in response to it.

What was he getting himself into?

He pushed through the throng, growling under his breath about the way people were hindering his progress and the growing awareness of his feelings towards Amber.

She was bait. It was just her blood making him act this way. And that was just a lie.

It ran deeper than blood. She had entranced him even before he had tasted her. It had been difficult to keep his eyes off her in the street when he had fought to protect her from the man, and in his car as he drove her to his apartment. He had been under her spell since the moment he had met her.

Amber meant something to him.

But she was human. She was beneath him, fit only to serve his kind.

Kearn broke through the crowd and out into the night.

He wished he could bring himself to believe that but he couldn't. She didn't feel as though she was beneath him. She felt above him, beyond his grasp. Human or not, he wanted her to be his.

He couldn't see her in the street. He searched all of the side roads that branched off the main road outside the club and then got into his car and drove around. The remnant of her blood in his veins wasn't enough for him to track her. Searching for her so randomly didn't have a great chance of success, but he had to find her. The vampire might have been at the club tonight and might have seen her leave. Without him, she was in danger.

He couldn't allow that.

He would keep his promise, no matter what.

He wouldn't let anything happen to her.

CHAPTER 7

Amber stormed along the street, walking blind in the hope of there being an Underground station ahead. She cursed her heels when her ankle gave out and hobbled on, defiant in the face of pain and the sliver of fear running through her veins. The streets were dark and there were only a few people around. What time was it? Judging by the lack of cars and people, it had to be close to midnight, if not already past it. She hoped she could reach the Underground before the last train. Her gaze darted around, taking in the dark brick and sandstone office buildings surrounding her, her heart beating fast against her chest. She couldn't believe that a club she had been to catered to vampires. A shiver bolted down her spine. How many times had she flirted with one? How close had she come to being nothing more than a midnight snack? And why had Kearn dressed her in such revealing clothing? She had never had to dress so sexily to fit in and attract attention at the club before.

Every man she walked past ogled her breasts and her thighs. It was freezing in the ridiculous stupid damn clothes that Kearn had bought for her.

And what good had they done?

The only men in the club who had shown the slightest interest had been a few less than savoury characters and Kyran. He had come over to her the moment he had spotted her and offered to keep her company, inviting her to meet his nice friends and keeping her away from the fiends that patrolled the club. He had been kind and attentive, ensuring that she felt included in his circle of friends. She hadn't minded the way he had remained close to her. It had been comforting and she had felt safe around him, protected from the vampires.

Kearn had gone and spoken to that other woman instead.

Her blood boiled.

Kyran had tried to stop her from leaving but she had been determined to get away. She had wanted out. Not just of the club but of everything. She didn't want to play bait anymore, not now that she had realised why she had agreed to it in the first place.

It hadn't been because Kearn could keep her safe and get rid of the man who wanted her blood.

It had been because she was attracted to Kearn.

The woman was a much-needed reminder that Kearn wasn't hers, and that he hadn't even hinted that he was attracted to her. He had seemed very comfortable with the young woman and hadn't looked at Amber once while he was with her. Kyran had explained that the woman was another Venator and Kearn had to greet her, but it hadn't made Amber feel any better.

A man wolf-whistled at her from across the quiet street. She stuck her fingers up at him and kept walking. She was sick of this stupid game of cat and mouse. Kearn could find himself a new mouse.

The low growl of an engine echoed around the street, bouncing off the office buildings around her and she walked faster. Lights punctured the dim street and threw her shadow out long in front of her. A moment later, the white Audi R8 pulled to a halt just a few yards ahead of her and she slowed down. He had found her.

Well, he was a hunter. She supposed that his kind could find anyone they were looking for. She smiled cruelly. Although he couldn't find his man.

"Get in the car."

Amber looked down at the open window and empty passenger seat.

She kept walking, sure that there would be an Underground station nearby. She had enough money to get a ticket back to her place and out of Kearn's crazy world.

A car door slammed behind her.

"I said to get in the car." Kearn's footsteps were loud in the quiet road.

"Clearly, I don't want to." She carried on. He wasn't going to order her around. Not now.

He walked past her and stopped in her path, his eyes narrowed with his frown. She looked into them, not hiding any of her anger or contempt, and they darted between hers, searching. Was he trying to see in them why she had left the club and was refusing to go with him? If he couldn't figure it out for himself, then he was a lost cause.

"Get out of my way." Amber went to pass him but he blocked her. She shoved him aside.

Kearn grabbed her arm and pulled her backwards, towards his car. That wasn't going to happen. She stamped on his foot, using her heel, eliciting a short noise of frustration from him. His grip on her arm tightened.

"Get in the car." Anger laced his dark tone, turning it blacker than a thundercloud and just as threatening.

"No."

"Why not?"

Amber glared at him. He glared right back. She didn't care if she had hurt his foot. He deserved it.

He deserved a lot more than it.

"You should go back to the club. Your girlfriend will miss you."

His dark silver eyebrows rose and his eyes widened. It was as though a light had clicked on in his mind and she was seeing the external effect.

Amber yanked her arm free and tried to keep walking but he caught hold of her again and pulled her back to the car. She stumbled and landed on the bonnet. Part of her wished she had hit it harder and put a dent in it with her backside. Perhaps that would hurt Kearn enough to satisfy her.

"I do not have a woman." Irritation joined the anger in his tone. Did her lack of obedience frustrate him? Good.

She pushed away from his car.

"Where are you going?"

Amber whirled to face him and his gaze dropped to her thighs. The motion had sent her black skirt flying out and had probably given him a view of her underwear. That drove her to confront him. She was going to give him a piece of her mind, set him straight, and then leave.

"I'm going home to get some real clothes." She started out small. Her insides fluttered at the thought of confronting him about everything. It was frightening but exhilarating at the same time, sending a dizzying rush of adrenaline through her.

"Those are clothes."

Every inch of her warmed as his gaze drifted over her body, leisurely taking her in, his pupils widening the whole time. She blazed so hot that her skin prickled, the cold forgotten. His eyes roamed over her again, from her heeled boots, over the tiny skirt and tight corset, to her throat and then her face. He stared into her eyes, desire visible in his.

Now he was eyeing her up? Too damn late for that.

"No." She placed her hands on her hips and his eyes settled there, burning into her, as though he was trying to see through the small black skirt to her knickers beneath. "This is something a whore wears. I don't know what circles you move in, but sluts dress this way."

Kearn was silent for a moment, a stunned edge to his expression.

"I thought it looked nice." No trace of anger touched his voice now. It was low and cautious, edged with huskiness. If he could sense her intent to explode, then he was stupid for complimenting her for looking good dressed as a two-bit prostitute.

"You would. You're a man! Or whatever it is you are." Amber turned on her heel and stalked away.

He was in front of her again before she could make it five paces.

"There are no Underground stations around here and you cannot walk to your home." The spark of desire that had been in his eyes was gone, but their green depths weren't empty. Concern filled them.

"I'll get a cab." She tried to step past him but he moved with her.

She wasn't in the mood to dance.

"And pay them with what?" He countered her again.

"With money at my flat." Amber curled her fingers into fists and tried to pass him.

He wouldn't let her. He blocked her path and stepped into her, forcing her backwards.

"And you have keys for that flat?"

Checkmate.

Amber cursed him under her breath. Her keys and things were at his place. She hadn't been planning to ditch him.

"Leave me alone," she whispered and unclenched her hands. Her shoulders sagged and she stared at the pavement. "I'm tired of playing slut for you and your vampire friends. Just leave me alone and find them yourself."

Silence.

She hated the sound of it. She wanted him to say something to make her stay, to make her feel as though she was more to him than just bait, but she knew in her heart that it wasn't going to happen and she had a feeling why.

"I need your help." His eyes shone in the light of his car, open and honest. He needed her help and she needed answers. If he gave them to her, confirmed her suspicions or put them to rest forever, then she would go with him.

Her fingers went to the bandage around her right palm.

She stared deep into his eyes, holding his attention. "Then you'd better be straight with me, starting with this."

Before he could move, Amber tore the bandage off and thrust her palm in his face.

He recoiled and turned away.

"No." She moved around him, unwilling to let him escape, her heart beating like a jackhammer against her ribs. "You're like them, aren't you? You're a vampire!"

She pushed her hand in his face, keeping up with him as he backed towards his car. He tried to swat her hand away but she wouldn't let him. She kept it in his face, wanting to see if she was right about him. He stared at her palm, his eyes so wide that she could see the whole of his irises, and swallowed hard.

"You want this."

Kearn grabbed her wrist, spun her around so quickly her head swirled, and pinned her to the passenger side of his car.

"Do not *ever* do that again." His voice was dark and low, a rumbling sound that echoed his anger. His grip on her wrist tightened until it hurt.

She didn't care.

All she could focus on were the red eyes staring into hers and the sharp fangs that showed between his lips when he spoke.

She had been right.

Kearn was a vampire.

Her pulse raced, body trembling, and her knees weakened. She was falling for a vampire. It would have seemed insane if she hadn't already accepted it on some level. She had known what he was and, although sense had said that she was foolish for still wanting him, her feelings hadn't changed in the slightest. It scared her, but she was determined to keep moving forwards on the path she was walking, to see where it took her.

She stared up into his red eyes, mesmerised by them, lost in the explosive combinations of feelings running riot through her. She wasn't sure whether to break free of his grasp or submit to him. Part of her wanted to run away and the rest wanted to run to him, to feel his arms around her and his mouth on hers.

Kearn's lips parted, revealing his fangs.

Reality check.

Would he bite her?

A spark of fear shot through her blood. Instinct said to escape. She wasn't ready for this. What had she expected from him? He was a vampire. Vampires bit people. She didn't want to be just another meal to him.

"Kearn?" she whispered, fearful of jolting him out of whatever thoughts he was lost in as he stared at her in case she prompted him to bite her.

He leaned into her, his body as hard as granite against hers. There was so much anger in his eyes but there was conflict too. Her blood was like a drug to vampires. Did he want it? Was that a bad thing?

He had told her that it was illegal to drink her blood. Would they punish him for tasting it? Was that the reason behind the battle playing out in his eyes?

Kearn bent her hand back and his red eyes shifted to her palm.

"I need to stop this damned cut from bleeding."

Amber's eyes shot wide when he licked her palm. She kept still, fascinated by the feel of his tongue stroking her skin. The moment he swallowed, he trembled and leaned more heavily into her. He turned his head to one side and gazed at her chest, breathing hard. The fingers of his other hand curled around her waist, digging in. He licked the cut again, harder this time, pressing his tongue in as though he needed more, and then released her arm. His hand claimed her neck, fingers against the nape sending a shiver down her spine, and he pressed his thumb against her jaw, tilting her head back.

His gaze tracked down her throat and then fell to her breasts.

This wasn't like him.

He pulled her closer, exhaled on a sigh, and ground his hips against hers. He was hard.

Her blood had this effect on vampires?

He was a different person now—his red eyes unabashedly taking in her body and his grip on her dominant. Gone was the man she had been speaking to a moment ago, replaced by something altogether more sensual and unrestrained.

His eyes narrowed on her throat and he lowered his thumb from her jaw and hooked it into the thick choker. She gasped when he tore it off and threw it to the ground. His hand claimed her neck again, rough and commanding. Her blood thundered through her veins in response, her heart whispering that he was going to bite her if she didn't do something.

"Kearn?" she whispered.

Before she could ask him if he was alright, his lips were on hers, devouring them in a hungry kiss. He pressed the length of his body into hers and forced his tongue into her mouth. It caressed hers, teasing her teeth and luring her into joining it. She couldn't stop herself. She kissed him back but failed to match his rough demanding passion. His mouth claimed hers with fierce possession, stealing her breath as their lips parted and met, their tongues tangling and breath mingling. Her pulse raced. A heady sensation of need ignited deep within her. Her tongue traced his teeth, finding no fangs, and she thrilled at the thought that they had been there a moment ago. He moaned and she threaded her fingers into his hair, twisting the silver lengths around them, and held his mouth against hers. It was too divine to surrender and she feared it would end too soon.

He thrust against her again and groaned into her mouth.

Was her blood making him do this, or had it only freed his desire? It had to be the latter. She wanted this to be about her, not her blood.

He slid his hands down to her hips, clutching her against him, and kissed her deeper, until she felt as though she couldn't breathe, but she wouldn't give him up. She wanted to drown in him.

Someone called over to them, making lewd suggestions.

Kearn was gone in a heartbeat. Amber slowly opened her eyes, dazed and warm all over. Her gaze sought Kearn. He stood with his back to her, the beam of his car's headlights on his legs.

Amber went to him and tried to touch his arm but he jerked away from her.

"Leave me." He took a step forwards. "Get in the damn car and leave me."

Amber backed away, her stomach heavy with guilt. She hadn't meant to upset him. The air around him felt colder than ever. It felt as though any chance she'd had of opening his closed off heart had disappeared.

Slipped through her bloodstained fingers.

She got into the car, afraid of upsetting him further by disobeying him this time. Her eyes roamed over his black shirt-clad back and down his arms. His fists trembled at his sides.

It wasn't just his fists shaking. His shoulders were too. When he had been against her, she had felt him trembling. If she had known her blood would induce such a strong reaction, she wouldn't have teased him with it.

Kearn raked his fingers over his silver hair and locked them around the back of his head. Why had he told her to leave him alone? Because he didn't want her?

A chill settled in her at that thought.

She wanted him. It was insane of her to want a vampire, but she did. Deep in her heart, she knew that Kearn wasn't like the man who had attacked her. He was doing all in his power to protect her. He had to feel something for her. It had to be about more than her blood and his duty.

He tilted his head back, his hands still clutching it, and then lowered it again.

Minutes passed and he still didn't move.

What was he doing?

Her heart said that she knew exactly what he was doing. He was fighting whatever dark desire she had awoken in him. She touched her bare throat. The way he had torn her choker away, ridding her throat of obstruction, still made her shiver, but not wholly from fear. Part of her had thrilled at the thought he might bite her. There had been visible struggle in his eyes before he had kissed her. Had he forced himself to do that in order to stop himself from sinking his fangs into her neck, satisfying his hunger with her kiss rather than her blood? If he came to her now, would he be a danger to her? Would he want to bite her?

He turned around, walked to the car, and got in. His eyes were green again. Did that mean he was back to normal?

He stared straight ahead. "Do not ever do that again."

There was no trace of anger in his tone, only a sense of weariness that left her feeling worse than if he had shouted at her. Amber shrank away and leaned against the passenger side door, looking out of it as he drove. The world flew by, all blurred coloured lights and darkness. She sighed and her breath fogged the window. It cleared a few seconds later, the misty patch creeping smaller and smaller until it disappeared.

Kearn didn't speak.

She wanted to break the oppressive silence but couldn't find the right words. How did you apologise to a vampire for tipping him over the edge?

How much danger had she really been in?

The kiss had been fantastic but if the man hadn't disturbed them would it have come with a high price? Would Kearn have bitten her? Drained her dry?

She felt as though she had flicked the latch on Pandora's Box and flung the lid open without considering the consequences.

"Where do you live?"

Amber blinked her heavy thoughts away. The hard set of Kearn's eyes couldn't hide the feelings in them this time.

He didn't want to ask that question.

Something inside her said that there was a more important one that he couldn't voice. She felt different again, as she had the night she had tasted the vampire's blood, only this time she felt out of place and unsatisfied. And worried.

There was an underlying sense of struggle and conflict too, and those were both of the feelings in Kearn's eyes.

She could feel him.

She almost laughed at herself but there was no other explanation. Somehow, she could feel him.

Was the conflict really about his desire for her blood or something else? Now that the moment had passed, she felt it was about something else, and she knew what it was. It was only natural for him to think it. After all, she had been afraid of the vampire who had attacked her.

Amber directed him to her flat, never taking her eyes off him. She tried to pick out the emotions that didn't feel as though they were hers. Whenever she had almost figured one out, it winked out of existence. They disappeared at the same rate as they did in Kearn's eyes, until she felt normal again and his eyes were empty.

He pulled the car to a halt outside her dull brick apartment building in the suburbs of London. His car couldn't have been more out of place surrounded by the hatchbacks, estates, and occasional four-wheel drive vehicles in the parking lot. None of them cost anywhere near half that of Kearn's two-seater sports car.

Amber stepped out of the car, resisting the temptation to say that it was a safe neighbourhood and his car would be alright. She didn't need to explain her life to him or apologise for the way she lived it.

Kearn's gaze scanned over the uniform rows of small windows on her four-storey building. It wasn't as impressive as his, but it was how normal people lived in London. He didn't say anything so she led the way to her flat. It was only when they reached her door that she remembered she didn't have any keys.

"The super has a spare set of my keys. There's a chance he might still be awake. Wait here. I'll go see," she said but Kearn shook his head.

She expected him to tell her to remain in the hall while he went to the super for her, but he stepped past her and waved his hand over the locks on her door instead. Each clicked. She couldn't believe her eyes when he turned the handle and her front door swung open.

Amber thanked him with a quick smile, trying to grasp what he had just done.

He could open things with just a wave of his hand. Hey presto! That would be a useful ability when breaking and entering to drink people as they slept soundly in their beds. Could vampires just walk in uninvited?

Her nerves got the better of her and her brain engaged babble mode.

"Do I have to invite you over the threshold?" she said with a giggle that came out sounding more like a hiccup.

"Your blood is invite enough... not just to your home." Kearn looked so serious that her heart leapt into her throat. She swallowed it back down.

Just what sort of things had she invited him to do? The light bulb in her head pinged on. She could catch a hint of his feelings. Did it work both ways? Could he control her as the other vampire had? The implications of what just a drop of blood could do suddenly seemed infinite.

She pushed the growing list in her head away and stepped into her apartment.

Kearn didn't follow.

He stood in the cream hall. The serious edge to his eyes hadn't gone anywhere.

She walked back to him, feeling that he wanted to say something. She felt conflicted again, and anxious.

"Do you fear me now?" He glanced away from her, casting his eyes downwards at the wooden floor in the corridor. "You may remain here if you prefer it."

He took a step back. She countered it with one towards him.

"No."

He stared at her, eyes empty and betraying none of the feelings inside her. He needed more than just that one word. He needed to hear her say it.

"You don't scare me," she said.

He didn't look as though he believed her. She wished he would because it was the truth. The fact that he was a vampire didn't frighten her, not as she had expected it would. He didn't feel dangerous to her. Being around him was exciting. Even when she saw his fangs and his eyes, he was still the same man to her. He was Kearn—the only thing that felt real in this strange fantasy world and the man who wanted to protect her from the bad guy.

He was her hero.

"We're partners, remember? We need to catch that man, and until we do, the only place I'll feel safe is with you." Her feelings lightened but Kearn's expression didn't.

"You are probably safer away from me," he said and then added in a whisper, "I cannot stop thinking about your blood."

Her heart missed a beat. His gaze darted to her chest. Of course he would hear it. It wasn't fear but strange excitement that had made it skip. Did he know that?

Amber held her hand out to him.

"Come in." She was glad her hand didn't tremble like the rest of her. "I'm sorry for what I did. I hadn't expected that sort of reaction."

He placed his hand into hers. "I apologise too for acting the way I did."

Amber didn't say anything. There was no need for him to apologise. The kiss had been amazing and she was glad that it had happened. Some small part of her clung to the hope that her blood wasn't the only reason he had kissed her. She wanted him to be attracted to her too.

His hand left hers the moment he crossed the threshold of her small flat and she closed the door. Kearn walked along the purple hall to the open door at the end and looked around her living room. There wasn't much to see. Now that she had been in his place, hers looked tiny. She could probably fit her whole apartment into just his bedroom.

She felt like apologising again so she turned right down the hall and went into her bedroom. She gathered clothes that would make her pretty but not like a slut, and then picked up her old gym bag and dumped it down on her double bed. The bag smelt a bit. A spray with perfume fixed that and she crammed her clothes in, tossing in some toiletries on top. Her whole life fit into a small bag. There was something sad about that.

She looked around her bedroom at her belongings, her gaze skipping over the stack of French books on her mahogany dresser, and realised that she didn't have that much to pack for her move after all.

Other than the photos of her brother at his Paris apartment and her parents at their villa in southern France that decorated her dresser and mocked her chilly British life with their warm smiles, there was nothing else she would take with her even if she were never coming back.

Amber stared at the French books next to the framed photographs, feeling none of the excitement she had before when looking at them. She felt less certain about her trip now, and it wasn't just because she knew that vampires existed and were likely to be in Paris too.

Her gaze strayed to the door that led back to the hallway and Kearn.

There was already a part of her that didn't want to leave him, and she knew that with every hour, let alone day, that she spent with him, that part of her would grow.

Moving to a new country didn't seem anywhere near as exciting as the past few hours she had spent with Kearn.

She picked up her bag, sighed, and walked back along the hall to him. He looked positively bored but his green eyes warmed when he turned to face her. She stared into them, remembering how red they had been and how sharp his fangs had looked.

She stopped just short of him, held her bag in both hands in front of her, and hesitated. He would be angry if she asked him, but she had to know.

"Do you bite people? Is that what you had for breakfast?"

He frowned. "No. I do not bite people."

Amber dropped her gaze and bit her lip, feeling her cheeks burn. At least he didn't look bored now. He looked mortally offended.

Finding her courage, she raised her eyes to his.

"What... what would happen... if you did bite someone?" It started out as a whisper but she was close to normal volume by the time she added, "Would they die?"

"No." His green eyes lost their hardness. "*You* would not die."

Her blush deepened. Was she that obvious?

"You would become like me."

"Just from a bite... no swapping blood. I would die and change just like that?"

"A single bite is all it takes to infect you. You would not die. Over a period of two years or less, you would gradually change until your thirst awakened." His expression turned serious again and his gaze fell to her throat. "It would not even take a bite. A scratch from my fangs would be enough."

The edges of his irises burned red and then faded to green when he looked away.

He wanted to bite her. She touched her neck and then dropped her hand before he noticed. He didn't need her drawing attention to it if he was struggling against a desire to drink her blood.

"Is it the same for all vampires?"

"No. Only those bitten by a vampire of the noble houses can do such a thing. A vampire born to parents of a pure bloodline."

"Like you?"

"Like me."

And Kyran. And she suspected those friends of Kyran's were probably vampires too. No wonder Kyran knew Earl Huntingdon. They were both vampires of noble blood. If she had kept reading the book, would she have found Kearn's name in there and that of his brother?

"How do other vampires... if that man bites me—"

"I will not allow that," Kearn interjected.

"But what if it did happen?" She had to know what she was up against and what might happen to her. She had always faced things and this time wasn't going to be any different.

"If he is like me, you would become like us." Something akin to concern shone in his green eyes.

"If he isn't?"

"You will die."

Three words that fell like lead on her chest. She would rather become a vampire than die.

"Why?" Her voice trembled.

"Because I doubt he would give you his blood to complete the process of a Commoner." Kearn walked to her and took her bag. The silver strands of his hair partially obscured his eyes as he frowned. "Something tells me that the man we seek is not of common blood though."

"That isn't comforting in the slightest, and it isn't the whole truth either is it?" Her bravery almost faltered. She had felt the lie in his words.

He shook his head.

"So stop telling me the bedtime story version." She tilted her chin up and straightened, denying her creeping fear. "What would they do to me?"

"Bleed you... without biting you."

"Kill me? For my blood?" A chill chased down her spine and arms. She could see herself tied up and slowly bleeding to death in front of that vampire while he grinned at her.

"No. Killing you would mean an end to the supply. They would sooner turn you, risking your blood gradually losing its effects with each day you progressed in your transition, than kill you. At least then they would have a year or two in which to harvest your blood." He paused and frowned, his expression turning troubled, and she sensed he didn't want to say anything else on the matter. She gave him a look that demanded he tell her and he sighed. "They would not kill you or turn you, Amber. They would take enough blood to keep you alive and weak, and under their control. I have seen it done. Whenever you recovered, they would take your blood again, harvesting it."

Amber gasped and shook her head. Tears blurred her vision. They were going to torture her by keeping her on the edge of death. If that man gave her blood again, she would do as he commanded—eating, drinking, restoring her blood so he could drain her again.

Her knees gave way but Kearn caught her arm, supporting her with one hand.

"It will not happen to you, Amber." There was a promise in his eyes. The terrifying vision of the man using her as a slave drifted away as she looked into them. "I will keep you safe."

Amber nodded and held on to his arm until her legs felt strong again. Her eyes didn't leave his. She drank her fill of the emotions in them. She could see beyond the barrier, down into his heart. She had opened it and she didn't want it to close again, even when she knew it would.

"So we're partners?" she whispered up at him.

A sense of sorrow and emptiness filled her and it was there in his eyes too. Loneliness.

He nodded and then turned away.

"Partners."

CHAPTER 8

Kearn's phone rang in his pocket when they were halfway to his car. He pulled the black mobile out and glanced at the display as he brought it to his ear. His brother.

"Where have you been?" Kyran's voice crackled. The reception was poor. "I have been trying to call you since you left the club."

"What is it?" He handed the bag to Amber and pulled his car keys from his trouser pocket.

"Your boy and his entourage were here."

Kearn paused with his finger on the button that would unlock his car.

"He was there?" He looked at Amber. Her eyes silently asked him what was happening.

"It might have been him. It was difficult to tell. I did not see his face but he was definitely a vampire, a Noble no less, and he stopped at the spot where I had found Amber and spoke to the bartender." Kyran sounded clearer now. Kearn unlocked his car and hurried to it.

"What did he say?"

Amber's eyes were still on him, burning into his back with their question. Her heart beat fast, calling to the blood in his veins. She was frightened but resolved. He was glad she had found the strength to come with him, although he wasn't convinced that she trusted him.

He had scared her. She could deny it but she couldn't hide such a thing from a vampire. His senses were tuned to fear above all over emotions. Blood tasted even sweeter when they were frightened.

Kearn got into the car and started the engine. Amber sat in the passenger seat, her bag on her lap, and struggled to buckle the seatbelt. Kearn didn't bother with his.

"I did not hear him, but Marshall did. The man asked about the woman who had been sitting there. He held the glass out to the bartender and threatened him. The bartender said she had left alone."

Damn.

"How long ago?"

"Fifteen minutes, not more. Marshall followed them to the corner of Wardour, heading down from Oxford Street. They are on foot."

"Thank you." Kearn closed the phone.

He knew where they were going.

A Noble. He wished it wasn't true. Noble blood was strong. How much had the man given Amber? There was a chance it wouldn't have left her system yet and the man had only been biding his time.

Kearn's gaze slid to Amber. Her eyes were glassy, fixed ahead, and it didn't surprise him when she spoke.

"Come to me, Lover," she whispered, distant and hollow. "Let me taste you like you let that damned Venator."

Lover?

Kearn growled.

Over his dead body.

He gunned the engine and sped through the streets of London suburbia, heading back into the centre of the city. He knew exactly where to find the vampire.

His heart beat harder, quicker, almost human in its speed. Amber's continued to race and her eyes didn't leave the road. She wasn't with him. She was miles away, with that bastard.

He had to calm down. Amber was supposed to be bait for the man, not bait for him, but the man was using Amber to lure them to him. Kearn wasn't sure what he was going to do once he got there. There had been three of them when he had saved Amber, but the warehouse had given him the impression that more were involved. He should have asked Kyran how many had been in the vampire's entourage and asked him to tell the Venator where to meet him.

One on one with a Noble, he would be able to cope without a problem. If there was more than one Noble, it was going to be difficult, or impossible if they had recently fed on forbidden blood.

And he didn't have his gun.

This was a stupid and dangerous move, but he had to make it.

"Ahead." Amber pointed. "Almost there."

The old redbrick factory building stood before him. What was the vampire playing at? Did he want Amber's blood so much that he was going to attempt to take her from him?

It seemed both he and the vampire were willing to take great risks to get what they wanted.

He pulled the car to a halt in the side road and turned off the engine and the lights.

"Stay close to me." He touched Amber's hands where they clutched the bag.

Amber looked at him at last. Her hazel eyes were still dull and empty.

Kearn hated seeing her under the control of the vampire, and he hated himself for allowing it. He wanted to use the connection between their blood to free her but he needed her to lead him to the man.

She stepped out of the car, placed her bag in the foot-well, and walked away. Kearn got out, closed his door and then the passenger side one, and locked the car. He followed her around to the front of the empty factory. His fingers twitched. Cold blue light crept over the marks, seeping along his fingers until they glowed, and then started over his hand. He shook it away, not wanting to waste his strength. He had to wait until he had the man in his sights. He couldn't risk draining himself, not when he didn't have his gun with him.

Amber pushed the gates open and continued. He let her remain a few paces ahead of him. She walked into the empty dimly lit building and through it, moving slowly across the bare concrete floor as though she was sleepwalking. In effect she was. The vampire had control of her body and she could only obey him. Kearn could end her living nightmare for her, could free her. He didn't want her to go near the vampire again.

But she was bait.

While he had been fine with it before, the thought of using her like that now left him feeling uneasy. He shouldn't allow a human to affect him in such a way, but he couldn't help it. He didn't want her to get hurt and he didn't want that man touching her. He wanted to protect her.

The kiss had changed things.

It had changed him.

Now that she knew what he was, he had no reason to wear a mask around her, and his heart wanted to open to her, even when he feared the consequences. A human had no place in his world.

The alternative didn't bear thinking about.

He wouldn't allow her to become like him.

Amber ascended the stairs to the next floor. Kearn followed in silence and focused on his surroundings. It was difficult to sense the vampires. It felt as though there was only one besides him. That couldn't be right.

She stopped at the top of the dark stairs. Could she see where she was going? Only the streetlamps outside lighted the floor and they barely cut through the darkness near the windows. The rest of it was pitch-black.

Kearn's eyes bled into red and his vision sharpened. The darkness lifted enough for him to see that the entire floor was as empty as it had been last night.

Amber started moving again, heading into the gloom. Kearn kept his distance and listened to the building. The vampire was still here somewhere.

Bright lights burst on, blinding him. His eyes switched back straight away but it wasn't soon enough. Spots danced across them, dulling his vision. It quickly cleared and Kearn didn't like what he saw.

Amber stood in the middle of the expansive grey room facing him.

A man dressed in a sharp black suit stood behind her.

The man was older than he was, his long black hair tied back in a ponytail. Kearn didn't recognise him but he was the same height and build as the man who had attacked Amber. The man grinned, revealing long canines.

Kearn's arm activated, the power rolling up it quickly this time. It glowed blue at his side and whispered to him, urging him into dispensing justice and feeding it the vampire's soul. It was hungry.

The man's red eyes fixed on the nape of Amber's neck.

Amber raised her hand, sensually running it over her chest and into her long chestnut hair, pushing it up and exposing her throat. She smiled at Kearn, tilting her head to one side. The sight of her pulse beating below her jaw was torture. He took a step towards them.

"What are you waiting for?" Her smile turned seductive and she lowered her hand, grazing her fingertips down her throat and over her cleavage. "I thought you wanted this, Venator?"

It wasn't her speaking. The vampire was controlling her. It didn't stop Kearn from wanting her. Her blood in his veins commanded him to come to her and fulfil her need for him. He took another step towards them, trying to figure out how to get to the man without hurting Amber in the process. The man was too close to her. If he attacked, he would hit Amber too. He needed to separate them.

"Come on, Lover," she husked and dragged her nails over her throat, scoring red marks on her pale skin. "I know you want this."

"Let her go." Kearn raised his right hand.

The vampire smirked.

"Let me go? I don't want him to let me go. I want both of you. I want you both in me." Amber caressed her hips.

Kearn growled. "Let her go!"

Amber laughed.

The vampire moved closer to her. He placed his hands on Amber's arms and she ran her fingers over her breasts and the black leather corset, heading downwards. She brushed them over her stomach and then dipped them in, touching her groin and raising her skirt. A flash of black knickers made Kearn ache for her.

That ache faded a moment later, replaced by a sense of fear.

Amber.

He shoved aside his desire and focused on her, communicating with her blood. He needed her to remain calm and fight the vampire's hold on her. Even though the vampire was a Noble and still able to control her, his blood would be growing weak in her system. If she fought hard enough, she could free herself. He would help her.

She blinked and dropped her skirt. The vampire frowned.

Kearn used the blood he had taken from her to break the vampire's hold on her. The moment it shattered, Amber ran forwards and fell on her knees at Kearn's feet. He was past her in an instant. The vampire didn't run. Kearn tackled him to the ground, landing on top, and wrestled with him, trying to pin his arms so he could use his right hand to kill him. The man sneered and threw him, and Kearn shot onto his feet, coming around and looking for another opening. The vampire picked himself up and glared at Kearn, red eyes narrowed and dark. He was strong but it didn't match Kearn's strength, not when he had a trace of Amber's blood in his veins and the desire to protect her fuelling him.

Kearn shot across the room, caught the man around the throat and hurled him, sending him slamming into the wall at the far end. Bricks exploded outwards and a wave of dust swept through the room. Amber screamed, curling up into a ball at the top of the stairs with her hands over her head. Kearn ran to the vampire and dragged him off the floor by his neck. The blue glow of his arm brightened and a command from the Sovereignty flowed through him. The vampire had tasted forbidden blood. He had no choice but to do as his duty dictated.

Before he could sentence the vampire, he kicked Kearn in the stomach, knocking the wind from him. Kearn dropped him and the vampire grabbed his arm, turned and launched him across the room. He spun in the air, hit the floor hard and skidded along it, ending up near Amber.

"Kearn?" she whispered, still curled up with her hands over her head and looking at him through her lashes. Her frightened heartbeat whispered a command to his blood that was stronger than the one the Sovereignty had sent to him. Protect her.

He pushed himself up off the dusty floor and focused, bringing his jumbled senses back into order and shutting down the deep throbbing ache in his bones. It wasn't just pain from the fight that pulsed through him. It was the effect of keeping his right arm activated too. Each second that ticked past stole a little more of his strength. He needed to end this before he didn't have the power left to sentence the man. He wouldn't let him have Amber.

"Go downstairs," he said and Amber nodded and ran for the stairs.

The vampire went after her. Kearn growled and intercepted him, grabbing the vampire and running past her, back the way the man had come. He slammed the man into the wall with his body, using the speed of the impact to weaken him. Without his gun to slow the man down, he had to use every method at his disposal to end this quickly, no matter how unrefined it was. He struggled with the vampire, pinning him with his body, and elbowed him in the face. The vampire snarled and tried to bite him. Kearn growled, drew back, and punched him hard on the jaw. His reward was a right fist in the stomach. Pain spread outwards from the spot in a hot wave. He snarled this time and threw another punch at the man. The vampire dodged it, grabbed his wrist, and twisted it, forcing him to bend over backwards. A deep throbbing wave washed through him and his right arm burned. He was getting weaker but he wouldn't give up. He would keep Amber safe and keep his promise.

The vampire threw him aside and ran for the stairs.

Kearn didn't give him a chance to go after Amber.

He focused all of his remaining energy on his arm. It was difficult to use it from a distance but he couldn't let the man have her. He unleashed the power and blue ribbons of light shot towards the man. They snaked around his body, wrapping themselves around his arms and legs and holding him. Kearn felt the shift in the power, the moment it went from merely containing the vampire to draining the life from him. The light from his arm and the threads holding the vampire turned red at first and then darkened to black. The vampire thrashed around, desperately trying to break free of the bonds that held him, snarling and growling like a rabid animal. A chill settled inside Kearn, growing in his heart and numbing him. He turned away when the black tendrils of his power crawled up the man towards his throat. He didn't need to watch in order to know what was happening. The black threads split, some covering the vampire's chest and the rest forcing their way into his mouth, slithering down inside him. The icy feeling inside Kearn grew worse and terrible darkness opened within him.

He severed the connection between his power and the vampire, and fell to the floor, his knees hitting it hard at the exact moment the vampire collapsed. He pressed a hand to his chest and then took it away when he realised it was his marked one. He hated it. He hated what he was and where he sent the vampires that he sentenced with the power given to him by the Sovereignty. He hated himself.

What the vampires did was deplorable, but sending them to the eternal darkness, a place where they existed without a physical being and endured endless pain, was even more unforgivable.

But he had to carry out his duty.

If he didn't, the Sovereignty would kill him instead.

His head felt light and his hunger was fiercer than ever, an inferno inside him that burned with such intensity that it threatened to control him. He slowly got to his feet, not daring to rush in case it made him pass out. He had killed enough vampires with his power to know his limits in the aftermath. He also knew the things he needed in order to recover. Blood and sleep.

Blood he had in the cooler in the bonnet of his Audi.

Sleep?

He hadn't slept well since this had started three years ago.

But now it was over.

The vampire disintegrated into ashes, leaving nothing more than a dusty mark on the floor. It was the fate of all those who were killed by the Sovereignty's power. Death by any other method would leave a body behind, but the Sovereignty believed that every trace of a sinner should be removed from the world, leaving nothing but a memory.

No body for their family to bury.

He closed his eyes against the memories that remained with him. He wished the Sovereignty would take those too.

Kearn looked at the stairs. He could feel Amber waiting below. What did he tell her? She was free. She could go home.

He didn't want to say those words.

He didn't want her to leave.

He went down the stairs and found her standing in the middle of the open low-lit room. She turned to face him as he approached and he stopped dead.

She smiled, her hazel eyes dull and doll-like.

Kearn's fingers twitched and he grabbed his right arm, trying to stop it from activating. Bastard.

He looked at the ceiling, towards the dead vampire, and then back at Amber.

"You did not think it was over?" She laughed. "Honestly... Venator... I would not allow it to end so easily. Our game has finally begun."

"Let her go." Kearn's senses reached out, sweeping through the building. There was no vampire in the vicinity except himself and the pile of ash upstairs. He glanced up at the ceiling again.

The vampire.

He had been a pawn, another under the vampire's control. The one in the street that night had been his real target, the mastermind behind everything, and he was the one who Kearn was going to track down and kill.

He would pay for using Amber like this.

Amber ran her hands over her breasts. "She really is a divine creature, isn't she? Does her blood taste as sweet as she looks?"

Kearn growled and his hand glowed blue.

He shook away the power and focused on Amber instead. He had to use his blood to protect her and shield her from the vampire's control. It was difficult when he was so weak from the fight and using his power, but he wouldn't fail her.

"The way you cope with it makes me suspect you are no stranger to blood from a Source."

Kearn hated to hear those words issuing from Amber's lips. She would remember everything that had happened. If the vampire revealed things to her about Kearn's past, how would she look at him then? He focused harder, determined to free her.

"Now, now. I will leave her since you are so persistent, and will offer you another chance to find me. Shall we make our game interesting? I may or may not make an appearance at Duke Montagu's ball tomorrow night. Are you brave enough to take the bait and face your demons, Venator?" Amber grinned and then collapsed in a heap on the floor.

Bastard.

Kearn ran to her and gathered her into his arms. They trembled and threatened to give out when he lifted her, cradling her close to him. He was as weak as a human right now but he had to get Amber to safety. He carried her out of the old factory building and back to his car. She didn't stir, not even when he placed her down on the passenger seat and secured the safety belt across her chest.

"Amber?"

She murmured.

Her heart was steady and her blood showed no sign of struggle. He went to the bonnet of his car and opened it. A white cooler filled the small space. He removed the lid, picked up one of the clear plastic packs and bit into it. It wasn't pleasant but it was blood. He swallowed it down, chucked the empty into the box and grabbed another. When he had finished that one too, he closed the cooler and shut the bonnet.

Amber looked at him from the passenger seat.

Kearn wiped the back of his hand across his mouth, walked around the car and got in, settling himself behind the steering wheel.

"How are you feeling?"

Amber looked herself over and her eyebrows furrowed. Tears lined her eyes. "A little strange… and a bit dirty."

He swallowed at the memory of her flashing her underwear.

"It was not you who did those things. Even if he is a Noble, his hold over you will fade soon. It was weak tonight. You fought it well." He smiled for her but she didn't blush this time.

She hesitated and then leaned across the car and rested her cheek against his shoulder. Kearn wasn't sure how to respond. Her hand pressed into his chest, her warmth burning through his black shirt and into his skin, filling him with an intense yearning to feel her fingers against his bare flesh. She shuffled closer, her cheek rubbing his left shoulder, warming that spot too, and he surrendered to temptation. He eased his arm out from between them, placed it around her shoulders, and curled his fingers around her bare upper arm. Her skin was cold beneath his fingers but smooth like satin. He stroked it, as much out of a need to feel her as out of a need to comfort her, and leaned towards her. Her dark hair tickled his cheek and he turned his head and breathed in her scent. The smell of her fragrance mixed with the divine aroma of her blood sent need spiralling through him and he opened himself to her, reforming the connection between their blood so she would feel him and would feel safe. He was weak right now but he still wouldn't allow anything to happen to her.

"We have to go to that ball," she whispered.

The soft waves of her hair obscured her face so he couldn't read her feelings in it. Her blood felt calm.

"It would not be wise," he said.

She looked up at him. He cleared the hair from her face with his right hand so he could see her hazel eyes. They were brighter now and shone with resolve again. He could see she wasn't going to give up. Perhaps she would if he told her why he didn't think it would be wise to attend.

"The ball is a masquerade. We will be at a disadvantage. It would be too dangerous," he said.

"I want to go. He might be there. We have to take this chance to catch our man."

Kearn held her shoulder, keeping her against him, and stared at the dashboard. When had the vampire become their man and not only his? Had the kiss changed her too?

Her forehead touched his neck. The feel of her against him was more than nice. He liked how she felt in his arms, and how warm she was against his side, and the way he could smell her scent and feel her heart beating.

More than that, he liked how it told him that she hadn't been lying. She wasn't afraid of him. He couldn't deny it now. Her heart was steady, her blood was calm, and she showed no sign of fear at being so close to him. Both he and Kyran had been wrong. He had thrown off his mask, revealing his true self, and she hadn't run away. She had only grown closer to him.

And she had only grown more determined to help him catch the vampire.

But was she really brave enough to attend the ball?

The vampire had chosen a brilliant stage for their next meeting. Kearn didn't want to face his demons and the vampire knew that, and all about him. He hadn't realised just how well his adversary knew him but now he was sure that the man was a Noble, he wasn't surprised. The noble houses knew Kearn's tale in all its sordid glory.

It was the reason he had avoided social gatherings since shortly after his family had cast him out. Everyone at the ball would recognise him and would know his history, especially the family hosting it. It would be difficult to focus on his mission when he would be in danger, having to watch everyone, on constant alert in case they attacked him. His presence at Amber's side would increase the threat to her. She would make an easy target for anyone wanting to hurt him.

Amber was right though. He couldn't pass up this chance. They had to take the risk and attend. He would do his best to keep his focus and keep her safe. If the ball became dangerous, or anyone threatened her, they would leave.

He wouldn't risk her to catch this man.

She was more important to him than his duty.

CHAPTER 9

She must be crazy.

Amber sat in the passenger seat of Kearn's Audi, heading to a ball full of vampires, with a chance of one of them attempting to capture her and bleed her.

The words had sounded good at the time, the right thing to say to make her appear strong to Kearn, even when she had been on the verge of breaking inside. The things the man had done to her with only his mind, the dark thoughts he had placed inside her, terrified her, and now they were heading into dangerous territory just for the chance of meeting him again.

Even Kearn thought she was crazy for suggesting they go to the masquerade. That had to be the reason he hadn't said a word all evening. He hadn't even complimented her when she had walked out of his bedroom in her ball gown. His eyes had remained cold and impassive. She had mentioned how handsome he looked and he had merely holstered his gun at his hip, covered it with his black mid-thigh length military-style jacket, and turned away towards the door.

He did look handsome though. No. He was gorgeous.

The black jacket had a double set of bright silver buttons down the breast, and silver-blue embroidery around the hem, cuffs and the tall collar. The thick material didn't conceal his physique. It stretched tight across his chest, emphasising his muscles. The finger-length silver strands of his hair brushed the collar at the back and by his ears, almost white against the contrast of black.

She looked across at him as he drove. They were heading out of central London, towards the suburbs. He changed gear and her gaze fell to his legs. They looked lithe but powerful in his tight black trousers that were tucked into black over-knee riding boots with bright shiny buckles.

The woman at the club had worn something similar. Was this Kearn's uniform? If human police wore such a thing, even more women would be falling over each other to get to them.

The car slowed and she faced front. Her heart pounded at the sight of the huge black wrought iron gates opening ahead of her and the massive sandstone house beyond. It was beautiful, impressive with the façade lit and every window on all three storeys emanating a warm glow. With the long corseted black dress she wore, Kearn in his uniform, and this house, she felt as though she had fallen back in time to a period when the rich threw balls full of ladies and gentlemen, like the romantic dramas on the television.

Kearn parked the car at the end of a row of sombre-coloured Bentleys and Rolls-Royces and flashy black sports cars.

Amber followed him out of the car. The golden gravel crunched under her black heeled shoes. She stood with her black gloved arm on the roof of Kearn's car and tried to take it all in. A large fountain stood in the centre of the courtyard, the water lit with the same warm lights as the house and flowing like molten gold. She had never felt so out of place. She had never imagined that vampires would live in a place like this. She had always thought they would live wherever they could, hiding in the shadows and stalking humans, like monsters, not that they would lead grand lives and be rich and powerful.

A couple walked past them.

And beautiful.

They both wore black and were talking and laughing just like people, only she could see a difference in them. The way they held themselves, tall and proud, posture perfect, set them apart from anyone she knew. They emanated a sense of nobility, of grace and power.

The brunette smiled at the man, her dark eyes melting into red, and placed a slim black mask across them. He smiled back at her, adjusting the mask so it settled over her eyes and tightly fitted her delicate features. He slipped his own mask on and preened his short sandy hair back.

"Countess Huntingdon and Marquess Pendragon." Kearn's voice was pure darkness.

Countess Huntingdon? Amber knew that name from Kearn's book. Could someone so beautiful really be so bloodthirsty?

When she turned to ask Kearn, he was staring at her dress. He had chosen well this time. She had expected him to buy her another ridiculous outfit, but it was glamorous and refined, elegant enough to make her feel as though she might fit in at the ball. The straps of the black satin corset were ribbon, tied at her shoulders, with tails that flowed down her back, tickling her. The long skirt almost reached the floor, cut in such a way that it didn't cling to her legs but still gave away their shape.

She had tied her hair up, twisting the lengths into a messy gathering at the back of her head, and had surrounded her eyes in dark make-up while painting her lips red.

When she had stepped in front of the mirror in Kearn's bathroom, her reflection had been exactly how she imagined a vampire looked—all sensual and seductive. She felt that way, especially now that Kearn's eyes were roaming over her body and leaving a hot trail in their wake. She kept still, not wanting his attention to leave her.

"You should take your hair down." His gaze touched on her throat and red ringed his irises.

Amber shook her head. Her neck wasn't on show to get the vampire's attention, or anyone's at the ball. It was to get Kearn's attention and it was working. She wanted him to want her. She wanted to lure him to her and have him kiss her again. She wanted his eyes on her and her alone tonight.

With so many vampires around, he would be distracted from her and would perhaps speak with some of them. It was selfish and childish of her, but she wanted him all to herself.

Kearn turned away and started towards the house. Amber hastened after him and fell into step beside him. Had she upset him by refusing his suggestion? No. He had been quiet since last night.

Amber tried to feel his emotions but wasn't sure how it worked. Before, she had felt things without even trying. Now, she was trying her hardest but she couldn't detect anything. Had the strange connection between their blood ended, or was he somehow blocking her attempts?

The bright foyer of the mansion was stunning. Gold candelabras lined the twin white marble staircases curving up in front of her towards a balcony and a massive crystal chandelier hung in the open space above her.

"Sir, I will need to see your licence."

Amber looked over at Kearn. He was with a man at the bottom of the left staircase. The vampire couple were near the top. The woman was walking very delicately, lifting the skirt of her dress with one hand and holding the man's arm with the other. He was still smiling and talking.

Kearn reached into the collar of his jacket and pulled out something on a silver chain. Amber couldn't see it clearly. The man blocking his way nodded and stepped aside. Amber hurried over to Kearn and glanced at the man. He wore a black tailcoat like a butler. There had been men outside in similar outfits. Staff? She supposed a house this big would need staff. Was he human or did some vampires work for other ones? That completely shattered her image of vampires. Did some of them have jobs? She supposed that Kearn did, although it seemed more like a calling than a profession. Before she had met him, she had thought that vampires would all be out for themselves, looking after number one, rather than serving others or caring for them. The idea that they had families would have seemed ridiculous. She had so much to learn about Kearn's world. Every moment she spent in it challenged her perspective of things and changed her forever.

She followed Kearn up the stairs. There was so much to take in and think about that it pushed her fear to the back of her mind, leaving only excitement filling her.

The vampire couple stopped at the top of the stairs. Another couple in front of them walked through a wide arch and disappeared from view on the other side. The sound of the orchestra and choir sent a shiver over Amber's skin and made her fine hairs stand on end. It was beautiful. Amber ran her black gloved hand up the bright brass railing of the staircase and looked into the foyer below. More vampires were following them, all wearing black. Laughter rang out from one group and she recognised one of the vampires from the club. Her heart beat quicker at the reminder that any of the men here could be the one after her blood. It snapped her back to reality. Her fascination with this new world and her breathtaking surroundings had made her forget why she was here.

Kearn's stern look said that he hadn't forgotten. His green gaze was on the group below them. The man was staring back at him, an equally dark expression on his face.

Amber moved closer to Kearn. He stopped at the top of the stairs and glanced at her. There was a flicker of something in his eyes that she couldn't quite interpret. Nerves? Fear? Worry? All she could feel were her own anxiety and excitement.

"Is it tradition for everyone to wear black?" She hadn't seen one person wearing another colour.

"Duke Montagu declared that his ball this year would be a midnight masquerade." Kearn adjusted the collar of his black military-style jacket. "Every year has a colour."

"Marquess Pendragon and Countess Huntingdon." A loud voice echoed up from the other room and the vampire couple at the top walked forwards. The man held his hand out, palm down, and the woman laid hers on top of it.

They were announcing the guests?

Amber swallowed. They didn't know her name. Would they even announce someone like her? Everyone would probably stare if they did.

"What happened back there with the servant?" she whispered to Kearn, remembering the licence the man had asked for.

"My appearance is not enough to confirm me as a Venator." He unclipped the stand-up collar of his black jacket and pulled out a small silver medal on a chain. She didn't have a chance to see it properly before he was putting it away again. "I need to show my licence to prove my status and to allow me entrance to this sort of affair where so many important people are gathered."

No emotion touched his voice and he didn't look at her. His green gaze remained focused on the entrance to the other room.

For a brief moment, she caught a glimmer of his feelings.

Nerves.

For some reason, that unsettled her.

Why was he nervous?

She forced herself to focus on something else. Would his family be on the other side? He had said he was of noble blood. Kyran was sure to be there. She couldn't imagine him missing something like this.

Amber looked back down the stairs. The group she had seen enter were all masked now. She didn't have a mask and neither did Kearn. He had said they wouldn't need one but everyone else was wearing them.

She turned to see Kearn standing near the arch glaring at her and hurried forwards, almost tripping on her dress.

"Do not say a word," he said when she reached him and she heard the nerves in his voice now. "Do not speak unless spoken to, do not stare, control your emotions as much as possible and remain close to me."

Amber glanced through the arch at the room beyond and her breath left her. Golden tones lit the expansive rectangular room stretching out below her, warming the dark red walls and reflecting off the ceiling height mirrors that lined the walls between equally tall windows. The choir rose with the orchestra and her heart fluttered. It was incredible. In the centre of the room, a river of black dancers moved at a swift pace, all of them in perfect synchronisation as though choreographed. More people lined the edges of the room, some walking around and others gathered in groups. She had never seen anything like it.

Kearn grabbed her arm and yanked her forwards.

"Pay attention," he hissed beneath his breath and she fell into line beside him at the top of the wide red-carpeted staircase that swept down into the ballroom. He let go of her arm and straightened his jacket out.

He wasn't the only one nervous now. Her heart jumped around all over the place and she tried to calm it but couldn't. Her throat was parched. She needed a drink. Something alcoholic, and strong.

The servant at the top of the stairs raised an eyebrow at her and then turned to face the room. She glanced to her right, at Kearn, and he titled his chin up. He looked so noble and handsome, proud and powerful like the Marquess Pendragon. She wanted to look that way too so the vampires would see they weren't the only ones who could do beautiful and graceful.

She raised her head, faced forwards, and took a deep breath.

Kearn's words echoed in her head like a mantra. Don't speak unless spoken to. Don't stare. Don't let her feelings get the better of her.

"Venator Savernake!" the man to her left announced.

Amber expected Kearn to offer his arm. He didn't. He walked down the stairs at a slow pace and she followed unsteadily on trembling legs, her ankles wobbling in the heeled shoes. It was impossible to calm her nerves.

The entire room had stopped.

A sea of red eyes stared at her from behind black masks and she felt their hatred deep within her.

She held it together and kept walking. Vampires waited at the bottom of the stairs, their eyes boring into her. Her hand twitched, tempted to touch her bare throat and cover it. She felt exposed and vulnerable. This was the craziest idea she'd ever had and something said that she was going to pay for it with her own blood.

"You said they wouldn't stare at me," she whispered.

"They are not looking at you."

CHAPTER 10

Amber looked at Kearn and then at the vampires. He was right. They were all staring at him with murder in their eyes and she could feel their hatred. Why hadn't he told her they would treat him this way? She wouldn't have insisted they come if she had known.

They reached the bottom of the stairs and Kearn stopped. A blond man stood in his path. Marquess Pendragon.

Kearn bowed his head and the man grinned, revealing the sharp points of his canines. His flinty gaze shifted to her. Amber bowed too, afraid of making the situation worse, and the marquess walked away.

Kearn kept his head bowed.

She didn't like seeing him so humble.

The room began to move again but their eyes were still on her. Kearn straightened and walked towards the right side of the ballroom. The people parted before him, keeping their distance, watching him pass with disgust. Her gaze fixed on his back and she wished she could see his eyes because she couldn't sense his feelings and it felt as though he was closing his heart again. Why?

Was it these people and the way they treated him? She had expected them to act like friends and acquaintances but they were behaving like the enemy. Was it all because he was a Venator or did they have another reason to hate him?

A sense of menace hung over the lavish red and gold ballroom. It hadn't been there before they had announced Kearn. An air of excitement had prevailed then. Even the large orchestra and choir that lined the room beneath the balcony hadn't drowned out the chatter and laughter. She had seen the smiles on the faces of the dancers. They were gone now, replaced by narrowed eyes behind black masks and low spoken conversations that she knew were about her and Kearn.

Kearn stopped near one of the full height mirrors and turned towards her, his expression grim. The reflection of the room in the mirror made her feel as though a thousand people surrounded her, all staring her way. Kearn's way.

Everyone near them swept away, heads held high and whispering to each other.

A wide ring of open floor grew around them, the vampires lining it watching her with contempt, and Amber felt even more in the spotlight than ever.

What had Kearn done to deserve such a reception?

Amber spotted Kyran surrounded by a group of women and men. She could recognise him even with his mask. He looked so much like Kearn. She smiled and he turned his back on her. Her smile fell away. Even Kearn's own brother wouldn't associate with him in front of these people. Her gaze shifted to Kearn. He stood with his eyes downcast now, his chin lowered, and it hurt her to see him so dejected. She wanted to talk to him, needed to say something to lift his spirits and let him know that not everyone in the room was looking on him with hatred burning in their eyes. Whatever he had done, it didn't deserve such a callous reception or such cruel treatment. He didn't deserve to suffer it, especially not from his brother. She went to touch Kearn's hand but he moved it out of reach. Didn't he want her to touch him? She only wanted to comfort him. Her eyes sought his and he looked at the mirror. Perhaps tonight had been a mistake. If she had known that it would be like this, she would have made him stay away instead.

Amber moved around him, stepping into his line of sight.

Kearn's green eyes finally met hers and the loneliness in them echoed deep within her heart.

She reached out to him and then paused.

A murmur ran through the crowd, growing in volume until the music died, replaced by the confident swift click of heels on the parquet floor. A tall man was heading towards her. The fine gold detailing on his black thigh-length jacket and tall boots, and the way the vampires parted for him, bowing their heads, spoke of standing and power. His long black ponytail made her think of the vampire but this man was taller and looked more heartless than the one after her. His red eyes glowed from behind his black mask, narrowed on Kearn's back, a hard edge to them.

Kearn turned and dropped to one knee before the man, lowering his head and pressing his right hand to his chest.

The man stopped and ran his gaze over her. Everything about him radiated power—the way he held himself, the way he looked at her, and the way he made her feel inferior without even trying.

She wasn't sure what to do.

Kearn's silver hair had fallen forwards to mask his face and she was too afraid to get his attention. He hadn't mentioned anything about a situation like this.

She went to bow.

"No." The man's deep voice sent a chill tumbling down her spine. She froze with her head only slightly dipped and looked up at him through her lashes. "Such grace does not need to stoop and bow before me. Only those beneath me should lower themselves to be there."

Amber glanced at Kearn. Beneath him? This man might be superior amongst his peers, but Kearn was a Venator and a Noble. Surely, they were on the same level in society?

The man removed his mask, revealing his slim face. It had a cruel edge to it when he smiled. He was older than Kearn by at least twenty years. Was that his reason for acting superior?

"I do not know why this Venator has dared to attend my ball, but if it is with the sole intention of presenting you to society, then I will accept his presence... if you will dance with me." The man extended his hand to her.

She didn't want to take it. Everything in her screamed that this man was dangerous. He frowned, clearly displeased. It was his ball. He had a right to dance with whomever he wanted and she was sure that she should be flattered and accept but she didn't want to dance with him.

"I am afraid I don't know how to dance."

She sensed that Kearn wasn't happy, and then she felt something else.

Being here was important to him and it wasn't just about catching the vampire.

She had to dance with the man or he would throw them out. She couldn't let that happen.

"It is truly a shame." He raised his hand.

Amber grabbed it and the whole room gasped.

The man's red eyes narrowed in contempt, telling her that she had done something wrong. She quickly released his arm. Her heart beat painfully fast against her ribs and she trembled under his scrutiny and that of the entire room.

"I didn't say I wouldn't dance with you," Amber said it so fast it sounded like one word. She took a deep breath to smooth out her feelings, aware that her racing heart was probably drawing as much attention to her as what she had done. "I only said that I didn't know how to."

He still looked as though he wanted to call the guards and have them kicked out.

His gaze roamed down to her neck and she was thankful when it carried on, running over her body. She preferred him staring at her breasts than at her throat.

There had to be something she could say that would please him and stop him from signalling security. She couldn't think with everyone staring at her. Their red gazes flustered her and she wished she could see Kearn's eyes, could stare into their cool green depths and feel safe again. Right now, she felt like dinner. If the man kicked Kearn out, would they let her go too, or was she facing death?

She felt as though she was staring it right in the face.

The man's red eyes met hers and he slipped his mask back on. She was failing. Think. It was too hard to when panic was turning her insides to jelly and jumbling her thoughts. Flattery. Flattery got you everywhere and she was sure that he would like his ego rubbed as much as the next man.

"I would not want to be a poor partner for you at your own ball." She made a dip of a curtsey, feeling silly for suddenly speaking so formally. The man smiled at last. "I only ask that you give me time to learn to be a worthy partner of such a prestigious man as yourself."

His smile widened to reveal sharp canines. Amber swallowed. Either she was about to become dinner, or he was pleased.

"Stand, Venator," the man barked.

Kearn got to his feet in one swift graceful move but kept his head bowed. He hadn't said Kearn's name since arriving. Why?

The man's eyes shifted to Kearn. "I will accept your presence here."

Kearn dipped his head lower. His hair parted enough for her to see his eyes. There was gratitude in them and deep inside she knew it wasn't purely because he would be able to continue his mission here tonight. Something else was going on.

"I am only glad my dearest sister could not attend." The man turned away and disappeared into the crowd.

The music started again.

Everyone slowly went back to dancing and talking.

Kearn remained with his head bowed, his eyes wide now and fixed on the floor. She felt strange inside, muddled and hurt.

"Kearn?" Amber whispered, wanting to look into his eyes and see if those feelings were his. She wanted to ask him what was going on and who that man's sister was.

"You are very brave to jump into the lion's den to save my brother." Kyran stood where the other man had been.

He smiled, his red eyes warm behind his slim black mask. His clothes were similar to all of the other men's, but Kyran's stand up collar jacket had black detailing and buttons. His highly polished riding boots reflected the golden light of the candles around the room.

"He is lucky this is our uncle's ball or your flattery would have been worth nothing."

"Uncle?" she said.

Kearn moved away a few steps and scanned the crowd. He was ignoring Kyran. Why? She caught a glimpse of his eyes. The hurt was still there in them, and in his feelings, and she wanted to know what was going on. If she went to him now would he push her away? Kyran shifted slightly and she looked back at him. As much as she needed to go to Kearn, it would be rude to leave Kyran alone when he had come over to them, risking the glares and whispers of everyone else.

"Duke Montagu is our mother's younger brother," Kyran said and glanced at Kearn, drawing her gaze back to him. "I admit, I was surprised to see Kearn here tonight, and yourself also. So you know about us now?"

She nodded. She knew all about him and the others here. Vampires. Kyran smiled and leaned in close to her, his red eyes fading slowly to blue. His fangs showed between his lips as he spoke.

"Are you scared?" he whispered and Amber lowered her gaze to his chest and studied her feelings. Was she?

Maybe she had been at first, but she wasn't now. Another feeling overshadowed her fear. Concern. She glanced at Kearn and then met Kyran's gaze and shook her head. He smiled, no hint of fang in it. His expression lost its cold edge and he looked her over, his gaze lingering on her throat and her dress before settling on her face again.

His smile widened, turning charming. "The duke is right about you. You are as radiant as the night, Amber. Breathtaking."

A blush scalded her face.

Kearn's eyes narrowed.

He had heard that at least.

His fists clenched.

Was Kyran trying to upset him? It was cruel to do so when he was already hurt and humbled by his own family and kind.

Kyran looked over at Kearn. "Nothing much has changed in the fifty years since you last dared to attend. It surprises me, but it seems as though the old man retained his soft spot for you. I had thought that out of the attendees, he would hate you the most. Do not expect others to show such restraint. Watch your back."

Kearn didn't even acknowledge him.

Kyran frowned, his irises bleeding into crimson and eyes narrowing into thin lines behind his mask. "Kearn?"

Kearn nodded but his gaze remained on the dancers.

"Would you like me to teach Amber some moves?" Kyran grinned and this time Kearn did turn to face them. His expression was black and his eyes were red. "I always was the better dancer."

Kearn shook his head and came to stand close beside her. Amber felt relieved to have him back with her, where she needed him to be.

A blonde and a redhead woman wearing fine black corseted dresses came over to Kyran and wrapped their arms around his. They sidled up close, all beautiful smiles directed at his face.

"Come away, Marquess Savernake. You would not want to sully our reputations by speaking with this Venator, would you?" The blonde woman smiled widely at Kyran and tilted her head to one side, causing her ringlets to sway. She looked like a doll.

"I would dearly love to sully your name another way." He patted her hand where it rested on his arm. The redhead on his other arm mewled in disapproval. He smiled at her too and touched her cheek. "I am quite adept at sullying more than one woman at a time, my sweet, no need to pout."

Kyran smiled at Amber and both women glared at her. They turned with Kyran and walked away.

"Bitches," Amber muttered under her breath. It seemed they were rampant in every walk of life.

"I can teach you to dance," Kearn said and her attention was with him again. The worry and hurt had left his eyes and she couldn't feel it anymore, but she wasn't convinced that it was gone.

"Was Kyran telling the truth?" The moment that question left her lips, Kearn was looking away from her again, staring into the dancers. He nodded. "If he is your uncle, why was he so cold to you?"

Did it have something to do with Kearn's mother, the duke's sister?

Kearn smiled at her. "It is a conversation best saved for another time. Come, I will teach you to dance. Have you ever danced a waltz?"

It was a very polite way of telling her not to ask and not to mention it again. It hurt that he had shut her out when she only wanted to make him feel better. She was sure that he would if he shared his pain with someone. She wanted that someone to be her. She wanted to know more about him.

"I danced a waltz once with my brother. I hit his feet more than I hit the right steps."

"You have a brother?" Kearn's silver eyebrows rose. She nodded and smiled.

"I'm a terrible dancer though. I don't hold out much hope of you being able to instruct me. I'm going to make a fool of myself out there." Amber looked at the dancers. Couples spun around the dance floor, elegant and graceful, their heads held high. Vampires or not, they were beautiful and everything she couldn't even dream of being.

Kearn cleared his throat. "Amber, would you allow me some freedom with your blood?"

A shiver danced down her spine. Her blood? Her eyes widened and her lips parted as her mouth turned dry. He wanted more blood?

Kearn smiled and it was warm and genuine.

"There is no need to panic. I do not need more blood. What little remains in mine is enough to give me control." His smile reached his eyes and her heart fluttered in her throat at the sight of him.

"You can control me like the other man," she whispered, lost in how handsome he looked now that he was smiling and no longer held hurt in his eyes. It distracted her from the topic of conversation, drowning out the fear she felt whenever she thought about someone using her blood to control her.

He nodded.

"I would never do such a thing without your consent though." He looked honest enough, his expression serious once more. "You have my word on that."

He didn't need to give his word but it was comforting to have it. The thought of anyone controlling her was disturbing, but the idea of Kearn doing it against her will hurt her. Her vision blurred as she remembered the events of the past few days. She didn't want Kearn to use her like that, making her do things like that terrible man had.

Kearn took a step towards her and her gaze met his again. The worry in his eyes warmed her heart and she shook away the dark memories of what the man had made her do and say, and nodded.

"Just enough to help with the fancy footwork," Amber said and looked across the room to the duke. He sat in a tall-backed gilt chair on a stage above everyone, surrounded by men and women of varying ages. They were all speaking to him but he was watching the dancers, putting them under incredible scrutiny. He seemed displeased with everyone. She thought they were all amazing and no one was putting a foot out of place. "I get the impression that if I fail to make an impression on his lordship we'll be going home early."

"He is not a lord." Kearn's tone was hard, matching his frown. "He is a duke and you must refer to him as such."

She nodded quickly, taken aback.

"Amber..." His look changed, softening instantly, and the darkness left his eyes. "The only reason we can be here is because of you... because you are... Amber, you are beyond merely beautiful and outshine the radiance of the night. You are as entrancing as the moon and as stunning as the million stars that glitter around her. You are breathtaking to behold, and I am honoured to be in attendance with you tonight."

Her heart doubled its pace, cantering in her chest. She stared into his eyes, lost in them and what he had said. He thought she was more than beautiful. Her cheeks blazed, burning with the intensity of the sun. His words had been so eloquent and poetic. She had never had a man speak of her in such a way and she was surprised that he had said it, and wished that he had told her earlier, before the duke and Kyran, but perhaps it was because they had voiced their opinion that he had found the courage to voice his too.

She wasn't sure how to respond so she went to look away but stopped. He hadn't touched her face, but it had felt as though he had. She had sensed his desire for her to remain looking at him, and had done so.

Was this Kearn controlling her? It hadn't felt as it had when the other man had done it, forcing her to do things in a way that made her feel as though she wasn't master of her own body. It had felt as though he had physically touched her to keep her attention on him.

"Thank you for doing such a thing for me," he whispered.

She warmed inside and smiled. "I haven't done it yet. Thank me when I don't make a fool of myself with the duke."

Kearn held his arm out. The music quietened. Amber hesitated a moment and then placed her black gloved hand on the back of Kearn's. It felt so formal that her smile widened.

Her nerves increased as they approached the dance floor. The vampires surrounding it parted to make way for them, their eyes on her. They wanted to see her make an idiot of herself. They wanted her to fail. She tilted her chin up. She wasn't going to fail. Kearn was with her and he would be a good teacher, she was sure of it.

"Have you danced many waltzes?" She glanced at him. He had his head held high, his profile to her, and his green eyes fixed straight ahead. The silver lengths of his hair caressed his cheeks and neck, shining in the warm light of the chandeliers. He looked like the other vampires—noble, beautiful, and powerful.

Her heart fluttered again but not out of fear. It fluttered over the sight of him, and the feel of his hand under hers, and the thought that soon she would be in his arms again.

"Several hundred. I attended the balls every year since I turned one hundred and sixty."

Amber stopped dead. A couple almost collided with her. They sneered in her direction and she couldn't believe her eyes. They were a young girl and boy. Neither of them looked over twelve but they held themselves with such poise that they were unmistakably of noble blood. Amber looked around her. There were other girls and boys, varying in ages from young children to teenagers. Had someone turned them?

Kearn moved his hand forwards, a silent order for her to keep walking, and she obeyed.

"They were born vampires," he said, as though he could read her mind. Did her blood give him that power too? It was a relief to know that no one had turned the children. Kearn had mentioned that he had been born to his parents. It was strange to think that vampires could have children and could age.

"How old are you?" She stared at his face, trying to figure it out. He must have been alive a long time on top of the one hundred and sixty years he had mentioned if he had clocked up several hundred waltzes.

"I was born in sixteen forty nine."

Amber stopped again. He was over three hundred and sixty. He looked at her with cool eyes as she struggled to comprehend it. He had been alive over ten times longer than she had, and yet he only looked a handful of years older. It didn't seem to bother him. She smiled at her thoughts. It was normal to him so why would it bother him? He probably thought it was strange that she was aging so rapidly.

"Come," he said. "We should not keep the dancers waiting."

"Wait." She held her hands up. "You can't drop a bombshell like that and expect me to just dance afterwards. It isn't normal."

"I assure you it is." He placed her hand on his again and started walking.

Amber had no choice but to follow him.

"My species ages at a different rate to yours. Initially, we take ten years to physically age the same as a human would in one year. Our bodies are different. Our heart beats only once per five seconds at resting pace. When we reach five hundred, around fifty in human terms of appearance, the aging process slows again, so thirty years is like one."

That was a lot to take in. She looked over at the duke.

"How old is he?" she whispered, afraid he would hear and throw her out for asking such a question.

"Duke Montagu is over one thousand years old."

Kearn stopped again with his back to the duke. Amber stared wide eyed at him over Kearn's shoulder. The duke was watching her now, a smile curving his thin lips.

He looked barely older than her father but he was really over one thousand. Incredible.

The music started again, low strings slowly working up to include the woodwind instruments. Her eyes gradually moved away from the duke. Kearn was watching her too, his green eyes warm with amusement. She smiled.

"Ready for your lesson?"

Amber didn't think she was.

But she nodded anyway.

Looking into his beautiful eyes, she realised that she didn't care if she made a fool of herself.

Not if she was dancing with Kearn.

CHAPTER 11

Amber looked around her to see what everyone else on the dance floor was doing. The ladies curtseyed to their partners so she did too, going low enough that she would make the right impression on Kearn and the watching vampires, but not so low that she wouldn't be able to get back up. She rose again and the ladies stepped forwards into their partners' waiting arms.

She went to touch Kearn's arm and take his hand.

Kearn stepped back.

"The first thing you need to know is never touch me or anyone above your rank." His voice was stern again. She had committed a faux pas by grabbing the duke. Everyone here was probably above her. "You must allow your partner to place your hands."

Kearn gently placed her right hand on his shoulder and held her left, their palms pressing together. His hand was warm and his fingers curled tightly around hers. Both of his hands were steady. Hers shook like crazy.

She swallowed to ease the dryness in her throat but it didn't help.

"I need a drink," she whispered and Kearn's gaze slid to her neck and then back to her eyes. A shiver tripped through her at the flash of red in his irises.

She jumped when his left hand settled against her waist and then they were moving. The tempo of the orchestra was slower than before. It was a triumphant sounding piece, with rising strings and deep brass. The choir sung beautifully but she didn't hear it. She was lost in Kearn's eyes and the way he was holding her, moving with her. They turned in slow circles and it didn't feel as though he was moving her feet for her. She felt in control.

"See," he whispered and smiled into her eyes, "nothing to it."

She smiled and his look turned serious, his head tilting to one side. His eyes dropped to her mouth, briefly enough that she might have missed it had she not been watching him so closely. Did he want to kiss her? She swallowed again. She wanted to kiss him.

"Tell me about your brother," he said.

She stumbled slightly. "I don't think this is the time for conversation. I need to concentrate."

"No, you do not. You will only make it more difficult for me. I can concentrate for both of us."

Amber tried to think of what to tell him. It was hard not to focus on her feet when she knew she was dancing.

"He's around your height and build, funny and smart, looks like a male version of me and lives in Paris," she said and no longer noticed the way the vampires stared, the couples glancing their way as they passed, or even the duke. The music and Kearn filled her world. He was so handsome, looking at

91

her with warmth in his eyes and no trace of loneliness. She felt as though she had helped erase his hurt after all. "He's always trying to get me to move to France and it must have finally worked because I'm going to Paris soon."

Kearn frowned. "You are leaving England?"

She nodded. "I'm moving there for work."

The warmth in Kearn's eyes dissipated, leaving ice in its wake. He turned his face away, looking in the direction that they were moving with the music, and her feelings shifted. The excitement and happiness she had felt on mentioning her move to Paris gradually changed into something darker.

Anger?

That feeling winked out of existence and she stumbled, barely keeping herself standing as she turned with Kearn again.

Cold swept through her.

He had shut her out, relinquishing control of her and leaving her in the dark about his feelings. Why?

Amber focused hard, biting her lip and tripping her way through the steps. This wasn't good. She panicked, the feeling blasting through her so quickly that her temperature shot up and her heart skipped. She caught her foot on Kearn's boot and her eyes leapt to his, her apology balancing on her lips.

It fell away when her feet suddenly knew the way and her legs no longer shook. Was he controlling her again? The anger she had felt before he had surrendered control of her wasn't there anymore. She searched his eyes for it and found nothing. The desire to question him burned in her heart but she couldn't find the courage to go through with it. What was she going to ask him?

Was he angry because she was leaving England? Didn't he want her to go to Paris? Did he want her to stay?

Did he want her?

Amber glanced down at the bright silver buttons on the breast of his black jacket, focusing on herself instead of him, studying her own feelings. What did she want? The thought of Paris had excited her before she had met him, but now her move felt like something to fear rather than look forward to. Her eyes roamed up over his chest and neck to his face, lingering on his sensual mouth. Fire skittered over her skin at the memory of their kiss. The thought of kissing him again excited her, sent her blood rushing and her mind leaping forward to imagine how everything would unfold from even the gentlest of caresses.

She forced her eyes onwards, until they met his. There had to be something that she could say to break the ice between them again.

"I'm not really sure I'll like it in Paris," she whispered, looking deep into his eyes. She had loved the thought of it just a few days ago but meeting Kearn had changed her whole world, knocking it off kilter, and now she wasn't sure of anything. She shrugged. "I'm not even any good at French."

Kearn leaned over and her eyes widened when his cheek brushed hers, heating hers through. He whispered in French into her ear, his breath tickling her neck, and continued to turn with her. Her eyelids fell to half-mast and she melted into him, savouring the feel of him against her and the relief that blossomed deep in her heart as she realised he was no longer angry with her. Only warm feelings danced inside her now, and a part of them were his. He drew back again and she shook some sense into herself, enough to look him in the eye.

"What did you say?"

He just smiled.

She wanted to know. Whatever it had been, it had sounded distinctly romantic.

The choir began to sing again, slower now but rising with the music, sweeping over the room and carrying her along. Their words sounded as beautiful as Kearn's had and she listened to them.

"Is that Latin?" She turned with Kearn. They had moved closer together. His chest brushed hers as they spun to the music, galloping around the room. It was still hard for her not to think about the steps. Whenever she stopped speaking, her focus went back to her feet. She used Kearn as a distraction, keeping her eyes on his face, and floated along in his arms.

He nodded.

"Do you understand it?" What other languages did he know? He was over three hundred years old. He had probably learnt many languages and studied all sorts of things in his years.

He nodded again and looked ahead of them.

"What are they saying?"

"You do not want to know."

Amber gasped when they collided with another couple. The sandy haired man glared at her. Marquess Pendragon. Had he bumped them on purpose? Amber didn't recognise the woman in his arms.

"Ignore them," Kearn said and she focused on him again, only this time the world didn't melt away. She was aware of everyone staring and the intent behind their glares. She could sense they wanted to harm her.

No, not her. She stared into Kearn's eyes. These were his feelings again.

The tempo of the music increased. Her legs were growing tired but she kept going, determined to finish the dance.

"You must curtsey to the duke and allow him to place your hands. Do not speak unless spoken to and do not look him in the eye. Keep your gaze on his chest." The warmth was gone from Kearn's face and voice, but at least he wasn't shutting her out again.

"Why?"

Kearn turned with her and she caught a glimpse of the duke. He was still watching her.

"Because regardless of what he said to you, you are beneath him, just as I am."

Amber wanted to ask why he was beneath the duke but the hurt was back in his eyes. Would he really tell her later or had he been using it as an excuse to keep her quiet on the subject so she would forget about it? She would never forget the way the people had treated him tonight.

"Remain polite at all times and maintain the proper distance between you and him."

Kearn's hand slid around her back and he drew her closer to him, until their chests were against each other the whole time they danced. That wasn't proper distance, but she didn't care. It felt too good to be this close to him, in his arms. It didn't matter that her feet were tired and her legs ached. She wanted to keep dancing so she could remain like this with him.

Her eyes met his just as he was about to speak and his mouth closed. He stared down into her eyes, warmth resurfacing in his. She was glad the loneliness was gone again. They shone now, and deep contentment filled her. It wasn't only her feelings.

Kearn raised his left hand and trailed his fingertips down her bare arm and then over her long black satin glove. The touch was light and sensual, teasing her and stealing her breath. Her lips parted and her gaze fell to his mouth. His parted too, an invite to a kiss that she wanted to take more than anything. The world disappeared again and she was drifting with him with nothing but the sound of her heart beating and the light strings of the orchestra filling her ears.

She raised her gaze to his. Red tinted the edges of his irises. What was he thinking to make them look like that?

The dance ended.

He took her hand from his shoulder, raised it to his lips, bowed low and pressed a kiss to it.

Amber smiled, warm all over, and then realised that she wasn't the only one looking at him. Half of the room had stopped to stare again and were whispering to each other. Her gaze stopped on Kyran. He stood a few metres away, blue eyes narrowed behind his black mask. The woman in his arms looked disgusted.

Kearn rose, turned Amber's hand in his, and led her from the dance floor. Either he was oblivious to the dirty looks they were receiving or he didn't care. They stopped in the spot where they had been before, near the wall and away from everyone.

"You danced well." He smiled.

Amber smiled too and touched the spot on her glove that Kearn had kissed. Was the kiss why everyone looked so shocked? She had wanted far more than such a tame moment of intimacy. She had considered kissing him on the mouth.

"That was quite a spectacle." Venom dripped from the male voice.

Amber looked up to see Kyran stood beside Kearn, glaring at him. Kearn's expression was void of emotion as he stared back. The tension between them was palpable. Kyran's red eyes darted to her and his lips compressed. None of the usual kindness and charm touched his face now.

"A Noble lowering himself to a human." Pure disgust tainted his expression and his tone. She had been wrong. The kiss hadn't shocked everyone. It was the fact that Kearn had bowed to her. Kyran smirked. "Do not expect such behaviour from Duke Montagu."

She wasn't sure how to react or what to say.

Kyran snorted in her direction and then grabbed Kearn's upper arm.

"Excuse me, I must speak with my little brother before he ridicules the entire family." He turned on his heel and dragged Kearn away.

Kearn didn't seem to care that he was in for an earful. He looked back over his shoulder at her.

"Do not move from that spot. I will not be long. I will bring you a drink." He actually smiled.

Amber's eyebrows rose. She stood rooted to the spot, watching the brothers. Kyran jerked to a halt and shoved Kearn out in front of him, pushing him back towards the wall near the corner of the room. She was too far away to hear them but their thunderous expressions said they were arguing. Kearn threw Kyran's hand from his arm and stepped up to him. She wanted to know what they were saying.

"That was quite a dance."

Amber turned quickly to face the owner of the female voice.

A short dark haired young woman and two other women, both of them closer to Amber's height, stood before her. They were all wearing black empire-line dresses with a lot of cleavage on show, and a lot of make-up in sombre tones. They looked like death, ashen and dull.

Amber smiled politely. Kearn had told her that there would be other humans at the ball and they might be unmasked. These women were going through the transition from human to vampire. If she were bitten, would she look this bad when changing?

Heat touched her cheeks when she thought about Kearn biting her. She had dreamt of it today while sleeping in his bed and had tossed and turned so much that Kearn had woken her by knocking hard on the door and asking whether something was wrong. She had blushed ten shades of red then and hadn't been able to tell him the truth. Instead, she had said it was nothing and had hurried into the shower. He had gone out and when he had come back, he had given her the dress.

She felt incredibly sexy in it.

Especially when he told her that she looked beautiful.

"He is quite the catch." The blonde woman in the group looked past Amber.

Amber followed her gaze. Kearn was still arguing with Kyran. The other vampires nearby had moved away and were warily watching them. What were they arguing about? It couldn't just be about her. Was it about their family name too?

"And so subservient."

She looked back at the three women. They all smiled at her. She didn't think that Kearn was subservient but she smiled anyway.

"To think a Noble would behave such a way." The short dark haired one cast a wistful look in Kearn's direction and then her brown eyes found Amber's again. "I have never seen anything like it."

The third woman, a brunette with a bob, stepped forwards and looked Amber over. "How far along are you?"

Amber glanced down at her stomach. She looked pregnant?

"I thought the dress was quite flattering." She skimmed her hands down her sides. Kearn definitely liked it, and she'd had a duke and Kyran call her beautiful too.

All three women laughed.

"In your turning." The brunette smiled. "You must be far along for a Noble to behave in such a way. It shocked the crowd something terrible."

Amber hadn't failed to notice that.

The blonde twisted her hair around her fingers. "I've almost completed my transition but my Lesser Noble won't even dance with me."

Kearn had also warned Amber that humans going through the transition never danced. Most Nobles and Lesser Nobles didn't associate with them until they had fully turned. It seemed strange that they went to the trouble of courting a human to convince them to become a vampire and then discarded them during their transition. It was almost cruel. Kearn hadn't said what happened when they had finished becoming a vampire.

"So how far along are you?" the brunette prompted.

Amber smiled politely. "I'm not a vampire."

They all laughed again.

"No." The blonde took Amber's black gloved hand and patted it. "You're what my Lesser Noble refers to as a chrysalis—the transition from disgusting worm to beautiful butterfly—and you must be close to spreading your wings."

Amber's smile faltered at the corners. "I'm afraid you're all quite mistaken. I'm the caterpillar."

They gasped and backed off a step. The blonde woman dropped her hand and wiped hers on her dress, glaring at her as though she had been the one to take hold of her.

"A human." The dark haired one sneered and flicked her long locks behind her shoulder, revealing a set of scars on her neck.

The three women turned their backs on her, looped their arms together, and moved off as one, disappearing into the black-clad crowd.

Heat burned through Amber, a remnant of her dream. Kearn had bitten her neck. She had worn marks just like that woman. If she did in reality, would Kearn treat her differently? Was he merely courting her with the intention of sending her through the transition and then discarding her until she had become like him?

No. He wanted to protect her, even from himself. He had slipped tonight and allowed a glimmer of his feelings to shine through, but she was sure that he wasn't out to make her into a vampire.

She turned to look for Kearn and found Duke Montagu standing before her. Instinct whispered that it was dangerous for her to be alone with him. He frowned over her head towards the women and then at her, his red eyes intent and cold behind his black mask. He was over one thousand years old. How powerful did that make him?

"I hope they have not upset you," he said with charm and grace. "If they have, I will see to it that the young Venator is punished."

Amber's eyes darted towards Kearn. He stood a few metres behind the duke, a glass of champagne in his hand. His eyes were wide. Stunned? She couldn't feel anything of the sort. He could definitely control the connection between them and had shut her out again.

"I was not offended." She smiled, not wanting him to punish Kearn for what he had done. It was an honour to have such a noble man lower himself to her regardless of the rules.

There wasn't a trace of cruelty in the duke's smile this time. His red eyes held hers.

"Jealousy is such an ugly thing." His eyes narrowed as his smile widened. "The presence of such a beautiful creature will always upset those desiring to attain beauty beyond their grasp."

Amber wished that Kearn had been the one to say those words. If he had been standing before her, telling her again how beautiful she was, she would have kissed him. She wouldn't have cared if they had thrown them out for it either.

She glanced past the duke to Kearn. He no longer looked stunned. The warm edge to his eyes told her that he believed the duke's words and what he had told her earlier. When he looked at her like that, with a shine to his green eyes and a smile starting to tease at his lips, she felt as beautiful as he painted her to be.

She blushed and looked back at the duke. He stared in the direction of the three women.

"They had hoped to believe you almost a vampire, desiring that they would become as beautiful as you on their transition, and that their master would show them such attention." His gaze dropped to her and a serious look replaced his smile. "They are still foolish enough to believe it will happen. What they will find when they join us is nothing more than they have now— empty vanity and a male who will move on to a new female."

The women had been nasty to her once they had realised that she was human but she felt sorry for them. They only wanted their vampire to love them. They were alike in that respect. She barely knew Kearn but she was falling for him, and she wanted him to fall for her too. She had come here tonight with the intention of keeping his attention on her, desiring him to be as lost in her as she felt in him. Regardless of their differences and the fact they walked in two different worlds, she wanted to be with him.

"But you," Duke Montagu said. "If you changed, you *would* attain that beauty and the heart of your Noble. You would rule absolute."

A shiver danced through her and her gaze roamed to Kearn. Would she really win his heart that way?

No trace of denial touched Kearn's features. His eyes were open, allowing her to read his feelings in them, but she couldn't decipher them and she desperately wanted to.

"I said a Noble." Duke Montagu's tone was darker, commanding, and her gaze snapped back to him. "Not a Venator. Such a creature is unworthy of you. I spoke of someone like myself."

In the corner of her vision, Kearn's eyes turned vivid red.

Duke Montagu raised an eyebrow and his gaze slid to the side, towards Kearn, but he didn't turn to face him.

"You dare to threaten me, Venator?" The duke's voice was pure ice. His red eyes narrowed behind his mask.

Kearn's irises melted back to green and he lowered his head.

Duke Montagu held his hand out to one side, towards the dance floor.

The music stopped.

The crowd parted and left the large dance floor bare.

"Allow me to show you how a true Noble behaves."

Amber looked at Kearn.

He cast his gaze to one side. She could feel hurt inside her, a dull ache in her chest, that wasn't just hers.

She followed Duke Montagu onto the dance floor, her heart too heavy to care whether she made a fool of herself. When she stopped opposite the duke in the middle of the dance floor, she glanced back at Kearn.

He was watching her now.

She wanted to go to him and tell him that he was worthy of her.

She didn't want the duke or anyone else for that matter.

She only wanted him.

CHAPTER 12

Amber didn't have much of a chance to ready herself. The moment the music started, Duke Montagu pulled her into his arms and swept her around the empty dance floor. The tempo was fast, the brass triumphant and the choir singing beautifully, but all of it was lost on her as she tried to focus on dancing. She lifted the hem of her black dress to stop herself from tripping on it and kept her gaze fixed on Duke Montagu's chest.

Her focus slipped but her feet kept going, galloping to the music. The pace was at least twice the speed of her waltz with Kearn. She tried to see him but the people lining the edge of the dance floor created a black blurry wall.

Her legs were already beginning to tire.

"You dance rather well for a woman who has only had one lesson."

"Thank you," she whispered, unsure what else to say.

"A little too well. I suspected my nephew had tasted your blood. Now I have proof."

"He was healing my hand." Amber remembered how it had felt to have Kearn's tongue sliding sensually over her palm, and the kiss that had followed in the aftermath. That had been divine. Her heart sped with the music and her head began to spin with the constant twirling as they raced around the dance floor. Each step made her feet ache in the heels and her ankles threatened to give out. "He's looking for a vampire who is interested in my blood."

"Because you are a Source Blood?" the duke said and she glanced up at him. Her gaze immediately dropped to his chest again. He laughed. "Do not seem so surprised that I can tell such a thing. There is more to your beauty than looks."

They danced on and Amber kept telling herself not to concentrate too much. She just had to keep upright and keep staring at the duke's chest. Kearn would do the rest.

The tempo of the music increased again. Christ. She would fall now.

"Shall we see how good the Venator is at dancing?" the duke whispered into her ear. "If you fall, you are mine."

No. She wasn't going to agree to that. The pace of the music was ridiculous. She was only human. She couldn't dance this fast and not fall. He was stacking the odds against Kearn.

She wanted to see him. Her vision was a blur of black and she couldn't make out anything.

But she could feel Kearn's eyes on her, intense and focused, and could feel him guiding her steps.

And she could feel the duke watching her. Waiting for her to fall.

Whatever civility he had been showing her before was gone now. He was as cold and distant as Kearn had been when they had first met. She didn't want to become a prize like those other women and she didn't believe a word the duke had said about her being able to win his heart. This man didn't have a heart. He treated his own nephew with contempt and was treating her as though she was something he could win, like a possession. Well, she wasn't and she would never belong to him.

The brass section blared out again, the strings joining it. The choir rose along with the tempo. He was making them do this. He had to be.

Her knees weakened and she felt sick from swirling so quickly in circles.

She was going to fall.

No. She wouldn't fall. She was doing just fine. She just needed to relax.

Amber looked around. Kearn. These were his thoughts somehow placed into her mind. Did her blood allow him to do this too? Last night, she had felt something similar, had heard a voice inside her that had told her to fight the man's hold over her. He was speaking to her through her blood. She relaxed as instructed and tried to see him. The tempo of the song finally began to slow and she gasped when Duke Montagu pulled her hard against him, so his body pressed into hers.

Anger surged through her.

He smiled. "If the Venator continues to threaten me, I will have to make an example of him."

Amber saw Kearn standing at edge of the dance floor, a gap between him and the other vampires. When she spun with the duke, she turned her head to face Kearn again. His eyes were bright red and his expression matched the outrage inside her. His anger. He didn't like the duke holding her like this.

A murmur ran through the crowd. Duke Montagu looked towards the entrance, and Kearn did too. She glanced over, curious about what had their attention.

The female Venator.

Duke Montagu stopped dead and Amber almost fell, but managed to keep upright with only a little flailing of her arms. She wasn't going to fall and be his.

He smiled ruefully.

"Excuse me. I must attend to some business. I am afraid we shall have to continue our dance later." He walked away without a backwards glance, heading straight for the stairs and the Venator. As if. Amber wasn't going to risk her neck by dancing with him again. She would leave before it happened.

She looked over at Kearn. He was gone. She scoured the crowd and saw him heading for the stairs too. Her heart ached. He probably had to greet the other Venator, just as he had the other night, but it didn't mean she had to like it.

Amber walked back towards the side of the room, distracting herself from her jealousy by congratulating herself on surviving such a fast waltz and planning how to avoid the duke for the rest of the evening. Couples moved in again to dance, blocking her path. She carefully squeezed her way through, afraid of upsetting any vampire when Kearn wasn't on hand to protect her.

She could see the edge of the dance floor when someone grabbed her arm and dragged her backwards. Their tight grip hurt and she tried to prise their black gloved fingers off her but they wouldn't let go.

The music started again at a fast pace. The man spun her, pulled her into his arms so her chest pressed into his, and started to dance with her. His grip was unrelenting, tight against her ribs and her left hand. She pushed at his arm with her free hand and then froze when she looked up into his red eyes.

Even with the slim black mask hiding the top half of his face, she swore that she knew him. Her head felt fuzzy and light, and her feet knew the way even when she didn't know the steps. A warm feeling suffused every inch of her and she drifted along in the man's arms, no longer wanting to fight him. It was nice. She was enjoying it.

And she wanted more.

His hand left her side, skimming her shoulder, and she shuddered when his fingertips traced tantalising lines over her throat. She smiled and her eyelids fell to half-mast. Her mind turned hazy and she could only focus on the delicious feel of his touch. She wanted this.

She tilted her head back and to the side, still waltzing with him, lost in the tempo of her heart and the music.

His thumb caressed the left side of her throat. She flinched at the sting of pain and then sighed when he drew her closer to him. His body was hard against hers, strong like his grip on her, and she closed her eyes when their cheeks brushed.

Taste me.

Something warm tickled her neck. A point above it burned.

The man stopped with her, lowered his mouth to her throat, and wrapped his lips around it. Amber sighed and then moaned when the man sucked on her skin and a dizzying rush crashed through her. She leaned back, arching into the man, seeking more than just the pleasure of his forbidden kiss.

It was enthralling.

Beautiful.

Bliss.

She wanted more.

The world around her wavered and became silent save for the beating of her heart.

The man kissed her neck, licking it and growling against her skin. She smiled at the ceiling and clung to him.

She wanted to be his.

She wanted to go with him.

She would go with him.

Lover.

CHAPTER 13

Kearn stood to one side, a few feet from Duke Montagu as he greeted the female Venator. He wished the man would hurry. Amber was still on the dance floor. Another partner had caught her. It had been bad enough seeing her in the arms of his uncle. Seeing her in the arms of a younger male made his blood burn for violence.

He clenched his fists and glanced over at them. They were still dancing. Amber didn't seem too afraid. Her blood was calm and she showed no outward sign of fear.

Lord Montagu and Earl Huntingdon glared at him from a short distance away. Both men were younger than he was and weaker, but this wasn't the time to be considering the outcome of a fight. He had to hurry through greeting the Venator so he could get Amber out of that damned man's arms and back into his.

The eyes of the vampires passing by and those around him bore into him, full of malice and laced with intent. He shut them out and focused on his business and Amber.

He had been prepared for the reception society had given him on his entering the ballroom but it had still hurt. Everyone had ensured that he remembered his status as an outcast. They had all tried hard to make him see how far he had fallen and how difficult it would be for him to regain his old place within his family and society.

And he wanted to.

Deep in his heart, he dreamed of retaking his place and longed to return to his family.

Being here around people who had once respected him and called him friend, people he had grown up with but who now looked down on him in contempt, made him feel as though he would never realise that dream.

He looked at his right hand and the intricate silver marks on his skin. He hated them for how they had altered his life and the duty they represented. He had never wanted it and the pain it had caused, and the way it had torn him away from his family and the world he had loved.

Kearn curled his fingers into a tight fist. It trembled. He hated being alone.

His gaze moved of its own volition over the heads of the dancers to find Amber. It was hard to spot her amongst the crowd. He searched for her a moment longer, needing to see her and know that he wasn't alone here, and then turned back to the Venator.

The smell of blood hit his senses like a bulldozer.

Amber.

He would recognise it anywhere.

Kearn was moving in an instant. He growled when he saw the man holding Amber close, his head bent to her throat and hers tilted back. Her arms encircled his shoulders, her fingers tangling in his dark ponytail.

Sheer bliss lit her face.

People blocked his path, heading towards the source of the smell just as he was, only they wanted to hurt Amber, not protect her.

Kearn's growl became a roar and his left hand went for his gun at the same moment as the marks on his right began to glow pale blue.

It was him.

The second Kearn drew his gun, the crowd screamed and scattered, running across his path and hindering him.

Amber.

His blood called out to hers and her eyes opened. They widened and then she struggled, trying to push the man away from her.

"Kearn!" she screamed.

He was coming.

Amber managed to break out of the man's grasp but he grabbed her wrist.

Kearn looked down the line of his gun at the man's back and kept running. The path between them cleared. He squeezed the trigger.

The man turned and flung Amber at Kearn. He reacted in an instant, jerking the gun up to the ceiling just as it fired so the bullet didn't hit her, and catching her with his other arm to stop her from hitting the floor. His knee hit the parquet and then he stood with her, holding her close to him. She was bleeding badly. The scent of it was strong and there was a trail of red down the left side of her neck and over her chest.

The man stood on the opposite side of the room, facing him, perfectly still. Kearn couldn't tell who he was with the mask on, but he was sure of one thing. This was the man he was after.

People ran between them, knocking them both in their panic and rush to safety, but they remained facing each other, staring into each other's eyes, unmoving.

Several people stopped near him, their red eyes on Amber, and then edged towards him.

Kearn growled and his eyes turned crimson. He swept his arm around, pointing his gun at all of them, trying to clear them away. It was her blood driving them crazy, not the gunfire or anything else. They bore their fangs at him. He sneered, revealing his, and swept his gun over them again. The moment he threatened to squeeze the trigger, they fled, leaving the area between him and his enemy clear. Kearn's focus snapped to him.

The man would pay for what he had done to Amber.

Kearn brought his gun around.

The man smiled.

Amber pulled out of Kearn's grasp and blocked his line of sight. She stood at a slight angle to him, a vision in black and scarlet, her left hand behind her and her right trembling at her side.

Her hazel eyes went as round as saucers and sheer terror filled them.

"Demon!" she screamed at the top of her lungs.

He shook his head and took a step towards her. He wasn't a demon and he didn't want her to see him that way. Blood ran down her throat and chest. Tears glistened on her pale cheeks. She clawed at her neck with her right hand, causing more blood to spill, and then held her trembling bloodstained hand out between them.

"You did this. Demon!"

Before he could react, she had pulled her left hand out from behind her back and attacked him. A flash of silver crossed his eyes. He raised his right arm to block her and cried out when the knife lodged deep in his forearm. Pain burned up his arm and he roared when Amber tried to pull the knife out to attack again. Her eyes were wild, wide and dancing around.

Kearn broke free of her grasp and pressed his hand against her head.

Sleep.

Her eyes slipped shut and she fell. Kearn caught her, grimacing at the feel of the short blade grating against the bone in his arm, and laid her on the ground. He hated to use such control over her but he couldn't risk her attempting to hurt him again. He had to protect them both. She would remember everything she had done.

Kearn raised his gun but the man was gone, the rushing crowd swallowing him. It would be impossible to find him in the chaos and he couldn't leave Amber. She was his priority. The man knew for certain now that she was a Source Blood. He would come for her again, and Kearn would be waiting for him.

He looked down at Amber.

Tears glittered on her solemn ashen face. She hadn't cried out of fear. She had cried because she had known what she was doing. He had felt her pain and sorrow in his blood, her hurt and horror flowing in his veins. Kearn touched her cheek in a light caress. He shouldn't have left her alone.

He pulled the knife from his arm and dropped it.

The dance floor emptied, most of the guests surging towards the stairs. Kearn growled at those who remained and dared to look at him or attempted to come near Amber, and put his gun away, leaving the knife on the floor. He cleared the brown waves of hair from Amber's throat, careful as he removed the strands that had stuck to the cut. There was so much dried blood around it that he couldn't see it clearly. He couldn't risk cleaning it away in case the bleeding worsened. The smell of it already filled his senses and pushed at his control. Everyone in the room would be feeling the same. If Amber lost more blood, it would be difficult to get her out of the building without a fight, and it would be impossible for him to resist his desire to taste her again.

He carefully picked up Amber, ignoring the pain in his right arm, and pressed his hand against the left side of her throat and the cut on it. He had to stem the bleeding.

"Calm down." Duke Montagu's voice rang out from the top of the stairs and echoed around the ballroom.

Silence fell.

Kearn carried Amber towards the tables that lined the sides of the room. There had been food there when he had gone to get Amber a drink. The vampires gathered near the tables moved away as he approached. The duke continued to talk, assuring everyone that it was over and they were safe. Kearn set Amber down on her feet near a long red table full of food and champagne glasses, keeping one arm around her back so she didn't fall. He picked up a wad of black napkins and pressed them against her neck. It was difficult to get her back into his arms when he needed to keep pressure on her wound and his right arm was on fire. Blood slid down it, soaking his black uniform. He needed to seal the cut with his saliva and bandage it.

By the time he was cradling her again, Duke Montagu had his guests under control and the orchestra were tuning their instruments. Servants were leaving the dance floor, one of them carrying the knife. No trace of Amber's blood remained on the parquet.

Kearn kept the pressure on her throat with the arm he had around her back.

It was as though nothing had happened.

Everyone appeared calm, all talking and laughing again. Some had even retaken their places on the dance floor.

The underlying sense of unease in the room gave away their real feelings. What they had witnessed and the smell of human blood that permeated the air was unsettling them.

Amber stirred in her sleep. Kearn walked towards the stairs, monitoring her pulse. It was quicker than normal but not fast enough to worry him. It would probably settle once he had sealed the wound and stopped the bleeding. He couldn't do that here. Duke Montagu was old enough to recognise that she was a Source Blood, and it wouldn't take much for others to discover why he had brought her to the ball. If they saw him drink from a Source Blood, even though it was to heal her, he would never be welcome in society again.

Kyran caught up with him at the top of the red-carpeted stairs. Kearn was about to mention his surprise at seeing his brother and ask whether Kyran intended to lecture him again, when he spotted that Duke Montagu was close behind him.

"I do hope you can see that I had nothing to do with this incident," Duke Montagu said and Kearn smiled inside, relishing the note of fear in his voice and highly satisfied by it.

"I will need to investigate before I can determine who was involved." He turned away with Amber and allowed himself a small smile. It disappeared when Kyran stepped into view. If Kyran saw his childish triumph, it would get back to the duke.

"Will she be all right?" The concern in Kyran's voice surprised him more than the fact he had come to see him.

After their argument earlier, he hadn't expected his brother to be so civil towards him. Normally when they fought and Kearn didn't back down, Kyran didn't speak to him for months, sometimes even a year or more when it was about their family.

Kearn nodded and kept the pressure on her neck. Her heartbeat was steadying. The fragment of a connection they shared assured him that her feelings were stable. She didn't seem in any immediate danger.

When they reached his car, he would check her wound. He couldn't seal it there though. He would fall under the influence of her blood and wouldn't be safe to drive. It had been dangerous enough when he had licked her hand and driven afterwards. He couldn't risk something happening now when she was injured. He would never forgive himself.

"You had better leave before you have to fight to stop her from becoming the main course." Kyran looked back towards the ballroom.

Kearn nodded. He could feel their eyes on him and sense their intent. They wanted Amber's blood. He relished its scent. It spoke to the trace in his veins, telling him to taste her again so he could form a stronger connection between them and could feel that way again. He wanted to feel the desire it provoked in him, the hunger for her.

He looked at her where she lay in his arms.

He didn't need her blood in his veins in order to feel that way. Just a glance at her tonight had been enough to make him yearn for her. Dancing close to her had pushed him past yearning to the point where he had been ready to act on his desires. He had kissed her hand in front of society, and Kyran had made sure he knew the full extent of their outrage over him committing an atrocity by lowering himself to a human.

Society had cast him out, yet it still cared about how he acted and still felt he should behave as his old position within it dictated. Did it still see him as a Noble? He would have laughed at that had it not been his heart's desire.

In that moment though, part of him hadn't cared what they had thought of him.

Amber had been all that had mattered.

Just as she was all that mattered right now.

He walked through the arch and down the stairs. Kyran continued to follow him. Kearn cast him a questioning frown.

"I will go with you. Safety in numbers." Kyran's blue gaze dropped to Amber again. A hint of red ringed his irises.

Was the smell of Amber's blood the reason Kyran wanted to accompany him? The scent was strong and it alone stirred his blood and made his hunger return with force.

"Just to the car. I have several Lesser Nobles' daughters to introduce to my wicked side." Kyran grinned.

Kearn wasn't surprised to hear that. Seeing those women with Kyran tonight had reminded him of when they were younger and had been the toast of all the balls. They had never stopped dancing back then and every daughter of a Noble or Lesser Noble had wanted to be with them.

He looked down at Amber. Things really had changed. He no longer wanted to dance with every pretty female who smiled at him. He only wanted to dance with her.

She was growing paler and it worried him. During the fight, he hadn't felt his own fear. It was only in looking back that he realised it had seized his heart and had controlled him. He would have done anything to protect her. He would have sacrificed himself.

"She really is a Source then," Kyran whispered, staring at Amber. "Her blood is potent."

"She is." Kearn walked out into the courtyard, his eyes on Amber's face, absorbing her beauty and feeling a ghost of the effect her blood had on him. "It is."

Warmth lingered in the air, lacing it with the scent of the sun even though it was past midnight. He carried her over to his car and set her down, leaning her against it. Kyran took hold of her and Kearn thanked him with a smile. He found his keys in his pocket, unlocked the car, and opened the door.

Kyran helped him manoeuvre Amber into the passenger seat, sitting her sideways facing the driver's side with her right cheek against the headrest. Kearn secured her safety belt and peeled the thick wad of black napkins away from her throat. He touched the spot where the dried blood was darkest. Small beads broke to the surface and formed a short diagonal line. Had the knife made the cut or the man's fangs? He covered it again and took a deep breath. If he'd had a god, he would have prayed that it was the knife.

He didn't want to lose her.

Kearn stroked her face. Her soft skin was warm and still damp with tears in places. He brushed them away with the pad of his thumb, taking his time and memorising the feel of her skin as he gazed on her. She was so delicate and fragile, but she had been so strong tonight, and he had meant what he had said to her with all of his heart and every drop of his blood. Her beauty was unparalleled and he was eternally grateful to her for giving him even the briefest chance to enter society with her on his arm. Drawing his hand away, he curled it into a fist as he thought about everything she endured for his sake. His gaze slipped to the wad of black napkins covering her throat. He was going to hunt the bastard down and make him suffer for this. Black rage curled through him and his fangs extended at the same time as a spark of blue lit his fingertips. He struggled to shut down his feelings and then stood and faced Kyran when he was back in control.

"Be careful." Kyran had removed his mask and his eyes were blue again, no trace of red touching them. They held a serious edge. "If uncle wants her—"

"I will not allow that to happen." Kearn's gaze dropped to her. The lights around the courtyard turned her skin golden. Her left black glove had slipped down past her elbow. He was tempted to smooth it up her arm again, to make her look perfect as she had done when the evening had started, but it wouldn't undo what had happened. The blood on her neck and chest was real. He had failed in his promise and it hurt because he wanted to protect her above everything. "She does not belong in our world."

"I am surprised to hear you say that considering the way you act around her."

Kearn closed the passenger door.

"Let it go." He walked around the car. He didn't want to have to explain himself to Kyran, not when he wasn't even sure what he was feeling. He opened the driver's door and glanced at the wide sandstone mansion. Duke Montagu was watching them from a window on the first floor. "Be careful and stay away from the blood. Someone has spiked it with Source Blood."

Kyran grinned. "I had wondered why I felt so giddy."

Kearn sighed and waved his brother away. He didn't want him on his list. Drinking spiked blood was a grey area in the law. Someone could easily deny knowing it had contained Source Blood and the Sovereignty wouldn't know any better. They couldn't hear normal vampires' thoughts. They could only see their actions.

Kyran would deny it if asked, even if he had known. All of his kind would.

It didn't matter. The Sovereignty would see the one who had spiked the blood and would send a Venator to deal with them.

Kearn got into his car, started it, and drove fast out of the courtyard. When he reached the main road, he pressed his left hand against Amber's throat, keeping the pressure on the wound. The trace of her blood in his body was fading and he couldn't sense her now that she had fallen into a deeper sleep. He wanted to know how she was feeling but he couldn't risk rousing her to see if she was in pain or in danger.

He removed his hand from the wad of napkins to change gear and then pressed it back over them again, speeding through the outskirts of London. They would be back at his apartment within fifteen minutes if the traffic was with him.

He ran all the red lights, not slowing down even for those with speed cameras. They couldn't fine him. His car was unregistered and he didn't even have a driver's licence to put points on.

In the human world, he didn't exist.

Amber's heartbeat quickened.

Kearn frowned across at her. A new line of blood was creeping down her chest. The wound couldn't have reopened by itself. Amber hadn't moved and it had almost stopped bleeding beneath the napkins. The vampire was doing something to her.

He growled and ran his hand across her bloodied chest. It was dangerous but the man left him no choice. He licked the blood on his fingers and shivered as he swallowed it. It instantly seeped into his, spreading fire through his veins and turning his mind hazy. Heat settled low in his abdomen, arousal stirring there, and he clamped his teeth together as his fangs extended. He growled and fought the effects, focusing on Amber to clear his mind. He wouldn't let it control him this time. Amber was in danger and he had to protect her. The connection opened between him and Amber, and he used it to check her feelings. She wanted to wake up. The man was trying to command her. Did he want her to attack him again? Kearn wasn't going to let that happen.

She had to stay calm and sleep. She was tired and she had to sleep it off. When she woke, her cut would be better. It was nothing for her to worry about. He would take care of her.

He shifted gear and ran another red light, narrowly avoiding a red double-decker bus. He couldn't slow down. He had to get Amber to his apartment and heal her wound. The blood he would take from her then would be enough to establish firm control over her.

Her heart missed a beat and then raced.

Sleep.

It slowed again, falling back into a natural rhythm. Kearn touched her face. She was getting colder. He was a fool. He hadn't considered the differences between their species and her heartbeat had convinced him she was safe.

A human was fragile compared with a vampire. Even with the cut not bleeding at a dangerous level, he could still lose her if the vampire had taken too much blood from her.

Panic rushed through his veins, blocking out every thought or feeling that wasn't about her. He had to get her to safety and help her heal. It was all he could do, but he feared it wouldn't be enough.

"Stay with me, Amber." He pressed his hand against her throat again. Her face twisted in pain and then turned calm once more. He hadn't meant to hurt her but he needed to make sure she wasn't bleeding now. He needed her to live.

Kearn used her blood to keep the connection between them open. The vampire was still trying to make her do things. He caught snippets of the thoughts the vampire was placing in Amber's head and countered them all with his own commands. She wanted to remain asleep and was very tired. When she woke, she would feel better and he would be there with her. He wouldn't let the vampire have her. He wouldn't.

The vampire sent a message to her that made Kearn growl and put his foot down on the accelerator.

He wanted her to come to him.

Amber wanted to go to him.

Bastard.

"Stay with me." Kearn sent the same words to her blood so she would definitely hear him.

She calmed again and it felt as though she had reached out to him in return, strengthening the connection between them. He focused and kept it strong, giving her reassurance and anything she needed. In this moment, it didn't matter if he looked weak or lonely, or if any of his growing feelings for her showed. It only mattered that she knew that he needed her with him, because then she would stay. He was sure of it.

Their blood bond grew stronger and he knew it was Amber's work. She was calling to him, reinforcing the link between them.

The vampire disappeared. Kearn's panic began to subside when he sensed her feelings. No pain or fear touched them now that the vampire was gone. She must have been trying to fight his hold over her by herself. Her heartbeat and feelings hadn't altered because she had been in mortal danger. It had been because she didn't want to leave him.

Her heart beat steadily in his ears.

Her warm scent soothed his senses.

The connection between them remained strong and open, tying their hearts together.

Kearn stared at the road ahead, his panic clearing and leaving reason behind. The vampire would have only taken enough blood to test it and control her. He wouldn't have endangered her when he wanted her alive so he could harvest her blood. She would survive the attack.

It didn't stop Kearn from worrying about her though. Every time he saw the blood on her, saw how pale she was, a voice inside him whispered that he was going to lose her.

She was human. Frail. He didn't know if she could withstand this sort of attack on her body and mind.

He drove down into the large empty garage beneath his apartment building. The metal shutter door creaked as it closed behind them. Kearn turned off the car engine and raced around to Amber's side. His arm hurt as he lifted her out of the car but he ignored it. He wasn't losing too much blood now. The pain was nothing. He bore it because Amber was more important.

He looked down at her peaceful face, monitoring her feelings as well as her heartbeat, and hurried to his apartment.

An image of her attacking him flashed across his mind.

The vampire had made her do it but it still upset him. There had been such genuine fear in her eyes. He had felt as though he was a monster after she had made him feel like a man, and he still felt that way.

He was a monster for bringing her into this. He hadn't even given it a second thought when he had decided to use her as bait, and had been willing to do so against her wishes. A monster without a heart.

She had changed him though.

She had opened his heart and he could no longer close it to her.

Kearn waved his hand over his apartment door and it opened. He closed it with the same gesture once inside and carried Amber across the large white room to his bedroom. He carefully laid her down on his bed. She didn't stir, not even when he turned on the light.

"Amber," he whispered and touched her cheek.

He lost his hold on her blood, the connection between them severing and leaving him cold and alone. She lay on his bed, white against the brown covers, looking like death.

Kearn tried to talk to her blood again. Nothing happened. She had passed out. It would keep her safe from the vampire but it worried him. He wasn't used to dealing with humans so didn't know how bad this was. A vampire could lose consciousness from lack of blood and come around only a moment later. He didn't know how long a human would take.

He removed his black uniform jacket and placed it over her to keep her warm, and then ran around the foot of the bed and into the bathroom. He wet one of the brown hand towels and came back to her, and drew the jacket away from her chest. Blood caked it in a thick line down from the left side of her neck. He gently cleaned it off her and then took the black napkins away from her throat.

Bits of the tissue stuck to the blood on her throat. He picked them off, careful not to disturb the cut, and then concentrated on cleaning around the wound.

The dried blood slowly cleared to reveal the cut. It was shallow and only half as long as his little finger, stopping just before her artery. Tonight would have gone differently if it had reached there. He would have had to seal the wound in the ballroom and suffer the consequences.

The precision of the cut backed up his earlier thoughts about the vampire. He hadn't intended to place her in any serious danger. He had only wanted to confirm her as a Source Blood and control her.

Kearn wrapped the damp towel around his fingers and dabbed at the cut. Tiny beads of blood lined it in spots where the skin hadn't begun to heal.

He reached over and turned on the bedside table light. It shone brightly on the cut and relief bloomed sweet and strong inside him.

The knife.

The vampire had cut her with the knife. The line of the wound was too clean for fangs.

She wouldn't become like them.

With his fear eased, his anger returned. What the vampire had done wasn't the only reason he was angry. It was the way the man had held her and the look of ecstasy she had worn. It was the fact that the vampire had made her hold him too and made her enjoy the feel of his lips against her throat.

Kearn's blood burned. His jaw tensed and he ground his teeth together, frowning down at Amber's throat. His heart demanded the life of the vampire in return for trying to take her from him.

The vampire wasn't the only one to blame for her suffering.

Kearn had failed her too. He should have assured her safety and then greeted the Venator. From now on, he had to place her before his duty. He wouldn't fail her again.

He put the towel down on the side cupboard and gently tilted Amber's head to her right, so he could see the wound. He needed to help it heal. The thought of running his tongue over her throat was potent and arousing, stirring him to hardness against his trousers even when he knew that nothing would happen between them. He had never touched a human's throat in this way before and wasn't sure if he would be able to control himself, but he needed to seal the cut.

With a deep breath, he kneeled on the bed and leaned over her, placing his hands on either side of her arms. His gazed fixed on her throat. He wasn't strong enough to do this. It would tip him over the edge, past the point of no return, and the effect on him wouldn't be because she was a Source Blood. It would be because it was her.

Tear tracks lined her pallid face, black make-up ringed her closed eyes, and her red lipstick had worn away, but she was still beautiful to him. She still captivated him.

Closing his eyes, he dipped his head to her neck and took another deep breath to regain some control.

The moment his tongue touched her throat, he was lost. The taste of her blood was sweet on his senses, rousing them and strengthening the connection to her. She surfaced from the black abyss of unconsciousness and wrapped him in invisible arms that held him to her throat. Her mind swam with his in the darkness of their joined blood. He licked her throat again, savouring her blood and opening further to her, allowing her in so more than their blood became one. Her feelings ran in his veins, all warmth and happiness, fear and trepidation, arousal and desire. His matched them but for different reasons. He feared what she would think of him.

She wouldn't think anything bad.

He desired to protect her.

She wanted to free him, to give him reason to fight, so he would never be lonely.

He was scared of the future.

She was unafraid of it, because he would be with her, and she would savour every moment of it, no matter how it ended.

Kearn wrapped his lips around her throat, unable to resist the call in her blood for him to take it, to bring her into his body so they could be as one for longer and remain together. It went beyond merely healing her, but he couldn't help himself. He needed her.

She moved against him when he sucked on her blood, taking a small amount and reopening the wound. His head felt heavy and light at the same time, his senses swirling and emotions spiralling out of control. He pulled harder, needing more, and a buzz ran through his veins when he swallowed the mouthful of blood. Not only his feelings but Amber's too. She wanted this. She wanted him. He licked the cut and kissed her throat, desperate to take things further, and then buried his face in her neck, sucking on her blood again. Images from his dreams ran through his mind. His arousal soared and warmth coiled in his abdomen. He groaned and longed to feel her naked body against his, her legs wrapped around his hips and their bodies truly as one. His heart beat harder, a dizzying rush in his veins that relaxed him and released his inhibitions. He wanted her too.

So take her.

Make her his.

His fangs extended at the command and he pulled away, afraid of catching her with them or giving in to his desire to sink them into her throat and seal her fate. He breathed hard, staring down at her, and struggled for control, grasping the bedcovers and drawing them into his fists.

He couldn't do as her blood bid. She had no place in his world.

Duke Montagu's words hit him with full force as his body still tingled from the taste of her blood and still ached to be inside her.

She would make a beautiful vampire.

While normal humans became weak vampires, Amber would become one strong enough to rival even the power of the oldest of his kind. Her blood would see to that, and it wouldn't become like a normal vampire's, strong and dull in taste. It would retain most of its fragrance, but would lose almost all of the effect it had on other vampires. That power would be hers then, locked deep in her blood, held out of reach of others. She would be a goddess with both beauty and power.

Kearn remained leaning over her, his gaze on her peaceful face. Feelings surfaced within her that threatened to shatter his control. Affection. Tenderness. Understanding. She wanted to be with him. He believed that deep in his heart. She was falling for him.

He lowered himself and pressed his lips to hers. She surprised him by responding, kissing him so lightly that he warmed inside and longed for more. His lips played against hers, parting and meeting, moving slowly over each other in a gentle caress that tested his restraint. His fangs grazed his lower lip and he was careful to keep them away from hers. They wouldn't go away as long as her blood was calling to him to taste it again. He took a deep breath, breathing in her scent and savouring it, memorising this moment in case it never happened again.

Amber tilted her head up towards his.

She whispered against his lips.

"Stay with me forever."

Kearn pulled back, eyes wide, the tips of his silver hair framing his vision of her.

He searched his blood but couldn't tell where her feelings ended and his began. Had she meant those words or had they been his voiced through her? His arms trembled, as though they could no longer support his weight, and his breathing became shaky. He was a fool.

He was falling for her, a human, and it was too late to stop himself.

She didn't need to become a vampire to win the heart of her Noble.

She had already captured it.

Her blood in his veins cried out for him. It called his name and he knew that the other vampire would sense it too. Kearn wanted nothing more than to take the offer to slake his desire for her by making love with her and taking her blood, but he couldn't.

She had no place in his world.

As painful as it was, he had to keep his distance from her. What they had could only be fleeting. He wouldn't make her a vampire.

His heart said that he would if she asked him. If those words that had left her lips had really been her feelings and not his, he would do as she bid, even if it hurt him. He could never refuse her.

Kearn leaned over her again and pressed a kiss to her lips. He supported himself on one arm, and touched her cheek with his other hand.

"Say those words to me again when my blood is not with yours," he whispered against her mouth and then sent her a command to sleep.

Her body relaxed into the bed and her mind emptied, her thoughts going deep. He pushed her beyond sleep so the vampire couldn't affect her while she rested, and lost the connection to her. It was better this way. He needed to clear his head and gain some perspective, and he couldn't do it when he could feel her calling out to him. He would give in to her.

Kearn pressed another kiss to her forehead and then went to the bathroom.

He looked back when he reached the door.

Did she really want to be with him forever? If she asked him, would he bring her into his world? She didn't want him to be lonely.

Kearn turned away.

He didn't want it either, but it was the path that he had chosen.

And one he had to walk.

Alone.

CHAPTER 14

Kearn closed the bathroom door and turned on the shower, avoiding his reflection in the large black framed mirror above the white oval sink. He couldn't look himself in the eye when he was thinking about Amber and whether he would go through with it. His blood hungered for hers, his body craving the taste and the effect it had on him. He focused on clearing his mind. With the connection between them closed, it was easier to purge his lust and the hazy feeling. A sliver of desire remained, not induced by her blood but by the feel of her skin beneath his lips and the taste of her kiss.

He stripped off and inspected the wound on his right arm, turning his attention there in an attempt to shut out the desire to go back to Amber and kiss her again. The cut was in a difficult place on top of his forearm, slicing through the silver marks there. He twisted his arm towards his chest and managed to reach it with his tongue. His saliva would speed the external healing process, stopping the cut from reopening, and his body would take care of the rest.

Kearn stepped into the shower. The hot water soothed his muscles, relaxing him even while Amber's blood flowed in his veins. He ran over everything that had happened tonight. Another chance had slipped through his fingers because he had placed Amber first when facing his enemy. He couldn't help it. When she was in danger, he could think only of protecting her.

He traced the evening backwards, looking for anything that could point to the man's identity. So many of the guests had drunk the spiked blood and shown trace effects that it had been impossible to detect the man from looking at eyes alone. The masks were another problem, hiding enough of the guests' faces that most of them looked the same.

It left Kearn with little to go on.

All he knew was that the man was of noble blood and that he would come for Amber again.

Kearn tilted his head back and the water bounced off his face.

The image of the man and Amber flashed across his closed eyes.

Bastard.

He clenched his fists. He wanted to rip the man's throat out for laying his hands on her and hurting her. Amber would wake knowing what she had done. She would remember it all. The cut on his arm stung under the hot water and he licked it again. She wouldn't forgive herself, even though it hadn't been her fault.

It was his fault.

He turned the water temperature down to cold but it did nothing to quell his anger and his desire for blood.

The man had to pay.

Power rose in Kearn's right arm, trickling upwards from his fingers, warm and fierce. He let it fade away. This wasn't about his duty now. It was about her. He wasn't hunting the man on orders, not anymore. He was hunting him to protect Amber, to protect the woman who had become the most precious thing in his dark world.

He couldn't deny his feelings for her. He loved her without a doubt, and even if there were no future for them, he would protect her, with his life if it came to it. Sacrificing his existence for the sake of hers would be an honourable death.

Kearn looked down at his right arm and the marks on it when they pulsed. Water streamed over his head, running in rivulets down the long strands of his silver hair like a waterfall.

He hated them. These marks were the reason he had to act so humbly around his kind, lowered to nothing more than a Commoner amongst them. He clenched his fist and cursed the power and the Sovereignty. If it weren't for them and his foolish acceptance of their offer of revenge, he would still be the man he had once been, the man he longed to be.

He looked at the wall separating him from Amber.

She meant something to him. If he hadn't walked the path he had chosen and had remained nothing but a Noble, he never would have met her and felt real love. He would have been lost to the darkness of lust, forbidden blood, and the life his parents had planned for him.

Status meant nothing in a world where he had no freedom and had no love. In his world without status, without rank amongst his peers, he had fallen in love with someone he never would have considered when he had been a Noble—a beautiful human woman.

Amber.

The marks on his arm flared into life and burned. He gritted his teeth and clutched it to his chest, screwing his eyes shut against the pain.

The water no longer touched his body. A chill breeze replaced it and he shivered as it froze the droplets on his bare skin. He opened his eyes and glared at the high dark grey stone arches of the cathedral-like room around him. The thick pillars supporting the arches and vaulted roof led his eyes down the length of the long dim rectangular room to the bright altar at the end.

The marks on his arm faded and the power disappeared.

Kearn cupped his groin with both hands to protect his modesty and frowned at the altar as he walked towards it. The dark flagstones were freezing underfoot. He had never seen any room besides this one in the building but they had shown him the outside once when he had asked about it. It was a gargantuan stone fortress hidden between planes, in neither Earth's realm nor the demonic one. It bridged the gap between them, and the Sovereignty watched all, ensuring none of the laws of the species it governed were broken.

When he reached the crescent-moon-shaped pool that arched around in front of the altar, set into the flagstones, he stopped. He wouldn't go any further. He had tried to once and they had punished him by sending him to the eternal darkness to suffer with the souls of those who had broken the law.

His gaze dropped to the still black water in the pool. It wasn't pleasant in there and he had no desire to make a return visit.

"I thought I said never to bring me here from my apartment?" Kearn glared across the pool to the altar.

Nine figures stood there, all veiled in translucent long white flowing layers. Pale light streamed in from an opening above them, causing them to glow ethereally and hiding their faces from view. They were female, he knew that much from their voices, and they were all the same height and had the same figure. And they weren't human or vampire. Whatever they were, they had long ago accepted the role of adjudicator over the nine species of demon, and they were the last of their kind, thousands of years old.

"We do so enjoy your visits," the one in the middle said. Her voice was the youngest, always lined with an edge of playfulness. She was the one he felt most at ease with and he often left wondering if she represented his species. "You are doubting us again."

He cursed under his breath. It was impossible for him to hide anything from the Sovereignty. They often watched him and were aware of every Venator from every species, and if they focused their power on him alone, they could sense his thoughts through the marks they had given him.

"I never stopped doubting you." He pulled his shoulders back and stood tall. He didn't care that he was nude before them because they had seen him naked before, but he kept his hands over his genitals, unwilling to give them a free show.

"Venator Greystone will visit you tomorrow night."

Was that the female Venator's name? A Lesser Noble. Greystone were one of the lowest ranked families. No wonder she had been so polite. His own family, Savernake, ranked third of all bloodlines, only lower than Montagu and the archduke's bloodline, Pendragon.

"And why will she visit me?" The darkness in the crescent pool shifted and revealed an image of the woman. She was talking to Duke Montagu at the ball.

"She has come to test you."

Kearn's head snapped up and he frowned at the nine Sovereigns.

A blood test?

His heartbeat quickened. He had taken blood from Amber, enough that it would put him over the limit. The Sovereigns had to be aware of what had happened to her and what he had done. Were they trying to turn a Venator against him? If he measured over the limit, Venator Greystone could easily spread word to other Venators that he had broken the law. Even if the Sovereignty didn't decree it, they could hunt him for it.

The Sovereign in the middle stepped forwards.

"It is important that you allow her to take your blood." Her voice echoed around the dark stone walls of the hall. "We need you to do it."

"Why? My blood will measure positive and she will—"

"You are not to question this order." She turned away from him.

He watched her walk through an arch at the back of the altar, fury sweeping through his blood at her behaviour and order. He wanted to go after her but didn't dare. The others turned and followed her, leaving him alone in the hall. He looked down at the moving image of the other Venator in the pool.

Why did they need her to test him?

If it wasn't to incriminate him, or set the other Venators on him, what reason could they have for doing such a thing?

The image in the pool faded and his arm burned again. He growled and held it, waiting for the shift between their world and his.

Light swallowed him and when his vision came back, he was in his apartment.

In his bedroom to be precise.

Kearn covered his groin and his eyes darted to Amber. She was still sleeping soundly, his jacket acting as her blanket. He cursed the Sovereign. She had placed him back in his bedroom on purpose. He hated it when they amused themselves with him. It wasn't as though he could return the favour. If he stepped out of line, they would kill him and send him back to the darkness.

He shivered at the thought and went into the bathroom.

The shower was still running. He turned it off, dried himself, and wrapped the brown towel around his waist. He was about to leave the bathroom when he caught his reflection in the mirror above the oval sink and black cabinet. Green eyes met his. Silver hair framed his face, icicles with staggered tips that brushed his nose, jaw and cheeks. Did Amber like how he looked?

She didn't know him any other way and was attracted to him, so she had to like his appearance. He looked hard at himself and swept the hair from his eyes. Perhaps it was part of the reason she was falling for him.

Much as he might not have met her had he not become a Venator, her feelings for him might have been different if he had blue eyes and black hair.

His appearance suddenly seemed less repulsive.

She was changing him. He no longer truly hated his duty and what he had become. He was starting to accept it because of her.

He took the remaining bandages from the black cupboard under the basin and walked into the bedroom. Amber was still asleep. He set the bandages down on the end of the bed and opened the left side of his wardrobe. He threw on a pair of black trunks and black trousers, and then tossed the damp towel into the bathroom.

Taking the bandages, he went to Amber and sat on the bed to her left. The digital clock on the bedside table read three in the morning. The Sovereignty had kept him a long time. He had gone into the shower around one thirty. Time always distorted when they called him to them. What was minutes there was hours on Earth. He was glad that Amber had remained asleep. If the vampire had attempted anything or had come for her, he would have made the Sovereignty pay for taking him purely to announce his impending blood test and to amuse themselves with his nudity. It wasn't the first time they had taken him from his shower or his bed. It happened at least once a year, and that was why he had forbidden it last time it had happened. He might be theirs to command, but he wasn't theirs to toy with.

Kearn tore the length of crepe bandage into two pieces. He wrapped one around the wound on his forearm, tying it tightly, and the other around Amber's neck, securing it with a safety pin. It would catch any blood and stop her from accidentally reopening the cut.

He touched the bandage on her throat and stared at his fingers. He didn't know what he would have done if the vampire had bitten her. Things were getting too dangerous.

Amber frowned in her sleep and stirred.

He smiled when her eyelids fluttered open to reveal her hazel irises.

He would keep her safe.

Because he loved her.

CHAPTER 15

Amber's head throbbed and it hurt to swallow. She blinked her eyes open and the world gradually came into focus. Kearn sat beside her on the bed, shirtless and with tender concern in his dazzling green eyes. They smiled at her and she could feel his relief. There were other feelings there, mingling with hers, but they slipped through her grasp and fell away. The light in his eyes began to fade. She wouldn't let him close his heart to her again. She still wasn't sure how the connection between them worked but she wasn't going to let him sever it.

His eyes held a hint of surprise and then his shoulders relaxed and he reached towards her.

The back of his left hand brushed her jaw and cheek as his fingers stroked her throat. She went to raise her hand and touch his but it felt too heavy. The soft warm bed was comfortable beneath her and she wanted to lay there with Kearn watching over her like a guardian angel.

She frowned when she remembered calling him a demon. Her memory of the night was hazy but she could recall some parts of it clearly. She had danced with Kearn and it had felt wonderful, and then she'd had to dance with Duke Montagu and she hadn't liked it, and then the man had appeared.

Her pulse doubled, blood thundering in her temples and making the left side of her throat throb. Her eyes widened as she remembered what had happened during her dance with the man. With a lot of effort, she brought her hand to her throat and felt a bandage around it. Panic washed through her, prickly hot and turning her insides. She held Kearn's gaze, silently asking him the question quivering on the tip of her tongue.

"You will be fine. The man cut you to test your blood," he said serenely and his fingers touched hers when he drew his hand away. "I have sealed the wound for you and I am using the blood I took from you to keep the man out. I will not let him control you again."

She continued to stare into his eyes, a little relieved but still trembling all over. The man had drunk her blood. He knew what she was now, and could control her again. Would he come after her? Would he make her do things against her will as she had at the factory?

"We almost had him this time." Kearn smiled but Amber felt only sorrow inside her.

Her eyes shot wide. The man had already made her do something.

She had attacked Kearn.

She went to sit up but he pressed his hand against her shoulder. Her head spun and she collapsed back into the bed, a deep wave of fatigue crashing over her. How much blood had she lost? Every inch of her felt drained and weak from just moving a small amount. Her heart beat feebly in her chest.

Her gaze shifted to the bandage around Kearn's right arm. A few spots of red marked the cream material. A terrible feeling twisted her stomach and she looked away. She could remember it all now. She had tried to kill him.

Tears filled her eyes and she wasn't strong enough to stop them from tumbling down her cheeks.

Kearn's hand was soft and gentle against her face and she closed her eyes, savouring the feel of his touch and the meaning behind it. He cleared her tears away and brought her head back around to face him.

"It was not you." His smile made her heart tremble and beat faster, stronger. "You were under his control."

He sighed and she felt the meaning behind that too. He wasn't happy. His words weren't what she was feeling inside. She felt upset, angry, and hurt, and none of them were her emotions. They were how he felt about her attacking him.

His hand left her face and became a fist.

"I let my guard slip. The vampire had your blood. I should have been more cautious... but I... I had to get you back." He looked down at his knees, the silver strands of his hair falling forwards to veil his face. "I had to protect you."

Amber gritted her teeth and told herself to move. She had to move. She slowly lifted her left arm, causing her neck to ache on that side, and swept the hair away from his cheek. His eyes closed when her fingers made contact with his jaw and she cupped his right cheek and held it.

His gaze met hers and she smiled with all of the feelings in her heart. Feelings for him. Affection, gratitude, and most of all love. She didn't fear loving him because she had never met a man like him—wonderful, protective, handsome, and caring. Someone she needed to love. Someone she needed.

"We need to be more careful," he whispered and took hold of her hand. She was relieved to have him take the weight of it so she didn't have to continue to support it. He brought her hand down to his lap but didn't release it. His fingers toyed with hers, softly stroking them. "If the vampire were to bite you, you would become like him."

"He's like you then." She wondered if Kearn knew that she could feel the anger behind his words.

The jealousy.

She had felt those feelings in him at the ball too. He had hated the duke dancing with her, and he had wanted to kill the man who was after her blood, and it wasn't because of his duty. She was sure of that, had felt it through their connection. He had wanted to kill the man because he had hurt her. She smiled and Kearn's expression turned questioning.

"Nothing." Her cheeks coloured. She wished she felt her usual self. She would have announced that he was jealous and that he wanted her all to himself just to see his reaction. For some reason, she felt shy around him now that she had realised the depth of her feelings for him. It was ridiculous of her to fall for a vampire, a man who would live beyond her and who would only look forty by the time she was seventy.

Unless she became a vampire.

A sliver of a memory surfaced with that thought.

"What is it?" Kearn's hand tightened around hers. It was warm and strong, and she could sense his desire to protect her. It flowed through her, a tangible thing that she felt she could reach out and touch. She couldn't so she took her hand from his and touched it instead.

"I had the strangest dream." She traced the silver marks on his right hand with her fingertips while she struggled to grasp hold of her dream, following the intricate tribal patterns over his fingers to the back of his hand. They were beautiful and she had wanted to do this so many times over the past few days.

They swirled and danced in a way that reflected her mind. No matter how much she tried to recall her dream, it evaded her, but she wouldn't let it escape. Her eyes roamed up his arm, fingertips tracing a route over the silver marks, following them upwards to his elbow and then over his bicep. When she reached his shoulder at the end of the pattern, her eyes shifted to meet his. His pupils were wide, his lips parted, and the unmistakable fire of passion shone in his eyes. He was watching her closely, his chest slowly rising and falling. His external steadiness hid the turbulent emotions she could feel inside her. Some of them were hers, but most were his, and they backed up the hunger in his eyes. She lowered her hand to his chest. His heart beat against it, as slowly as he had told her, a strong steady drumming on her palm.

She smiled at him when it came back to her. "I dreamed that you were with me, here, and cleaned my neck."

"I did." He feathered a caress down her throat and the edges of his irises turned red. "It was not a dream."

"It had to be… I kissed you… and then I said—"

Kearn stood sharply, his face frozen in darkness. "You must rest. Sleep now. I will be in the other room should you need anything."

She reached out to him but he walked away, closing the door behind him.

The room felt cold. She held his black jacket over her chest and breathed in the scent of him that lingered on it as she stared at the door.

It hadn't been a dream.

She had told him to stay with her forever, and it had upset him. Why? He was a vampire. If he felt something for her, surely he would want her to become one too and stay with him?

Wasn't he falling in love with her?

She laughed internally at her girlish thoughts. She was bait to him.

Foolish Amber.

She was probably muddling up their feelings, thinking that hers were actually his. He hadn't given her a reason to believe that she was anything to him other than a way of catching his man. The kisses they had shared had been induced by her blood.

But the way he had acted at the ball.

He hadn't tasted her blood then and he had broken conventions. He had kissed her hand and had lowered himself to her in front of everyone.

And the way he had felt when she had danced with the duke and the other man. The anger and the jealousy.

She hadn't imagined those feelings.

She sighed and turned her gaze to the ceiling.

Perhaps he was falling for her too, just as she wanted him to, only he was fighting his feelings. If she went into the other room and kissed him, would he kiss her back or would he push her away? Her heart hurt at the thought he might turn her away and treat her as coldly as he had just now. He hadn't liked what she had said.

Amber closed her eyes, feeling drowsy, and tried to recall what had happened.

She saw his face again and felt his surprise. And she remembered the kiss that had followed—the sweetness and tenderness that had laced it and made her fall deeper in love with him.

Then he had spoken to her.

His words swam around her head, colliding and refusing to fall into order.

He had touched her face.

She stroked her cheek, mimicking his actions.

He had looked down at her.

She stared at the ceiling.

And he had told her…

To say those words again when their blood wasn't together.

He hadn't believed her.

No. She rested her arm across her eyes, shutting out the room.

He had believed her and it had frightened him. Why? She couldn't remember the way she had felt or what feelings had been in his blood. It wasn't clear in her head. The ball came back to her. She had heard Kearn's thoughts as her own. Did he think that she had only voiced his feelings and thoughts?

He was as big an idiot as she was if that was the case.

Amber closed her eyes, a wave of fatigue sweeping over her. Thinking hurt her head and she couldn't focus, but she tried. She forced herself to think about her blood in the hope of connecting to Kearn's somehow.

It hadn't been his feelings that she had voiced. Those words had been wholly hers.

Sleep beckoned her but she wouldn't surrender, not until she was sure that he knew.

She wanted to stay with him forever.

CHAPTER 16

Kearn couldn't remember a time he had felt so grouchy. Sleeping on the couch had put him in a bad mood and having to leave Amber alone in his apartment while he had his blood tested wasn't helping. He paced across his bedroom and stopped near the side of the bed where Amber had slept. He touched the pillows and drew a deep breath, catching her fragrance in the air. His focus switched to her where she sat in the living room watching the television.

He had heard her this morning before she had fallen asleep. She had forced a connection between them that he hadn't been able to resist or refuse.

And she had sent that same message to him.

She wanted to be his. Forever.

Part of him doubted her but the rest at least wanted to believe.

She didn't know what she was asking though. She must have seen the women at the ball who were going through the transition. He didn't want to put her through so much pain and bring her into his world.

His heart called him a liar.

He couldn't stop dreaming of her. Not just lustful dreams full of sex and blood either. His dream of her today was slower, nothing more than kissing and tender touches, and he had bitten her again. He always bit her.

His fangs ached to extend. He wanted to bite her now. He wanted to walk out into his living room, pull her into his arms and give her a kiss that was eternal, one that would bind their hearts forever.

He wouldn't do to her what other Nobles and Lesser Nobles did to those they convinced to go through the transition. They were only interested in increasing the numbers of servants they had.

He was only interested in making Amber his and his alone for eternity.

A voice in his heart contested his desire. The Savernake ruling line never turned humans. Their blood was pure, their family tree filled with only those born to vampire parents, not those turned. It was a matter of pride and principle. Better to marry a purebred Lesser Noble than bring a human into the family, no matter how strong their blood was. Turning humans was something they left to the lower ranks, those who only served the titled vampires in the family and higher ranks.

His senses latched on to Amber, until her blood sparked into life inside him, relaying her feelings to him and filling him with their warmth and contentment.

He didn't care what his family thought. They had cast him out and no longer ruled him. He was free to do as he pleased, and he wanted to make Amber his. He wanted to be with her forever.

If she became a vampire, he would worship her, cherish her, and would give her everything. She would be his whole world and he would love her until the end of time.

No. Not only if she became a vampire. He would do all of those things for her right now, even though she was human.

He picked up his black shirt from the end of the bed, stepped out of the bedroom, and looked at her. She turned to face him and smiled, pausing with her hands against her rich brown hair.

There was colour in her cheeks now. The evening light of sunset streamed in through the wide bank of windows and warmed her skin. Blue jeans hugged her slender legs and a black flared-sleeved top crossed over her breasts at the front and revealed enough cleavage to make him want to growl. There was something so feminine, so beautiful and alluring, yet so strong about her. It was more than her blood.

She finished tying hair up in a ponytail, exposing her throat. The crepe bandage around it didn't show any sign of her bleeding.

He dragged his eyes away from it.

Amber stood and walked towards him, her footfalls quiet on the wooden floor. She stopped close to him and he couldn't bring himself to look at her, not when his irises were close to changing. She hadn't been afraid in the times he had lost a sliver of control and it had shown in his eyes, but he didn't want to risk it.

He went to put his black shirt on but halted when she reached out to him. His gaze tracked her hand as it edged towards his right arm. Was she going to touch him again? He swallowed at the thought and anticipation churned his insides, his breathing coming quicker as he waited to see what she would do. He wanted to feel her hand on him again, her warm fingertips caressing his skin, but he wasn't sure he could take it.

Kearn shivered when her fingers touched his right arm, close to his wrist, and he lowered it, letting his shirt drag on the floor. His gaze darted to her face. She was watching her fingers again, desire widening her pupils and beating in his blood. He kept still, frozen to the spot, only able to watch as she carefully traced each jagged spike and curving spiral on his arm. He felt her slight tremble in her touch and sensed the hint of fear in her. It wasn't what he was that she was afraid of, it was fear of touching him, excitement and anticipation that matched his own.

The fascination on her face, shining in her eyes, spoke to him, flooded him with a need to tell her to keep going, to do as she pleased with him because he was a slave to her. She could command him with nothing more than a touch or a thought, with only a feeling in her blood.

Warmth spread down his arm and over his chest and back when she reached his upper arm, her progress slowing as she swirled her fingers over his skin, following the silver marks. When she reached the ones that bled over his shoulder and danced down towards his chest, he could barely take it. Hunger swept through him, wildfire that consumed and burned out of control. Her touch drove him to burn and thirst for her, pushed him to his limit.

His eyes met hers and he breathed hard, struggling for control and the strength to resist surrendering to the desire in her eyes and in his blood. He wanted to act on it, needed to drag her into his arms and kiss her again, yearned to have her lips on his and her sweet taste filling his mouth.

Her hazel gaze fell to his mouth and he wet his lips, close to doing as she bid and kissing her. He lowered his mouth towards hers and then shifted course and pressed a kiss to her forehead instead. He lingered there, blood rushing, heart thundering, trembling with the need to have her touch him and kiss him.

Sheer desperation pushed him to give in, to forget his duty and slake his thirst for this woman who had changed his whole world, who was his whole world, but he resisted.

Kearn closed his eyes, breathed in her soft scent, and then stepped back.

"I have to go out," he said thickly and tugged his shirt on. He lowered his gaze away from her as he buttoned it and tried to get his feelings back under control.

The calm edge to her blood disappeared. Her worry swept through him.

"I will only be outside. I need to meet..." He considered not saying it and then couldn't help himself. He wanted to see her reaction and feel it in her blood. He wanted to test her. "I need to meet Venator Greystone."

Amber's eyes widened and then she went back to the couch, sat down, and started changing television channels.

He had expected a better reaction than her snubbing him. Wasn't she jealous? He tested her blood with his and smiled inside when he felt it. She was hiding it well.

Kearn took a step forwards, hoping to get her attention. It remained fixed on the television. When he reached the door, he sensed her eyes on him and looked over his shoulder at her.

"Kearn?" She pulled her knees to her chest, holding them there with one arm. Her toes curled.

"Yes... Amber?"

"Don't be long, okay?" She looked worried.

Kearn walked back to her, rounding the other black couch that faced the window, and stopped in front of her. He placed his hand against her right cheek.

"I will keep an eye on you," he whispered and some of the fear in her eyes faded. "I will come if I sense anything. If you are scared, call out to me. I will hear you."

She nodded. He smiled for her and she smiled back.

Before he gained enough sense to stop himself, he bent over, tilted her head up, and pressed a kiss to her lips.

"Keep the door locked."

She nodded again.

Kearn walked over to the door and out into the hall. He closed the door and swept his hand over the locks, clicking them all into place.

His senses delved deep into his blood, opening the connection between him and Amber. It was still strong. He closed himself off to her and walked down through the building. She didn't need to know his feelings while he was with the Venator and he knew that she would be trying to if he left the connection to him open. She had figured out that something happened between them when he had tasted her blood. She was a bright girl.

And beautiful.

Kearn wiped a hand down his face and sighed, trying to expel that thought and the feelings attached to it.

She was bait. It didn't matter what her blood had told him or how he felt about her. When this was over, they would part ways and never see each other again.

Was he alright with that? No, but it was how things had to be. As much as he desired her, wanted to give her the gift of immortality, he couldn't go through with it. What life would she have if he did? Condemned to spend eternity despised by humans and vampires alike, in danger every day, and with only him for company.

He stepped out of the front door of the apartment building and spotted the truck parked up on the side of the quiet road.

A blood bank van?

The smile touched his lips before he could contain it. It seemed the Sovereignty had developed a sense of humour. They used to be more subtle.

He rapped his knuckles on the side door. It opened and the female Venator looked down at him with emotionless eyes.

"Venator Savernake." She bowed her head.

It was strange to have someone act humbly towards him when he had been the one behaving that way last night. He wanted to tell her that he didn't deserve such respect, but he took it all instead, enjoying how it made him feel—strong, proud, and cruel.

Her behaviour unleashed a side of him that he had forgotten. He felt like the man he had been before becoming a Venator.

He stepped up into the truck, glanced around the white insides without hiding his disgust at having to do such a thing for the Sovereignty, and then stared at the woman.

"Venator Greystone. You witnessed what happened last night at my uncle's ball." His voice was pure ice and darkness. A thrill bolted through him when she lowered her head and nodded. "Then you are aware that I took blood from that human so she would heal."

That human?

Amber. She had a name. Was his desire for his old life so strong that he would cast her aside to reclaim it?

"Such information is inconsequential," Venator Greystone said in a small voice. He felt her fear inside him—the tremble that gave away more than just her awe at his position and strength. She dared to look up at him. Her pupils were wide, admitting her desire to him. Such a female would look to mate with a strong male. The tip of her tongue caressed her lips and she swallowed. Her eyes could barely hold his. Did she honestly expect him to want such an inferior and weak female? Her bloodline was worthless. "I only need to test for large quantities, not trace doses, my lord."

Her lord?

He grinned the moment she dropped her head again. That was right. To her, he was the highest echelon of society. A Noble of house Savernake.

Large quantities?

Sense crashed over him. He had taken more than a trace from Amber. He had wanted to drink her all down and savour every last drop. The vision of her drenched in red, her black bodice barely holding her breasts in, and his marks on her throat hit him hard. He wanted that.

He shut out the image, sat down on the black leather patient's chair, rolled up his right shirtsleeve and stared at Venator Greystone.

"I am busy. Let us get this over with." The coldness in his voice didn't go unnoticed by her. She dropped her gaze and nodded, as though shamed by wasting his time.

Her touch was light on his forearm, tracing the marks on his skin. The feel of her fingers on him turned his insides and made him want to tear his arm away from her, or knock her hand aside. He didn't want her hands on him. He wanted the human's.

Amber.

The way she had touched him had set his blood aflame, burning with the desire to kiss her and claim her body as his own, to sink his fangs into her throat and join them eternally.

He would kill for that.

Venator Greystone went to a long row of white cupboards, opened a drawer and took out a needle and a tube. His heart gave one hard beat at the sight of it and the thought of what she was going to do. He couldn't refuse to be tested. It would only look suspicious if he did that. The Sovereignty had told him to do this. It was an order.

"This won't take long, my lord."

Those softly spoken words drew his gaze to her face. Her pupils were still wide. Amber had looked at him like that more than once. She had watched his mouth with eyes full of fire and hunger. She had wanted him to kiss her.

And he wanted it too.

Kearn closed his eyes and leaned his head back into the chair. The Venator tied his arm and the whole of it felt tight, the blood trapped there. Blood. He reopened the connection between him and Amber, needing to feel her. She wasn't just a human to him.

He focused on her. The Venator spoke to him but he was high above them, within Amber, trying to hear her thoughts and feel her feelings. He wanted to know her from the inside.

Her blood had said she wanted him. It asked him to drink it.

He had never experienced such a thing. He had only ever drunk from another vampire. His parents had believed it too unrefined for their children to hunt. They had brought them the finest blood from the hunts they had led.

He only knew that to bite someone was profound. To surrender to his instincts and bite another vampire had been intoxicating. More thrilling than sex or Source Blood. It had addled his mind and driven him to behave like a beast. It had freed him.

Biting a human would be different.

What would it feel like?

He latched on to Amber's blood, sensing her through it. She wanted him. Would she cry out if he bit her or would she moan into his ear?

In the darkness of his mind, he could easily imagine how it would play out. It would be perfect. An intense moment when his lips touched her neck and then her shiver of pleasure when he eased his fangs into her flesh. There would be nothing quite like it. His arousal soared at the thought and he reached out to her through their blood. He felt her awareness, sensed her own desire flare at the image of him biting her throat and holding her close, never to let her go. She wanted it.

He could never do such a thing.

His heart reproached him for his false chivalry and empty nobility. It was all a lie, something he kept telling himself because it was the right thing to feel in the situation. Only it wasn't. It wasn't what he wanted.

He had done nothing but lie to himself since meeting her.

He wanted her.

He would bite her and suck her blood like a beast, feasting on it and slaking his unending thirst for her, and he wouldn't give her a choice. She wouldn't be able to stop him. He would do it without consent and make her belong to him.

His heart darkened at the thought of her hating him but he wouldn't care as long as she was his.

Kearn cursed himself for being so inhuman and then almost laughed out loud. Inhuman? He couldn't be such a thing when he wasn't human. He was a vampire and desired to do what his heart and his blood dictated.

He would make Amber into a vampire.

And she would stay with him forever.

"Lord Savernake?" A voice reached through the haze of hunger and he slowly opened his red eyes.

The female Venator leaned over him, her long silver hair caressing her face.

"I thought you had passed out." Her eyes told him something different to her words. Something she feared saying and with good reason. It didn't matter if she had noticed his aroused state and was openly inviting him to take her body with her parted lips and wide eyes. It wasn't going to happen. He shut down his hunger so she would no longer sense it and stared at her, cold and hard. "I had not expected you to be so very docile, Lord Savernake."

Kearn realised with a spark of panic that she had strapped him into the chair. He quelled his fear before she detected it. It had been a few years since his last blood test but he hadn't expected any of the process to have changed in that time.

"Is this standard protocol now?" He raised a dark silver eyebrow at the leather wrist cuffs and experimentally tugged at them. They were tight and strong, reinforced inside with steel by the cold feel of them.

"We need to take more blood now since it was discovered that only taking a small vial could give false readings. It is only a pint. It should not take long."

"So why the restraints?" He eyed them again, unable to bring himself to trust the woman now that she had tied him down.

"Some Venators have an adverse reaction to having such a quantity of blood taken. It… it awakens our nature."

Their nature? That was a very polite way of saying he was about to become little more than a beast. Was only a pint enough to trigger that? He had lost a lot of blood in the past due to injuries and only once had it been enough to prompt such a reaction. He had killed every vampire present at the time.

He corrected himself.

He hadn't killed them.

He had slaughtered them.

Venator Greystone swept her hair aside, exposing the left side of her neck. "It isn't that I do not trust you, Lord Savernake. It is that I fear your strength."

Thick ragged scars cut over her skin, distorting it. She would have come close to dying from such a deep wound. It was understandable that she was cautious now, especially around a Noble of his bloodline. He was far stronger than she was. If he lost his mind to his instincts, she wouldn't stand a chance.

He looked up at the ceiling.

And neither would Amber.

Her blood was with his. After killing the Venator, he would go after her to satisfy the gnawing hunger he had felt since first tasting her.

He nodded to Venator Greystone.

She picked up the needle and carefully eased it into the soft flesh on the inside of his elbow. It didn't hurt. The yellow tube turned deep red and Kearn leaned back.

His focus drifted to Amber and he closed his eyes.

"It will not take long, Lord Savernake."

That name brought him back to the truck. It grated on his nerves now. He hadn't been Lord Savernake in over sixty years, and the Venator knew it, so why was she persisting in calling him that. Venator Savernake. That was his only title now, and it was as worthless as her bloodline.

A deep sense of discontent stirred within his heart. It grew as he lost more blood and he began to feel the effects. His defences dropped and his instincts pushed for control but he didn't allow them to take over. He was strong enough to keep a level head. It was only a small amount of his blood and there was no threat to him. Hunger gnawed at his gut and the memory of Amber's blood made his own call out to her. He wanted her to come to him, to straddle his lap, and let him sink his fangs into her.

He imagined her above him and it was as though she was there with him. Her hands came to rest against his chest and a smile curved her lips when she glanced at his bound wrists, as though she enjoyed the thought of him being at her mercy. He was. He was a beast at her mercy, tamed by her and longing for her to whisper him a command. He would obey.

She leaned over him and the waves of her long brown hair caressed his bare chest. Her fingers followed suit, tracing the line between his pectorals while she purred her approval of his body. He liked the way she looked too. He tried to reach for her but the cuffs stopped him. Her smile widened and she raised herself, so her face was above his. He tilted his head back to keep his focus on her and she rewarded him with a kiss. Not searing or passionate, but slow and tender. A kiss that fanned the flames within him and his desire for her blood.

Her lips left his and trailed along his jaw and then down his neck. She kissed it, licked it, branded his flesh with her scent until he could barely contain himself, and when he was on the brink of snapping the restraints to get to her, she did the one thing he had never considered in all of this.

She bit him.

Her dull teeth dug into his throat. He bucked his hips against hers and roared. It was divine, turning his blood to fire in his veins until it burned through him, driving him over the edge.

His fangs extended and his eyes switched.

Amber drew back, a trace of blood on her lips. The sight of it fascinated and enthralled him. She had broken the skin. She had tasted him. He groaned and craned his neck to reach her. He wanted to bite her. She had to let him bite her now. It was only fair.

He thrilled and grew hard when she reached around her head and pulled the hair from her neck, holding it back. It was the left side and the cut was still there. A mark made by another man. A mark he would erase.

Kearn growled when she lowered herself, acceptance shining in her hazel eyes. She wanted this. She wanted to be with him forever and she would be.

His lips touched her throat and he lost control. He wrapped them around the cut and then sunk his fangs in. Amber moaned into his ear and her fingers tensed against his chest, nails digging in. He groaned and sucked hard, desperate for her blood and desperate to make her belong to him. She belonged to him.

He wanted to hold her against him but couldn't get his arms free. The feel of her fingers threading into his hair and holding his mouth against her throat was enough to placate the desire. He fed deep, drawing greedy mouthfuls of her blood and savouring every one. The moment he felt her weaken, he released her neck and licked the cut, carefully sealing it and being gentle so he didn't hurt her any more. He would never hurt her.

Not now that she was his.

"Lord Savernake?" The voice was dull. He ignored it, wanting to stay with Amber, wrapped tight in her embrace as she held him close to her, as a lover would. "Lord Savernake?"

The world shook and he frowned at it when Amber disappeared.

He fluttered his eyes open and stared at the bright white ceiling. Where was he? Where had Amber gone?

An unfamiliar face appeared in view. It took him a moment to gather himself. The vision had been strong. He had never experienced anything quite like it. Had Amber seen it too?

He reached out to her. She was sleeping. He sensed desire in her and deep contentment. His eyes widened at the thought that she might have experienced it too. If it hadn't been just his imagination but a vision created by their joined blood, then she had offered her throat willingly.

She wanted to be like him.

"Lord Savernake?" Venator Greystone said again and he snapped himself out of his thoughts. She removed the needle from his arm. "Did you experience any adverse effects?"

He shook his head.

Only the most fantastic vision he'd ever had.

"It will take a short while to test your blood. I have to keep the restraints in place until we are done. I hope that does not offend you, Lord Savernake."

Kearn shook his head again. The restraints didn't bother him as much as her persistence in using his former title did. It brought back the ball and the way the man had held Amber. He had felt a violent urge to kill the man with his bare hands, had wanted to unleash his power on him, even before he had known who the man was. He had never killed another vampire without orders to, but he had wanted to butcher any who had dared to look at her. He had wanted to fight his own uncle.

He closed his eyes and sighed. What was becoming of him?

Not only did he consider killing without orders but he also wanted to turn her into a vampire without consent. Was he that caught up in her? Did he honestly love her?

Kearn.

He frowned.

Kearn? He hadn't taken long to come back. He felt tired still but rubbed it away and then opened his eyes. Only he didn't see the truck. He saw a dark room. His apartment.

Who had turned out the lights?

Was it Kearn? Had he come back so soon?

A shape came out of the darkness. Red eyes. Sharp fangs. It wasn't him. Another man materialised from the shadows. He shook his head. His panic rose and his heart raced so fast that he felt sick.

It wasn't him.

Kearn!

There were men in the apartment.

Amber. Kearn growled and tugged at the arm restraints, gritting his teeth against the pain and calling all of his strength. Someone was up there with her. Her fear strained the connection between them, distorting it until he couldn't sense her clearly.

Run. Amber. Run. Hide in the bathroom. He was coming to protect her.

CHAPTER 17

Kearn pulled at the restraints again. The metal bit into his wrists, filling his senses with the smell of blood, but he struggled on, determined to break his bonds and save Amber.

"What's wrong, Lord Savernake?" Venator Greystone's eyes were wide, showing her fear. She thought he was suffering a delayed attack from having his blood taken. He could see it in her wary expression.

"You have to unlock me." He clenched his fists and growled, tugging the cuffs. "Amber is in danger. I need to go to her."

Venator Greystone's expression filled with astonishment. "How much blood did you take from her?"

His patience snapped when he felt Amber trembling, felt the threads that bound them quivering with it and sensed her panic. She didn't want to die. Her blood called to him. It demanded that he go to her.

"It was a deep wound," he snarled and the Venator stepped backwards, away from him. "I had to seal it!"

He fought again, until blood covered his wrists, the chair creaked and the entire van rocked from his struggle. He wouldn't let her die. He wouldn't let the man take her from him.

"What are you doing? You can't break those." The Venator's words were lost on him.

Amber screamed.

Strength surged through him. His eyes burned red and his fangs sharpened. He roared and lifted his arms, snapping the metal in the cuffs and tearing through the leather.

"Lord Savernake!" The fear in those words satisfied him. He would hear more like it soon. He would murder those fiends for daring to go near his woman.

He was out of the van before Venator Greystone could interfere and was running up the stairs towards his apartment.

Hide, Amber. Hide. He willed her to do it, sent the message through his blood, but none came back. The connection was weakening. The man was fighting him again. He wouldn't let him have her.

"Kearn!"

He heard her this time. He bolted down the corridor to his apartment and kicked the door in. A man held Amber from behind as she flailed and screamed for her life.

Kearn lost it.

In the blink of an eye, he was behind Amber and tearing the man away. He threw him across the apartment, sending him crashing into the kitchen island

and toppling the stools, and then pulled Amber back against his chest and covered her eyes with his left hand.

"Do not look," he whispered close to her ear, his eyes scanning over the two large men dressed in black, assessing them. They were strong. Worthy opponents. He was stronger. "Do not listen."

His arm glowed blue. Not a reaction to the two vampires but a reaction to his desire to protect Amber. He couldn't use it. These men were clean and he had no order to kill them. He would use his own powers this time, and obey his own command.

He would destroy them.

They rushed him but didn't reach within five feet of him before he raised his arm and sent a telekinetic wave deep into their minds. They stopped dead and he grinned, revealing his fangs, and narrowed his eyes on them. The blue light from his arm brightened until it lit the apartment and their faces. Die. He wanted them to die.

Violence rose within him, black ribbons edged with red that wound around his heart, and he surrendered to his lust to see their blood painting his walls.

He sent a shock into their minds, stronger than any he had dared used before in his lifetime. Their faces twisted in agony and he kept applying the pressure, kept feeding the hatred within him into them. They screamed and clutched at their heads and he tilted his back, looking down on them. Feel the power of a Noble. Know that this is the end.

Kearn closed his hand into a fist, gathering his strength, and then flicked his fingers open.

A shrill cry pierced the night.

The men shattered and exploded.

He quickly raised his hand, palm facing outwards, and formed an invisible bubble around him and Amber. Blood splattered over it so it ran as red as the walls of his apartment and covered the floor in a slick pool that glowed in the light of his arm. He wanted more. A deep sense of dissatisfaction blazed inside him. It had been too easy. He needed more to quench the fire. His eyes dropped to Amber's throat. He needed her blood.

Kearn breathed hard, struggling to regain control, and held Amber to him. He wouldn't do that. The blood rolled off the shield around them, revealing the gruesome sight of his apartment, and he let it fade and disappear. He kept his hand firmly over her eyes, pulled her backwards into his bedroom and closed the door before releasing her. The sickening stench of vampire blood crept in under the door. He needed to get Amber out of the apartment. It was bad enough that she would smell the blood and had heard the death cries of the men who had dared to frighten her. He couldn't let her see what he had done.

He held her at arm's length, clutching both of her arms, and dipped his head so he could see straight into her eyes. She panted, her racing heart speaking of fear, and shook beneath his hands.

Had she seen anything? He didn't want her to witness such atrocity.

"You are safe now." He could almost see her strength leave her, as though it was a tangible thing.

Amber stood there a moment with tears lining her lashes and her face a mask of fear, and then she was against him, her hands pressing into his back and holding him close to her. He hesitated, his fingers flexing as he considered holding her, and then placed his arms around her. It felt so good to have her nestled close to him, safe in his arms, unharmed, that he sighed and pressed a long kiss to her hair. Her body trembled with her sobs, shuddering against his. He stroked her ponytail with one hand, clutched the nape of her neck with his other, holding her against him, and vowed never to leave her alone again, not until this was over, not if he could help it. The man had shown his intent and the lengths he was willing to go to now. Nowhere was safe for them.

Or was it?

"Are you hurt?" He couldn't smell any blood on her. The only blood he could smell was that of those wretched men and his own cut wrists.

She shook her head but didn't emerge from his embrace.

"Are you—" He couldn't bring himself to ask that question. He had done something terrible and he feared that she was shaking because of it, and not just because of the attack on her.

She was afraid of him now.

Amber drew back. Tears shone in her beautiful hazel eyes and stained her cheeks. He didn't dare move and wipe them away for her. He didn't want her to fear him.

"You... I was so scared." Her voice was small and she dropped her gaze away from his. Her hands didn't relinquish their grip on him and he was thankful for it and the fact that she remained close to him. "You saved me... you must be getting pretty tired of me and my damsel in distress routine."

He smiled at her although she couldn't see it. Her damsel in distress routine? She hadn't chosen to become a victim or thrown herself into the path of the man. She hadn't asked for any of this to happen to her.

Kearn placed two fingers under her chin and tilted it up. His eyes searched hers. He needed her to say it again. Even though he was a beast, a creature who would shed blood without hesitation or regret, he still had the heart of a man. He still needed to hear the woman he was falling in love with tell him that he hadn't destroyed their future. He could live with her hating him, would bear that cross when he finally succumbed to his nature and turned her, but he couldn't live with her fearing him.

Her fingers brushed his cheek. He closed his eyes and then opened them again, wanting to see her feelings when she said it and wanting to feel them in her blood. He needed proof that she wasn't lying.

"Thank you for saving me, and for protecting me. I don't know what you did, but you did it for me." She tiptoed and pressed a kiss to his lips.

It was over before he could respond but it left his senses reeling and his head was full of her again. He took hold of her arm and she frowned when she looked down at his wrist. She turned, released him, and gently caught hold of his arm.

"What happened?" she whispered, her dark eyebrows furrowing with concern, and took hold of his other arm. She held them both in front of her, her gaze scanning over the cuts and the blood, and then looked up into his eyes for an answer to her question.

"I was having my blood tested when I sensed you were in danger. I had to break the restraints."

The soft warmth in her eyes heated his chest and he frowned when she lowered her mouth and pressed light kisses to his wrists, worshipping them with affection that eased the fear in his heart. She wasn't afraid of him. She still wanted him.

When she raised her head, there was blood on her lips. He shook at the sight of her and the memory of his vision, and his desire returned, fiercer than ever, burning in his blood and fraying the tethers of his control. He reached out and swept his thumb over her lips, erasing the blood, and they parted. Her breath was warm against his thumb but the way it made him feel couldn't compare to the hunger that surged through him when she poked her silken pink tongue out and swept it over her lips, capturing the remnants of his blood and touching his thumb in the process.

Kearn waited with his heart in his throat, expecting her to be disgusted by the taste of his blood and what she had done.

She didn't retch or spit it out. Instead, she tiptoed again and kissed him, and he could taste himself on her tongue. He pulled her close, tangled his tongue with hers, and unleashed his need for her, pouring it into his kiss so she would feel everything that he was—fear, relief, love—all of it.

"Thank you," she whispered against his lips and her forehead touched his, the tips of their noses pressing against each other. She stroked his cheek and briefly kissed him again before settling back on her feet.

Kearn wasn't sure what to say or do. She had tasted his blood and his desire to do the same with hers, to sink his fangs into her throat, was overwhelming. He drew a deep breath and the stench of dead blood filled his senses, tamping down his hunger and reminding him that now wasn't the time for such things.

"We need to get out of here." He took hold of her arm and led her to the bed, unwilling to risk leaving her near the door in case she tried to open it.

She might think he was the prince charming to her damsel in distress, but she would think him evil and a monster if she saw the other room. She sat on the bed and placed her hands in her lap. Very behaved. He could sense her curiosity even if she wasn't showing it. Her blood whispered her deepest desires to him. She wanted to see what he had done in order to protect her.

He went to the bathroom and washed the blood off his hands and wrists, and then licked the cuts to seal them, his senses fixed on Amber the whole time. She kept still but he knew she was looking at the door. He walked into the bedroom and grabbed his gun and holster from the side table, and put it on.

Her gaze followed him now. He shoved some clothes and ammunition into a black holdall that would fit in the space behind the two seats of his car. He placed it beside Amber and then took her clothes and handbag and piled them into the bag on top of his things.

"Where are we going?"

Kearn glanced at her. What he was considering was either a wise move or insanity.

"Down to the car." He took the bag from the bed and slung it over his shoulder. "You will have to close your eyes again."

She looked nervous but nodded. Kearn scooped her up into his arms, angling her so she faced his chest as he cradled her. He couldn't let her walk. She would slip on the blood or would see it on her shoes.

He stared at the door. Nerves twisted his stomach.

Amber looked up at him.

"Promise me you will not look." He needed to know that she wouldn't see what he had done, what he was capable of because of her. "And take a deep breath and do not let it go until I tell you."

"Promise," she whispered and buried her face in his neck. He heard her breathe in and motioned with his hand, opening the bedroom door.

He was across the apartment in a heartbeat and out of the front door. He shut it behind him, shifting the locks into place, and walked down the hall. When he reached the end he said, "You can breathe now."

He would need to contact someone to clean his apartment. He knew a man who could take care of it. Once he had Amber somewhere safe, he would see if they were available for an immediate clean up, and would ask them about improved security for the building while he was at it.

Kearn set Amber down when they reached the ground floor and drew his gun. His arm tingled and then blue light shone from the marks on his fingers. He shook it away. The vampires who had attacked him hadn't taken forbidden blood. The man was playing one hell of a game sending innocent vampires his way. It wasn't as though he wouldn't kill anyone who stood between him and his quarry, and who tried to harm Amber.

The blood bank truck door was open and the smell of vampire blood was strong in the air.

Venator Greystone.

He dropped the bag from his shoulder and holstered his gun.

He found her sitting on the floor desperately trying to heal a deep cut on her arm. Blood covered her black jacket sleeve and the metal floor, stark against the silver material and pristine white environment. Her fear tainted the air. Her bloodline was weak enough that she could bleed to death from the right sort of wound.

This one looked right.

He went to mount the metal steps into the truck to help her but stopped when he sensed a shift in Amber's feelings.

A glance over his shoulder confirmed that she was watching him, her eyes narrowed in a challenge. She hadn't shown her jealousy earlier but it was painted in neon across her face right now. He wanted to tell her that his helping the Venator meant nothing. There was no reason for Amber to be jealous. He had no interest in the other woman.

Amber's eyes widened an almost imperceptible amount and he knew she had picked up the message from his blood. She blushed. It was a delightful colour on her. He saw a flash of her on her back beneath him, her cheeks crimson and flushed, her lips parted with staccato breathing and her neck bloodied, marked by two puncture wounds.

The vision faded and he stared at her.

She didn't take her eyes away from his while she raised her hand to her throat. Her fingers grazed the bandage there.

Kearn turned away, clearing the vision from his mind and closing the connection between them a fraction. Her blood was influencing him too much and he needed to think straight. He stepped into the truck and took the Venator's arm. She tried to pull away but he didn't let her go. He tore the sleeve off her black jacket, revealing a long gash down her upper arm. Part of him didn't want to heal her, not when Amber was watching, waiting for him to make a wrong move like this, but he had to help her. He licked the wound until he was sure that it had stopped bleeding and then grabbed the bandage she held and wrapped it around her arm.

"I apologise, Lord Savernake." Venator Greystone bowed her head. "Men came after you had left. They were too strong for me. One wore a mask."

Kearn sensed Amber tense.

"They attempted to kill me. I managed to get one of them." Venator Greystone tried to stand. Kearn stood and offered his hand. She took it, pulled herself up, and held her arm. "The vial. I had finished testing it when they attacked me. They took the vial. It tested positive."

Venator Greystone glanced at Amber and then looked back at him. Her green eyes shone with understanding.

"I can see you were only helping the human survive and will report so. I must report what happened though, Lord Savernake."

Kearn nodded, wishing that she would stop calling him that name because Amber stared at him every time.

"I will file a full report." He intended to do no such thing. The Sovereignty already knew what had happened and that he would test positive. There was no point in reporting it.

His name was on the screen of the laptop on the white work surface above the cupboards, along with the results of his blood test. It troubled him that they had taken the vial. Did they intend to blackmail him?

If they threatened him, if they wanted Amber in exchange, he couldn't do it. He wouldn't let them have her. He hoped they were only after the remnant of her blood in his but he couldn't think why they would need it.

He bowed to Venator Greystone and she lowered her head.

Amber backed down the steps when he approached her and stood on the pavement.

"Where are we going?" The lingering trace of her fear still ran in his veins, tainted by jealousy and a hint of anger.

He stepped down from the truck, his expression pensive.

There was only one place where they might be safe.

It would be almost impossible for the vampire to get Amber while she was there. He would make her stay there while he hunted the man alone. She wouldn't like it, but he didn't have a choice. It was too dangerous for her to go with him. He had to keep his promise and protect her.

He was getting ahead of himself.

He had to get them to accept his request first and that wasn't going to be easy.

Could sixty years heal the pain he had caused?

Kearn stared at Amber. There was no other way. The man had compromised his apartment and he needed to take her to a safe place. He could only hope they wouldn't turn him away.

If they refused, it would be the final blow.

He would bear the pain and sever ties with his family forever.

CHAPTER 18

Amber sat in the passenger seat of Kearn's car. The silence was oppressive but her thoughts weighed so heavily on her that she couldn't find her voice to break it.

Everything had happened so quickly back at Kearn's apartment and she was still trying to catch up. She had fallen asleep on the couch and had a fantastic dream about him biting her that had felt incredibly real and then she had awoken to the sound of the door opening. She had fought the two men, all the while calling out for Kearn.

And then she had known he was coming for her.

Amber looked at him out of the corner of her eye. He was deep in thought, his silver finger-length hair swept back out of his face to reveal his handsome profile, but that wasn't the only reason he was quiet. He was worried.

"I knew you were coming for me," she whispered, afraid to voice it any louder in case he thought she was insane.

"It is my blood." He glanced at her.

His blood. She touched her lips. Her curiosity had driven her to taste it and she had been surprised to find that it tasted the same as hers did—metallic. She had thought that vampire blood would taste different. Perhaps it was because she had blood like a vampire's that hers tasted the same.

Did they taste the same to him? He had licked his own blood and even that other Venator's without taking any pleasure from it. When he licked her blood, it was as though he had tasted something intoxicating and heavenly, and she always had the feeling that he wanted more.

His gaze dropped to her throat and then he fixed it back on the dark road ahead of them.

"Your blood is still with mine. A theory says that it is your blood transmitting back to you from within mine, causing a cycle within us both—a connection," he said.

Maybe she wasn't insane then. There really was a connection between them and she really had felt his feelings. And he really could turn it off. She frowned when she realised that she couldn't detect his worry now. He had shut her out.

"It is how I knew you were in danger." He turned a corner. They were heading down onto an empty motorway. Where was he taking her? "Your blood called to me and mine relayed my feelings back to you."

Amber went quiet again. At the truck, she had felt what he had wanted to tell her. He didn't want the female Venator. He desired her.

She blushed and felt his eyes on her.

The silence grew heavy again and she tried to think of something to say. The only thing that leapt to the front of her mind was probably something she shouldn't ask, but she had to know.

"At the apartment... what did you do?"

That question hung in the air between them. Kearn's look darkened and he glared at the road.

"You do not need to know." He seemed to think there was a lot that she didn't need to know, but she did. She had to know what he had done and why he hadn't wanted her to look. Was it so horrible that he hadn't wanted her to see?

"Why?" She turned on the seat to face him. He put his foot down and the engine roared. The world sped past in a constant line beyond his profile. His grip on the steering wheel tightened and his jaw tensed. She felt a glimmer of anger within him and something else. Fear. "Because I'm just a human? I won't tell anyone... no one would believe me."

"No!" The force behind that word made her jump. His tone softened. "No... not because of that... because you would fear me."

Amber felt the pain in him. He didn't want that to happen. She reached over and touched his left arm, curling her fingers around it.

"I already told you that I'm not afraid of you... Kearn," she whispered and meant every word with all of her heart. He looked at her, his eyes fixed on hers, dark in the low light, and kept driving. She smiled. "That does frighten me. You can drive without looking."

He smiled, and he was beautiful. The hope in his eyes, the fear she could feel mixing with relief, and the warmth. Everything about him in that moment was beautiful, and she wasn't afraid of him. Whatever he had done, it had protected her from those men.

"Where are we going?" She tried it again.

He looked back at the road.

"My home."

Amber frowned. "We were just at your home."

"No." The note of worry was back in his deep voice. "My family home."

She swallowed at the thought of being around so many vampires again. Would she be safe there? Would his family protect her? Kyran had been cruel to Kearn at the ball. What if his family were like that too? She didn't want him to go somewhere that would hurt him just to keep her safe or to find the man.

Kearn touched her knee and her gaze fell to his hand. It was pale against her dark jeans. Her thigh warmed beneath it, a buzz tingling where it rested.

"I will not allow my family to harm you."

As she stared at his hand, it dawned on her that she wasn't worried about herself. She was worried about him again and wanted to tell him that but the words evaded her. She stared into the darkness beyond him, thinking everything over. Back at the ball, women had called Kyran Marquess Savernake. Tonight, the Venator had kept calling Kearn Lord Savernake.

142

"Your family is powerful, isn't it? That hunter... she was almost subservient."

Kearn nodded. "The house of Savernake is a Noble bloodline and one of the three strongest and oldest. The Montagu bloodline is above mine, and above that is the family that has ruled us all for centuries. Pendragon. Their annual visit to my family is due shortly, but if we are there, I will not need to attend the formalities, and neither will you."

Amber raised her eyebrows. "Because you're a Venator?"

His expression turned grim and he nodded.

Just how lonely had his life been? How did he feel about killing his own kind? She couldn't imagine what it would be like to take someone's life. Had he grown used to it? He hadn't hesitated back at the apartment. She had been too scared at the time to wonder what he had been doing but now she wanted to know. Had he killed them with his arm, with the power he held in it, or did he have other powers too? The more she knew about him, the more she realised that he had only shown her the tip of the iceberg. He had kept her in the dark and she wasn't going to let it continue, not anymore. She wanted to know him, even if some of it frightened her, and she wasn't going to give up until she did.

First, she wanted to know why his own species despised him.

She couldn't quite believe it was because he was a Venator. They hadn't treated the other Venator with contempt.

Was there another reason why?

Amber stared ahead at the road. Kearn pulled off the motorway and drove onto a smaller road, heading into the countryside and away from London.

His family were powerful. Their house would be as grand as Duke Montagu's, she was sure of it. Would Kearn receive the same cold welcome there?

CHAPTER 19

Nerves rose in Kearn with every passing second of the long drive from the gates to the main house, until they gnawed at his insides and whispered dark words in his mind. He was insane to bring Amber to such a place, to return after all these years without warning, but he had no choice.

He stared always ahead, his eyes fixed on the golden wide façade of the palatial house. Most of the windows in the three rows were unlit. If he were lucky, the majority of the residents would be out hunting or on errands. If he wasn't lucky? Well. He glanced at Amber. He could only hope that things didn't turn violent. He didn't want to have to fight his own family.

Amber was staring at the house, her mouth slightly open and a sense of awe in her blood. It was larger than Duke Montagu's house and had been in his family since they built it around three centuries ago. Before that, another house had stood on the same ground. Vampire hunters had burned it down.

He gripped the steering wheel and scowled at the house as his father's voice echoed around his mind along with his tutor's, telling him of his family's bloodied past and the night many of them had died to protect their duke and duchess.

His parents.

Kearn had only been young then and had been afraid during the hunters' attack. The smell of blood and fire had choked him. Kyran had held him close, using his body as a shield and whispering soothing words to him as they escaped the inferno and the battle, and then hid together. In human terms, they had been only five. While it had horrified him, given him nightmares that had lasted almost a decade, Kyran had taken it in his stride.

He had protected him.

Kearn had always been weaker than he was. The firstborn son inherited strength from their father. The second only inherited a fragment of it, and the rest from their mother. Their mother was weak in both mind and body. Her fragility was the reason he was so reluctant to set foot on this land, to enter this house again without permission.

He parked the car next to a row of black Bentleys in the lit area in front of the house. The tall double doors of the sandstone mansion opened and a man scurried towards them, his footsteps loud on the gravel.

Kearn stepped out of the car and the man immediately stopped, turned and hurried back in.

They remembered him at least.

He stared up at the grand façade of the house, a feeling of dread settling in his stomach and weighing his feet down. It was a mistake to come back here, but it wasn't that which worried him, which had his heart whispering to him to leave because it wasn't too late yet. They could find somewhere else to hide.

His gaze shifted over the white roof of his car to Amber. She stood on the other side, staring up at the building just as he had been. He could feel the tension and trepidation in her blood. It called to him and it would call to others. The vampire would know her fear, and so would every member of the house of Savernake if he took her in there.

They would know she was human.

Could he commit such an unforgivable sin?

Bringing her, a human, uninvited into the home of a bloodline, a home that had lost many due to the vampire hunters' inferno, was a worse sin than those he had committed in the line of duty.

His family would never forgive him.

It struck him that he didn't want their forgiveness for doing it. He would pay the price for bringing her into their sacred place and accept whatever punishment they saw fit, so long as they would protect her.

"Amber," Kearn whispered and her gaze met his.

Fear shone in her eyes. Her heart beat hard in his blood.

He walked forwards and she mirrored his movement, meeting him at the back of his car. He looked deep into her hazel eyes, memorising the way the warm light from the house played on her face, and then took her hand. She started and then relaxed when his fingers interlocked with hers and he pressed their palms close together.

The doors to the house opened again but no one was there.

An invite.

It was a more civilised reception than he had expected. He had thought they would send out the guards to take him and Amber by force.

Kearn walked forwards, his pace slow, assessing the house and the potential danger. He would be powerless against his family should they attack her. He wasn't strong enough to fight so many Nobles and stop them all, not even with her blood in his veins. The amount he had taken was too small to significantly increase his strength or evoke the true effect of her blood.

Amber's hand trembled in his. He didn't have the words to calm her down so he used his blood instead, opening the connection between them and subduing his feelings to give her a sense of calmness in him that wasn't real. She didn't need to know that being here frightened him. She needed him to be strong and to give her a sense that he would protect her.

Because he would.

It was suicidal but he would fight his family for her sake. He wouldn't choose them over Amber. She was the most precious thing in the world, and even though she drove him near to losing control and becoming a beast, he would never leave her side.

He looked down at their joined hands as they walked, constantly aware of the soft feel of her fingers against his knuckles and the warmth of her palm on his. He had never held anyone's hand quite this tightly or been so afraid of losing them.

Never.

They passed through the open doors and into the main vestibule of the house. The wide stone staircase in front of him split at the back wall, heading left and right up to a balcony on either side. A huge chandelier hung from the high ceiling. He had always run under it as a child for fear of it falling on him. The dark red walls echoed the colour of blood. It was exactly as he remembered and it hurt to see it again.

His family watched from the shadows. He could feel eyes on him, intent and threatening.

It was a struggle to find the strength to keep moving, to head into the house in search of his parents and face his family. Amber's hand squeezed his. He didn't dare look at her but was silently thankful for the show of support. He must have failed to control his feelings for a moment and she had sensed the sorrow and pain beating in his heart. The fear.

He walked forwards, waiting for his family to make themselves known. It had been so long since he had set foot in the house but it still felt as though he belonged. Even though he knew that they wouldn't welcome him, he couldn't help hoping, imagining, that they would. It was all he wanted in his heart. He wanted to return to his family.

His gaze moved to Amber.

He wanted to be loved and no longer alone.

"Remain silent, no matter what happens," he said and she nodded. "I will handle it. I will not allow anything to happen to you."

Kearn took another step into the house and no fewer than twenty of his kin stepped out from the doors to his right and left. They filed in and blocked his way in those directions but he walked forwards, undeterred.

Another two dozen walked down from above, barricading the stairs and leaving only the exit open to him. He stopped under the huge crystal chandelier. The crowd on the stairs parted and a broad-built man stepped forwards. His black eyes narrowed in contempt and then bled to red. Kearn refused to rise to the threat. It sickened him but he lowered his head, acting humble even though the man bore no title and was only one of the many serving families within his bloodline.

Amber moved closer to Kearn.

Strength rose within him, brought about by a need to show his family that he was still the man they had once known, and that he had only grown stronger in their time apart. He wanted to put them in their place and teach them never to look down on him. His other hand curled into a fist, trembling with power as it had done back at his apartment. He wanted to paint the walls a fresh shade of red.

Amber's heartbeat echoed in his mind, a reminder that he couldn't allow this to become a bloodbath. He wouldn't be able to fight them and protect her at the same time.

For her, he would humble himself.

Only for her.

The vampires closed in until they were only ten feet away, some of them moving to block even the exit now. Their eyes changed as one, burning red with their hatred and lust for blood.

Amber clung to his arm, her heart thundering against it and her cheek pressed against his shoulder. He clutched her hand tightly and told her through their connection that she was safe. He would protect her with his life if it came to it. It didn't calm her. It only made her worse. She tugged on his hand, urging him back towards the door. She wanted to leave but he couldn't allow it.

The men all took another step towards him, the broad-built one leading the way. He looked like a guard, a man who loved nothing more than violence and bloodshed. The man bore his fangs. Kearn's eyes changed and he growled, his other hand going to Amber's shoulder and moving her behind him. His senses swept out in all directions. The vampires surrounding him snarled. The sound sparked his own desire for blood into life and it rose to meet the threat as he readied himself, tensing and calling every ounce of strength he had so he could meet the first attacker head on.

The man stepped forwards.

Kearn narrowed his eyes. Amber clung to his back, her fingers twisting his black shirt into her fists, and her body shaking against his. Her heartbeat was off the scale, pounding in his blood and demanding he protect her and keep her safe.

He lowered his other hand and focused his power there.

He hadn't come here to shed blood, only to ask for assistance. He didn't want to fight but they were leaving him no choice. His heart reached out with that thought, running through the house, searching for someone who would hear it and listen, and believe him.

He only wanted somewhere safe.

Where safer than his home?

The man launched himself at Kearn and Kearn brought his hand around to face him. The world stopped before he could unleash his power, leaving the man hovering in mid-air.

Sheer confusion distorted the man's face and then he dropped to the ground in a heap, writhing and crying out.

"Allow my son to pass." The deep voice boomed around the vestibule. A shiver of recognition bolted through Kearn. He had been on the receiving end of such anger before in his lifetime. Kearn's gaze shot up to the balcony on his right.

Father.

His father looked down on him, strands of his long silver hair brushing his slim handsome face, and his green eyes full of fire and the fierce anger held in his words.

The vampires around Kearn immediately moved away, disappearing into the rooms they had come from and leaving just the man on the floor. He continued to writhe. Kearn's father had heard his call and had come for him. His own father. He had helped him and had protected him. He had done to the man what Kearn had wanted to but feared. And he had called him son.

It honoured him to hear his father use such a word for him.

Kearn dropped Amber's hand and went down on one knee, bowing his head and pressing his right hand against his chest.

It honoured him to have his father come to his aid.

"What business have you here?" The anger had gone from his father's voice but Kearn sensed it still in his blood, a connection between father and son that was inerasable.

He kept his head bowed.

"I come to ask something of you, my honourable master." Those words were easy to say. Respect for his father had always made Kearn humble before him.

"Enter then, and ask of me what you will."

Kearn rose to his feet. His father walked down the stairs, his long black coat flowing from the waist down and trailing behind him. One day Kearn would wear such clothing. The uniform of a retired Venator. His father turned the corner on the stairs in front of him, all grace and nobility, an air of pride and power about him that Kearn could only wish to achieve. The silver-blue detailing and bright buttons on his father's coat gleamed in the light from the chandelier.

Kearn bowed his head again when his father reached him and Amber, and sensed his father's eyes settle on her. He would have realised long before arriving at the scene that she was human but he didn't say anything about it. Perhaps it was his years as a Venator, a protector of humans, holding his tongue about what Kearn had done by bringing Amber into the house of Savernake.

His father walked on towards the doors to the left of the entrance and Kearn turned and followed. Amber hurried to be beside him, close enough that their hands brushed as they walked through the black painted gallery that led to the main reception rooms of the house. Kearn could sense her desire to have him take her hand again but he couldn't, not in front of his father.

Light shone in through the rows of tall windows to his left, illuminating the paintings on the black wall opposite. Family portraits. His eyes trailed over them as he walked. His grandfather and grandmother, painted beautifully for the time they had been done many centuries ago. His father, standing tall and noble beside his seated mother against a backdrop of the house and grounds. The vision of her hurt him. She was beautiful, delicate, a pale rose that his father cherished and with good reason. Kearn had never understood why his father doted on her so much, bent to her will and gave in to her every whim, until he had met Amber. For Amber, Kearn would do anything. Whatever she asked of him, he would make it his mission to do it. She ruled him absolutely.

Kyran looked proud in his painting. Kearn had sat for his portrait at the same time, when they had reached twenty in human years, only a year before the events that had led to him becoming a Venator.

He looked away when he reached the space where the next painting should have hung. It pained him to see it missing and to see the scratches in the plaster. Anger still emanated from them. Hatred. He had hurt his mother so much that he deserved nothing less than her eternal damnation of him.

Amber's gaze fell on him. She didn't say anything but he knew she had seen the empty space and the plaque beneath that bore his name. Kearn Savernake.

Outcast.

Murderer.

His father opened the dark double doors at the end of the gallery and strode into a large black-walled reception room lavishly furnished in red and gold. Memories of playing with his brother in the room assaulted him but he pushed the pain deep into his heart, locking it away.

Kearn stopped near the door and waited for his father to seat himself. His gaze followed his father's back as he crossed the room to the two gold coloured antique couches that stood facing each other in front of the elegant black marble fireplace on the wall opposite him. When his father was seated on the couch to the right of the fireplace, furthest from him, Kearn took measured steps forwards, leaving Amber at the door, and came to stand before him. He couldn't sit on the couch behind him, opposite his father. Not without permission. Even then, he wasn't sure if he would. He didn't deserve such an honour.

He placed his right hand on his chest and bowed his head.

"Duke Savernake, I thank you most humbly for granting me an audience with you, my honourable master."

His father made a dismissive noise but Kearn didn't raise his head. He kept his gaze fixed on the wooden floor. He wasn't fit to look at him.

"Why have you come home?" his father said without any trace of anger or any intonation.

"I am in pursuit of a man and have been for three years. He is a Noble. I have come close to fulfilling my duty with the help of this human. She is a Source Blood and the man wishes to claim her and harvest her blood."

"You wish this not to happen."

Kearn swallowed. "I have vowed to protect her from the man I seek."

"And that has brought you back here?"

"The man has proven his determination. He attacked her in my own home." Kearn sensed the ripple of anger that ran through his father. To attack a vampire in their home was unforgivable. A Noble or Lesser Noble would never do such a thing. Their home was a sacred place, their sanctuary from the human world.

"Is this the same man who attacked the human at Montagu's ball?"

Kearn did look at his father now. He nodded, surprised that his father knew. Had Kyran told him, or was his father aware of the things he did and what happened to him? The Sovereignty remained in contact with Venators even when retired. Would they have told him?

"I seek your permission to remain on Savernake grounds." His voice trembled but his father didn't seem to notice.

He was assessing Amber in the same way Kearn had done the night they had met. She might look frail but she had proven herself strong more than once.

"How is your life as a Venator?" His father's green eyes moved back to him. It was a loaded question and one he hadn't expected. His father wasn't only asking how he had been doing these past sixty years but how he felt.

Lonely.

Kearn sent that feeling to his father through his blood, unwilling to say the word aloud.

His father nodded and understanding filled his eyes when he looked back at Amber. Kearn hadn't meant to allow his father to see his growing attachment to Amber too, but it was impossible to hide things from him. The bond they shared was too deep. Even if he had tried, his father could have broken through any defence and seen the truth without even trying.

"How is mother?" Kearn's voice trembled fully now. "Has her pain lessened?"

Would she ever forgive him?

His father leaned back in the couch and crossed his long black-clad legs, his expression thoughtful.

"You are fortunate that she is away now visiting Montagu."

Kearn bowed his head again and closed his eyes when his hair fell forwards and masked his face. It had been too much to hope that his mother would have forgiven him and would welcome him in her home. If she had been here, his father wouldn't have seen him.

The guard would have escorted him from the grounds as he had been that night sixty years ago.

The memory of it still brought back every ounce of pain. He hadn't forgotten one moment of it. Not the look on his mother's face, or the way she had spoken of him as though he was no longer her son, or how she had dragged him to the entrance and thrown him down onto the gravel drive. Her reproach and anger had chilled him, and he had felt empty for the first few months, doing his duty without feeling or care. Injuries had gone unchecked and he had risked his life, not caring whether he died or not.

It had only been after a year had passed that things had changed for the better. He had met Kyran by chance and his brother had spoken to him. It had given him hope that one day he could return to his family and he had felt alive again. Things between him and Kyran had been tense at first but, over time, they had begun to grow closer again.

Would Kyran speak to his mother for him? He knew that Kyran never mentioned their meetings to her. It went against her rules and would upset her if she found out, but if Kyran spoke to her, perhaps Kearn could return, or at least gain an audience with her. He needed to make her see that he didn't want to be a Venator and he hadn't wanted to do what he had done. She had to understand.

"Her pain has not lessened," his father said and Kearn clenched his fists.

The spark of hope inside him that he had been nurturing for decades, that he had kept alive and that had grown tonight into a tiny flame, sputtered out and died.

"Then it is hopeless," he whispered. A desire to scream welled up inside him, to shout and argue his point with his father, to cry and beg him to speak with his mother for him. He held them all inside and cursed himself instead.

"Nothing is hopeless."

Kearn was surprised to hear Amber speak. He looked through the lengths of his hair at her. His father watched her too. She stood in the doorway, twisting her hands in front of her, staring at her feet. Crimson stained her cheeks, an outward sign of the embarrassment blazing through her blood. She knew she had broken his rule about not speaking, but he couldn't be angry with her, not when she had said the words he had needed to hear most.

"The human female is correct." His father sat up. "Perhaps in time you will do something that will gain you the forgiveness you seek."

Perhaps he could wait for Kyran to do something unforgivable again. He cursed. He didn't want to believe that his mother would never forgive him and welcome him back into the family, but he did.

"You may stay with the human in the lodge at the gate." His father stood and stepped up to him.

Kearn dropped to one knee again and bowed his head. "Thank you, my honourable master."

His father gave another short noise of disapproval. It didn't matter what he wanted. He deserved to have Kearn's respect, even if he didn't like it.

"Archduke Pendragon will visit."

Kearn nodded. It was both a warning not to show his face and a warning that his mother would return soon.

Would she throw him out again when she did?

He needed to keep Amber here. If his mother wanted him off the estate, he would beg her to let Amber remain at the lodge in exchange for him leaving. Kyran would keep her safe for him.

His father left the room. Kearn remained kneeling a few seconds longer and then stood and turned to face Amber.

If he had to, he would leave her here.

He would hunt the man alone.

He would protect what was his.

CHAPTER 20

Amber walked in silence through the large house, trailing behind Kearn. They passed back through the gallery and she glanced at the empty place on the black wall. Long gouges marked the plaster. Whoever had removed Kearn's painting had been very angry with him.

His mother?

She had felt his emotions when he had spoken of his mother. The pain had been raw and intense, strong enough that it had felt as though they were her feelings, not something she was merely sensing in him. His despair and his words of failed hope had forced her to speak. Whatever had happened between them, she was sure that it was the reason he wasn't welcome in his own family's home.

She was sure because his father was a Venator too.

They reached the red lobby and she spotted Kyran at the door.

Kearn raised his head.

Kyran smiled.

His blue eyes were bright in the warm light of the chandelier. It reflected off his black hair, highlighting it with threads of gold. He leaned back against the elegant wooden doorframe and folded his arms across his chest, an imposing figure when dressed head to toe in black. The last time she had seen him, his clothing had been more formal. Tonight he was dressed as Kearn was, in a shirt and trousers.

A noise on the stairs caught her attention. Three women stood on the left side of the stone staircase, all of them wearing flowing long black dresses and scowls. Amber moved closer to Kearn.

"There is no need to fear the dogs." Kyran's voice echoed around the high ceiling of the expansive room, intentionally loud, as though he was making a point. Who was he making it to, the women or her and Kearn? She brought her gaze back to him. He grinned. "They would not dare bite you. It is Kearn's blood they want."

Everyone seemed to want his blood. Just what had he done to deserve such cold and cruel treatment?

Kyran stared at her, the smile fading from his face and his eyes losing their brightness.

"How is your throat?"

Amber touched the bandage. Had Kyran helped when she had been injured? She looked at Kearn but his back was to her.

"Healing." Her cheeks blazed and body burned with the memory of what Kearn had done and how good it had felt.

"You should take more care of yourself." Kyran walked past Kearn and touched her left shoulder. His gaze traced her neck, lingering on the bandage around it. "That blood of yours is very valuable."

He smiled and then passed her. She looked over her shoulder at him, watching him walk up the grand stone staircase to the three waiting women, and touched her throat again. Kyran pushed one of the women's arms so she started walking and then nudged the other two forwards to follow her. They lowered their heads and did as he said without protest. Amber frowned at his treatment of them.

"Come. It is not wise to linger here." Kearn walked out of the door.

Amber followed him to his car and got in without another word. She was silent the whole of the short drive, mulling over how Kyran had treated the women. Was he like Duke Montagu too and believed that women were inferior, something to possess and control? She had never noticed it about him before. He had always seemed so nice around her and hadn't treated the women at the ball in such a disrespectful way. She glanced at Kearn. Did he harbour such tendencies too? He looked at her out of the corner of his eye and she faced forwards.

The moon shone brightly down on the lodge by the gate, casting pale light over the square sandstone building and reflecting off its bay windows and slate roof. It wasn't a small house as her mind had conjured up on hearing it referred to as a lodge. It looked large enough to have at least four double bedrooms on the upper floor.

Kearn pulled the car to a halt near the dark painted front door and turned off the engine.

Amber stared at the lodge, thinking about what had happened back at the house with his father and his family, and then looked over at Kearn.

"What was that all about?" she whispered, amazed she had found the courage to ask.

Kearn's eyes narrowed on the black steering wheel and he sighed.

"It has been many years since I have been welcome here." Pain laced his voice, a hurt that she felt deep inside her.

"What happened?" Amber covered his hand with hers and held the steering wheel with him. Her brow furrowed and she leaned forwards to see his face. He stared at the dashboard, his green eyes distant and cold, belying the increasing hurt within him. "It can't be because you're a Venator because your father is one."

"No... it is not because of what I am... but because of what I did." He looked at her out of the corner of his eye. "It is because I killed my mother's younger sister."

Her hand tensed against his and her eyes went wide. "Why—"

"It was my duty to. She had been purchasing Source Blood. She was an addict."

They had made him kill his own family? What sort of terrible people were in charge of the Venators? They had sentenced him by making him do such a thing. They had condemned him to a life alone.

"My mother tried to convince me to go against the Sovereignty. I did not, and instead carried out my duty, and she has not spoken to me since." His hoarse low voice conveyed his hurt as clearly as the way his hand trembled beneath hers.

Amber placed her other arm around his shoulders and pressed her forehead against his temple. She wished she could take away his pain. She didn't want him to feel it. She didn't want him to feel lonely.

"How long has it been?" she whispered against his cheek.

"I have not set foot in that house since nineteen forty seven."

Amber felt terrible for him. Sixty years of never seeing his family. Sixty years of suffering such callous and harsh treatment by his kind.

"You have your brother at least," she said, trying to find the bright side so his pain would ease.

Kearn shirked her embrace and got out of the car, slamming the door behind him.

She didn't understand.

She stepped out too and found him standing near the bonnet, staring up at the moon. It cast silvery light down on him, kissing his hair and face, turning her demon into an angel. His eyes shone, tears reflecting the moonlight. She took his hand and longed to kiss away his tears and heal his pain. She wanted to tell him that he was no longer alone. She was here now and she wasn't going anywhere.

"What is it?" She touched her throat again, rubbing the bandages.

"Do not be fooled," he whispered up at the moon, his silver eyebrows furrowing. "My brother has hated me since I became a Venator."

Amber frowned. Kyran hated him? They had their moments of tension but she had never suspected that Kyran felt that way. She couldn't bring herself to believe it. It didn't seem possible.

Kearn looked down at her, straight into her eyes, stealing her breath away with the tenderness in them and the need.

She wanted to give in to him when he looked like that, when he looked as though she could save him from his pain. She would do whatever it took. Would she go as far as to become his forever if he asked it of her? She wasn't sure.

"Why?" she said.

A hint of a smile touched his lips and then disappeared.

"Because as eldest son, he should have become a Venator, not me. That is the tradition and the way it has always been. The Sovereignty changed it and took Kyran's dream away, and gave me this nightmare."

Kearn stared back towards the house. Amber covered his hand with both of hers and her eyes traced his profile. If the Sovereignty had followed tradition and given the role of Venator to Kyran, Kearn's life would have been so different. He would have been so different.

Even if he had never met her, she wished his life had followed the course it should have and he had never become a Venator. She wished it because she knew in her heart that he would have been happy then.

Kearn turned back to her. She touched her throat again.

"Is something wrong?" He brushed her hand aside, his long fingers caressing the bandage in their place, his gaze following them.

Amber thought about it. "It stings a little."

Kearn kept hold of her hand and led her into the dark lodge. He turned on the lights in the small dull cream entrance and then walked through another door and turned on the lights in that room too. It was a large pale living room.

There wasn't much furniture. Two dark red armchairs stood either side of an old stone fireplace to her right, with a small wooden coffee table. An empty Welsh dresser lined the left side of the wall opposite her, beside a closed door.

Kearn walked forwards, forcing her to follow, and stopped under the naked light bulb in the middle of the room. He tilted her head up and removed the bandage from around her throat.

His expression darkened.

And then the edges of his irises melted into red.

"You are bleeding." His jaw tensed and his eyes slowly turned green again. "And I took you to the house."

Amber touched her neck and felt the wet blood.

"No." She lowered her hand and his gaze left her throat to meet hers. "It was okay a moment ago... when I was in the house it was fine... it was only after that."

It was after Kyran had asked how it was and she had rubbed it.

"Keep still," Kearn whispered and she snapped back to the room and him. His hand caught her under the jaw, his touch light yet as commanding as his words. She stood still, her head tilted back and held by him, and tried to follow his movements with her eyes.

He leaned in, focused on her throat. His green eyes bled into crimson, so vivid in colour that she was sure she would never forget this moment and the sight of them. Kearn's true nature. The man he had hidden from her. A man he thought she would fear. He had given her no reason to feel such an emotion towards him. She only felt a growing sense of need and affection.

Her lips parted with the first brush of his tongue over her neck and her eyes fell shut with the second caress. The fingers of his other hand wrapped around her left upper arm and his other thumb pressed into her jaw. He tilted her head back further and licked her throat again, sweeping his tongue along the length of the wound. His fingers trembled against her and his blood spoke to her, conveying the way his whole body quaked from the taste of her alone.

Amber frowned when his grip on her arm tightened.

He licked her neck harder, stepping into her at the same time. The fingers holding her jaw tensed and he no longer shook. He dragged her against him, his grip on her so tight that she flinched.

And then it tightened further, and she felt as though he would snap her arm. Her fingers numbed.

Kearn wrapped his lips around her throat and sucked. She gasped when her head spun and the wound stung. He wasn't healing it. He was reopening it.

His hand left her arm and pressed into her back, crushing her against his body until she couldn't breathe. His own breathing was rough in her ear, laboured and fast, an intermittent sound that broke the silence between his suckling. She felt his intent.

She felt it deep within her blood and she feared it.

She feared it for both of their sakes and the feeling wasn't wholly her own.

"Kearn." Amber tried to wriggle free but he held her tighter and sucked harder on her blood. Anger and fear collided inside her, exploding into panic, but she could feel other things too. Hatred. Self-loathing. Sorrow. Kearn's feelings. Her head spun again. She had to make him stop. "You don't want to do this. You'll never forgive yourself."

Nothing.

His lower teeth touched her neck and then he pressed his fangs against her flesh. It was the front of them, not the tips, but it was enough to make her fight him. She couldn't let him do this. She could sense in her blood that he was torn about this. He wanted to bite her but hated himself for it at the same time. There was so much pain inside her, screaming in her veins, but so much need too. She couldn't let him do this, not now, not like this. He lived in a world without love, where all those who had once been close to him now hated him, and if he did this, he would despise himself too.

"Kearn, no! You'll hate yourself!"

He pulled back and laughed, his arm still around her and his fangs sharp in the light.

Amber put her hands against his chest, using the opportunity to restrain him.

"I already hate myself." He grinned.

"I know that isn't true," she said. He met her words with another mirthless laugh. "I know you don't want to do this."

His red gaze bore into hers, his expression deadly serious all of a sudden. "Oh, I do. You cannot tell me that you did not see that vision of us... and that you did not like it."

He tilted her head back again and appraised her throat. She had seen the vision of him at her neck, and she had liked it, but it had been nothing more than a dream. This was reality and it was beginning to scare her.

He grinned again, revealing his fangs.

"Your blood calls to me." His voice was a low whisper that sent a shiver down her spine. She couldn't deny that either. "It wants me to take it."

This wasn't like him. It wasn't. She refused to believe it. He was acting just as he had done the night she had confronted him and discovered that he was a vampire. It had to be her blood that had changed him. He just needed to get control of himself again, as he had in the street after the club. She needed to gain some space between them. She was sure that if she did, he would fight the effects of her blood and be normal again.

He went to pull her back to him but she shoved him hard and broke free. She ran to the closed door and yanked it open. The kitchen. She skidded on the tiled floor and ran to her right. There was a set of stairs and nothing else. Amber bolted up them, aware of Kearn chasing her in the darkness and that she was heading towards a place where she wouldn't easily be able to escape.

Her heart pounded and panic fuelled her. She turned this way and that through the dark winding hall, bumping into the walls and desperately trying to reach the other side of the house. There had to be another set of stairs that led down again. If she could reach them, she might be able to get out of the house. Had Kearn locked his car? It was her only hope. She wouldn't be able to outrun him on open ground. She had to reach his Audi and lock herself in, giving him time to calm down.

She didn't make it.

Kearn grabbed her arm, spun her and dragged her against him.

"Do not fear me," he whispered against her throat and licked it.

She wasn't afraid. It was a lie, but she told it to herself so she would remain calm and not drive Kearn into doing something he would regret. It was her blood making him like this, out of control and wild, like a beast. The conflict inside her grew, becoming a violent battle waged in her blood. Kearn's battle. A fight that he would win given time. She needed to buy him that time. She had to do something to soothe him and help him.

He pressed into her and she stumbled backwards, falling through a door and into a room. She managed to keep her footing and slammed into something hard and cold. Her fingers groped it in the darkness. A sink.

She threw Kearn off balance and dived to her left, hoping that she was going the right way. She had to clear his head and there was only one method open to her. Her heart beat in relief when she hit a bath and she had one of the taps running before Kearn grabbed her again. She leaned forwards as his body touched her back, tipping him over her shoulder, and landed heavily on top of him in the bath.

He growled.

He actually growled like an animal.

Amber pressed down on him, trapping him beneath her, and fully opened the tap, thankful that the water was cold.

He struggled but she didn't budge. She wouldn't move until he had either calmed down or drowned. The icy water saturated her clothes. He coughed and spluttered beneath her, his struggle lifting her up and sending panic racing through her blood. He was too strong. She leaned over and pinned his shoulders, making sure to keep his arms trapped beneath her backside and legs, and prayed that she could hold him. The water drained the heat from her fingers and they stiffened and hurt as she gripped him. He growled again and lurched, almost throwing her off his chest, and kicked against the bathtub and the wall. The tiles splintered. Amber grabbed him by the jaw and forced his head further under the water.

With the lights off, she couldn't tell if he was back to normal yet. She needed to see his eyes but couldn't risk getting off him and trying to find the light switch.

"Kearn?"

His skin was freezing beneath her aching fingers now.

She could feel him breathing.

She hoped she wasn't crushing him.

"Kearn?" Amber risked it and brought his head out from under the water.

"I am sorry."

She could feel the depth of meaning behind his apology. His blood relayed jumbled thoughts and feelings to her. She couldn't make sense of them but she could make sense of what he had said and his tone of voice.

Amber turned off the tap and leaned down. She pressed her forehead against his and felt his breath against her face.

"Apology accepted?" he whispered.

She nodded and pulled herself off him. She bumped into the sink and heard Kearn leave the bath. The light burst into life a moment later and she blinked against the suddenness of it. When she looked at Kearn, he was staring at his drenched black shirt. His silver hair hung in wet tendrils against his face and spiked out at the back near his neck.

His irises were green again at least. She took it as a positive sign.

"You didn't really want to hurt me."

His eyes rose to hers. They bled back into red. Instinct said to take a step backwards but she stood her ground.

"It was my blood making you like that." She wanted to believe those words, but the hungry way Kearn's eyes bore into her throat made it impossible.

He laughed again.

"Do not cover the truth with lies, Amber. It will bleed through!" His eyes narrowed on her neck and his fingers curled into fists. "I did want to hurt you. I wanted to sink my fangs into your delicate beautiful throat and quench my thirst for you."

Amber shook her head. "You would hate yourself."

"I would." He stepped towards her. She backed into the wall and wished she'd had the sense to go towards the door instead. There was no escape this way and Kearn had proven himself more powerful than her. If he wanted to bite her, she wouldn't be able to stop him. "I would hate myself... you would hate me... but I would not care... not as long as I had you."

Her eyes shot wide.

"Do I frighten you now? You should be scared." He stared hard at her throat and reached a hand out to her. She tensed and shook when his fingertips stroked lines either side of the cut on her neck and his lips parted, exposing the tips of his fangs. "You should fear me… because I want your blood… I want you… and nothing on this Earth can stop me… nothing but myself."

"Not even me?" she whispered, looking down at his hand. His touch was light, his fingers trembling and cold.

His eyes shifted and locked with hers, blood red and darkened by his dilated pupils.

"Not even you."

His hand slid around the back of her neck and she was in his arms before she could blink. He grabbed her right hand and stared at the scab on her palm, and then at her throat. She kept still, afraid of pushing him over the edge again and forcing a reaction from him they could both regret.

Kearn licked the cut on her palm and then the one on her neck. He held her close to him, so gently that she almost relaxed. He kissed her throat and sighed against her skin.

"When the time comes… when I can no longer control my need… I will…" His tongue brushed her neck again and he shivered against her. He pressed his cheek to hers and whispered into her ear, "You will be mine."

Amber stared over his shoulder at the white tiles covering the wall opposite her, absorbing those words and struggling to grasp them. His dominance didn't surprise her, or even frighten her. Having seen the way the other male vampires acted towards women, and having felt the depth of Kearn's need for her, she could accept his behaviour and his desire to make her belong to him. What she couldn't accept was that he wouldn't give her a choice.

Didn't he care about what she wanted?

Her dreams of them together, of him biting her, had been erotic and tantalising, but reality was nothing like a dream. She had seen the turned women at the ball, and the way their men had treated them, and she didn't want that. Part of her was willing to go through with becoming a vampire if it meant she could remain with Kearn, could be with the man she was falling for, and could put an end to his loneliness, but the rest needed reassurance. She needed a promise that she wasn't making the same mistake those women had by giving herself to her Noble only for him to cast her aside and use her to populate the ranks of his servants.

She didn't want to live eternity watching Kearn moving from woman to woman, creating a harem of slaves. She wanted him to be hers and hers alone.

"Does that frighten you?" he breathed against her neck.

"No." Her voice shook and betrayed her turmoil. She wasn't sure of her feelings yet, but she didn't want to fear him or anything that might happen between them because she knew that it would hurt him.

"Liar," he whispered and she shivered this time.

She couldn't fear him because some part of her did want it too.

Amber wrapped her arms around his shoulders and held him close.

"You embrace me as though holding a lover, not a man who will destroy you." He tried to pull away but she didn't let him go.

"You won't destroy me." She placed a kiss on his neck, a sign that she could overcome this fear just as she had overcome her fear of him being a vampire.

"I want to." His hands settled against her lower back and then he rested his head on her shoulder and sorrow filled her.

"No, you only want to end your loneliness. I can understand that." Her fear faded as she held him, her blood feeding his feelings to hers. They were clearer now. He wasn't lying to her. He did want to make her forever his and it was becoming difficult for him to resist.

She stroked his wet hair, running her fingers though it, feeling calm inside now. Could he feel that in her? Did he know that she wasn't really frightened of him?

"It will not save you." He pulled her closer to him and rested his head more heavily on her shoulder. He sounded tired and felt it too. Not normal tiredness but a deep weariness. Was he weary of being lonely? Was that why he so desperately wanted to keep her with him? He didn't want her to leave and he feared that she would. "Your belief in me... it will not save you. I am a slave to my instincts... you make me a beast and I cannot fight it. I want you."

Amber closed her eyes and tilted her head so her cheek brushed his jaw.

"So take me," she whispered.

Kearn tensed.

Amber remembered saying that to him through her blood the night he had healed her neck.

Stay with me forever.

She didn't say it aloud but sent the message through her blood and her body to him.

If it would ease his pain for only a moment, she would give herself to him. All she would ask in return was that he didn't discard her as the other Nobles did when they turned a human, but rather cherished her as Duke Montagu had said she would be by her Noble.

Amber pushed Kearn back and looked deep into his eyes. She touched his cheek, stroked his jaw, and caressed his lower lip, all the while thinking about what it would be like to be with him forever. She sent the message to him again, expressing without words that it had been her desire she had uttered that night, not his.

His lips parted.

She dipped her thumb in and her heart beat so hard against her chest that it felt as though it would smash through her ribs. He became very still and opened his mouth to her. She stared at his fangs, scared but excited, and ran her index finger down one, from the root to the tip. She was careful not to cut herself. He wouldn't want it to happen that way.

He needed to bite her neck, to do it that way, not by accident. It had to be special to him.

He shook beneath her wandering fingers, his red eyes fixed on her mouth. She swept her fingertip along his lower lip again and his breath shuddered against it.

"You do not know what you do to me," he whispered. "How hard this is for me."

"I know." She saw it in his eyes and felt it in his blood. His need ran through her, so deep and strong that it stirred her own, and she knew that it was the reason he had become so possessive and dominant. It wasn't about her blood. It wasn't just what she made him feel or want to do. It was that she had ended his loneliness and he was afraid to go back there. He needed her, and his blood whispered that he couldn't live without her. He didn't have to.

Amber leaned in and pressed a soft kiss to his lips, reassuring him without words that she understood and could come to accept this too. She wouldn't fight him if he gave her the reassurance she craved.

He returned the kiss, his mouth moving slowly against hers, and she smiled when their tongues met and she realised his fangs had receded. His tongue brushed hers, soft and sensual, his gentle kiss brimming with love and warming her heart. Her whole body lightened, her fear melting away, leaving only deep affection flowing through her. Not only her feelings, but his too, joined within their blood, leaving them open to each other. The strength of them gave her a sliver of the reassurance she needed from him, but it still wasn't enough to convince her to step into his world. She needed more from him. She needed to know that his heart belonged to her before she gave hers in return.

The kiss ended too soon. He drew back, his green eyes full of the mixture of awe, gratitude and love that she could feel within his blood.

"I must go out." His tone was distant as though he didn't want to and she nodded.

She had known the moment he had brought her here that he was going to do this. It seemed as though he couldn't hide anything from her anymore. His blood had made it clear to her, relaying his thoughts throughout their journey and some he'd had at the house. It had told her that he wanted to keep her here, where it was safe.

"You will be fine here. I will lock the doors." He placed another kiss on her lips and then he was gone.

Amber stared at the empty room in front of her.

Her fingers stroked her neck.

The thought of becoming a vampire frightened her.

But not as much as the thought of being parted from Kearn.

If she was going to be with him, she had to walk in his world and leave her own behind.

She had to become like him, give herself to him, and trust that he would surrender his heart to her in exchange.

She had to.

She loved him.

CHAPTER 21

It was a delicious dream. Each detail of it slipped through Amber's fingers the moment it had passed but she knew Kearn was in it and that he had bitten her again. She smiled at him and he returned it, full of brilliant warmth and happiness. Would he smile like that for her when she was like him? She was insane to be considering it but the marks on her throat were always there in her dreams. She wanted it or she wouldn't keep dreaming it.

A sense of awareness rolled through her followed by an unsettled feeling.

She fluttered her eyes open and frowned across the bright sunlit room to Kearn where he stood in the doorway, bare-chested and watching her.

Amber sat up, holding the covers to her naked body with her right arm and propping herself up with the other.

He looked irresistible like that, wearing only his black trousers and leaning back so every muscle on his pale torso was on show. Her gaze trailed over his body, the sight of it stirring arousal in her as much as her dream had.

She had fallen asleep in this room before he had returned. Now it was day. How long had he been gone? He looked tired in his face but his eyes were alert, burning into her. They dropped to her neck and she touched it. She had bandaged it again so it wouldn't stir him when he came back. His gaze moved on, gliding sensually down over her chest and remaining there. It felt as though he was looking straight through to it to her heart.

"Couldn't you sleep?" she whispered and his eyes leapt to hers.

He said nothing.

He stalked towards her, kneeled on the end of the bed and crawled up the cream duvet towards her.

Amber leaned back, her head hitting the pillows and her arm still clutching the covers to her chest.

"What are you doing?" She stared into his eyes. They narrowed on her and a smile tugged at his lips. Her stomach fluttered at that look and the fire in it. She knew exactly what he was doing.

He reached her and knelt with his hands either side of her head, splayed out against the pillows, trapping her beneath him. His green gaze held hers.

"I am going to make love to you." The way he said it stole her breath away.

There was such passion in his voice, such hunger that rippled through her in response, that she almost closed her eyes to savour it.

He wasn't asking her permission to make love with her. He was going to seduce her even if she said no and for some reason she was fine with that. She wanted it but feared it at the same time. If they did this then it would change her completely. There would be no going back.

She would never be the same.

And neither would he.

Her eyes slipped shut the second his lips touched hers in a searing caress that claimed her breath and made her heart explode against her chest. She released the blanket and wrapped her arms around his, moaning when his body settled on top of hers. The weight of him was divine and everything she had dreamed. She no longer cared if this changed them. She didn't want to go back to a world without him anyway.

He kissed down her jaw, devouring her and making her tremble. She tilted her head up, eager for more, and shivered when he pressed a long kiss to the bandage on her throat and then leaned his cheek against hers.

"Do not fear," he whispered into her ear, his breath soft and warm, tickling her and heightening her arousal. "I am in control, and if I lose it, I will leave for now... but I need you."

His weight was gone from her. She opened her eyes, settling them on him as he closed the pale bedroom curtains and then undid his belt. This was really happening. He was going to make love to her. Every inch of her hummed with desire and called to him, begging him to come to her and be one with her at last—to live out their dreams and the visions they had shared through their blood.

She wasn't afraid when he stripped, revealing his hard length and toned thighs, and she wasn't afraid when she pulled the covers back to expose herself to him and invite him into the bed. She feared none of it. Not even the thought that he might lose control. She wanted this moment too much. She wanted it enough to risk the consequences of surrendering to her desire. In the heat of the moment, if he couldn't stop his urge to bite her, she wouldn't be able to stop him either. She would want it.

She would welcome it.

Kearn lay against her and she tossed the duvet over him. The feel of his bare body against hers was delicious. Warm and hard. She looped her arms around his neck and drew his mouth down to hers. He groaned when she kissed him, her lips playing lightly against his and her tongue stroking the seam of his mouth, and opened to her. Their tongues brushed, each caress stoking the fire that had ignited in her veins.

His hand claimed her left breast, his thumb circling the nipple until it was hard and aching for more, sending shivers of tingles through her body from its centre. She moaned into his mouth and writhed against him, her thighs rubbing together to make the most of the sweet moist feeling between them. She wanted him. She needed him inside her.

He pushed the covers back and lowered his mouth from hers to her neck, kissing it while he grazed the backs of his fingers downwards over her stomach towards the apex of her thighs.

"Amber," he whispered against her throat between kisses.

His fingers lazily stroked her thighs, teasing her with their proximity. She wriggled her hips and he pinned her right side with his body, his hot hardness

165

pressing against her, trapped between them. The feel of it increased her hunger for him. Just the thought of him inside her was making her crazy with passion.

"Amber," he said again and licked just below her jaw.

Did he want to bite her?

He kissed across her chest and up the other side of her throat, his mouth hovering there over the cut. She swallowed and trembled. Her hand went to the bandage but he caught her wrist and pushed himself up.

"Don't you want my blood?" she whispered, confused as to why he had stopped her. She had thought he would want it now more than ever—that he would want her blood as well as her body.

He shook his head, sending the silver threads of his hair swaying, and his green eyes narrowed on hers.

"No... I want you like this." He released her hand and ran his over her left breast. She arched into him, pressing into his palm and sighing at the feel of it against her. "I do not want you while I am under the influence of your blood... never like that."

She stared into his eyes and felt the truth in her blood. He meant it. She smiled, threaded her fingers into the hair at the back of his head and lured him down for a kiss, rewarding him with it and hoping he could sense how he had made her feel. She was warm all over, heated not by arousal but by the thought that he wanted this to be about their feelings rather than his hunger for her blood.

His hand glided down over her stomach and she groaned into his mouth when he covered her mound with it, his fingers dipping in to tease her.

Amber surrendered to him when he deepened the kiss, stoking the flames in her and making her melt into the bed beneath him. His tongue played with hers, keeping tempo with his fingers as they combined to take her out of her mind. Her body tightened and she tensed, making the most of each sweep of his fingertips over her most sensitive flesh.

He lowered his hand at the same time as he lowered his mouth. His lips claimed her left nipple, drawing it into his mouth, and his fingers slid down to her slick opening and eased inside. His deep groan filled the silence. She unleashed a moan of her own as he buried his long fingers inside her welcoming body and screwed her eyes shut.

"I need you," Kearn whispered against her chest between hungry kisses, his voice full of urgency that echoed within her.

She could sense his need and it matched her own. She was too hot, burning too fiercely for him. She needed him now, wanted her first climax with him to be when they were as one, their bodies finally together in the way she had ached for since meeting him.

Amber ran her hands down his strong back and shifted her hips against his, rubbing his hard length with them. He moaned again and sucked her nipple, palming her other breast with his hand.

"I want you," she uttered and arched into his hungry mouth.

His knee pushed her legs apart and her heart fluttered at the thought of him filling her, his body moving against hers. Her groin throbbed and ached. He moved between her knees and covered her with his body, his mouth reclaiming hers with a searing kiss that sent her temperature soaring. She matched his passion, her teeth clashing with his as she tried to release the need building inside her and find relief. His tongue swept over hers, caressing it in a sexy way that made her grind her hips against his, rubbing herself on his length. Sparks chased through her, warmth skittering over her skin at the feel of him pressed against her sensitive flesh and the thought of what was to come.

He moved back and she froze as sense reared its ugly head.

She gripped his shoulders and he looked at her, green eyes full of confusion as to why she had stopped him.

"Do we need protection?"

Mood killer.

He smiled a brilliant smile.

"No." He moved back to her mouth, pressing light kisses to it. "A human and a vampire are not compatible like that. When you become a vampire, you will be fertile to me."

If he hadn't been kissing her so sensually, sending her out of her mind, she would have been coherent enough to pick him up on his presumption. She might not want to become a vampire. She might run away from him before it could happen.

Neither of those things were what she wanted, but the thought of him being so damned commanding made her want to say them.

They would hurt him though. Even if she said them as a joke, retaliation against his possessive tone and the way he treated her as though she was already his to control, they would cut him deeply.

"Amber?" He drew back.

She dragged his mouth back down to hers and kissed him, trying to reignite the fire within her and stoke it back into the inferno it had been a moment ago.

He pulled away from her and broke free of her grasp. "You already despise me, don't you?"

She cursed him for being stronger than her and being able to sense her feelings from her blood. Sometimes she wished she could turn off the connection as he could.

"No." She caressed his cheek, and brushed his hair from his face, absorbing the soft look in his eyes and how handsome he was. "I don't. Honestly. I just... maybe I don't want kids."

A faint smile touched his mouth. "Are you sure that is all?"

She hesitated and he frowned.

"Tell me," he whispered and leaned down, peppering her face with kisses. "I can take it."

"That's just it... you take what you want. What about what I want?"

He drew back again and his eyes searched hers.

"I have hurt you." There was a note of defeat in his voice and he moved off her and sat on the edge of the bed with his back to her, the cream duvet over his lap. "I am sorry if... I... I need you."

He was sorry that he needed her? That wasn't what he had wanted to tell her. Amber sat up and went to him, kneeling behind him. She wrapped her arms around his shoulders and locked her hands in front of his chest. Her breasts pressed against his back and she rested her chin on his right shoulder. He sighed and she ran her right hand down his arm, fingers tracing the silver markings, as she thought about what to say.

"I know you want to make me like you... and that I might not get much choice... but there are things we have to decide together and I've always been able to stand on my own two feet."

"What is that supposed to mean?" His voice was a bare whisper.

She sighed. "I've seen the way men treat the women in your world. I... don't think I can let you control me like that. I don't want to be made to feel inferior to you."

"Inferior?" He turned to face her so fast that his head hit hers. She grimaced and rubbed her forehead. His fingers eased hers away and he kissed the spot he had hurt, softly murmuring his apology against her skin.

She savoured the gentle way he held her and the love she could feel in the embrace, but drew away so she could see his face when he spoke. She had to see his feelings in his eyes as well as feel them in his blood.

"You are anything but inferior," he said and stroked her face. "Duke Montagu was right that night at the ball. You are beautiful, and you rule the heart of this Noble. There is nothing I would not do for you, Amber. If you told me you did not want to become a vampire, I would fight my desire to make you one for the rest of my years."

"You can't fight it forever though or you wouldn't have told me everything you did in the bathroom."

"It is growing more difficult to resist my desire to claim you as forever mine." He turned away again.

Amber leaned her head against his back and sighed.

"I meant what I said to you," she whispered and he tensed. She grazed her fingers down his forearm and stared at the marks that danced across his skin. "I meant every word and every feeling the night of the ball. You're so distant right now, so full of self-hatred and fear that what I'm about to say can't possibly be your feelings this time. These are all mine, as they were that night. I'm not afraid of the future, Kearn, because I'll be with you, and no matter what happens it will be worth it. I want you to stay with me forever."

He sighed and took hold of her hands, holding them tightly.

"What are you afraid of?" he said in a quiet voice.

"I'm scared I'll wake up the day after you've bitten me to find you acting like those men at the ball... I don't want to be like those women... I don't want you to discard me as though I mean nothing to you." Tears lined her eyes but she didn't let them fall. She took a deep breath to steady her emotions and closed her eyes. "Promise me that it won't be like that."

"Amber," he breathed and she was in his arms, held close to his chest. She curled up against him, listening to the slow beat of his heart against her ear. The sound of it frightened her, a reminder that he wasn't human that seemed more real than the eyes or the fangs. Would her heart beat so slowly if she became a vampire? She didn't think she would be able to get used to feeling such a leisurely rhythm as her pulse, but she supposed it was better than no heartbeat at all. He pressed kisses to her hair and combed his fingers through her ponytail, chasing away her fear and soothing her. "Amber, it would never be like that. If you allowed me to bite you, I would cherish you more than I do now. I would dote on you and do everything in my power to make you happy. It is all I can do for you... my most precious Amber."

She cursed him when tears tumbled down her cheeks and wiped them away with the heel of her hand. She didn't want to cry. How could a man who had appeared so cold and emotionless at first be so full of warmth and love?

Drawing away from him, she placed her hands against his bare chest and looked into his eyes. The love in them was overwhelming. A love that would last forever. All she had to do was reach out and take what she wanted, just as he was willing to do.

She nodded and he frowned, clearly not understanding her.

"When the time comes," she brushed the hair from his forehead, sweeping the silver lengths out of his eyes so he could see her properly when she took the leap, "I won't stop you... I won't be afraid. Not anymore."

Her eyes widened when he grabbed her and pressed her down into the bed, his mouth capturing hers again. His rough passionate kiss stole her breath and fanned her desire back into life. She smiled and wrapped her arms around him, tangling her fingers in his hair and keeping his mouth against hers. The warm pulse of arousal beat through her. She rubbed her knees together in anticipation and ran her hands over his strong shoulders and down his spine. Every muscle shifted under her touch, speaking of his power and making her hum inside. She wanted to feel him against her, inside her. She wanted to show him how much she loved him and that she wasn't afraid of him. She would give herself to him.

His lips left hers, trailing down her neck to her breasts. He palmed and kissed them, until she longed for his body and for completion. She lifted her leg, rubbing her calf against his buttocks, and clutched him to her breast. A low rumble echoed through him, causing his chest to vibrate against hers. He growled. She really did turn him into a beast.

Amber caught him under the chin and brought him up to her. She didn't want to wait any longer. The fire had come back fast, burning through her, and only he could save her from it.

Kearn kissed her again and moved between her thighs. She moaned when he thrust his hard length against her groin, teasing her moist flesh.

"Say you will be mine," he whispered against her mouth and the connection between them became clearer, so that she could feel everything he did. He needed her so much.

She needed him too.

"Always." She raised her knee, trying to spur him into taking her. She was too hot, burning fiercely for him, to wait any longer.

He growled and shifted his hips back and then he was in her, deep and hard. The sting of pain was nothing compared to the feel of being one with him. She stilled beneath him, focused on the point where their bodies joined, and memorised the feel of him stretching her, filling her until she was content at last. He withdrew and thrust in again, as hard and demanding as his kisses. She didn't care. She gave herself to him, wrapped her legs and arms around him, and let go.

Kearn growled again, loud against her face. He buried himself deeper and groaned with each meeting of their hips. Amber raised hers, letting him in further, opening herself to him fully. He slammed hard against her, his long length hot and rough inside her, the intensity of their coupling driving her out of control too, until she was moaning with him, clutching and kissing him, desperate for release and to feel him climax inside her.

He pulled her closer, one hand under her back, so their stomachs and chests pressed against each other. It was incredible. Each deep thrust of his hard length into her tore a groan from her throat and made her writhe in sheer maddening pleasure. Sweat beaded against her skin and her heart galloped. The strength of his thrusts had them both moving upwards and she pressed one hand against the headboard behind her, trying to anchor them as they spiralled together, soaring towards their climax.

Kearn's grip shifted to her hips and he held her hard, pumped deeper with his hips, claiming her body as hungrily as he had claimed her blood.

She groaned and arched, screwed her eyes shut as the hot buzz built inside her, and her thighs tightened around him. Kearn kissed her and swallowed her moans. Her mind filled with their combined feelings and the sound of his heart beating, faster now, a pace that almost matched hers. He clung to her, fingers pressing into her flesh, and she sensed he was close, that he would come undone soon and would fall from the dizzying height of desire he had built them up to and slip into hazy bliss with her.

Kearn moved faster against her, curling his hips and driving himself deep into her warm core. She couldn't take the way his pelvis brushed her sensitive flesh and his length teased. She tilted her head back, opened her mouth in a silent scream and shattered into pieces.

Her body quaked around his, milking him and encouraging him to release himself, to lay claim to her and change things between them forever.

He groaned into her ear, his pace quickening and turning frantic as she relaxed beneath him, floating on warmth and lost in the ecstasy of her release. She didn't feel the pain of his grip on her hips or the roughness of his thrusts. She felt only pleasure and happiness, and a deep awareness of his feelings.

Kearn buried his face in her neck and slammed to a halt inside her. His hands trembled, clutching her hips, and his breath shook on her throat. She wrapped herself around him and held him gently while his body quivered, his length throbbing and spilling his seed within her.

He held her like that for long minutes, neither of them moving. She listened to his blood, to his emotions, and they echoed her own. She loved him. She stroked his hair and let him feel that within her blood, knowing that he needed it. The words were too difficult to say right now, but in time, she would find a voice for them and the right moment, and so would he.

For now, they could say it without words.

He relaxed on top of her, his breathing slowing and his heart calm again. She didn't protest when he rolled onto his back, pulling her on top of him. His arms were steel bands around her telling her that he wouldn't let her go even if she did try to move off him. If he was comfortable beneath her weight, then she was happy to sleep like this, tangled around him, her head on his chest and their bodies still joined as one.

Amber closed her eyes and listened to his heart beating.

Her heart.

She smiled.

She had won the heart of her Noble.

She would give hers in return.

Eternally.

CHAPTER 22

Kearn wasn't quite sure how to act around Amber. He pottered about the living room of the lodge, flicking through one of the books he had found but not seeing any of the words on the pages, and occasionally glancing at her where she sat by the fire. It was cold in the stone lodge even though the night outside was warm, so he had brought wood in and lit the fire for her. The smile she had given him for doing such a thing had been dazzling. It seemed small things could count as much as big gestures. He had a lot to learn about women and how relationships worked if he was going to treat her the way she deserved.

He reined himself in. It wasn't the time to become lost in her. Until he had sent the man to the eternal darkness, Amber wasn't safe. He couldn't afford to get complacent.

It still didn't stop him thinking about what she had said. She might not want children. He supposed that it was as much her decision as it was his, but he had always imagined that he would have children, many of them. Two boys at least. Before he had become a Venator, it had been his duty to produce heirs to the dukedom of Savernake. After becoming a Venator, he had been too busy with his new duty and then he had been cast out of society. All hope of finding someone to spend his life with had disintegrated. He hadn't thought about children after that and all that had been in his future was his calling. Now things were different and he found himself thinking about all sorts of things.

Not just what it would feel like to bite her, but what it had felt like to make love with her. He had tried hard to contain his strength, fearing that he would be too rough and would hurt her. She was strong for a human, but her body was frail compared to his. He would never have forgiven himself if he had injured her in any way. She had enjoyed it though. Her blood and her scent, everything had told him that she had been there with him in the moment, feeling nothing but sheer bliss at their coupling.

He had never been with a human before. Since the events that had led to him becoming a Venator, he had closed off his heart to women completely. Amber had forced it open again and shown him that there were people in the world capable of love deep enough that it transcended boundaries. And that he could love again.

He wanted to keep that feeling forever by making her immortal.

What would his family say to that? If he told them that he wanted to turn a human, they would see it as a lowly desire, one that would taint the pure lineage of his family.

He didn't care. His family had cast him out. They had made it clear that he was no longer a part of them, and that meant they no longer governed him.

They could think what they liked about him. All that mattered to him now was having Amber at his side eternally, and he wouldn't hear a word against it or against her. He wouldn't let anyone call her weak because she was a turned human and not a pureblood vampire, or attempt to harm her because of it. He would challenge them all and protect her. He would make them see that she was strong and deserved recognition as a Savernake.

"You're very quiet," Amber said and he looked at her. She curled up on the red armchair and faced him, tucking her feet in near her bottom. The firelight shone on her, darkening her jeans and the hooded zip-up black top she wore but highlighting her face and hands, turning her skin golden. "Thinking?"

He nodded.

"About the man?"

"Amongst other things." He crossed the room to her, placed the book down on the coffee table and sat in the armchair opposite her. She was beautiful today. There was a glow about her and it seemed she couldn't stop smiling. He had frightened her yesterday but there was no trace of fear in her now. She grinned.

"You probably shouldn't think too hard." Amber reached across and ran her thumb up his forehead between his eyebrows. "You frown too much when you think. Can vampires get wrinkles?"

He nodded.

"Then you definitely shouldn't think so hard." Her grin widened.

Was that her way of saying she didn't want him to get wrinkles? He had many years before that happened. He studied her face. She was still young for a human but they aged so rapidly. He wanted her to look always as she did now. He couldn't have that, but he could have her age at the same rate as him. He could live with her for centuries.

He wanted that more than anything.

Kearn stood with the intent of kissing her but stopped when he heard a knock. He frowned and walked out into the small entranceway. Someone was at the door. They were weak. He opened it. A servant looked up at him and then bowed her head. Her dark hair fell across her face. She placed her hands in front of her, clasping them together.

"Your presence has been requested at the house, Venator Savernake."

Kearn looked over her head towards the brightly lit mansion in the distance. He was about to ask who had requested him, thinking it would be Kyran, when she spoke again.

"Archduke Pendragon desires to meet you and the female human."

Kearn's heart dropped into his stomach. The archduke wanted to meet Amber? He didn't want to take her to the house but he couldn't refuse the man who ruled over the noble bloodlines, not even when he was no longer a welcome part of them.

"May I relay your answer to Duke and Duchess Savernake?"

His father knew about this? His mother was home? His head spun at the thought of seeing her. She wouldn't want him in the house. He would hurt her by going.

But he couldn't refuse.

"You may tell them we shall be there directly." His tone was flat, without inflection, and he stared back at the house. What was he doing? It was madness to take Amber to the house to meet with the archduke. His father had made it clear he wasn't to attend. But then his father had sent the servant.

Could he show up without Amber?

Even as he thought it he realised it wasn't an option. The archduke would see it as a mark of disrespect and no excuse would save him from punishment.

He closed the door, distant in thought as he walked back into the living room. Amber's gaze was immediately on him. He wanted to tell her to stay in the lodge but couldn't. The archduke had to be curious about her to request her attendance. He had to bring her with him.

"Who was that?"

Kearn looked at her, still frowning, and tried to think of what to say.

"We have been called to the house." He could see she didn't understand. She frowned back at him, stood and moved around the armchair to face him. "You recall my father mentioning Archduke Pendragon?"

She nodded.

"He has come, and he wishes to meet you."

Her hazel eyes went wide. "Me?"

He heard her heartbeat accelerate and felt the fear in her blood. It whispered to him and his spoke back, assuring her that he would keep her safe. Nothing would happen to her. They would leave if it became dangerous and he would risk the archduke's anger.

"He's important isn't he? I remember you mentioning Pendragon before."

"They rule us. I cannot disobey. I desire to, but it would only incur his wrath and place you in more danger."

She nodded and looked herself over. "Should I dress up?"

The honesty in her eyes when she looked at him brought a smile to his face. Here he was worried about keeping her from harm, and she was more concerned about her outfit. Was her belief in his ability to protect her so strong that she didn't fear meeting such a powerful vampire?

He moved across the room to her and touched her cheek, his eyes holding hers. "You are beautiful as you are."

Her cheeks coloured, darkening delightfully in the firelight and warming beneath his fingers. He dipped his head and raised her chin. The kiss was soft and he sent a sense of reassurance through the connection to her so her belief in him would only strengthen. He wouldn't allow anything to happen to her.

He skimmed his hand down her arm, claimed hers, and led her to the door and out into the night, walking past his car and towards the house. The night was beautiful, full of stars and a bright crescent moon. He was in no hurry to be mocked and humbled. The archduke and his family could wait.

Amber's hand shifted in his, interlocking their fingers so her palm pressed against his.

The whole world could wait when Amber was with him.

It was dark out on the lawn. He kept the connection to Amber open so he could monitor her feelings and she could feel the calmness of his. She was relaxed too and more than once he felt her eyes on his profile. He smiled. It felt nice to walk with her like this, just enjoying being with her and not thinking about the next moment or the past. He only wished it didn't have to end.

The house loomed ahead of them.

They would see the archduke and then leave. He had meant to go back to London tonight to hunt the man but he would stay with her instead. She would worry without him and he didn't want to leave her alone in the lodge when there were vampires from outside his family in the main house. He doubted anyone from the Pendragon bloodline would try anything but he didn't trust them.

The female servant was waiting at the entrance to the house. She bowed to him again, opened the door and walked in. The moment they entered, Amber's hand left his. She was learning about his kind. The sight of a human touching a vampire of the rank he had held would only stir trouble amongst the lower ranking men and women of the house.

He followed the servant left, through the long black gallery. They wouldn't stop in the first chamber this time. The archduke would be waiting in the grand reception room, and he wouldn't be alone.

Kearn glanced at the painting of his parents, his eyes fixing on his mother, and then strode on. He raised his head and straightened his back. His family may have cast him out, but he had lost none of his pride. He would face his mother and show her that he had only grown stronger in their time apart. He was a worthy son of the Savernake line.

Amber was muttering things. He caught snippets of them. She was trying to calm her rising nerves by chanting the rules he had told her at the ball.

She glanced up at him.

"Follow my lead. We will not linger. I will have you back at the lodge soon." His words did nothing to alleviate the fear in her eyes.

Against his better judgement, Kearn stopped. Her eyebrows furrowed. He smiled and cupped her cheek, using touch to reinforce their connection.

"You will be safe. It is a promise," he whispered and she surprised him by raising her hand and placing it over his, holding it against her face. Her eyes closed and she leaned into his touch. He had never felt so warm, or loved. Or needed.

The servant watched them. He no longer cared if it was improper for him to touch a human, or to show such feeling towards one. He took Amber's hand in his and turned with her to face the servant. She bowed her head and kept walking.

Amber's hand shook, conveying the nerves he could already feel in her blood. He would hold it until they reached the archduke.

His nerve wavered when he stepped into the first chamber and saw the gilt doors to his right that led through into the grand reception room. He would hold it until he reached those doors at least.

The servant opened them, revealing the warmly lit stately red and gold room beyond. Amber's hand left his. Had she sensed his intent to let go? Had it hurt her to feel that in him? She smiled at him, no sign of anger or upset in it.

"Venator Savernake," the servant announced.

A sudden wave of anger crashed over him.

Mother.

He swallowed and went to step forwards but Amber caught his arm. Why had she stopped him? He heard her thoughts plainly in her blood.

She was there with him. He wasn't alone. They would face this together.

He nodded and touched her hand. She released him and he walked forwards with her at his side. He wouldn't let her walk behind him. She wasn't inferior.

Archduke Pendragon stood directly before him at the other end of the long room. The lowest ranking vampires crowded the area near the entrance, quietly standing with their heads bowed and right hands against their chest, all facing the archduke. Kearn walked forwards along the corridor they had created. He took in everything—the red walls and high ceilings, the warm light emanating from the candle sconces that lined the walls and the two small chandeliers, and the sheer number of vampires in the room. There were at least one hundred. Guards from the Pendragon household formed a barrier between his bloodline and the titled vampires where they stood on a raised platform.

Kyran stood far to the left of the row, dressed formally in black with his head held high and a glass of blood in his hand.

To Kyran's left sat their mother. It seemed she didn't deem Kearn worthy of a proper greeting. She wasn't even looking at him. Her head remained turned away as he approached the platform, her sleek black hair forming a barrier across her pale face and blending into her black dress. Her anger radiated through him, pulsing deep in his blood, and he cast his eyes downwards for a moment, struggling to bear it. A sense of calm flowed into his blood and he looked up at his father where he stood beside his mother, wearing the long black coat of a retired Venator. His green eyes were on him, shining with a touch of concern but also with pride, and Kearn straightened, raising his chin again, bolstered by his father's feelings and Amber's eyes on him. Kearn's gaze moved to the man next to his father.

Archduke Pendragon.

He was older than his father by almost five hundred years but only around fifteen years senior in appearance, and was not a handsome man. Battles throughout the centuries of his existence had left him scarred and he had a dark personality to match his cruel visage. Kearn had only met him as a child, when the hunters had razed the Savernake mansion, and Archduke Pendragon had hunted them in the name of Savernake.

He had butchered them and revelled in the glory, becoming a beast and slave to his bloodlust. The Pendragon bloodline was strong, and every vampire in it made Earl Huntingdon look kind in contrast.

Kearn stopped in line with the vampires from the Pendragon house and went down on one knee. Amber followed him this time. She was definitely learning. The archduke wouldn't be as kind to her as Duke Montagu had been. To him, all humans were a threat, pests to eradicate.

Whispers started at the back of the room. Kearn kept his head bowed, feeling everyone's eyes on him, including his mother's now. Her cold glare cut into his heart.

"Rise, young Savernake." The archduke's voice was emotionless.

Kearn could sense nothing from him. His age defied all attempts to grasp his emotions and his intent. He rose to his feet and Amber followed suit. She kept her head bowed, her hands resting in front of her stomach, and he hated seeing her so meek.

"You have grown well, young Savernake. I have heard much of you."

"Thank you, my most honourable lord and master." Kearn kept his feelings in check and tried not to think about Amber. Archduke Pendragon would be able to read him openly, without much of an effort. If he sensed Kearn's feelings for Amber, it would only make things worse.

"Come, child." Archduke Pendragon stretched a hand out and motioned towards himself.

To his horror, Kearn realised that the archduke was speaking to Amber. She raised her hand, her eyes hollow, and walked towards the archduke. He was trying to control her.

Kearn reacted on instinct.

He moved in front of her and blocked her path. Archduke Pendragon glared at him.

"My apologies, my most honourable lord and master, but I cannot allow the human to come any closer." Kearn dropped his head and his heart raced. He was stupid. He shouldn't have interfered but the thought of Amber being near the archduke turned his stomach. He wouldn't allow it. She would be in too much danger.

He tried to use his blood to release the archduke's hold on her but the connection closed.

She couldn't do such a thing. She didn't know how.

The archduke towered above him on the small platform, a displeased look on his dark face. His black eyes narrowed on Kearn and he felt the power in him, and knew he didn't stand a chance.

Archduke Pendragon moved onto the bottom step of the platform, raised his right hand while holding Kearn's gaze, and backhanded him across the face. The force of the blow sent Kearn down, his left knee and hand hitting the wooden floor so hard that the impact jolted every bone in his body. He closed his eyes to stop his head from spinning, and then pushed himself up, coming back to stand on trembling legs between the archduke and Amber.

"You dare deny me!" Archduke Pendragon growled the words and the whole room tensed.

Kearn felt his parents' eyes on him and the strength of their anger in his blood was overwhelming.

He wiped the back of his hand across his lip to clear the blood away and breathed hard. Another one of those and he would probably pass out. It was madness to stand against such a powerful vampire, but he had promised to protect Amber.

He faced the archduke again, standing tall and proud, showing no weakness in the face of his enemy.

"I will not allow her to be touched," he said, even and measured, and resisted his desire to change and release his true nature. Threatening the archduke would only lead to death at either his hands or those of the Pendragon guards.

Archduke Pendragon smiled.

It was thin-lipped and knowing. A smile that set Kearn's nerves on edge.

"Spoken like a man in love," he said and Kearn's heart lodged in his throat. He had thought or felt nothing of the sort but his actions had given away his feelings. "In love with her or her blood?"

The archduke stepped down to the floor and whispers rushed through the room. It was unknown for someone of his rank to lower themselves to be level with a man of Kearn's.

"How many times have you tasted her?" Archduke Pendragon glanced at Amber. Kearn kept the path to her blocked. He could sense her awareness coming back but the connection between them remained closed. Archduke Pendragon's voice dropped to an accusing whisper. "How many times have you wanted to bite her?"

Kearn raised his chin. He would not answer that. It was not for anyone here to know.

"Stand aside, young Savernake." The archduke stood toe to toe with him. He could kill Kearn with a single blow at such a distance but he wouldn't comply. He couldn't.

"I cannot do that, my most honourable lord and master."

"I will not have you stand in my way!" Archduke Pendragon's eyes changed to red and Kearn felt the threat in every cell in his body.

Power shot up Kearn's right arm and he backed off a step and raised it, pointing his palm at the archduke.

"I will not let you pass!" He struggled to calm his desire to unleash Hell on the archduke. It was bad enough threatening him, doing so with a weapon that he could only use in the line of duty was shameful, but he needed to protect Amber, and it was the most powerful weapon in his arsenal.

The air in the room darkened and tensions rose, filling the space with a sense of danger that set him on edge. His senses scattered, monitoring anyone who would be a threat to either him or Amber, including his family.

"Stand aside and lower your weapon," Kearn's father said but he didn't move.

"No." He reached around behind him and caught Amber's arm, pulling her close to his back. His right hand shook with the power surging through it, whispering dark desires to his heart, encouraging him to let go and use it. "Doing so would go against my duty to protect her."

Was he answering his father or the power?

"I mean her no harm." Archduke Pendragon's eyes returned to black and the aura of anger around him faded. "If you are so concerned, bring her to me yourself."

Kearn glanced over his shoulder at Amber. She touched his back. Her eyes said to let it happen and her blood backed them up, telling him it was the only way of stopping things from becoming dangerous to them both. She didn't want to see him hurt. Being able to feel her again soothed his ragged nerves and he relented.

He moved aside, took her arm with his left hand, and then lowered his right. The blue light still shone from it, illuminating his feet. He wouldn't deactivate it until Amber was safely away from the house.

The archduke moved back to the grand gold seat on the platform and sat down. He swept the greying strands of his long dark hair from his face, and motioned for Kearn to approach.

Kearn did so, bringing Amber with him, wary of the archduke and the vampires around him. When he reached the archduke, he bowed his head, feeling lucky that he still had one. If they had been alone, the archduke would have killed him for his insolence. It was only the presence of his family that had saved him.

He looked out of the corner of his eye at his mother. She was staring at Amber with a strange look in her eyes. He couldn't read her at all. She had closed her heart to him.

His father's heart spoke of disappointment but also pride. Why? Because he had defended Amber? He hadn't really done it out of duty. It had been done out of love.

He released Amber's arm and stepped to one side.

Archduke Pendragon leaned back in the chair, his dark gaze appraising Amber from head to toe and back again.

"She is very pure," he said in a thoughtful tone, his eyes not leaving her. "She must tempt you since you have tasted her, young Savernake."

"There is no temptation, my honourable master." Kearn bowed his head again but didn't miss the look the archduke gave him. He wasn't convinced.

Kearn frowned when Archduke Pendragon held his hand out to Amber and she moved towards him. He stepped forwards with her, unwilling to let her out of his reach. She placed her hand into the archduke's and several of the Pendragon vampires rushed forwards. Archduke Pendragon raised his other hand and dismissed them with an impatient wave. They moved back into position but didn't take their red eyes off Amber.

It was not acceptable to have a vampire, let alone a human, touch a vampire of the archduke's standing.

It was not acceptable to Kearn to have any man touch Amber.

Archduke Pendragon raised her hand to his face. He breathed in her scent and his eyes closed. Amber didn't seem frightened but Kearn had lost his connection to her again the moment she had touched the archduke. Was he hiding something? Kearn should have been able to sense him vicariously through Amber's blood in his veins when they had touched. The archduke had blocked it.

"I can see why she needs protection," Archduke Pendragon whispered against her hand and then released it.

Amber stepped back, visibly trembling, her skin drained of colour and hazel eyes wide. Kearn wanted to go to her but it was too obvious. He had already upset everyone. He couldn't do anything else to jeopardise her safety.

Archduke Pendragon stood and regarded him.

"I believe you should take your leave now, young Savernake, and never dare to show me such disrespect again. Next time I will not allow you to live."

Kearn bowed low and pressed his right hand against his chest. It still glowed. He tried to deactivate it but it wouldn't. His desire to protect Amber was so fierce that it remained active, even though he knew he could never bring himself to use it without the blessing of the Sovereignty.

"My sincerest apologies, my most honourable lord and master." Kearn closed his eyes and bowed lower, and then rose and bowed to his family.

His mother looked away, her long tresses of black hair covering her face. She had remained seated again, deeming him unworthy of her respect. He held the hurt inside and turned to Amber, caught her arm and was striding down the corridor between the vampires before another heartbeat had passed.

The tense atmosphere didn't leave when he exited the room. There were vampires from his household in the first reception room too now and in the gallery. They watched him, their intent clear. If he made a wrong move, they would fight him.

He kept Amber close, feeling her shaking and slowly regaining the connection to her. She wrapped her hands around his arm and hurried along beside him. He shouldn't have come. He shouldn't have brought her here. And he shouldn't have dared to threaten Archduke Pendragon. He had only made more enemies tonight and solidified his family's hatred of him. He cursed himself and stepped out of the house and into the waiting night. The scent of it filled his lungs and eased his heart, soothing it and reassuring him that they were safe now in her embrace.

They were halfway between the house and the lodge when Amber finally released his arm. He looked at her. She was pale in the slender light of the moon and her eyes still held fear. She had been afraid to go to the archduke but she had done it anyway, just as she had feared Duke Montagu but had danced with him, all for Kearn's sake. She faced the most terrible vampires for him.

He was surprised she wasn't scared of him too. He had chased her, threatened her, told her that he would turn her against her will, and she still held him close. She had embraced his darkness. Could she embrace his world as easily?

What world was he bringing her into? He would keep her safe though and protect her. He wouldn't allow anyone to touch her, not without his retribution, not even if he regained his standing in society. He would slaughter any who dared.

"He knows something," Amber whispered and he stopped dead, wondering if he had heard her right. She looked at him with large eyes and then back at the house. "That man knows something."

"Archduke Pendragon?" he said and she nodded slowly. "Are you sure?"

She touched her hand. "I felt it."

Kearn had wanted to know why the archduke desired to meet them but had known that he wouldn't be able to sense it without touching him. Amber must have picked up his desire during their brief connection in the reception room. She had sensed it for him when she had touched the archduke.

Archduke Pendragon couldn't have realised that his hold over Amber had slipped for a moment, giving her a chance to feel Kearn's need to know his intent.

Or had he?

It was possible that the archduke had done it on purpose. His father and mother were old enough to sense the connection between him and Amber. Perhaps Archduke Pendragon had severed it to keep them unaware of something.

The something that Amber had mentioned.

Kearn hurried with her to the house, aware of how easily the sound of their conversation would travel to any vampires patrolling the estate grounds. He closed the door behind them and joined her in the living room. The fire was low. Amber placed some more of the split logs onto it and sat in the red armchair she had occupied before.

He sat opposite her and waited.

"I need to know what he knows, Amber," he said when she didn't speak.

She curled up on the armchair and stared into the flames. Their connection relayed her confusion and struggle. It would be difficult for her to discern the archduke's feelings from touch alone. Kearn tried to help her, searching for the man's intent in her blood, but it wouldn't come to him either.

"He said I had very pure blood."

"You do." He had told her this before. Her docile expression worried him. Were the thoughts the archduke had placed in her mind confusing her? It was possible. Someone inexperienced would have difficulty with anything relayed through touch rather than a blood connection.

She blinked slowly.

Kearn leaned forwards and took hold of her hand. "Your blood is precious. It would make whoever drank it incredibly strong and dangerous."

"Like you were?"

"More so." He had only taken traces of her blood and he had felt amazing, indestructible. If he took enough to feel the true effects, he would be powerful enough to defeat even Archduke Pendragon with ease. "That is why I brought you here, remember? So you would be safe while I hunted the man who wants to hurt you."

Her eyes gradually widened. "I can go with you... like bait... partners... remember?"

There was such a distant note in her voice and her eyes. What had the archduke done to her?

"No... not now." He stroked her hand and she looked confused. "I cannot use you like that."

"Why?"

He didn't answer. He stared at the fire, trying to think of a different reason to the one in his heart. Archduke Pendragon had been right. He loved Amber. He loved her so much that he couldn't risk her anymore.

"I've got it!" she said and his head snapped around to face her, a jolt running through his veins at the thought that she had figured him out. She grinned, more like her normal self. "He wants to meet you."

"Sorry?" he said and then realised she was talking about what the archduke had planted in her mind. "When?"

"Tomorrow. He has something." She frowned, pensive and focused, and then her hazel eyes met his. "He has your blood."

Kearn stood and stared towards the door.

Archduke Pendragon had his blood? How had he come across it? Had the man after Amber given it to him? He wanted to go to him right now and ask but couldn't. He had to wait and do as the archduke ordered if he was going to get the vial back and discover what was happening.

Amber came to stand in front of him. Her eyes held his, intent and focused, as though she was trying to read something in them.

The answer to her earlier question?

He would give her it.

He lowered his head to kiss her.
A knock sounded.

CHAPTER 23

It was Kyran at the door. He stepped past Kearn before he could say anything and walked into the lounge, casting his gaze around it in disgust. It was nothing compared with the quarters Kyran had at the main house or even Kearn's apartment, but it was safe and warm, and that was all that mattered to Kearn now. He didn't need modern comforts or even the luxury of furniture. He just needed somewhere safe for Amber.

"They will blacklist you for being here." Kearn closed the front door.

Kyran shrugged and undid the top set of buttons on his stiff formal black jacket. "The old man has always liked me. I'll live."

Kyran smiled at Amber and then settled himself in one of the armchairs. The warm firelight did nothing to brighten Kyran's appearance. It only made his hair and eyes look darker.

"I ordered some food." Kyran ran a hand over the messy threads of his black hair and sighed as he slouched into the armchair.

"You can order that?" Amber's voice was a high squeak. "Like we're just meat?"

Kyran laughed. "No. Food for you."

He reached into his jacket pocket and tossed a blood pack across the room to Kearn. Kearn caught it. His brother was up to something.

"And that's food for him."

"Thank you." Kearn lowered his hand to his side.

"Not hungry? Have you taken that much from her?" Kyran smiled at him but Kearn could see through it. He was bored and had come here to stir trouble.

Kearn stared at him, unflustered. "This isn't a good place for it."

Amber looked at the blood pack.

"She won't mind." Kyran waved a hand her way.

She snapped herself out of whatever trance she had been in and looked at the fire instead.

Kearn dropped the blood pack onto the coffee table. "Later."

He could sense Amber hesitating. She wanted to say something.

Heavy silence filled the room.

"I thought... you really can't bite people?"

Kyran grinned, his fangs slightly extended. "Not anymore. Back in the old days, we could get away with murder. It's harder to cover up now. Besides... Kearn isn't even allowed that freedom. If he kills a human, the Sovereignty would revoke his licence. They would probably toss him into the dark beyond."

Amber gasped. Kearn frowned at his brother, unimpressed by his attempt to frighten her.

"Consensual biting only for our boy." Kyran slumped further down the armchair with a long sigh. "Of course, there are vampires who still kill people, and those bloody Commoners can bite all they fancy."

"Because they can't turn people without giving them blood too," Amber said.

His brother raised a single dark eyebrow at her. "Kearn has been telling you all about our sordid little world, hasn't he?"

Kyran seemed disappointed. Had he wanted to upset Amber and cause a rift between them? Kearn had told her enough that she would be prepared in his world and would know what awaited her when he brought her over.

Amber looked at him. "Have you ever drunk from someone?"

Each of those words fell like lead on his chest and before he could even look at Kyran to tell him not to say a word, he was on his feet and speaking.

"Only another vampire, eh, brother?"

Kearn scowled.

"She was a feisty little thing too… went after you with a vengeance. A real firecracker and one hell of an introduction to the pleasures of mating. What a fiancée to have!"

Amber's face dropped.

A moment later, her expression was flat but she couldn't hide the hurt from Kearn. She smiled, shrugged, and looked as though she might laugh. It didn't lessen her pain. It radiated through him, her blood cursing him, and then the connection between them severed, leaving him cold and alone.

Had she done it?

He tried to speak to her blood again but felt nothing.

Kyran's eyebrows rose. "Have I said something wrong?"

"I need to sleep." Amber hurried past both him and his brother, heading for the kitchen door, her fingertips grazing the bandage around her throat.

Kearn punched Kyran as hard as he could manage, knocking his head to one side and toppling him. He wanted to knock it off.

Kyran rubbed his jaw, picked himself up and glared at him. "What was that for?"

"You know damn well what it was for." Kearn looked up at the ceiling. He could only sense Amber as a human in the building. He could feel nothing from her. He growled at Kyran.

Kyran smiled, dark and vicious. Victorious. "Oops."

There was another knock at the door.

Kyran passed him and went through the entranceway to the front door. He opened it and pushed past the man standing there. The man looked at Kearn.

His brother really had ordered food for Amber.

Kearn dug his wallet out of his pocket. The pizza delivery man took the money and handed him the flat white box. The smell of it turned Kearn's stomach, worsening the ache there.

There was so much pain in his heart that it felt as though it was going to stop. There was so much sorrow. It wasn't only his this time. Amber's feelings were beginning to trickle through to him again and he didn't think he would be able to bear the weight of her emotions if the connection fully reopened.

He dropped the pizza box beside the blood pack on the coffee table and went upstairs to the bedroom where they had slept together. The door was closed. He tried the handle. Locked. He knocked but she didn't answer.

Kearn spread his hand out against the door, feeling her on the other side. He could open the door if he wanted to, but it wasn't his decision to make. She had to allow him back inside, into her life again. In order for that to happen, he had to be honest with her and tell her about his past.

He turned and sat on the dusty wooden floor, his back against the wall, and rested his left elbow on his bent knee and stretched his right leg out. He pressed his foot against the other side of the low-lit hall and sighed.

It would hurt to dredge up memories he wanted to forget but he would bear the pain so she would see that what had happened was far in the past and there was no need for her to be upset.

"Will you listen to me?" He felt foolish for talking to the wall opposite. His senses locked on her, giving him a point of focus, and he felt her move. She didn't come closer. She remained at a distance.

It seemed she wasn't going to speak to him.

He would speak to her then, confess all his sins and hope she would return to him.

"I was young and stupid. My family arranged our engagement at birth. A prosperous marriage to improve relations between two bloodlines. It was all I had been good for back then."

Silence.

He picked at the knee of his trousers and tried to feel her. She was closing to him again.

"Kyran had been due to receive the duty of Venator from our father. I was only required to produce sons that could possibly inherit the duty." It pained him to think of how his life had been. He longed for the past but had never once desired to return to a world where he was married off and expected only to procreate and continue the ruling line. "It was nothing but a marriage of convenience to a house beneath my own... politics and money... more about power than anything else."

He sighed again and pressed the back of his head into the wall behind him. Telling her this made him realise just what an idiot he had been as a youth. He had blindly followed his parents' wishes. He hadn't thought to question them or persuade them to let him live his own life and find his own love, and then it had been too late.

"It was all I was good for and I went along with it."

"What happened?" Amber whispered and he smiled at the sound of her voice and the comfort it gave him.

She sat on the other side of the wall, her back against his, and he liked the feel of her close to him.

"My fiancée was sleeping with Kyran too. I realised that it was not love I had found but lust—a shallow craving for her brought about by her tainted blood. She had made me drink from her the first time we met and every day after that. I had thought the way I had felt was the giddiness of love, but she had been feeding on Source Blood."

Kearn stared at the wall. He still felt betrayed and broken. The countess had sought to enslave him using her blood, keeping him doped enough that he would go along with anything. She had been as beautiful as any of his kind, but only on the outside. Inside she had been wretched, rotten with her desire for power and standing, and willing to bed anyone to achieve it.

Even his own brother.

"How did you know about Kyran?"

He clenched his fists at the memory and took a deep breath.

"I caught them together in the orchard one night, Kyran with her pinned to the largest apple tree and her legs wrapped around him. The sounds of their moans haunted me that night and I soon discovered from some of the servants that it had been happening since her arrival at the house."

"That's terrible," Amber whispered and her blood opened to him again. Only sorrow came through their connection.

"I cannot blame my brother for what happened. It took only a little research to discover that the countess had a reputation amongst servants, and not only those of my bloodline, for scandalous behaviour. She would bed anyone who might give her power... seducing them for it. She had been acting the wanton whore for many years in Europe before her family forced her to uphold her part in our engagement and come to me."

Something in Amber's blood spoke to him, relaying the things that she couldn't say. She didn't understand why he couldn't bring himself to blame his brother for his part in what happened. It was the one area where Kearn was stronger than his brother was. Kyran had a weakness for women. The slightest smile from a beauty and he would pursue them with the intent of bedding them. It was his Achilles' heel and the countess had used her knowledge of it well in her quest for power. Kearn still wasn't sure whether she had intended to marry him and continue sleeping with his brother, or whether she had intended to swap them and marry Kyran instead. There was more honour in marrying a Venator, and more power came from it. It made sense that she had planned to marry Kyran and had only remained engaged to him as a fall back in case things didn't work out.

"What did you do?" Amber moved on the other side of the wall, turning towards him.

"I was a mess. I wandered into the woods one night looking for something... pain, something to kill, some way of undoing what had happened, an end perhaps... what I found was a new beginning." Kearn turned his head to one side, trying to get closer to Amber. He wanted to feel her arms around him and hear her say that they were going to be alright. He wanted her to love him. "The Sovereignty took me. They told me to have my vengeance by their decree."

"And you did?"

"And I did." He sighed. At the time, he hadn't realised that they had been testing him. "I came back to the house and I used the power they had given me to kill her. It was terrifying to feel the hideous power of the Sovereignty flowing through me and into her, sucking the life out of her and taking her soul to the eternal darkness. I could feel everything that she did... I was connected to her through the power... and I realised that she had been with child."

"Was it yours?"

Her blood demanded an answer.

"No."

"Kyran's."

"Yes." He paused. "I never told him. The Sovereignty brought me back to their world and announced that Kyran had committed unforgivable sin and would not become a Venator. He was forfeit and his blood impure. I tried to argue. I'd had my revenge and wanted nothing else. I was sick to my stomach from experiencing killing with the power and in no fit state to do what they were asking of me. I wanted nothing more to do with them. It made no difference."

He could still see the grey stone hall and everything that had happened that night. He had returned to the Sovereignty, bloodied from his first kill, pained by what he had done to the woman and what she had done to him. He had expected them to take away the markings on his arm and they had refused. He had argued so violently, threatened them, tried to hurt them, but nothing he had done had changed their minds.

"They made the marks on my arm permanent, changed my appearance so I would be recognised as a hunter of theirs, and pronounced me Venator of house Savernake. I returned to my family to find them gathered in the grand reception room. Kyran, mother and my father were there." He could picture it clearly—the door ajar, his father's proud expression as he addressed Kyran, and his mother's smile. He had shattered the happy scene. "My father told Kyran that his duties had ended. I walked in at that moment, wanting to explain."

Shock had rippled across their faces and they had stared at him, Kyran most of all. The pain had been clear in both his eyes and his blood. That night Kearn had cursed the strength of their familial bond. He hadn't wanted to see the pain he had caused let alone feel it. He had been desperate tell Kyran that he would fix everything with the Sovereignty. Kyran had only ever spoken of becoming a Venator. It had been his dream.

"Kearn?" Amber's soft voice drifted through the wall, through his blood, her concern overwhelming.

"Kyran tried to kill me before I could utter a word. Our father separated us and when I explained what had happened, Kyran was cast out, disgraced."

"But he's back now."

"Since I killed my aunt... Kyran has become mother's favourite... welcomed back to stop my mother from descending into madness. She begged my father."

"And instead you took his place." Amber opened the door and he looked at her. She knelt in front of him, her hazel eyes reflecting the worry and sorrow that he could feel in her blood. What a beautiful creature she was to look at him like that after everything he had done. She cast her gaze downwards to her knees. "Did you love her?"

Kearn reached over and stroked her cheek, bringing his fingers slowly down to her chin. He tilted it up so she would see the truth in his eyes and feel it in his blood.

"Not love," he whispered, fascinated by the shyness in her eyes. "Not like I feel for you."

Amber's arms were around him in an instant, her lips against his. She kissed him softly enough that his heart expanded and beat harder, filled with warmth and happiness. He rose with her and gathered her into his arms, his mouth moving against hers, taking all of her into him. He wanted to devour her. He wanted all of her forever.

She moaned quietly, driving him on, and he parted her lips with his tongue. Hers came to meet it, tangling gently and stirring his blood until his need for her filled every inch of him, every cell in his body screaming out for her. A soft gasp escaped her when he scooped her up and carried her into the bedroom. His body hardened at the sound and the thought of being inside her again. He would be gentler with her this time. His desperation had passed and her consent to be his had assuaged his hunger to bite her.

Now he could control himself and make love to her as he had wanted to their first time.

CHAPTER 24

Amber was beautiful beneath him, stripped bare and laying on the bed with her long dark hair fanned out across the pillow. Kearn ran his fingers lazily down her side, considering where to start. The bottom up. He wanted to be starving for her kiss by the time he reached her mouth.

He moved to her feet and stroked the arch of her left foot. Her soft laugh was music to his ears. He smiled, raised her foot and kissed it and then her ankle. He slid his hands up her leg to her calf and glanced down at the apex of her thighs. Dark curls hid heaven from view. Just the memory of how hot and tight she had been had his hard length bobbing for more. He groaned and dragged his eyes away. He would never reach her lips if he kept looking there.

Amber sighed when he kissed along her slender calf and then her thigh, careful to feel and taste every inch of her. She had strong legs. He grimaced at the recollection of their first meeting and how his groin had been on the receiving end of her knee. He kissed the knee in question and continued upwards, playfully nipping her hip with his blunt teeth.

Hunger surged through him and he did it again, harder this time. Amber's low moan sent a shiver through him and his eyes switched to crimson, his senses and vision sharpening. He pulled away the moment his fangs extended, kneeling between her spread thighs and breathing hard to regain control.

"What is it?" Tenderness shone in her eyes. She smiled and reached out to him. His heart melted. She was reaching to him even when his eyes were red and his fangs sharp. He had never met such a beautiful woman.

He abandoned his desire to kiss her all over and lay on top of her, seeking her warmth. She gently wrapped her arms around him and he rested his head against her breasts. Her heart beat steadily against his ear.

His heart.

Her blood called to him and his heart obeyed, coming to meet hers, until they were beating together. It was dizzying to experience such a fast beat but he wanted to be one with her completely. He wanted them to be forever as one.

"Kearn?" she whispered and he murmured his reply. He grazed her stomach with his fingertips and then placed his hand over her right breast. He thumbed her nipple, feeling incredibly content lying naked in her arms. "If you want to…"

Her heart gave a harder beat against his ear.

He pushed himself up onto his right elbow.

Scarlet touched her cheeks.

She didn't have to finish her sentence. Her blood whispered it to him. He refused to let his gaze fall to her neck. He wouldn't bite her. Not yet. His fangs receded and his eyes changed back to green. He felt a spark of hurt in her but it disappeared when he smiled.

"Not now." He leaned over and claimed her lips with his. Perhaps he would explore her from the top down instead. He poured his feelings into the kiss and allowed her to sense them in his blood. Love, happiness, contentment, possession, desire and awe at what she had offered him. He showed it all to her so she would know what it meant to him. He would take it one day, but not today.

He had only changed because he had bitten her too hard with his blunt teeth. He wouldn't make that mistake again and risk her. When he bit her, it would be special, the start of their new life together. Her new life. He would make it a moment she would want to remember forever.

Amber kissed him deeper and took control. Her hands skimmed down his back, warm on his skin, and she brought her leg up, her knee caressing his hip. Awareness of where his hips were spread through him.

A shallow thrust of them elicited a delightful moan from her, breathed into his mouth. He did it again.

"Kearn," she uttered against his lips and he felt every ounce of her need in his name. He would satisfy her hunger in time. For now, he wanted to drown in her sweet lips and her soft caress.

Her hands roamed up his back and then down his arms, curling around his biceps. She brought his hand to her breasts and moulded it over her right. He took the hint and broke away from her lips to worship it. She groaned and arched when he sucked her right nipple into a hard peak. His tongue flicked the bead and her fingers threaded into his hair, clutching him against her.

He denied her, moving downwards, kissing the subtle planes of her stomach. Her fingers left his hair and he looked up to see her grasping the pillows. Her teeth teased her lower lip. The sight of it made him growl with the urge for her blood. She didn't release her lip as he had expected. Her teeth remained firmly planted in it. His vision sharpened and her pupils dilated, her eyes darkening with hunger.

Did the sight of his red eyes arouse her? What fantasy was she living out in her mind? He tried to tell from her blood but it only whispered to go on, to do what he wanted with her.

Kearn did so without changing his eyes back. The sight of them aroused her and he wanted her to scream his name when she climaxed. If touching her when he was half in his vampire guise would make it more pleasurable for her, he would remain like it.

He skimmed his hands over her thighs and spread her legs. His eyes met hers again and her cheeks blazed. Her blush sent a pulse of desire shooting down to his groin and he groaned, his hard length straining for contact with her. He wanted to fill her up and take out his growing hunger on her body, ravaging it.

Instead, he lowered himself to her and kissed the neat triangle of curly hair, working his way downwards. He slipped his fingers in and opened her to him. The heat of her arousal and her sweet scent tore another groan from him and he swept his tongue over her, hungrily devouring her. It wasn't enough. He wanted more of her than this. All of her.

He flicked his tongue over her pert nub, loving the way she gasped with each contact. Her fingers tangled in his hair again, grasping it tightly and holding him to her. He wasn't going anywhere. He licked her, mercilessly teasing her body, and she moaned his name. He needed more. He slid his hand down and growled when he slipped his middle finger into her warm core and pumped slowly. She was so wet. He ached to replace his finger with his cock. She tensed around him and he barely held it together. He thrust harder, inserting a second finger, and groaned at how tight she was around them.

Kearn devoured her. He tasted every inch of her, suckling and becoming rougher as his hunger to be inside her built. She bucked her hips, riding his fingers. His erection throbbed each time they slid into her. Her moans filled the room, urging him on, and she tugged his hair.

She stiffened, her hips rising off the bed, and then jerked with a loud cry of his name as she climaxed. Her warm body pulsed around his fingers and he shuddered at the delicious feeling.

Amber released his hair, relaxed into the bed, and stretched out. Her contentment ran in his veins, causing his own need to abate. He watched her, smiled, and enjoyed the sight of her so thoroughly satisfied. He would make her like this forever. Every day he would send her into a deep sleep after making love to her for hours. He would never tire of it.

He crawled up the length of her and her hazel eyes opened. They shone with happiness. He smiled again when she stroked his cheek, his brow and then his lips. The touch spoke volumes, all of it about love.

Kearn eased back, took hold of his erection, and positioned it. He slid slowly into her, joining their bodies peacefully this time, and she sighed. Her arms encircled his neck and she brought his head down. She kissed him as he moved deep within her at a gentle pace, and her feelings spread through him. Her blood conveyed everything she felt as his communicated back to her, joining them completely until they were both feeling the same thing. Bliss. Happiness. Love.

He had never felt so content and as though he belonged anywhere as much as he felt he belonged there, inside her, alone with her, as one.

He kissed her softly, revering her and the emotions she evoked within him. With each thrust of his body into hers, he told her through his blood that he loved her.

Amber moaned and he felt the change in her blood, felt her respond to him as her hand grazed his face, her emotions those of tenderness and deep affection. She loved him too. She wanted to be with him forever.

He closed his eyes and held her close to him, until their skin stuck together with the heat of their lovemaking and his heart felt as though it couldn't take any more and would burst with their combined feelings. He moved deeper inside her, capturing her moans with his lips, savouring the sound of each one.

Her body tightened and her blood begged him to make her climax again and to find release within her. He gritted his teeth and pressed his cheek to hers, struggling to control his hunger to thrust harder so he could bring her to a sweet climax, one full of love.

Amber moaned into his ear, uttering his name in a way that drew a groan from him. Her heart beat in time with his, slow and steady. Soon it would always beat as his did. Soon he would have her completely. She would be always his. Forever. Eternally. His Amber.

She bucked up against him and arched into his chest, moaning her release. Her body pulsed around his, luring him to his own climax. He plunged deeper, harder now, his body tight and ready, and his desire pushing him onwards. Close.

Amber kissed his shoulder, his neck, teased him until he was on the brink of insanity and surrendering to his desire to take her roughly. He needed to come. It felt as though he was going to explode.

She saw to it that he did. Her lips brushed his shoulder and then she bit gently.

Kearn's eyes shot wide and he jerked hard inside her, his length throbbing with his release, spilling his seed into her waiting body. He trembled and collapsed against her, aware of the point where her teeth still pressed into his flesh.

She had bitten him.

He breathed hard against her throat. The smell of her blood wafted back at him. His fangs extended.

He had seen her as a vampire above him, moving on his hard length, her head thrown back in pleasure. She had leaned over him, her teeth sharp, and he had bared his neck to her because it was forever hers and hers alone. She had sunk her fangs into him and he had experienced his first bite.

"Kearn?" She stroked his back in slow gentle circles as though seeking to soothe him.

His blood was rampant, speaking words to her that were probably frightening. He wanted her to sink her fangs into his throat so he could wear her marks and everyone would see that they were together, eternally bonded, exclusively each other's.

"You okay?"

He stared at her neck and the bandage on it. He wanted to taste her.

Her fingers appeared in view. She untied the bandage and pulled it down. His gaze shifted to the cut on her neck. His neck. His and his alone. He would heal it for her and look after her forever so she would never be hurt again.

"You can if you want to," she whispered and her blood backed up her words. She wasn't trembling because she was scared. She trembled out of desire. She wanted him to take her blood again.

He wouldn't bite her though.

He would only calm his hunger and strengthen the bond between them.

Kearn retracted his fangs, closed his eyes and licked the length of the cut. She hissed out her pleasure and he licked it again. It was still bleeding in spots. He covered it with his mouth and sucked to reopen the wound. Amber held him closer, one hand against his back and the other on the nape of his neck. She cradled him to her, giving herself to him, body and soul, and he felt awed.

Honoured.

He held his fangs at bay and sucked harder, until blood trickled into his mouth, sending his mind swimming and reigniting his lust. He held that in too, unwilling to become a slave to his desires when under the influence of her blood. He would never do that. They would only ever be together because of their feelings, not because he was drunk on her blood. He drank deep, satisfying his need for her. The connection grew stronger, until he easily felt her emotions and her heart beat in his veins. They hadn't gone this deep before. Would it frighten her? She would feel everything he did and his heart beating within her. She would know him wholly. He wouldn't be able to hide anything from her.

Her mind would be open to him.

And his would finally be open to hers.

With this much of her blood in him, he wouldn't be able to deny her or close the connection, not until it began to fade again.

He stopped drinking and licked the cut, cleaning every drop of blood off her neck and sealing the wound.

Amber held him as she had done the night he had told her that he would bite her, embracing him and accepting him without words. He kissed her throat and reaffixed the bandage, and then leaned his head on her shoulder, fatigue washing through him. He could sleep like this forever with her—his body half on hers, naked against each other, content.

She placed a kiss on the tip of his nose with the corner of her mouth, sighed and rubbed it. She was tired too. He listened to her blood and drifted away with it into a deep sleep.

When he woke, he would meet with Archduke Pendragon and discover what he knew about the vial and the man he was after.

Until then, he would rest soundly in the arms of his woman for the first time, safe from the world and content at last with his duty and life.

CHAPTER 25

"Wake up, Amber."

The voice drifted into her mind through pleasant dreams, shaking her from sleep. She frowned and rolled over. She didn't want to wake up. It felt so nice under the covers, warm and relaxing, and the dream was so good that she wanted to catch it and bring it back.

"Amber." Someone shook her.

Her eyes fluttered open. Kearn stood over her, dressed in his black shirt and trousers, with his hair wet as though he had showered.

"What is it?" She rolled over again.

"We have to leave." Kearn caught her arm and pulled her into a sitting position.

There was worry in his green eyes.

"Has something happened?"

"We are not safe here." He pulled her out of the bed and shoved her clothes at her. "Get dressed."

She frowned when he left the room, rubbed the sleep from her eyes and tried to figure out what was going on. Had something happened with the archduke? The curtains were open and it was night outside. She threw on her jeans and hooded top, zipping it up over her chest, and then put on her shoes.

Kearn came back in, his holster around his shoulders now and the gun in his hand. The marks on his right arm weren't glowing. The man couldn't have come for her. Kearn would have been using his power if he had.

"Did something happen with the archduke?" she said and Kearn didn't reply.

He took hold of her hand and led her down through the house to the door. He held it open for her and she walked out into the night. It was pitch-black save the single light emanating from the door behind her and the distant house. She went to go to Audi and Kearn grabbed her arm, tugging her right instead.

There was another car there. A large black Bentley with a dark haired female driver.

"Why aren't we taking the Audi?"

Kearn opened the rear door of the Bentley for her and held it. She stopped and looked back at the Audi. It seemed strange that he was leaving it behind.

"Where are we going?" She looked up into his eyes. They were dark, emotionless except a spark of anger that she couldn't feel in him.

In fact, she couldn't feel anything in him.

He had taken her blood last night and the connection between them had run so deeply that she had been aware of him as though he was a part of herself. Now she couldn't feel anything. Had he shut her out again?

She walked forwards and went to get into the car, and then straightened again and looked at him. Something wasn't right.

"Where are we going?" She wanted an answer this time.

"Get in the car."

"Tell me where we're going."

His jaw tensed.

Amber's mind felt heavy. It spun and twirled, sending her vision out of focus, and she closed her eyes. A deep throb pulsed through her and then cold darkness swallowed her.

Her head was splitting when it receded and the world slowly came back. Sound came first, trickling in through her thick mind, and then she managed to open her bleary eyes and the haze in her head cleared enough for her to take things in, only there wasn't much to see.

A dark room.

Was she back in the lodge?

She tried to sit up but her head spun and she collapsed back again. She fumbled around in the dark. Soft padding cushioned her back and her right side, and formed a pillow beneath her head. Her left leg dangled over the side. She touched the top, fingers tracing the elaborate carving there.

A sofa?

She hadn't seen one in the lodge.

She sat up more slowly this time, clutching the back of the couch to steady herself.

Was she in the main house?

Her head throbbed and she closed her eyes. She touched her temples, feeling her blood pounding through them, and held it together. She didn't want to pass out again.

Amber tried to think back to what had happened.

She had been going somewhere with Kearn. He wouldn't tell her where. He had looked angry and then she had felt incredibly tired and sick.

Had he hit her?

It was a ridiculous thought. Kearn would never do such a thing and she hadn't seen him move. All he had done was look at her.

Maybe he had used his powers to knock her out.

She frowned in the darkness. Maybe everything was getting to her. She had felt sleepy last night after making love with him, so bone deep tired that she had slept through to tonight. Kearn hadn't even woken her when he had left the bed.

Bright light flared into life, chasing back the darkness, and she squinted against it.

"How are you feeling?"

Kearn.

It was good to hear his voice. She tried to look at him but her head hurt and the light was too bright for her eyes.

"I've been better." She squinted until her eyes adjusted and then looked around the room. She didn't recognise it, but it definitely wasn't the lodge. The room was large and stately, with antique gilt-framed furniture and old oil paintings hanging on the deep green walls. She cast her gaze around, scanning over the Chinese rug covering most of the dark wooden floor, and the beautiful inlays on the black cabinets. Kearn stood to her left, a closed mahogany door as his backdrop. Was she somewhere in the main house?

Her eyes settled on Kearn when he moved towards her. He was shirtless, his toned muscles shifting deliciously with each step, and his hair was damp again. He knelt in front of her, concern bright in his green eyes, and placed his hands over hers, bringing them away from her temples.

"Let me see," he said and searched her eyes, and then checked her over, touching around the side of her head and running his fingers through her hair. "You had me worried."

She wished she could feel that emotion in him as well as see it in his eyes.

"What happened?" She struggled against the pain throbbing in her skull.

"I am not sure, but I believe it might be related to the stress you underwent when meeting the archduke. It must have been difficult for you to cope with him communicating with you through touch alone." He sighed and held her hand, and warmth travelled up her arm and into her heart. His smile soothed some of her hurt, chasing away the darkness inside her, and she nodded. It made sense. She had felt strange and out of sorts after meeting the archduke. Her head and body hadn't felt as though they were her own, and some of her memories of meeting him were still tangled into tight knots that were impossible to undo. Kearn squeezed her hand. "You are feeling better though?"

"A little," she said and his smile widened. There was relief in his eyes but she couldn't feel it in him.

Amber focused on him and closed her eyes, trying to sense his feelings. Nothing came to her. He was a void before her. Why had he shut her out? He had been so open with her, and she had felt as though he loved her too, but now he had closed himself off again. Had she done something wrong?

She wanted to ask him whether his feelings had changed, but she was afraid of the answer. She had begun to believe in his fairytale of undying love and being with him forever. He had said that he would cherish her and treat her like a queen when he made her into a vampire. Right now, she felt as though he would treat her as those women at the ball had been by their men.

"What happened back at the house?" She opened her eyes and searched his.

"We had to leave." Annoyance laced his voice.

Was it because they had left the safety of his family's estate or something else? She studied his eyes, trying to decipher the truth and his feelings from them. They were cold now, as emotionless as they had been when they had first met. She hadn't seen them like that in a long time.

She started when his fingers brushed her cheek. They were warm against her and she was tempted to lean into his touch because she was cold. Only his warmth could chase away the chill in her heart.

"The Pendragons turned against us." The look in his eyes when hers leapt to them said that he had been shocked too. She caught a glimmer of his anger. "The archduke is in league with the man we are after. That is why he had my blood."

She believed him. When she had met the archduke, she had felt his power and had been afraid. She hadn't wanted Kearn to go alone to see him and had meant to tell him that she wanted to go with him, but it had slipped her mind last night and then he had gone while she had been asleep.

"Your neck is bleeding again."

Amber felt his eyes on it, burning through the crepe bandage. She sensed his intent and his desire. He wanted her blood.

Before she could utter a word, he was removing the bandage. His hands skimmed her throat, sending shivers tripping over her skin and building the anticipation inside her. It didn't frighten her when he drank from her. She knew in her heart that he couldn't help his hunger for her and that it wasn't only her blood that evoked such a strong response in him. It was his feelings too. He needed her.

His cheek warmed hers and he held her waist and drew her closer to him, until her bottom was resting on the edge of the sofa and he was between her thighs. He breathed in deep and then sighed.

"You smell divine," he murmured against her neck and heat flashed through her.

He kissed her throat and her eyes slipped shut. His tongue traced a line over the wound and it stung but the pleasure eclipsed the pain. He was gentle with her, softly licking her throat. It was nice to have him being so tender. It made her feel that he did love her after all.

He sighed again. "We need to be ready for the man. He will come soon, I am sure of it."

She barely heard the words. He uttered them quietly on her throat, his breath tickling and teasing her.

"You must give me enough blood for me to feel the true effects so I can be strong enough to protect you."

Those words frightened her a little. How much blood was he talking about? He had taken quite a lot in the past and hadn't shown the effects that he had told her about. It hadn't made him invincible and stronger than anyone. The archduke had felt ten times more powerful than Kearn ever had to her.

She nodded anyway and swallowed her trembling heart. She had to do this for him. She needed him to defeat the man so they could be together.

Kearn's lips closed around the cut and he sucked. It hurt at first and she felt lightheaded. She had never felt so conscious of her blood leaving her before.

He was sucking hard, his fingers closed tightly over her ribs, squeezing as though he wouldn't let her escape.

She clutched his biceps when her neck hurt again, fiercer now, and squeezed her eyes shut. How much blood was he taking? The sound of his suckling turned her stomach. She wanted to push him away but he needed her blood and she had offered it. She had to give him the advantage over the man so he would survive the fight.

Her heart missed a beat. Her head spun and her grip on Kearn slipped, her hands falling to her lap. She was too tired to hold him now. Would he ever stop drinking? Every inch of her felt drained, as though he was sucking the life out of her.

His tongue traced her throat, sparking her arousal. He murmured quiet words against her skin about the sweetness of her blood and how he loved the taste of her. Desire chased away her fatigue but couldn't erase it completely. Not even the feel of him sealing the cut could bring life back into her veins.

The connection between them reopened and she was glad to feel him at last, and to feel his hunger for her and his desire to protect her and keep her safe. He wanted her to be his, and she wanted nothing more. She wanted to give herself to him so his loneliness would end. She would be with him always.

"I want to bite you," he whispered in her ear, low and sultry, his hot breath tickling her. "I want to make you mine. Do you want that too?"

Amber closed her eyes. "I want to be yours."

"Soon." He pressed a kiss to her throat and she trembled. "I will not let anything happen to you. You are mine now."

Amber smiled and ran her hands up his back and into his hair.

She froze. Long lengths were under her fingertips, tied in a ponytail. Kearn's hair wasn't long enough to tie back. She pushed him away and her eyes widened, terror gripping her heart when she saw his face.

"You." Her voice quivered and her heart thudded hard against her ribs, making her dizzy.

He grinned, revealing fangs.

It wasn't Kearn.

It was the man who wanted her blood.

He had been Kearn a moment ago. She hadn't been dreaming it. He had worn Kearn's face and had Kearn's voice. He had felt love towards her.

Amber panicked.

She lashed out, slapping him hard across the face, and quickly brought her feet up and kicked him off her. He fell backwards, landing on the Chinese rug, and she scrambled towards the back of the sofa. He caught her ankle before she could clamber over it and dragged her towards him.

Her chin hit the wooden frame and her skull ached, sending deep throbbing waves through her body. Amber kicked him in the chest. When he stumbled away from her, she broke for freedom again. It was no use. He lunged at her, knocking both her and the couch over backwards.

She landed awkwardly with it, her legs in the air and her back on the floor. He was on top of her in an instant, painfully twisting her arms and pinning her wrists to the floor.

"You shouldn't fight me," he whispered with a smile, his red eyes burning into hers and his bloodied fangs showing between his lips as he spoke. She shook at the sight of them. He had been at her throat and could have bitten her and drained her dry. As it was, he had taken enough blood that she was close to collapse. But he had been Kearn then. She was sure of it. He lowered his face to hers and his smile widened. "You're mine now. You said you were."

Amber struggled against him but it was no use. "I'll never be yours. I'm Kearn's."

The man laughed. "The Venator?"

His grip on her wrists tightened and she cried out when it felt as though her bones would break.

"He won't give you what you need." The man smiled slyly. She wasn't going to believe him. He was just trying to hurt her and make her his. Well, it wasn't going to happen. She believed everything Kearn had said to her. "The Venator wants nothing to do with you... a human... a Noble vampire could never feel anything for a human."

She wouldn't believe that. Kearn felt something for her. It wasn't an act just so she would become a vampire. She had felt it in his blood. He wasn't like the other vampires. He loved her and he wanted to be with her. That was why he wanted to turn her. It was because he needed her, and he couldn't live without her.

"How would you know?" she whispered, feeling defiant.

The man grinned. "Because I am one."

Amber fought him again. He pinned her arms so she kneed him in the groin. He growled and struck her hard, sending her head spinning, her brain rattling around it from the force of the blow. It took her a moment to get her vision back.

"The Venator thinks only of duty. His duty to defeat me, and his duty to strengthen his bloodline. He told you his past, yes? His only point in life was to increase the numbers of his family. Why else would he want to make you a vampire?"

"Because he loves me."

The sight of his fangs when he laughed unnerved her. He could have bitten her and she would have believed that it was Kearn. She wouldn't have known until it was too late.

"Loves you?" His expression turned deadly serious. "His only feeling towards you is lust... lust caused by your blood."

Amber grimaced when he yanked her hands above her head and pinned them with one of his. He lowered his free hand, skimming it down her arm, and settled it over her right breast for a moment before moving it to rest over her heart.

"Pitter patter... pitter patter... is it fear or thoughts of the Venator that stirs you so?" His red gaze fell to his hand and his look turned to fascination. "It makes beautiful music. Just as it did the night we danced. You wanted to be in my arms then... and you wanted it again tonight. You want me."

"I want Kearn." She glared at him. "You disgust me."

His eyes darkened and then he smiled again, cruel this time, his lips compressed into a thin line.

"Your body wasn't saying that a moment ago."

"You were Kearn then... I swear... I don't know how the hell you did it, but you looked like him."

She glanced around, trying to find a way to escape. There was only the one door. Could she reach it before he caught her? Could she even get him off her? His grip on her wrists was so tight that she wanted to cry. Her gaze met his again and, for a moment, he was Kearn.

She couldn't bring herself to believe that he could change his appearance and look like Kearn. It seemed incredible even when she had witnessed it with her own eyes. Did her blood give him this power, or was this something the man had always been able to do? He had looked precisely like Kearn, had even sounded and felt like him. It must have been easy for him to get onto the Savernake estate and kidnap her. He had fooled her.

How long had he looked like him?

Her heart pounded at the memory of last night and making love to Kearn. She was sure that he had been the real one. The man must have used Kearn going out to meet the archduke as his opportunity to seize her, which meant he had known about it.

Had the man been waiting for this opportunity to capture her?

Had he orchestrated the whole thing?

Amber stared into his vivid red eyes and fear gripped her heart, squeezing it tight in her chest. Just what did he have planned? He had been toying with them from the moment she had met Kearn. The false lead at the club, the ball, the attack on the apartment so he could take Kearn's blood from the other Venator. It had all been part of the man's plan and Kearn had done exactly what he had wanted.

She willed her heart to slow. Hunger rose within her, a thirst for blood so strong that it sickened her. The man's feelings. They were all dark now, black thoughts that chilled her. He wanted her blood, but more than that, he wanted Kearn. Why? She had to find out.

She tried to read his blood but the connection severed.

"Now now," the man said with another broad smile. "If you really want to know what will happen to the Venator, and in turn yourself, you only have to ask, Lover."

She shivered at the use of that word. She wasn't going to become this man's lover.

Her mind reasoned that he had her blood and she was weak. If he sought to control her, she wouldn't have any choice in the matter. She was his slave now. The vision of her bound and bleeding flashed across her mind. It would be as Kearn had said. He would drain her until she was close to death and then control her to make her eat and rest, so he could bleed her again.

Unless Kearn could save her.

Her blood reached out to him but she couldn't feel him. Was it distance stopping her or something else? The man smiled cruelly, darkness in his eyes. He was stopping her, using her blood to close the connection to Kearn. Kearn would sense the loss of connection and return to the lodge and discover her gone. He would search for her. Wouldn't he?

"You want him to come here." She held the man's red gaze and realised that Kearn was about to do exactly as he had planned again.

"I want to make him pay for the things that he's done." He slid his hand over her chest to her neck and wrapped his fingers around it.

"Why?" She squeezed the word out, her throat tight at the thought of him hurting her.

"I will make the whole of the Savernake family pay... I will tear them down and end Kearn's line." His gaze was distant, fixed on her throat and his fingers.

Amber frowned. "What has he ever done to you?"

The man's hand shook and she sensed something in him. Anger. Bitterness. An evil so dark that she severed the connection herself, afraid of it.

"He took my future from me, and I will take his from him... starting with you." His cold tone rang with the hatred she had felt in him.

Amber's eyes widened and she didn't want to believe what had dawned on her. Kearn had taken this man's future. It couldn't be. It just couldn't. It would break Kearn and his suffering would be eternal, just as he felt it should be, if he discovered the true identity of the man he had been chasing for three years.

The man he had to kill.

She shook her head. It would destroy him.

"Kyran," she whispered, her voice full of the shock and dismay in her heart.

His image changed, his red eyes fading into blue and his long black hair shortening into soft spikes that swept across this forehead. She stared up at Kyran, unable to believe what she was seeing. His jaw tensed.

"Now you've gone and done it, Lover."

There was a dull pulse deep in her mind and the world disappeared.

CHAPTER 26

Archduke Pendragon handed the vial to Kearn, his face a mask of darkness. "The man who gave me this seemed quite intent on selling the blood it contained."

Kearn uncapped it and drew a deep breath. It was definitely his blood. He could smell Amber's in it.

"I refused his offer, of course." Archduke Pendragon reclined in the gilt chair in the grand reception room. He crossed his legs and his look hardened as he stared at the blood in Kearn's hand.

The room was empty save Kearn and the archduke, although guards waited in the first reception room beyond the closed doors. Whatever the archduke was going to tell him, he didn't want their families finding out.

"What did he want?" Kearn lowered the blood to his side. The glass was warm under his fingers and the scent of Amber lingered in the air. He wanted to be back with her at the lodge, wrapped in her arms and making love to her again. His precious Amber. Soon he would bring her into his world and make her his without a doubt. She would wear his marks and be with him forever.

"He desired my strength and wished to gain me as an ally." Archduke Pendragon stood and walked down the steps of the wide stage to come level with Kearn. There was worry in his eyes but Kearn couldn't sense his feelings.

In fact, he couldn't sense anyone's. Even Amber's were gone from his blood.

That unnerved him, increasing his desire to return to her a hundredfold. Perhaps it was the distance making it difficult to sense her or she was in a deep sleep. Perhaps the man had come and captured her.

His heart beat hard at that thought. No. The man wouldn't have made it through the gates. The security around the estate was tight, with regular patrols day and night. There was no way he could pass through undetected. The only people allowed into the grounds were those of the Savernake line, expected visitors, or human delivery people.

Amber would be safe enough at the lodge.

"When I refused, he became violent. He threatened me."

"Threatened you?" Kearn said.

Archduke Pendragon glared at the blood in Kearn's hand. "He said that he would end the Pendragon line and his house would take their place and rule."

"What house?" Kearn clutched the vial, eager to hear if the archduke knew. Archduke Pendragon was old and powerful enough to know the rarer Noble houses. Perhaps the man was from one of them, or from overseas, and that was why Kearn didn't know him.

The archduke looked troubled. "The man was hiding his true identity."

"He was wearing a mask?" The female Venator had said the same thing. The man had worn a mask over his eyes when he had attacked her.

Archduke Pendragon shook his head. "Not a mask as we wear at balls, young Venator. He wore the mask of illusion, and it was powerful."

"Illusion," Kearn breathed, surprised to hear him say it. It was a rare ability, often only appearing once every ten generations. He had never met a vampire who possessed it.

"Yes, a very potent power that only a few bloodlines have mastered." The troubled look in the archduke's eyes increased. Kearn felt his reluctance. It was frightening to be able to sense something in the archduke. The feeling would have to be strong enough that his age couldn't deny those around him the ability to detect it.

"Which bloodlines?"

"Pendragon, Montagu and... Savernake."

Kearn took a step back and his senses reached out through the building, searching for a sign of the man. He had never heard of a Savernake possessing the ability to cast illusions.

"I sense dark times ahead, young Venator, if the man cannot be stopped." Archduke Pendragon placed his hand on Kearn's shoulder. It was heavy and Kearn felt the weight of his words on his heart. It was his responsibility to stop the man and he would do just that. "My refusal angered him greatly. He will seek to harm my bloodline and I fear that with such strong Source Blood as the female possesses, even I will be no match for him."

A shiver danced down Kearn's spine.

The archduke was right. If the man had enough of Amber's blood, he would become a living god. No one would be able to stop him. He would destroy the Pendragon bloodline.

But how was Kearn supposed to find him? His enemy had the power of illusion. He could mask his appearance and it had to be the reason why the Sovereignty had been unable to determine who he was all this time. They couldn't see through the illusion either.

Kearn thought of the people he had met. Any one of them could have been the man and he wouldn't have known it. Just how many times had they come close to him? His illusion could be constant to some. He could always look different to the Sovereignty or certain people. It was a powerful technique indeed, but Kearn wasn't about to let him take Amber.

"Return to the Pendragon estate and fortify it. I will try to get word to the other Venators and will join you there shortly," Kearn said.

The man had given him a location and he wasn't going to disappoint him. He was sure that together they could defeat him. Not even a god could stand against the combined strength of Pendragon and the Venators.

He turned and left the reception room, striding down the gallery towards the main entrance. He had to get Amber and then get word to the Sovereignty about what they were up against.

His arm burned and pain rolled up it, engulfing it from fingertip to shoulder. His fingers tensed and the vial smashed, the broken glass cutting into his right hand. Each wound closed instantly, erased by the power of the Sovereignty. He gripped his arm close to his chest and gritted his teeth against the pain.

Not now.

He had to get to Amber first.

Kearn took a step forwards and the world became cold around him. He cursed the sight of the long dark grey hall and its massive stone arches, and strode towards the brightly lit altar, determined to get the Sovereignty to send him back to the estate straight away so he could make sure that Amber was safe.

"We have a problem." He halted in front of the crescent moon shaped pool that curved around the steps where the nine white-clad Sovereigns stood.

"A problem indeed," the one in the middle said and indicated the black pool.

Kearn saw Amber with himself in it. He was kneeling in front of her while she sat on a dark couch, her face pale. He touched her cheek and affection shone in her eyes. That never happened.

He looked at the Sovereigns as it hit him.

The man had her.

"The human female has at last identified the man you seek." The Sovereign's white veil shifted with the words. She glowed ethereally under the light streaming down from above.

Amber had?

He growled and his heart clenched when he saw the man feeding from Amber's neck. He couldn't have bitten her. Amber belonged to him and no one else. The man couldn't have taken her from him.

"A woman will do a lot for love, it seems."

Kearn growled at the Sovereigns now. Why hadn't they called him sooner? This had clearly already happened. They had watched events unfold and then called him only once they had known who the man was. They had used Amber. How far would they have allowed it to go before calling him? Would they have let her die?

His fangs extended and his eyes switched.

"You dare to threaten us, Venator?" All nine Sovereigns spoke at once, their combined voices echoing around the grand hall.

He roared.

"It is not us who should feel your anger, Savernake, but that of your enemy." The Sovereign in the middle waved her hand towards the pool again and his attention fell there.

Amber's words drifted up to him, her belief in him touching his heart and her love for him consolidating his need for her. She fought the man and he listened to everything they said, searching for a sign of the man's identity.

Amber's expression changed to one of shock and then she said something that turned Kearn's insides and sent a wave of disbelief crashing over him.

She called the man Kyran.

And in that moment, the illusion lifted to reveal his brother.

His flesh and blood.

His own brother.

Kearn shook his head, unable to believe what he was seeing. It burned his chest and wrenched his gut to know that his enemy was Kyran. He stared at him, still unable to understand what was happening before his eyes. Kyran hated him for what he had done but they had started to move past it. They had grown closer these past few years and not once had his brother shown a sign of being the man he was after. He had been supportive of him and kind towards Amber. It wasn't possible. He couldn't believe it. Perhaps this was only another illusion. The Sovereignty had no proof. They watched everyone on their list. Surely, they would have known before now that it was Kyran.

"We know what you are thinking, Venator."

He didn't doubt they did. They knew everything.

Everything but the fact his brother was his mark.

How was it possible they hadn't known?

"We do not have the power to see through an illusion. Your brother has been wise to us. He never once changed form while we were watching him. Tonight, he revealed himself to us and we saw through the veil to the man beneath."

"What does that mean?" Kearn knew in his heart exactly what it meant, but he wanted to hear the Sovereigns admit that they were as fallible as the demons and humans.

"Your brother had been destined for the role of Venator." The one in the middle stepped forwards so her reflection appeared in the crescent moon pool, hovering around the frozen image of his brother. Kearn stared at him, trying to grasp everything that had happened and wondering how long Kyran had been fooling the Sovereignty. "He can sense when we are watching him. It is a gift given to the eldest male child of a Venator, so they are conscious of us and behave accordingly so they will be worthy of the position we will grant them."

"Only Kyran used it against you." Kearn glared at them and clenched his fists, anger rolling through him. "This is all my fault. My brother would never have done such a thing had he achieved his dream and became a Venator. No. This is all your fault... you did this on purpose. You wanted to hurt my brother and drive him to despair so he had little choice but to succumb to his desire."

Kearn stepped forwards, until his toes of his boots touched the raised edge of the pool. He stared hard at the Sovereign in the middle, the one he thought watched over the vampires.

His insides twisted and tightened, rage gripping him as he thought about everything that had happened. Kyran had wanted nothing more than to become the Venator for Savernake. Kearn had taken his future from him, and now he wanted to take his. He wanted to take Amber and his family from him. And it was all the Sovereignty's fault.

"If you hadn't tricked me into becoming a Venator, he would have been happy. You took that away. You're as much responsible for this as I am!"

"Kyran chose his path by committing unforgivable sin."

Those words silenced his anger. He hadn't been brave enough to question them about that the night they had made him a Venator, but he wasn't going to let the chance slip by now. He had always thought they had banished Kyran for his acts of debauchery with the countess and for having drunk Source Blood. Now he suspected there was more to it than that.

"What sin?"

"Kyran's heart is impure. We felt it was so as we watched him become an adult and he prepared for his role as a Venator. He desired to grasp the power of the Sovereignty in order to rule his kind."

Kearn's heart leapt into his throat.

"No." He leaned forwards with his deep desire to cross the pool, take hold of the Sovereign and shake some sense into her. "I will not believe that. Kyran wanted nothing more than to become a Venator."

"Your brother sought to become a Venator so he would gain power, not so he could protect." The Sovereign's soft voice echoed around the dark cold hall, wrapping itself around him. The sound irritated him now. He curled his fingers into fists to restrain himself. He wouldn't believe her. "He and the female conspired to raise his power further via Source Blood. He was tainted. We could not allow him to become a Venator and challenge us and the balance which we create."

The female?

They were talking about the countess. The Sovereignty had played him from the start. They had only given him a chance to have his vengeance in order to eliminate one of the threats to them, and then forced the role of Venator upon him to eliminate the other.

They had manipulated him the whole time.

Their game was as sick as Kyran's.

His gaze fell to the frozen image of Kyran and Amber. She looked terrified. His blood reached out to hers but there was no connection. Was Kyran blocking him or was she unconscious? He had vowed never to let another man touch her and that he would kill any man who dared.

But killing his brother?

The thought of having to face Kyran was an icy shard in his chest. He had already taken so much from Kyran, and from his family. He couldn't bear the duty of taking his life too. He loved his brother and didn't want to kill him. They shared a bond and Kyran had reached out to him when he was alone.

Kearn's thoughts turned towards Amber and he stared at her image in the pool, his heart aching with the need to reassure her and protect her. She had reached out to him too. She shared something deep with him and he loved her with every part of him—his breath, his heart, and his soul.

He couldn't sacrifice her because of his feelings for Kyran, but killing Kyran was asking too much of him.

"Kyran has taken Source Blood. Send a Venator to judge him. Leave me out of this. I only want Amber back."

Could he really save Amber and leave the duty of killing his brother to another Venator? It wasn't possible. He knew deep inside him that Kyran would kill every Venator Kearn sent his way until he was the only one left.

For Kyran, these past three years had been a game with him, not the Sovereignty. Kyran wanted him and he had no choice but to fight and defeat his brother so his family and Amber would be safe.

It didn't matter that it was Kyran. His brother had chosen his path and Kearn would kill him for what he had done to Amber. He would do all in his power to protect her. She was his whole world and he wouldn't let anything happen to her. Resolve flowed through him and he stepped backwards, away from the pool and the Sovereigns.

"You cannot leave." Their combined voices echoed around the dark grey hall.

The light in the hall dimmed and the chill increased, an icy breeze sweeping up from below and encompassing him. He tried to move but couldn't.

The Sovereign in the middle stared at him.

He could feel her intent and her anger. Because he refused to play their games?

"We are powerless if his new plan comes to fruition. He would be cleared of his sin," she said and held her hand out to him, shifting her white veil with it.

"What is that supposed to mean?"

The scene in the pool rewound to the point where Kyran had looked like him and had been at Amber's throat. Her words stabbed him in the heart, each of them a cold needle that buried itself deep within his flesh.

She had consented to be his.

He shook his head.

No. She had consented to be his brother's without realising it.

"If he claims her, it will be consensual. She has given herself to him in word but not yet in body. You cannot allow that to happen. If it does, the sin we have proof of is erased. All blood he had taken from her will be marked as consensual too and we will be unable to touch him. There are others who share his ability and could have perpetrated the other sins. He could deny all knowledge of them and we cannot prove his involvement. You must defeat your brother before this happens."

Kearn's eyes bled to red and he glared at Kyran, watching him reveal himself to Amber.

It didn't matter what the Sovereignty wanted. He wasn't following their orders anymore. He was going to do this out of loyalty to Amber and his need to keep the promise he made to her. Kyran wouldn't get a chance to take her from him.

She belonged to him.

He loved her. Needed her more than anything. She was the most precious thing in his dark world and he couldn't live without her.

He didn't care about the threat to Pendragon or his family, or even the Sovereignty. The sight of Amber with Kyran sickened him. The thought that his brother had lied to him, had hurt Amber, had held her close in his arms and drunk from her, ignited a black rage within him, until the only thing he cared about was saving Amber and killing Kyran.

But how?

Amber's blood was very pure. If Kyran had taken enough, he could easily overthrow any who opposed him. It didn't matter. Amber's blood was still in him, increasing his strength enough for him to attempt to fight Kyran. His mission right now wasn't to kill his brother. It was to rescue Amber. Once she was safe, he would finish this.

"We will warn your father and the other Venators, and send them to protect the Pendragon, Montagu and Savernake families."

Kearn nodded his thanks to the Sovereign. He didn't think the Venators would stand much chance against Kyran if he had drunk enough of Amber's blood, but they could hold him off at least or perhaps combine their strength to defeat him. They had to stop him somehow.

There had to be a way.

Kearn's heart said that there was. Amber's blood whispered to him, her fear trickling through now and her need for him running in his veins. If he had more of her blood, he could defeat his brother.

If he had her.

His fangs extended and a dark desire burned within him. He couldn't wait any longer. This threat to Amber was his breaking point. When she was back in his arms, he would make her forever his.

Kearn cried out when tremendous pain gripped his arm and he clutched it to his chest, blinded by the brightness of the blue light that shone from it as it activated. He clenched his jaw and closed his eyes, trying to shut out the pain. The cold disappeared and spots of water hit him, heavy drops that bounced off his face and soaked into his scalp. The smell of wet earth filled his senses and he opened his eyes.

He was back at the lodge, standing outside in the rain.

Kearn pulled his keys from his pocket, unlocked his car, and jumped in. He gunned the engine into life and sped towards the main gates of the estate. They barely had time to open before he was driving through them at breakneck speed.

He knew where his brother would be.

There was only one place nearby that he would take Amber.

Earl Huntingdon's house.

It didn't take long to reach the gates of the Huntingdon estate. They were open, an invitation that he wasn't about to refuse. The rain lashed down, hammering hard on the windscreen of his Audi. Kearn drove up to the grand Georgian mansion. Its elegant columns and delicate façade belied the beasts that dwelled within its walls.

The only car outside the house was his brother's black Bentley. Kearn parked beside it, his gaze on the unlit mansion. There wasn't a sign of life.

His heart whispered dark words to him about Amber and Kyran, until he was on the verge of leaping from his car and running into the house, gun blazing. It was a fool's move and one he wouldn't make. Even if he were furious, desperate to spill blood for the things that had happened and to have Amber back in his arms, he wouldn't succumb to his desires. He had to keep his head or he would lose it. Kyran could easily defeat him if he ran headlong into the fight, not thinking clearly and not aware of the situation in the building or the layout. As much as he hated it, desired to surrender to his need for violence, he would assess everything and then make his move.

His senses reached out, dulled by the heavy rain, and searched his surroundings. There were vampires in the house but they were very still. It was night so it wasn't likely that they were sleeping. There wasn't a trace of blood in the air either, so his brother couldn't have killed them.

Was Earl Huntingdon involved in Kyran's plan, or had he not been included? The gathering of signatures and lack of patrols pointed towards the latter. Kyran must have taken the Huntingdon family hostage. If that was the case then he was likely to be at the other end of the house, as far from potential danger as possible.

Kearn scanned the length of the mansion, the windscreen wipers working furiously to clear the rain from his vision, and stared hard at the other end of the building to his right. He could sense people there. The signal was weak, indicating a small number of people, but he couldn't tell whether they were vampire or human.

He would start there.

He turned off the engine, reached behind his seat and took his spare gun from the box there. He checked the clip, chambered the first round, and then opened the car door and stepped out into the rain. The second he had closed the car door and locked it, he was running across the gravel drive to the portico of the house. He leaned his back against the damp sandstone wall near the dark wooden double doors and listened. Only the sound of rain filled his ears and he couldn't sense anyone on the other side.

The handle was cold under his fingers. He pushed it down and the door opened. It confirmed his suspicions. Kyran was holding the Huntingdon vampires hostage. Vampire families never left the door unlocked if it was unattended. Uninvited guests were a nuisance, especially since they were usually vampire hunters.

Kearn stepped into the foyer and closed the door behind him. His eyes changed to red, his vision sharpening as they did so, and he scanned the darkness for a sign of trouble. Nothing.

The door opened again. Kearn spun on the spot and aimed his gun at the intruder.

His finger froze against the trigger.

"What are you doing here?" He kept the gun fixed on her, unwilling to trust anyone right now.

"The Sovereignty sent me to help you." Venator Greystone pushed her long wet silver hair from her face. The tangled threads clung to the black jacket of her uniform.

Kearn lowered his gun but didn't put it away. He kept his finger on the trigger, ready to shoot her if she tried anything. His brother's illusions were strong. For all Kearn knew, he could be staring at Kyran, not the female Venator. He moved to his right, towards two doors that led deeper into the building, motioning for Venator Greystone to follow him. He would see how this played out. She had come in from outside and he hadn't sensed anyone there with him earlier, so she might have just arrived. The signal at the end of the building was as weak as it had been before, indicating that the same number of people were there. There was a chance that he was wrong and she wasn't his brother, but he wasn't prepared to risk it.

Venator Greystone followed him, her footsteps as silent as his were on the parquet.

His blood reached out to Amber's. Only a glimmer of her feelings came through the connection. It wasn't enough to comfort him. He needed the connection between them to be open again. He needed to feel her and know that she was safe and to tell her that he was coming for her. He would save her from Kyran and he would make her his.

The scent of Amber's blood drifted from one of the two corridors in front of him. He stopped and breathed deep, trying to discern which one would lead to her. The scent was strongest from the left door. Kyran was holding her at the rear of the building and he wasn't being discreet about it. His brother wanted him to find her.

It was fine with him. He was ready to make Kyran pay for taking her and for playing such a vicious game with them. He advanced slowly down the dark corridor with Venator Greystone trailing behind him.

"You know about the situation?" he whispered and waited for her response. If she slipped up at all in the next few minutes, he would attack.

"Yes." She moved closer to him. "They explained about your brother and the human female."

Kearn still couldn't quite bring himself to believe that Kyran had orchestrated such a plan and was doing this. He didn't want to believe it, even when he knew it was true. He kept hoping that he would discover it was all a mistake and the image of Kyran was in fact another illusion, a mask worn by the real culprit.

He followed Amber's scent through the maze of corridors at the back of the house. It was easy for him to use his senses to guide him in the darkness so he wouldn't bump into anything. Venator Greystone would find it more difficult. Lesser Nobles had weaker senses than Nobles. She would need to follow him rather than her own senses. Presuming she was just a Lesser Noble and not a Noble in disguise. He moved faster, seeing if she could find her own way in the darkness or was really relying on his position to help her.

She bumped into something and growled.

"Wait," she whispered and he didn't. He kept striding along the corridor.

The smell of Amber's blood grew stronger near a set of stairs that led upwards. He peered up them and reached out to her with his senses and his blood. She was there. Somewhere on the first floor. He waited at the stairs for Venator Greystone to catch up with him and then followed them to the next floor. The wooden treads creaked under their feet. He scanned the darkness ahead to see if anyone would hear it but it was empty.

The first floor was more spacious but just as dark. He couldn't risk lighting the way with any of his powers. It would give away their location to anyone in the vicinity. They had to keep moving forwards in the darkness until they were closer to Amber and his brother.

His senses sharpened enough for him to be able to see a ghost of his surroundings in his mind. A gallery. They were at the front of the house now. He moved to his right, towards where the windows were, and found a set of heavy velvet curtains. Pulling one aside a fraction, he peered out into the night. It was raining harder now, saturating the world. His car was bright in the grey night, parked a short distance from the Bentley.

He frowned when he didn't see another car and then realised that he hadn't heard one arrive when Venator Greystone had appeared. His senses fixed on her. How had she arrived at the estate only a short time after him? Even if the Sovereignty had seen him arrive at the house and transported her to them in order to give her the mission to assist him, she wouldn't have arrived so close to him. Time moved fast in the Sovereignty's dimension. Venator Greystone had arrived only minutes after him.

Or she had been here the whole time.

His grip on his gun increased. He tensed on the inside but didn't let it show on the outside or in his feelings. A Noble vampire would be able to sense a change in his emotions.

She came forwards so the dim light from outside touched her face and looked at him in the way she had done when testing his blood—a blatant attempt to get into his good graces and his underwear. He wasn't interested in her. The only reason he was even looking at her was because he was trying to figure out whether or not she was his brother.

He turned away and carried on down the gallery, following the scent of Amber's blood, only part of his senses were now fixed on Venator Greystone, monitoring her closely in case his suspicions were correct and she was in fact his enemy.

She hadn't done anything suspicious other than arriving at almost the same time as him, but his brother had never done anything suspicious around him either.

Kearn had never had the inkling that Kyran was his enemy. Kyran had played him well.

He sensed two people in a room ahead. He stopped and turned to Venator Greystone, only able to sense her form in the darkness and her feelings. She was nervous.

"We should prepare." He continued walking, his fingers flexing around his gun and his heart picking up pace. If she was going to make a move, it would be now.

"I am already one step ahead of you, Lord Savernake."

Before he could turn to face her, something heavy and blunt struck the back of his head. Dark waves threatened to pull him under but he fought them.

"Damn you." Venator Greystone struck him again, hitting his right shoulder this time. "You should be out cold."

He would have been if he hadn't taken so much blood from Amber so recently and hadn't been anticipating the attack.

"I knew it was you." Kearn growled and tried to focus through the pain.

"You knew it was who? You don't have a clue, Lord Savernake. You never have."

He could only stare as her fingertips began to glow blue. It wasn't an illusion. His power rose in response to hers and the connection their calling forged between them opened. She was a Venator.

Not an illusion.

Kearn brought his gun up and fired before Venator Greystone could move out of the way. She shrieked as the bullet tore through her right upper arm. The blue light faded from her fingertips. He had to injure her arm to stop her from using her power as a Venator against him and to slow her down further. His head was killing him.

He shot her again and his right arm ached, the power in it activating. Blue light punctured the darkness, chasing it back and revealing Venator Greystone. He dived to one side as she raised her own firearm and rolled out of the path of the bullet. She shifted aim and fired again. Kearn flipped backwards to dodge it and then brought his gun around and shot her right shoulder. She growled and shifted backwards, away from him. She wouldn't be fast enough to escape him now.

The stench of her blood filled the air, swamping his senses and making it impossible for him to smell the sweeter scent of Amber's blood. His head spun as the entirety of his arm became active, the symbols on it glowing brightly. It drained his strength and he couldn't allow that, but no matter what he did, it wouldn't deactivate.

And he knew why.

The Sovereignty had judged her.

Venator Greystone moved back, clutching her arm and scowling at him. "You were supposed to be out cold."

There was a pout in her voice. He had followed their plan for him to the letter but he didn't want to play anymore. They had threatened Amber and finally revealed themselves. Now that he knew who he was dealing with, he was going to finish it.

"I always have been a disappointment." He brought his arm up. The blue glow dampened his vision but he could still see his target. He could see her trembling and see the fear surfacing in her eyes as she shook her head.

Her heart beat loud and fast in his ears. She had honestly thought he would be that easy to defeat or capture. Her lust for power had only brought her an early death.

She growled and her eyes bled into red. "You were supposed to be an easy mark! That human female wasn't supposed to get in the way."

Kearn realised that he had altered Kyran and Venator Greystone's plan before tonight. The female Venator was supposed to have seduced him, to have lured him in with her flattery and acceptance of him. She had done her best but she wasn't the one who had become his distraction.

Amber had been it instead. Only she had made him stronger and had given him reason to fight.

Kearn slipped his gun back into the holster at his hip and gripped his right wrist with his left hand, steadying his arm. It whispered hungry words to him, encouraging him to kill Venator Greystone. He would, but not yet.

"What does my brother plan to do?"

Venator Greystone smiled. "You will find out soon enough, my lord."

He frowned and then his eyes widened when he sensed a presence behind him. Just as he turned, Venator Greystone came forwards. He didn't have a chance to block her. She kicked him hard in the head and the world wavered in front of him, his brother twisting and distorting with it.

Kyran raised his right hand and, without any trace of emotion in his cold blue eyes, closed it into a fist. A tremendous heavy feeling settled in Kearn's mind. Kyran was trying to knock him out but he wouldn't go quietly. He fought it, clearing his head long enough to break free of his brother's mental grasp, and lunged at Venator Greystone.

Her scream filled the silence in the gallery as his hand connected with her chest. Bright shining blue threads of power burrowed into her body and she thrashed around, lashing out at him in a desperate attempt to free herself. It was too late. The ribbons turned black and Kearn took his hand away and turned to face Kyran. He sensed her life force fade as she fell into the eternal darkness and then the connection to her severed.

Kyran raised his hand again, his red eyes boring into Kearn's, and started to close his fingers. Another heavy dull throb pulsed through his mind but he wouldn't let it stop him. He needed to get to Amber and make sure that she was alright. Kyran wouldn't have bitten her because that would change her blood and make it less potent and less valuable, but Kearn needed to see it with his own two eyes. He needed to keep his promise and take away her fear.

He ran at his brother and was within striking distance when Kyran swept his hand to one side, using his power to throw Kearn against the wall. He slammed into it and dropped to the floor, plaster raining down on him. His head spun. His brother was too powerful to defeat right now. With so much of Amber's blood fresh in his veins, Kyran was a god.

Kearn pushed himself up onto his hands and knees. Kyran laughed. The sound of it grated in his ears and drove him to stand. The power of the Sovereignty whispered insidious things to him and he obeyed them for once. He would give it everything he had. He wouldn't let his brother defeat him here. He would save Amber.

Focusing on his arm, he gathered all of his power there, both that of the Sovereignty and his own. With an ungodly roar, he unleashed everything he had in one cataclysmic burst aimed straight at Kyran. The windows exploded outwards, plaster tore off the walls, turning to dust and filling the charged air around him, and Kearn breathed hard, choking and struggling to remain conscious. His arm trembled, weak and numb like the rest of him.

Had he done it?

Was Kyran dead?

CHAPTER 27

Amber jumped when another huge explosion rocked the building, shaking fragments of plaster from the ceiling. She clutched the edge of the couch, listening hard and afraid that Kyran would defeat Kearn. She was sure it was him out there, battling his brother. She had felt his presence in her blood and a sliver of his feelings, and then Kyran's dark emotions had clouded her mind and severed her connection to Kearn. Kyran had left after that and then the sound of fighting had grown louder and more violent.

Cold fingers threatened to squeeze the air from her lungs and grip her heart so tightly it would stop.

She leaned forwards as everything went still.

Was it over?

Amber tried to stand to go to the door but her head spun and she collapsed back onto the couch. If she couldn't even make it to the door, she would never be able to fight Kyran and escape. She was relying on Kearn now.

Kearn.

Her heart ached at the thought of him having to fight his own brother. He loved Kyran and felt responsible for him losing his chance to become the Venator of their family. Discovering that Kyran was behind everything must have hurt him and now he had to fight him. Would he even be able to bring himself to kill Kyran? Couldn't the Sovereignty give the task to someone else? It was cruel to expect Kearn to take Kyran's life when he already felt as though he had, and had already hurt his family once.

The door burst open and she jumped. Kearn walked in, his silver hair stained with blood and a weary look on his face. Her heart leapt into her throat but she swallowed it again, her mind overruling her desire to go to him and telling her that it was Kyran only pretending to be Kearn.

A bright blue light shone out from Kearn's side and she realised that it was his arm and that he was dragging someone behind him by their shirt collar. Black hair. Black shirt.

Kearn dropped him.

It was Kyran and he was unconscious.

Kearn had defeated Kyran. Her chest warmed and her heart raced, overruling the voice that told her not to believe what she was seeing. He had defeated his brother and come for her.

She went to go to Kearn but he held his hand up.

"Take it easy," he said and she nodded.

She could feel his emotions flowing into her, all warmth and relief, and they matched her own, bringing them to the surface along with the fear that had been pressing down on her. Tears rose into her eyes, hot on her lashes, and spilled down her cheeks. There were so many things that she wanted to ask him but instead she drank in the sight of him. He was hurt, but he was here. He smiled, crossed the room to her, and pulled her into his arms, holding her close to his chest. His heart beat against her ear, familiar in its slow pace, and the connection between them deepened. She pushed away from the voice in her heart, not willing to believe that this was another trick. When Kyran had masqueraded as Kearn, it hadn't felt like this. This felt real. This was the Kearn that she knew.

He pressed a kiss to her hair and sighed. "I thought I would be too late. It is over now."

Relief filled her but it only lasted as long as it took for him to speak again.

"You seem weak." He pulled back, holding her by her shoulders at arm's length. There was darkness in his green eyes, anger that she felt deep in her blood. "How are you feeling?"

Amber touched her neck and more tears came when she recalled Kyran feeding from her, pretending that he was Kearn. She had promised herself to him and Kyran had made it clear that he intended to make her his, but now Kearn was here and she was safe at last.

The anger within her increased. It burned like rage through her veins, igniting her own feelings and rousing them. She was angry too. She wanted Kyran to pay for what he had done to her but she didn't want Kearn to have to suffer sentencing him.

She cupped his cheek. His skin was cool beneath her fingers and he leaned into her touch. She sighed at the sight of all the cuts and the blood on him. He had already fought his brother for her, and she couldn't thank him enough. She was sure that if he hadn't come to her tonight that it would have been too late for her and too late for them. She would have belonged to Kyran.

"I'm tired," she said and the anger in his eyes became concern, but the feeling inside her didn't change. He took her hand from his face and held it tightly. "I feel so weak."

Red tinted the edges of his green irises. His other hand shifted to her face and his eyes slowly changed. Her gaze fell to his lips as he spoke and she saw flashes of fangs.

"I cannot lose you," he said in a strained voice and lowered the hand on her face to her neck.

She sensed his intent in her blood and fear seized her again.

"Is it that bad?" Her voice trembled and her eyebrows furrowed. Was becoming like Kearn her only option for survival? She didn't think Kyran had taken that much of her blood. She just felt a little tired and she was sure that after a good day's rest she would be fine again.

Kearn nodded.

His thumb pressed into the underside of her chin and he tilted her head back. Her heart pounded. Her blood chilled. It didn't feel right. His body pressed into hers, his other arm slid around her waist, and he dipped his mouth towards her neck, his lips parting to reveal his fangs. It didn't feel at all as she had expected.

She felt anxious, not excited. Something deep within her cried out for her to escape and filled her with panic, fear, and anger.

Kyran murmured where he lay sprawled out on the floor. Her gaze fell to him.

Her anger increased when his eyes snapped open and she realised that it wasn't her feeling. It was his.

He was on his feet before she could blink, his hand gripping Kearn's shoulder and tearing him away from her. She stumbled backwards and fell onto the couch as he tossed Kearn across the room, sending him smashing into the wall. Kearn fell to the floor just as her backside hit the couch seat.

Amber stared up at Kyran, her hands pressing into the padded seat either side of her knees. Her heart lodged in her throat and fluttered there.

Kyran frowned at her, and then down at himself, looking at his hands, and then turned to face Kearn. She couldn't watch as they clashed. She curled up and closed her eyes, afraid of seeing the fight. The sound of it alone was terrifying.

"Run," Kearn said and she wanted to, only she wasn't strong enough. She could barely walk.

"Stay right there," Kyran shouted and she looked at him. "Do not believe a word he says. That is not me!"

Amber stared at them both, catching glimpses of their faces as they fought, punching and kicking, moving so quickly it was hard for her to keep up. She didn't know what to do or who to believe. Conflict reigned in her blood. She watched them, trying to figure everything out.

"This is an illusion, Amber, and you know it is," Kyran said and she shook her head. She wouldn't believe him. He was a liar and he had hurt her.

"Run, Amber, get out of here. Leave us alone," Kearn said and looked at her, his eyes pleading her as much as her blood was. She pressed her hand to her chest and then gasped when Kyran punched him, sending him crashing to the ground. He was on his feet again in an instant, growling and throwing himself at his brother.

"Do not listen to him, Amber! Listen to your blood." Kyran threw Kearn across the room again, shattering the plaster on the far wall.

Amber did. She focused on her blood just as she had been practicing and tried to open a connection to the real Kearn. It was hard to tell who was who even in her blood. She wasn't any good at this. She couldn't tell, couldn't get the myriad of feelings in it straight.

Kearn threw himself at Kyran, knocking him down and pinning him to the ground. She couldn't watch as he hit him, knocking his head back and forth, bloodying it with a quick succession of punches.

Her heart ached.

Panic filled her.

What if she was wrong? What if Kearn really was Kyran and Kyran really was Kearn? She had to do something. She had to find out the truth.

It hit her like a freight train and her head snapped around to face them.

"Tell me something only you know, Kearn," she said and then realised that she really hadn't thought her plan through. What would Kearn know that Kyran didn't, but that she would actually know herself?

Kyran forced Kearn across the room, throwing him with nothing more than a wave of his hands, and got to his feet.

He turned to her, his blue eyes shining with regret.

"I killed my pregnant fiancée... and the child was Kyran's."

Those words fell like lead on the room, causing immediate silence. A sense of anger and disbelief filled her blood. She looked at Kearn. The expression of sheer horror on his face was enough to confirm that it was his feelings, and that he hadn't known.

Amber immediately reached for Kyran and was in his arms the moment their fingers touched. He held her close, cradling her against his chest, and ran out of the room. The lights in the hall outside came on, illuminating a wide gallery. Cold wet air blasted in through the broken windows, tousling the torn curtains, and most of the plaster on the walls was either missing or fractured. He leapt over a buckled and broken patch of the wooden floor and kept running. Was this the result of the explosions she had heard?

"We have to get you out of here," he said and she hoped that she had made the right decision. It felt wrong to be in Kyran's arms. If she was mistaken, she had just signed her own death sentence. "I cannot risk fighting him alone, and with you here. I do not intend to break my promise to protect you."

The lights came on in a large room they passed through and Amber realised that it was his power doing it. Just as he had unlocked her door without a key, he could make the lights come on without having to flip the switch. As they reached a grand set of stairs and the foyer of the house, Kyran's face began to change. The blue in his eyes faded to green, and his hair lengthened and turned silver.

Amber threw her arms around Kearn's neck and held on to him, tears running down her cheeks. She closed her eyes and didn't let go. She would never let go.

"Where are we going?" she breathed against his neck. He smelt like Kearn.

"To my family's estate. They will protect you while I take care of Kyran." He paused and then held her tighter against him. He was trembling. "I almost lost you. I cannot... I will not risk that happening again. I need you, Amber."

She knew in her heart what he meant by those three words.

He was going to bite her.

Before, she had been afraid of stepping into his world, but she wasn't now. When she had realised that Kyran would make her into a vampire purely to spite Kearn, she had also realised how much she wanted to be Kearn's forever.

She wanted it more than anything.

She had only known him a short while but she couldn't imagine her life without him, and she didn't want to spend only a few short years with him as a human. She wanted to spend centuries with him as a vampire. Kyran was wrong about Kearn. He wouldn't treat her like other Nobles treated humans. He would dote on her, dedicating himself to her and loving her forever.

The cold damp night air broke over her, drizzle saturating her hair and clothes. Kearn's car was bright in the low light, parked near the Bentley that Kyran had forced her into. How far was it to the estate and whose house was this?

She looked over her shoulder at the mansion. It was dark on the outside but lights on the inside marked the path of escape they had taken. She traced it back to where they ended. Kyran was still alive. He would come after them.

There was a commotion from the other end of the building.

"We must leave," Kearn said. "The Huntingdon family will be out for blood. My brother played a dangerous game by holding them hostage."

"Will they kill him?" Amber whispered, too tired to raise her voice any louder. Kearn set her down in the passenger seat of his Audi and buckled her in.

"No. Earl Huntingdon and the countess will forgive him. Kyran will convince them to join him in his fight for power. Lesser Nobles such as the Huntingdons and the Greystones are easily swayed."

"Greystone? Like the female Venator?"

He nodded, closed her door, rounded the car and got into the driver's side.

"She was in league with Kyran." Kearn started the car and reversed fast, spinning it around, and then drove away.

Amber looked back over her shoulder at the house.

"Was?" She frowned at the black Bentley. It couldn't have been. Now that she was thinking about it, the driver had looked a little like the female Venator.

"I took care of her. The Sovereignty commanded it and I could not have her interfering in my fight against Kyran." Kearn drove fast through the gates of the estate and out onto a quiet road.

Amber didn't recognise her surroundings. She had been unconscious for the whole journey to the Huntingdon estate. It surprised her when they had only been driving a short time and they reached a road that she recognised. They had driven along it when heading to his family's estate from London.

"The Huntingdons live close to you?"

Kearn nodded. Minutes later, they were heading through the heavily guarded gates of the Savernake estate.

"What's going on?" Amber looked around her at all of the people in the grounds. Some of them had silver hair and wore a uniform like Kearn's black and silver clothing. More Venators. Could they trust these ones?

"We are on alert. Kyran intends to kill Archduke Pendragon and any of Pendragon blood who stands in his way, and then destroy the house of Savernake to seize power."

She gasped. He would kill his own parents and family? Kyran had never struck her as that sort of man. He had always been smiling and had always been proud of his family. She couldn't imagine him wanting to kill everyone like that.

"He wants me to pay for what I did to him, and he wants mother and father to pay for exiling him. Archduke Pendragon refused to buy your blood and help him, so now he will pay too."

"He wants it that badly? Can he even fight the archduke? You said he was power—"

"Believe me," Kearn interjected, "right now, Kyran could take on the Sovereignty themselves and win."

He was that powerful?

"It's my blood isn't it?" She touched her neck. "Kyran took a lot from me. Enough that he gained the true effects."

Kearn nodded and pulled the car to a halt outside the lodge. He gripped the steering wheel and his hard expression softened, the corners of his lips tugging into the barest of smiles.

"I can defeat him."

Amber ran her fingers over the cut on her throat. "If you have my blood too."

He nodded again. Her hand fell from her neck and rested in her lap.

"I do not just want your blood, Amber... I... I want you too," Kearn whispered, an ardent look filling his green eyes.

Her heart skipped a beat and then pounded hard against her ribs. She could only think of one reason why Kearn had stopped at the lodge rather than going to the main house. He was going to bite her now before anything else happened.

She touched her throat again, her fingers trembling against it. Kearn's gaze fell there and his eyes turned red. Intense need flowed through her. His feelings. He couldn't fight it anymore. His hunger and need were so strong that she couldn't deny him. This was how she had expected it to feel—thrilling, deep and incredible.

"I need to know that you are mine, Amber, and mine alone... forever." He reached across and touched her face. His fingers trembled against her cheek and she was tempted to close her eyes but kept looking into his, seeing everything her blood was telling her reflected in them. "Say you will be mine."

Amber placed her hand over his and flattened his palm against her cheek. "I will always be yours."

He closed his eyes and she felt his relief deep in her heart, and his happiness.

"I will give all that I can to make you strong enough to defeat Kyran."

His eyes opened to reveal the shock she felt in her blood. The surprise receded, leaving warm feelings in its place. She meant what she had said. She would give him everything if he needed it to survive the coming fight. She didn't want to lose him.

He left the car and rounded it to her side, opening the door for her. Amber stepped out and into his waiting arms, settling herself close to him and looking up at his face. The silver threads of his hair fell forwards when he looked down at her, his eyes vivid red and full of hunger.

"Are you certain about this?" he whispered and touched her cheek again. He pushed his fingers back, through the tangled lengths of her ponytail, and then ran them down her throat. "You will be weakened by my taking your blood but I will keep you safe. I will protect you this time. Do you trust me?"

Amber nodded and touched his shoulder. "I am, and I do. I'm not afraid... because... I love you."

Kearn frowned, pulled her close, and kissed her hard. It was a struggle to breathe with his grip on her so tight but she kissed him back, her lips playing against his, revealing all of the passion and desire, and the need that she felt for him.

She had meant what she had said that night.

She wanted to be his forever. She wasn't afraid.

He broke away, swept her into his arms and carried her into the lodge.

CHAPTER 28

Amber sat on the end of the bed, trying to read Kearn's feelings in his blood but her own nerves drowned them out. Kearn removed his black military-style jacket and sat beside her, his eyes firmly fixed on hers. She smiled but it faltered when he touched her knee. Was she really ready to do this?

The implications frightened her. She was going to leave her world behind, her family, her friends, and become a vampire, but she loved Kearn and knew that he felt the same way. He needed her love and her by his side, and he would have them forever.

Her nerves melted away, taking her rising fear with them, when she felt every feeling that was in his green eyes—love, need, devotion. He had never bitten a human before, had never made anyone into a vampire, and the emotions in her blood said that this meant something and that something was the world.

Amber reached around the back of her head and cleared the hair from the left side of her neck. When she tilted her chin up, offering her throat to Kearn, his eyes shifted there and turned red, but none of the feelings in them disappeared. Even in this state, they showed his love for her and how deeply this affected him.

His eyes met hers briefly and then he pulled her into his arms, settling her on his lap. Any feeling of self-consciousness she had from sitting on his thighs disappeared when he pressed a kiss to her throat. Her awareness of the world became an awareness of only Kearn. Where his hands touched her back, how delicious his arms felt around her, and the feel of his soft breathing against her throat, all of it stole her attention until there was only them, in an endless void, together and about to become that way forever.

"Do not fear me," Kearn whispered on her throat and leaned his cheek against hers. She closed her eyes and savoured the feel of their skin touching. "Do not fear this, Amber. My heart is yours until the end of time, beyond forever, and I will worship you endlessly and never stop loving you."

Tears filled her eyes. She could never refuse him. She wanted to be his and wanted to live out the fairytale he had planned for them, no matter how dark it was.

Kearn drew her closer to him, lightly kissing her throat in a way that spread warmth through her. Her heart floated in her chest. There was so much love in the way he was holding her, kissing her, and in his blood.

"I do not want to hurt you." He kissed her throat again. His blood backed up his words and Amber wrapped her arms around his neck, her fingers tangling in the silver threads of his hair and holding him to her. She knew that. And she knew it was going to hurt. But she didn't care, because he needed

223

this. "I wish I could make it painless... nothing but a scratch on your fingertip... I would... but I cannot, Amber."

His fingers stroked her throat and he sighed.

"I need to mark your throat. I need everyone to see that my beautiful Amber is mine and mine alone." He leaned his head on her shoulder and Amber held him, giving him time to say everything that he needed to.

His words touched her deeply. He needed to bite her throat and she wouldn't have it any other way. If they were going to do this, she wanted it to be as special for him as he needed it to be, and she wanted to do it properly. A bite on her neck seemed most appropriate, and she knew that it meant the most to him. He didn't want to do things half-heartedly. He had to do it correctly. He needed to.

"I want to wear your marks, Kearn." She rested her head against his, sighed and flipped his hair around her fingers. Her Noble. When she had first met him, she had never believed he could be so gentle and loving with her. "I want to be yours. I want you to stay with me forever."

He drew back and looked at her, deep down into her heart through her eyes. "Say it again."

She smiled. "Stay with me forever."

A smile curved his lips and his gaze moved to her throat and then back to hers.

"It is I who should be saying such a thing to you." He touched her cheek, brushing the backs of his fingers across it. "My beautiful Amber. Will you stay with me forever? You have tamed this Noble... you rule me absolutely... and I will ensure that you want for nothing, and that you will have everything that you deserve."

"There's only one thing I want, Kearn. There's only one thing I desire... you. So I'm offering this to you," she tilted her chin up to expose her neck and brought his hand down to press against the spot over her heart, "so I might have you forever too, and when I'm like you, I'm going to bite your neck so the world can see that you're mine and mine alone."

Kearn dragged her against him and kissed her, stealing her breath with his passion. She tried to keep up as his lips moved roughly over hers, his tongue plundering her mouth, but by the time she was moving with him, not against him, he broke away and was staring into her eyes again.

His were wide and green, full of emotions that made them sparkle in the warm low light of the bedroom.

"I love you," he whispered.

Amber couldn't help smiling.

"I love you," he said again and pulled her back to him, his hands pressing between her shoulder blades. He breathed against her neck. "I love you."

Amber closed her eyes, sensing his intent in her blood, and tried to relax.

"I love you, forever," he whispered and then his lips grazed her throat and a sharp pain shot out from where they touched.

She flinched but the pain only lasted a second, giving way to dull throbbing warmth. She felt queasy from the awareness of his fangs in her but suppressed the feeling, not wanting Kearn to sense it in her.

It hurt when he sucked and her head spun. She held him close, tangling her fingers in his hair to show him that she wanted this. The slow speed of his drinking and the gentle way he held her surprised her. She had expected him to act as he had when he had taken her blood and told her that he would bite her but he was so tender instead. Calm washed over her and it no longer hurt when he pulled on her blood. The connection that opened between them when she relaxed was incredible, stronger than it had ever been, and she could clearly feel all of his emotions. It meant so much to him to do this. There was a sense of reverence about his actions, about the way he was holding her and the gentleness of the bite. She could feel the deep awe within him, the happiness and the love.

Amber opened her heart to him, letting him feel everything that she was. She wasn't afraid of him, or of doing this, not anymore. She loved him and she wanted it too. This didn't just make him happy, it made her happy too. She didn't fear stepping into his world and leaving hers behind. It would be just as he had said. She had his heart and his love forever.

And he had hers.

Her head spun again, dizziness making her stomach turn, and she frowned. She didn't want him to stop drinking, wanted him to have all the blood he needed so he could defeat Kyran and they could be together, but she was growing weak.

Kearn's fangs left her throat and she mourned their loss and then sighed when he licked her skin. He wrapped his lips back around the bite and suckled slowly. Each drop of blood that he drank increased the connection between them, until she could no longer sense where his feelings ended and hers began. Her head was swimming with them, with the love and tenderness, with the need and desire.

He pressed a kiss to her throat and then licked the marks.

"I love you," he whispered into her ear and Amber smiled through the growing haze in her mind.

Darkness encroached and she tried to fight it, but she was too tired. She opened her eyes, wanting to see him, but they were blurry and she couldn't make out his face.

Her head spun again.

Amber managed to touch his face before the darkness took her, and whispered, "I love you too."

CHAPTER 29

Kearn carried Amber towards the open double doors of the main house, cradling her gently in his arms. The twin puncture marks on the left side of her throat were red and sore. He had been as careful as possible but he had still hurt her. She had borne it well, trying to hide her pain from him with her love, but he had sensed it deep within her. He wished that he could have done it without hurting her. He'd had to bite her neck though. He couldn't have it any other way.

He sensed vampires ahead of him.

What would his parents make of what he had done?

He told himself that he didn't care what his family thought about him choosing to turn Amber but it didn't stop the nerves from churning his stomach, eating away at him and increasing his anxiety. He wasn't sure how people would react to her now that he had begun her transformation into a vampire and he needed to keep her safe now more than ever. She was his to protect and he wouldn't fail her. Fear laced his blood as he cautiously looked at the lower ranking vampires and guards in the vestibule. They stared at him, and he held Amber closer to him, afraid that someone would try to harm her.

The vampires parted for him and his eyes switched to red when some of them dared to look at Amber. She belonged to him now. His love. His forever.

When he had bitten her, he had felt all of her feelings in his heart. He had felt her love for him and her fear of losing him, and it had made him feel as though he finally had a place where he belonged again. He desired nothing more than to protect her, the woman who was the most precious thing in the world to him, and he loved her more than anything. It honoured him that she had given herself to him and that she wanted to be his.

The connection between them had been so strong, and when she finally became a vampire, that same connection would return, linking them forever as one. They would always be able to feel each other, and she would grow as strong as he was and gain all of his abilities and powers.

Amber stirred, her eyes fluttering open. She looked up at him, the dark circles beneath her eyes concerning him along with the sense of weariness he could feel in her.

He stopped in the gallery that led to the main reception room. Daylight flooded in through the windows to his left, shining on her and making her pale skin glow. Fear threatened to seize his heart but she smiled and his blood felt the strength returning to her. It was a relief to see that he hadn't taken too much from her and that she would recover.

Kearn smiled for her and a hint of colour touched her cheeks. He would never tire of that reaction. She was beautiful when she blushed for him.

"I am sorry that I hurt you," he whispered.

She shook her head a fraction. "It didn't really hurt."

Her voice was quiet and weak. His concern returned and he held her closer. There was such deep affection in her hazel eyes. She touched his cheek and then her fingers curled around the back of his neck and she lured him down to her. He knew what she wanted.

Kearn raised her and kissed her gently, slowly, and with all the love that he felt for her.

She sighed when he lowered her again and smiled at him, brilliant and wide. He sensed the happiness in her and it stirred his own.

"I could feel you," she whispered and placed her hand on her chest, resting it over her heart. Her eyes held his. "I already feel different."

He smiled again. She did feel different. She felt stronger. Her body had begun the transition from human to vampire. Her hand pressed against his chest.

"I can feel you." She blinked slowly. Her tiredness ran in his veins, a feeling that he couldn't easily shake. He wanted to tell her to stop talking and to rest, but felt she had to say what she was going to and he had to hear it. "There's a connection... like a red ribbon tying our hearts."

Kearn sighed and smiled down at her, absorbing the love in her eyes.

"Uniting our hearts," he said and her eyes brightened with her smile. "We are one now."

She frowned. "A master and servant."

"No." Kearn shook his head. "Equals... lovers... you will never be inferior to me. My heart is yours, just as the duke said."

Tears lined her eyes. He wanted to wipe them away for her but she was too weak to stand on her own while he did so.

"Do not cry."

"I'm not sad," she whispered and closed her eyes. "I'm happy... and tired."

"Rest then. You will be strong again soon." He leaned down and pressed a kiss to her hair, and at the same time gave her feelings a slight push, enough to send to her sleep. She rested heavily in his arms but he didn't feel her weight. She was as light as air to him. His Amber.

Kearn waited until the connection between them became weak and he knew that she was in a deep sleep, and then continued along the hall. There were people in the reception room ahead. He could feel them. Their presence ran deep in his blood. His mother and father.

A maid at the dark double doors opened them for him but didn't honour him with a curtsey. She didn't even look at him. If the maid treated him as though he wasn't welcome, then how would the mistress react?

Kearn walked into the richly furnished room. The memories of playing here with his brother caused even more pain now and this time he couldn't push them away. He remembered how their mother would chastise them for drawing on the black walls, or for spilling blood on the furniture even though it had been upholstered in lush red then, and not gold as it was now. They had always been causing trouble one way or another.

"Out!" A high female voice shook him out of his thoughts and he stepped back towards the doors when a wave of anger hit him.

His gaze snapped to his mother when she stood, leaving his father sitting alone on the gold couch to the right of the black marble fireplace.

The rage in her dark eyes made Kearn hold Amber closer to him. His mother stalked towards him with intent and he resisted his desire to change. He couldn't threaten her.

"Leave my house." She flung her arm towards the doors.

She looked so slight and small in the black corseted dress and he couldn't remember a time she had felt so weak to him. The initial anger he had felt in her had covered the fear he could now sense, and the hurt. His father must have told her what had happened and why they had to guard the house.

His mother no longer had any children.

She would have banished them both.

Kearn stood his ground, unwilling to leave the safety of the main house when Amber was still recovering. She had to remain here, even if he couldn't. He would beg his mother for her sake.

His mother stopped a short distance from him, the long sleek locks of her black hair shining in the firelight at her back, her face shadowed. She stared at Amber and then frowned, her delicate features growing dark with it.

Her eyes turned red.

She took a deep breath.

The moment she did, her eyes widened and she hesitantly stepped forwards, her hands dancing around in the air, as though she wasn't sure what to do. Her gaze didn't leave Amber and Kearn was tempted to step back again until his father stood, an incredulous look on his face.

"You took her humanity?" His mother's voice was quiet and trembling.

Kearn nodded and held Amber closer still when his mother took another step forwards.

"She is weak. You took too much blood from her... she is too weak." The note of panic in her voice surprised Kearn. "You took too much!"

"Kyran took too much," he countered and moved back a step. His mother looked furious. "I only took a small amount, enough to tie us and to give me the strength to fight Kyran."

His mother reached out a hand but Kearn moved Amber away from her. He wouldn't allow anyone near her, not when she was so fragile. He couldn't trust anyone with her.

"Amber is strong. She will survive." He didn't have a chance to move back again.

Before he could take a step, his mother was right beside Amber, her hands fluttering over her, checking her throat and then touching her face. Kearn held the growl inside when he saw how gentle his mother was being and felt her fear deep in his blood. This time it wasn't fear of Kyran coming for them. It was fear for Amber.

He didn't understand.

Instinct told him to keep Amber away from his mother but he caught his father's gaze and saw his smile, and his blood told him to stay still and allow his mother to check Amber.

"She needs rest... and warmth. We must make sure she is warm. She is so pale. So much blood taken from her yet her heart beats strongly still. Rest and warmth." His mother frowned at the maid who had opened the doors for him. "Bring the others, and ready a room, and tell the kitchen to ready themselves also."

Kearn could only watch his mother. Her hands danced over Amber, touching and caressing. Her feelings collided within him—concern, fear and affection. He wasn't sure what to do.

And then his mother tried to take Amber from him.

Kearn growled and stepped back, pulling Amber close to his chest to protect her.

His mother looked horrified, her wide dark eyes sparkling with what looked like tears.

Tears?

His father came forwards and his mother turned to look up at him, her eyebrows raised high in an expression of pleading.

Pleading him why?

Kearn kept Amber close to him.

His father touched his mother's shoulder and she looked back at Kearn and Amber. There was so much warmth in his mother's eyes.

"The maids will make her some food... and tea, yes, she needs some tea to bring back her colour and her warmth. Humans like tea."

The sight of his mother so concerned about Amber broke through some of Kearn's defences. He searched their connection, trying to discern whether she meant Amber any harm. She seemed genuine enough, but why had she suddenly changed towards him and Amber? Was it purely because Amber was becoming like them now? He had expected his parents to be angry with him for bringing a human into their ruling line, not this.

His mother looked back up at his father, her eyes filling with affection.

"She needs me to take care of her," she whispered and his father nodded.

"Let your mother have her way, son," his father said in a soft voice. "Your female will be safe."

Kearn was only considering releasing Amber when his mother was in front of him, taking Amber from his arms. It was strange to see such a slight woman carrying another in her arms as though she weighed nothing, but it was even stranger to watch her walk away singing a lullaby.

He recognised it. His mother had sung it to him and Kyran when they were small.

Kearn went to follow her, intent on remaining close to Amber, but his father's hand came down heavily on his shoulder, stopping him. He stared after his mother, a deep need to go with Amber filling his blood.

"Do not worry, son. Your mother would never harm Amber, not now." His father smiled warmly. "You have achieved the forgiveness you seek. How does it feel?"

Kearn looked at him, into green eyes and at silver hair that matched his own. He didn't understand. His gaze went back to the gallery but his mother was gone. He could still feel Amber and would be able to follow the feeling to her whenever he wanted, but he didn't like her being out of his sight in his family's home. He wanted to go to her and make sure that she was all right.

His father walked around him and closed the double doors. He smiled.

"You have given your mother that which I could not and that which she has wanted above everything else—a daughter."

Kearn stared at him. "A daughter?"

He had never realised. He had known that his mother had wanted more children, but he had never known that she had dreamed of having a daughter. She had never acted so motherly towards the countess. She had always been cold towards her. Had she felt that the countess was rotten inside, unfit to be a part of their family? Such a thing would make his mother despise her.

Amber was strong though, and would become a vampire fit to rule the Savernake bloodline. She would be fit to rule all of their kind. And she was pure, kind-hearted, and most of all in love with him. Had his mother seen all that in Amber and did she know that Amber had chosen to become like him, to join him in his world, forsaking her own so they could be together?

If his mother truly saw Amber as her daughter now, then his father was right. His mother would never harm Amber. She would dote on her.

"Leave them alone for a while. Come and sit with me. We must discuss what we shall do when Kyran arrives."

Kearn followed his father to the two gold antique couches that stood either side of the fireplace and sat on the one opposite his father.

"She feels happy," his father whispered and looked at the doors. There was so much warmth in his eyes. He looked happy too. "She will love and care for her as a daughter, Kearn. Your love is in safe hands."

Kearn lowered his head, honoured to hear his father call him by his name and to know that his mother had welcomed him back into the family. He hadn't expected it. Everything had happened so fast that he was still trying to come to terms with it. He had turned Amber out of selfish need for her, to have her as his for eternity, because he loved her. He had never considered that it would also reunite him with his family.

Society would be different now. He could take Amber out without fear of any Lesser Nobles or Nobles attempting to harm her. She would be safe wherever they went, protected by his kin rather than despised. He would have been able to bear their treatment of him, but he had never wanted it for Amber.

And now he didn't need to fear it.

His mother would announce that he was a lord of the Savernake bloodline again, and Amber would become a lady of Savernake. His lady.

"I need mother to keep her safe here, when Kyran comes."

"He will come then?" his father said and Kearn nodded.

"I am afraid so. If Pendragon cannot defeat him—"

"You are sure he would go to Pendragon first?" his father interjected.

Kearn frowned. He had been certain that Kyran would go after the strongest family first. His senses reached out to Amber. What if Kyran came to destroy him first in order to take her again? Kyran would have all the power he needed then. He could drink from Amber to restore his strength and then go after Pendragon.

Kearn went to stand but his father raised his hand. He stopped and lowered himself back onto the couch.

"But what if you are right?" Kearn's heart beat fast and it wouldn't slow down, not while he was convinced that Amber was in danger. Not only Amber, but his mother too. She wouldn't stand a chance against Kyran.

"Kyran will not come now, when it is daylight. The Sovereignty informed me that you found him at the Huntingdon estate. The Lesser Nobles are weaker in daylight."

His father was right. The sun was high right now and, under such strong sunlight, the Lesser Nobles would be in danger. Kyran would wait until it was dark enough for his army and then attack. That was only a few short hours away.

"We still have little time to prepare." Kearn's senses reached out to Amber again, latching onto her for comfort. The connection was still weak but she felt warm and happy. Was she dreaming of him?

"The guards have been notified and the Sovereignty has sent us several of their best Venators. We are well protected."

"Guards and Venators will not be enough." Kearn stared at the fire, trying to find a plan amongst the flickering flames. It mesmerised him and his mind emptied as he began to relax. He looked away, needing to keep his edge in case his father was wrong and Kyran was already on his way. "Kyran has taken a lot of Amber's blood."

"We will be ready for him," his father said. "You have also taken Amber's blood and are strong enough to win this fight. Kyran has chosen his path and you must choose yours. I will lose one son this coming night. I know it will not be you."

The confidence in his father's eyes was also in his blood. He was so calm even at a time like this, showing strength that Kearn could only dream of achieving. His father had been one of the top Venators and Kearn had to live up to that reputation and earn such respect for himself. He had never wanted to become a Venator, but he was one now and that was all that mattered. He had to do his duty, and he would do it well so he would only strengthen the name of Savernake.

Kearn fell silent and stared at the fire again, mulling over his father's words. The outcome of this fight would hurt his mother and father regardless of who won. They would lose one of their sons. He wished with all of his heart that it didn't have to be that way, but Kyran had chosen to threaten their family and Amber, and Kearn couldn't allow that. He would defeat his brother, no matter what pain it caused him.

He sensed Amber stir.

Kearn stood.

"Your mother will not harm her," his father said as though he had read his mind.

Kearn focused on Amber's blood. The connection between them was growing stronger again. She was close to waking. He couldn't allow her to wake with only his mother and maids for company. It would frighten her.

"I know." Kearn walked to the dark double doors. "But I must go to her."

He opened the doors and strode down the gallery, heading for the entrance hall. His senses reached out and locked on Amber, and he followed them to her, climbing the elegant staircase and turning right at the split to continue upwards. Her scent filled the sunlit gallery that ran along the front of the house on the first floor. He walked swiftly down the corridor and then turned left when her scent was stronger, and then right at the end of that hallway. His mother had taken her to the guest quarters at the back of the house.

Two young maids stood outside a room on the left hand side in the long corridor. They curtseyed when he approached. It was strange to gain such a reaction from them. His mother must have informed the family that he was a part of it again.

He sensed Amber alone in the room and waved the maids away. He opened the door, stepped into the large dark room, and closed it behind him. A pass of his hand over the locks and they clicked into place. He placed a message on them, telling anyone who tried to open the doors to keep away on pain of death. He had been kind enough to his mother, giving her time with Amber that was rightfully his. He needed to tend to her now.

A thin ribbon of light streamed in through a chink between the closed curtains beyond the bed, and he was tempted to open them to light the room, but wanted some privacy for Amber. Instead, he waved his other hand in the direction of the double bed to his right and the lamps on the bedside cabinets either side of it glowed into life, filling the room with soft warm light.

Kearn frowned at the sight of Amber. She lay under the black covers, her shoulders bare and her wavy brown hair tied up in a knot at the back of her head. He didn't doubt that she was naked and was glad that only women had attended to her.

There was no trace of blood on her throat now, leaving the cut and the pronounced marks of his bite on show. The sight of them filled him with a hunger to kiss her throat and taste her, to reignite the deep passion he had felt during biting her.

She stirred, a frown wrinkling her nose, and wrestled her arm free of the thick covers. They fell back, exposing her left breast as she rubbed her face. Kearn stepped over to her and covered her again so she didn't present such a strong temptation. He sat beside her and she peered up at him.

Her hazel eyes widened when she looked around the large bedroom and a spark of panic laced her heartbeat.

"Where am I?"

"In the main house," he said in a low voice, not wanting to break the intimacy between them, and stroked her brow to soothe her and let her know that she was safe. She was warmer now and had more colour compared to his pale skin, but her blood still felt weary, heavy in his veins. He smiled for her when she glanced at her bare chest. "You were well attended to. My mother seems to have adopted you as her daughter."

Amber's eyebrows rose high. "Daughter?"

"You have gained me not only an end to my loneliness, but a way back into my family. My mother will dote on you as she would have a daughter. I never knew, but my father assures me that my mother wanted a daughter more than anything."

She looked worried. Kearn smoothed the wrinkles from her furrowed brow and smiled again.

"There is no reason to fear, Amber. I will not allow anyone to harm you, and I do not believe my mother means any such intention towards you." He traced his fingertips down over her right temple and cheek, watching her closely and monitoring her blood. The fatigue was still there, lacing all of her emotions. "How are you feeling?"

Amber rested her hand above her head on the dark pillows. Her skin looked so pale against the black. He wished his mother had chosen a nicer room to place Amber in, one that had more colour and looked less funerary. He didn't like the sight of her surrounded by so much darkness when she was weak.

"Tired." Her smile was playful and her eyes narrowed on his. "Not too tired though."

She reached up to him with her left hand and Kearn leaned down, following her silent command. He pressed his lips to hers, kissing her lightly and savouring the scent of her and the feel of her mouth on his. There was strength to her kiss and it flowed through her, chasing back the weariness that had been there a moment before. Perhaps he had sensed sleep rather than fatigue. She had only just awoken after all. Now she felt stronger, more like her usual self, and the heavy feeling in his blood disappeared.

He drew back, not wanting to tire her out. She smiled broadly at him, her hazel eyes warm with it, and he touched her cheek and sighed. She was so beautiful, and so brave to step into his world for him. He would never be able to find the words to convey just what it meant to him, and just how honoured he was that she had sacrificed her humanity, giving herself to him.

"Is something wrong?" she said with another frown.

He smoothed that one away too and shook his head.

"Nothing for you to worry about. You should be resting."

Her frown returned. "Kyran is coming, isn't he?"

Kearn couldn't lie to her. He didn't even need to open his mouth and tell her the truth. The understanding that dawned in her eyes and her blood said that she had sensed it in him.

And in the house.

There was an air of tension in it, a cold gloom that he could feel in his blood and that Amber would sense through him. Preparations were underway and even the servants were being instructed on how to fight. He had never experienced anything like this. Never in his lifetime had his family had to prepare themselves against a foe this strong.

He stroked Amber's cheek, trying to clear his blood of any negative feelings so she wouldn't pick them up. She didn't need to fret. The Savernake guards were stronger than the Huntingdon vampires, and he would deal with Kyran.

He wouldn't let anything happen to his parents.

He wouldn't let anything happen to Amber.

He would keep them all safe.

Even if the only way of defeating Kyran was to go with him into the eternal darkness.

CHAPTER 30

Amber gazed up at Kearn, trying to decipher from his blood what was playing on his mind. He had been quiet for a few minutes now and it worried her. The emotions she had sensed in his blood, the concern, the fear, and the anger, had disappeared one by one, replaced by a feeling of calm that felt false.

Was he lying to her through his blood?

She hated the thought that he would do such a thing and told herself that he wouldn't. He was probably trying not to frighten her. She did need to believe that they would survive the fight against his brother, but she needed even more for him to be honest with her.

"Are you giving me the bedtime story version again?" she whispered and his green eyes met hers. The feelings in them matched those in his blood. He was surprised, amused, and worried.

"Perhaps." His fingers halted against her cheek. They tickled as he lowered them, grazing her jaw and then her throat. They stopped on the point where he had bitten her. It was still sore but she didn't regret it, and she was happy that it had gone the way it had, and that he hadn't done it against her will. He stared at her throat and his fingers, and a small frown creased his brow. "Kyran will try to take you."

"I know." That wasn't her fear. She knew deep in her heart that Kearn would do everything to protect her from his brother. That was what scared her. She feared she might have entered his world only for him to leave it and she didn't want to lose him.

On impulse, she took hold of his hand and brought it away from her neck, clasping it and holding it against her cheek. She leaned into it, pressing a kiss to his knuckles, and closed her eyes.

He sighed.

"Do not be afraid, Amber. I will not let him near you."

Amber opened her eyes and looked into his, trying to memorise the way he was looking at her with so much love and warmth, and praying that this wouldn't be one of their last moments together.

"That's what I'm afraid of," she said and he frowned, clearly not understanding. Her heart ached at the thought of losing him and her throat tightened. "I'm afraid that you'll leave me here alone."

"I will stay right here with you if that is what you want." He smiled.

He hadn't understood.

She squeezed his hand and sniffed back her tears, wanting to be strong even when she felt weak inside. "No, you won't. You'll be here but you'll fight him, and if all else fails... I'm not... I don't want you to do that for me."

His smile disappeared. "I will protect you."

"Regardless of the outcome… of what I want?" Amber sat up now, not caring that the black duvet fell away to reveal her bare breasts. She dropped his hand, threw her arms around his neck and buried her face into it. "Please don't. I don't want you to do that for me. I don't want to be without you."

He sighed and wrapped his arms around her. The feel of them strong against her sides and his hands pressing into her ribs brought more tears. They were hot as they ran down her cheeks and she pulled in a deep breath and fought for control over them. She didn't want to cry.

"These aren't happy tears now, are they?" He pressed his cheek against hers.

Idiot.

Of course they weren't happy tears. He was considering sacrificing himself in order to keep her safe. There was nothing to be happy about.

"What would you have me say, dearest Amber?" His voice was soft against her neck.

"That you'll never leave me and I'm imagining the intent I can feel in your blood… that you won't do this and you won't leave me alone… I wasn't afraid of the future only because you were in it. If you aren't in it, then I don't want to liv—"

Kearn roughly pushed her back and pressed his fingers to her lips. Tears scalded her cheeks and she stared wide-eyed at him. He was angry.

"Shh." He released her mouth, his emotions subsiding and calm returning. "Do not think such things. If it pains you so much, if my leaving this world would only cause you to follow me, then I only have one path open to me."

He brushed her hair back behind her ears, carefully tucking the loose strands away, and then smiled into her eyes.

"I will have to win."

Amber kissed him and it became an outpouring of her feelings. Each brush of their lips and sweep of their tongues was full of the love, the fear and the need she felt inside her. She couldn't lose him. His mouth moved against hers in a light caress that brought her sadness to the surface and fresh tears came as she tried hard not to think about a world without him or the fight ahead of them.

She believed in him. She had to believe in him. It was the only thing that would keep her going. And if he even showed a tiny sign of considering sacrificing himself, she was going to fight too. She wouldn't last five seconds against Kyran, but she wasn't going to give up her future with Kearn. She was going to fight for it, even if it meant dying with him.

"You should not think such things," Kearn whispered against her lips.

She hadn't kept her feelings in check and he had sensed her intent from her blood as easily as she had sensed his. She looked away, staring at the black covers on the double bed and considering what to say. She tried to get her feelings back into place but they wouldn't go.

"I love you," she said in a small voice, tears blurring her vision.

"And that is why you think such things?"

Amber looked at him and blinked to clear her sight. The tears tumbled down her cheeks. Kearn frowned, sighed, and then gently wiped them away. His fingers were soft against her, so careful that more tears came. She sniffed them back, searching for the strength in her heart to say what she needed to.

"Isn't it why you think them too?" she whispered and Kearn's beautiful green eyes filled with sadness.

They were no longer cold and empty. Now she saw emotions in them whenever he looked at her, and every time they were different. She wished they were constant, only love and confidence shining in them. She wasn't sure how to handle the combined weight of their sorrow in her veins and in his eyes but it told her something. He feared the coming battle as much as she did.

If he could face it, then so could she.

She wouldn't give up and she wouldn't let him sacrifice himself. No matter what orders he gave her, she vowed to break them and help him if he needed it.

Kearn stroked her cheek. "It is because I love you that I can think such things. It is not out of duty as a Venator, or for any other reason."

"Then don't think them." She took hold of his hands and toyed with his fingers. Strong hands. They had saved her more than once. Her fingertips traced the silver tribal markings on his right hand. He had incredible powers. He only had to believe in them and fight with his heart, and she was sure that he would win. "Don't think about dying because you love me... think about living because you love me."

Amber looked into his eyes.

"I want you to live for me, Kearn... not die for me."

Kearn smiled and she blushed at the intensity of love in his eyes and in his blood. She dropped her gaze but he took his right hand from hers and pressed his fingers under her chin, raising it so their eyes locked again.

"I will try," he whispered and she knew it was all he could give to her, and it was the closest thing to a promise that she would get. "I do not want to leave you. I brought you into this world because I could not live without you, and because I needed you at my side forever. I do not intend to leave it now that I have you. I would be less than a man if I left you now to go through the transition alone. I will fight for you, my precious Amber, and only you... because my heart commands it."

He lowered his hand to her chest, pressing his palm flat against the space between her breasts.

His heart.

He had said that she ruled his heart. Had he taken her words as an order? If it would stop him from leaving her, she would order him a thousand times over to live for her.

Amber knelt on the bed in front of him, pressed her hands against his chest, feeling his muscles beneath his black military-style jacket, and leaned towards him. His gaze fell to her mouth as she approached, his dark pupils widening, and his lips parted.

"Make love to me," she breathed.

"You are weak still." Kearn grasped her shoulders, stopping her, and an incredulous look crossed his face.

"I can handle you. I feel better. I want... I don't want you to go into this without... I need this, Kearn... do as your heart commands and make love to me."

His frown stuck and then he smiled. "Commands? You are growing a little too used to ordering me around."

"Will you refuse?" She brought his hands away from her shoulders and down to her breasts. The moment she put them there, he was curling his fingers around to cup them and gently squeeze.

He shook his head, causing the silver threads of his hair to fall down across his eyes. Amber swept them back, loving the soft feel of them as they slipped through her fingers. He looked at her, his green eyes full of warmth and love again at last. There wasn't a trace of sorrow in his blood. Need and desire had replaced it—a heated feeling that made her lick her lips and lean in to kiss him again.

Amber pressed her mouth to his, parted his lips with her tongue, and kissed him. He responded with gentle force, his tongue coming to meet hers, sliding silkily along the length of it and tangling together. His hands clutched her breasts and she moaned when he thumbed her nipples, sending a wave of sparks dancing outwards across her body.

Every inch of her responded to his touch, growing warm and hungry for him. She pressed her hands against his chest and slid them over his tense muscles, towards the twin rows of silver buttons that formed a V down the jacket. The first set she chose didn't open.

Kearn pulled back, smiled down at her hands, and moved them to the opposite set of silver buttons. She began to undo them. When she reached the bottom, she pushed the thick jacket off his shoulders and then started on his black shirt. Her fingers slowed as she undid each button and she savoured the way it opened little by little to reveal the defined muscles of his bare chest. The heat pooling at the apex of her thighs increased and she ached to feel Kearn inside her.

Her gaze fell to his crotch as the last of his shirt buttons gave way.

The black material of his trousers didn't hide the hard outline of his erection.

Clearly he wanted to be inside her too.

Kearn groaned when she stroked his length. She stared at his face, relishing the way his eyes closed and his teeth sunk into his lower lip.

His eyes opened and the desire in them and in his blood astounded her. He narrowed his gaze on her and then lowered it to her body, slowly and sensually taking her all in. She burned under his perusal, hungry for his touch. When his gaze reached her hand, she ran it along his erection again, eliciting a groan from him that set her blood on fire. She licked her lips and continued to stroke him, enjoying the feel of him and his reaction to her touch.

He tensed and leaned back, giving her a wonderful view of the muscles of his torso. She leaned forwards to devour every inch of his delicious body but Kearn was on his feet before she could reach him, slipping free of her grasp.

Amber sat back and watched him undress instead. He shirked his jacket and shirt, letting them fall to the floor, and then removed his boots. Her mouth turned dry when he undid his belt and his trousers. A new flood of desire washed through her, and she wriggled on the bed as he kicked off his trousers and underwear, and ran his right hand down his hard length.

She wanted that. Now.

Lying back on the bed, she tilted her head to one side and crooked her finger at him.

He growled.

A thrill chased through her.

Animal.

Kearn kneeled on the bed and then leaned over her, his hips nestling between her thighs. She brushed her fingers across his cheek and then down his neck and over his shoulder, feeling the power in his beautiful body and his blood. He smiled when she hooked her hand around the back of his neck and lured him down to her. His kiss was sweet and slow, gradually stirring the embers of her desire into flames that scorched her skin.

He rested on one elbow above her, his other hand skimming down her right side. It tickled, causing her to wriggle beneath him, and then her eyes slipped shut as his fingers brushed across her stomach and downwards. A groan escaped her when he slid them into her warm folds and teased her. The feeling was too much when she was burning with hunger, balanced on the precipice of her desire and ready to fall into bliss with him.

His fingers moved downwards and anticipation coiled in her stomach. She raised her hips hungrily into his hand and sighed when he eased his finger into her body and slowly pumped her. She wanted to feel him inside her. The thought of being so close to having him there was maddening. She writhed against his hand, trying to encourage him to make a move.

Kearn kissed her throat and, even though she knew that he wouldn't bite her or take blood from her, it was thrilling to have him there again. She wanted to feel it but knew he would refuse her while she was still recovering.

Each kiss on her throat sent a shiver tripping through her body, down over her breasts and stomach to the point where his finger teased her.

She moaned and raised her body into his, eliciting a growl from him when her hip rubbed his hard length. She slid her hand downwards. The moment it wrapped around his shaft, he thrust against her, pushing himself through her tight grip. His finger moved deeper inside her, sending her desire spiralling until she wanted to burst.

"Kearn," she whispered into his ear and kissed it, licking the lobe and tempted to bite it to make him do as she wanted.

He pulled his finger out of her and moved between her legs. The weight of him against her was divine. She wanted to be one with him again, connected in their feelings, their blood, and their bodies.

Kearn moaned when he eased his hard length into her and she joined him, releasing a long sighing groan of satisfaction. He drew back and then slid in again, his pace slow and threatening to drive her as crazy as his finger had.

The connection between them deepened and their feelings became one. It was dizzying to have him like this, to feel everything that he could and know it was a reflection of her own feelings. She loved him more than anything and never wanted to be apart from him. She wanted this to last forever.

Kearn wrapped his arms around her, settling one in the arch of her back to hold her to him, and hooking his other hand over her shoulder. He moved slowly and deeply, and each thrust heightened her feelings and their connection a little more, until she was drowning in a warm hazy sea of bliss and she didn't care.

Amber kissed along his jaw and found his mouth. She lost herself there, drifting along with him at a slow pace, memorising every moment of being with him. Everything disappeared, melting away until there was only Kearn and nothing else. There was no coming battle. There was no fear of the future. There was only him and this moment, together with her in bliss and love.

Her heartbeat slowed even as her desire rose, her body tightening with need and arousal. She hooked her legs over his hips and he deepened his thrusts, moving slowly into her. She groaned and kissed him. Kearn pulled her close to him and her heart beat hard. It felt as though his had beaten at the same time.

She drew back. He smiled, as though he knew her silent question.

"My heart," he whispered and kissed her again. It was all the explanation he gave. Did their connection now run so deeply that their bodies were one, their hearts beating in time and their breathing in synchronisation? It was incredible.

Amber drifted away again, lost in the feel of him moving inside her, and the growing tightness in her abdomen. His kisses grew more desperate and she could feel he was as close as she was, reaching for his climax. Amber tensed her body around his and he groaned into her mouth. He thrust deep into her, brushing her sensitive flesh, and she came undone, her body trembling around his. Warmth ran in her veins, sedating her and carrying her away.

Kearn moved slower, deeper, and then stilled and moaned with his climax.

Amber wrapped her arms around his shoulders and held him to her, relaxing into the bed with him on top of her, still intimately entwined. He sighed and kissed her lips, her cheek, her throat, before settling his head on the pillow besides hers. His breath caressed her throat, tickling his marks there.

"Sleep a while." She could feel his fatigue running through her blood. He sighed again. She stroked her fingers through the silver threads of his hair, her focus wholly on him.

She waited for him to protest and leave, but he didn't. He remained in her arms, his weight heavy but nice against her, and his body acting as her blanket. She would never be cold when he was this close to her.

Amber closed her eyes and tried not to think about what was coming.

She wanted to savour every drop of this moment with him.

She didn't want it to be their last.

She wouldn't let it be.

CHAPTER 31

Kearn's gaze scanned the room for what felt like the millionth time. The three male Venators he had assigned to remain with him stood at the other end of the black reception room, dressed in their black uniforms just as he was. One of them paced near the door to the gallery while the other two stared out of the windows into the dark night. It felt as though the whole house was on edge, awaiting the impending attack but never knowing when it would begin. Amber's weariness and fear ran in Kearn's blood, flowing strongly and calling to him. He turned to her, offering a comforting smile when she looked up at from him the gold couch to his right.

His mother sat next to her, holding Amber's hand, gently chafing it.

He went to Amber and she held her left hand out to him. His mother released her as he took hold of her hand and pulled her into his arms. He held her close, one arm wrapped around her waist as his other hand held her head to his chest. Her fear abated a sliver when he stroked her long brown hair, toying with her ponytail, and he closed his eyes, sending her a wave of reassurance through their bond.

He refused to feel scared, or any amount of fear. He needed to be strong for Amber, so she would sense it in his blood and her own fear would lessen.

Amber drew back, away from him enough that he could look down into her hazel eyes. He grazed the backs of his fingers across her cheek and her eyes closed, and she leaned into his caress. She was beautiful. His Amber. His love. The marks on her throat were visible above the low-slung collar of her black hooded top. He trailed his fingers down to them and stroked the marks, feeling the pronounced bumps. It would be weeks before they had healed and even then they would remains as scars. She would always be his.

She smiled up at him, warmth travelling in her veins and through his, and her feelings lightening. Kearn dipped his head and pressed a soft kiss to her lips, oblivious to the five people watching him.

When he pulled back, the three Venators and his parents looked away.

His moment of peace shattered.

The strong smell of vampire blood alerted Kearn to the start of Kyran's attack. It drifted on the still night air, creeping into the house until it reached him. He faced the dark double doors, his senses scanning the estate grounds.

So far, he could only sense Lesser Nobles. They were easily detectable by their weaker blood.

His eyes narrowed on the doors.

Sometimes he despised Lesser Nobles. They were wretched families with little power of their own and aspirations beyond their reach, attempting to gain the power of Nobles. Tonight the Huntingdon family would learn their place.

He would remind them of it personally. They were inferior. Beneath the Nobles. There was a reason his kind ruled. They were superior in every way—breeding, strength, power and sense. A Lesser Noble was no match for them.

His hearing picked up the fight outside. It seemed his father did too because he turned to his mother.

"Come, it is time." His father took his mother's arm and led her into the grand reception room beyond the gilt double doors.

Kearn turned to Amber. She smiled but he could feel her nerves rising again. He wished this didn't have to happen. He didn't want to fight Kyran, just the thought of it cut him deeply, and he didn't want Amber to witness such a thing. He wanted things to continue as they had been only a few short hours ago when he had made love to her and slept in her arms. It was all that he longed for.

He signalled to the three male Venators waiting near the tall rectangular windows behind him, silently telling them to remain where they were. He had chosen them because they looked as though they would gladly fight both vampires who had tasted forbidden blood and those that hadn't, and they were the strongest. They would serve as backup when Kyran showed his face, keeping the other vampires out of his fight.

Amber stood and his attention returned to her. She was still smiling at him with love in her eyes. How could she look at him like that when she knew that he was going to fight his own brother? He wouldn't be able to look himself in the eye for a long time after tonight, and he wasn't sure how he would face his parents. Part of him said to allow his father the honour of taking his son's life, but he couldn't go through with it. Kyran had chosen to make an enemy of him, even though he knew Kearn had fought the Sovereignty's decision, and was intent on making him pay. He would harm Amber to achieve it, and then kill their parents before finally attacking him.

Kearn couldn't allow that.

He would protect his love and his family at all costs.

Amber's hazel eyes narrowed on his. She had sensed his feelings and wasn't happy. He pushed thoughts of fighting his brother to the death out of his mind and remembered that he had promised that he would live for her, not die. He would win. His love for Amber would give him the strength he needed to defeat Kyran.

He held his hand out to her and she slipped hers into it. She was quiet as they walked towards the grand reception room where his parents waited.

"You will be safe in here." He smiled for her and let her sense that he wasn't lying.

His need to have her and his mother near to him wasn't the only reason he had brought them here. This was more than a reception room. It was a safe room for his family in case they ever came under attack. The walls were reinforced and windowless, impossible to break through even with Kyran's strength. There were steel doors set into the wall above the wooden ones, ready to slide into place if his mother pressed a button on the other side. He had given her orders to if something happened. She would protect Amber.

Kearn looked back at the first reception room. Kyran would expect him to bring Amber and their parents here, and he would have to go through him in order to get to them.

The reception room wasn't ideal for fighting, but the close quarters would aid his side. The power of the Venators, his father, and himself, would be too much for the Lesser Nobles. The only ones that would pose even the slightest threat would be the ruling line of the house, and Kearn suspected that Earl and Countess Huntingdon would soon fall back after leading the attack through the lower guards surrounding the estate. Kyran might have the power to sway the other Lesser Nobles of the Huntingdon bloodline, but the earl and countess wouldn't be foolish enough to risk themselves against any of the stronger vampires of the Savernake bloodline.

"Do not be afraid," his father said and Kearn looked his way.

His father was holding his mother close, smoothing her long black hair down the back of her corseted dress. She tilted her head back when his father touched her cheek and smiled up at him. Something told Kearn to look away, and not intrude on this private moment between them, but the sight of his father drew his attention. He had never noticed before just how different his father was around his mother. He no longer looked strong. Kearn could feel the fear in his heart and it matched his own fear for Amber. It was overwhelming, crushing his chest and making him weak.

His mother reached up, swept the long strands of his father's silver hair from his face, and her smile widened.

"Stay safe." His father pressed a kiss to her lips.

Kearn did look away now. There was only so much affection a son should see between his parents. His gaze strayed to Amber. His father loved his mother so deeply, and Kearn felt the same about Amber. His heart belonged to her forever. Nothing would change that. He loved her until death and beyond.

"Protect Amber." Those words leaving his father's lips surprised him.

His mother nodded and her gaze shifted to Amber. She held her hand out to her.

Amber went to go to her and then stopped. She looked over her shoulder at Kearn, past the waves of her brown hair, her hazel eyes searching his, and then turned back.

He smiled when she kissed him, slowly and deeply, and he held her close, returning the kiss with all of the passion and love he felt for her, reassuring her of his feelings. He wasn't ashamed of his parents seeing him like this. He loved Amber and he would never shy away from his feelings, no matter who was watching. He had lowered himself to her and kissed her hand in front of all society, and he would do so again at the next ball and the rest after that. Everyone would know that he loved her and that she had won his heart.

She drew back, smiling wide through the fear he could feel in her, and brushed her fingers across his cheek.

"Be careful," she whispered and her blood said more than that. It told him to fight, and to keep his promise and come back to her.

He intended to.

"Call out to me if anything happens." He walked her over to his parents. His mother took her hand and started chafing it again in both of hers as though Amber was a child in need of comfort. "Do not open the door."

Amber nodded.

Kearn stepped back, away from her, and his father walked past him to the door. It was hard for him to leave Amber, even when he had to. He wanted to stay with her. He hesitated a moment, his eyes locked with hers, drinking in the sight of her and the love that he could sense in his blood, and then followed his father.

His father closed the gilt double doors when they were through, stealing Amber from view so he could only feel her in his blood. Her fear increased. He cursed his brother. He didn't want to fight him. Even after everything Kyran had done to him, Kearn still loved him. He was still his brother.

Kearn walked to the three male Venators and the windows they guarded. He looked out of the one nearest the doors, searching the night for a sign of his enemy. The fighting had reached the house. The smell of blood was stronger now, swamping his senses and calling to his instincts. His fangs extended and his eyes changed, his vision heightening until he could see through the darkness to the fighting. They were near the house, on the drive that lined the front of it.

His fingertips tingled.

Kyran was coming.

He could feel him in his heart, the blood bond they shared as brothers allowing him to glimpse his feelings. He was angry and bent on revenge, his heart dark and cold. Kearn clenched his fists and readied himself. The guards at the house were stronger, able to defeat all but the highest ranking of the Huntingdon bloodline, but the enemy were numerous. Some would get through and he would be waiting for them.

"They are coming." His father walked to the double doors that led onto the gallery.

Kearn could hear them. The fight was spilling into the house and the noise was loud enough that he was sure even Amber would hear it soon. He tried to keep his feelings calm, knowing that she would be reaching out to him through their connection.

There were voices in the gallery.

Power surged up Kearn's marked arm, making it ache and throb, until it glowed bright blue. It whispered dark words to him, encouraging him to take the lives of those daring to approach him with such evil intent. Kearn didn't listen. He cursed it instead and the Sovereignty for giving him such a terrible weapon. He hated the words it spoke to him and its hunger for vampire souls.

The doors burst open and two men ran in, both from the Huntingdon family. His arm didn't react to them. They hadn't taken Source Blood. He began to attack them with his own power, but his father raised his hands and the men were on the floor, writhing and screaming. His father was a formidable foe—the strongest of their bloodline and with power beyond a Lesser Noble's dreams. Another three clambered over the bodies of the first two, breaking their way into the room, and attacked with their own power, flinging their hands forwards and attempting to throw his side off balance with telekinesis.

Kearn held his left hand up and halted their attack. Fear whispered in his blood. Not his feelings but Amber's. Before he realised it, all three vampires were twisted and dead, their blood coating the open doors and the walls. He breathed hard from the sudden drain in his power. He hadn't been in control. Amber's feelings had made him react without thinking.

"It takes a little more practice to control your power when under the influence of another's emotions," his father said from behind him.

Kearn jumped back to be level with him. His desire to protect Amber was so strong that whenever he could sense her fear, he wanted to rip his enemy limb from limb. He wanted to protect her so fiercely that he would do anything, even shed his breeding and all sense of etiquette and let his lust for blood run free and unchecked. He would become the beast he had thought she would see him as. He would do that for her, and only her.

He focused on the enemy. More were coming. They were stronger but they were only getting through because of their numbers. His family were still fighting in the gallery and in the entrance hall.

The three Venators moved forwards and the blue glow of their hands filled the corner of Kearn's vision. He looked at his own right hand. It wanted souls to satisfy its growing hunger. It would have them soon enough. He could sense at least five vampires coming.

They broke into the room and Kearn's arm responded, the markings burning against his skin and glowing brighter. It seemed these men were on the list of the Sovereignty.

He signalled to the other Venators and they nodded and then dashed forwards to attack the vampires. Kearn moved across the room in the blink of an eye and punched one hard across the jaw. He couldn't use his power at a distance. He had to conserve his energy for his fight against Kyran and would have to kill these men the old-fashioned way.

The young dark haired man he had attacked fought back, clawing and then punching. Kearn tried to evade him but backed into another of the Huntingdon vampires. The man's fist caught him hard in the throat and pain blasted out, making it difficult to breathe. He growled, grabbed the man by his shirt and threw him into the wall. Turning, Kearn caught the man behind him too. This one was older and stronger, but still no match for him. He clutched the man's long hair, brought his head down, and smashed his face on his knee. The man fell backwards and one of the Venators caught him and pressed his glowing hand against the man's chest.

Kearn didn't watch the man die. His scream pierced the noise of battle, ungodly in its sound. Everyone would hear it and know what had happened to him. They would know what awaited them in this room.

He attacked the young dark haired vampire again, leaving the other three to the Venators. The man dodged his first punch, but Kearn caught him in the stomach with his second and then flicked his left hand, tossing him through the air. He slammed into the wall beside the doors to the room where his mother and Amber were and they shrieked.

Amber's fear lanced through him and Kearn gripped his arm, struggling to control his dark urge to shatter the man into pieces. He ran at him instead, and pinned him to the wall before he could recover. Their eyes met and Kearn didn't flinch away. He pressed his right palm against the man's chest and released the power in his arm. The man screamed, tilting his head back into the wall. Black ribbons crept out from Kearn's hand, penetrated the man's chest and crawled up his neck to his mouth. They slithered inside and the man's eyes opened wide and terrified.

Kearn watched. He had to. It was his punishment for committing such atrocity in the name of the Sovereignty and for sending the man to such a dark unholy place.

The young vampire's eyes rolled back and he convulsed against the wall. The black ribbons burrowed deep into his body and his skin greyed. Kearn released him and turned away. He had seen enough.

His father's gaze caught his but he couldn't hold it. How many lives had his father taken in the centuries he had been a Venator?

Had he ever felt so disgusted at himself?

Sympathetic feelings flowed into his heart and Kearn looked at his father, knowing they were coming from him and not Amber this time. Perhaps he wasn't the only Venator who had felt ashamed at times.

Two more screams punctured the air and Kearn went to help the other three Venators. All three men were fighting hard, two of them in the midst of sentencing their opponent, and the other fighting the remaining man.

Before Kearn could assist him, the Venator had the man in a headlock, his forearm tight across his throat, choking him. The Huntingdon vampire struggled but it was useless. His face reddened and his movements weakened. The Venator released him, spun him on the spot, and shoved his glowing hand against the man's chest. There was such glee on the Venator's face as he watched the man die. Kearn had never seen a man take such pleasure from killing another vampire, especially when sending him to the eternal darkness.

Kearn shifted his senses to the Venator, trying to detect what family he was from. He was a Noble. His strength and the underlying power Kearn could sense in him said that he was from a strong bloodline too.

"You do not seem to recognise your cousin. Is it so long since you have seen him?" his father said.

Cousin?

Kearn couldn't believe his eyes. He looked hard at the Venator, past the short silver hair and the green eyes, trying to see if it was possible. It had been a long time since he had seen Traegard Montagu, almost a century in fact. He hadn't realised that he had become a Venator or that he had grown so strong.

Traegard wasn't the son of Duke Montagu, but they were cousins by the bond between their families. In the Montagu family, the ruling line weren't Venators. Duke Montagu's mother had been eldest, and had gone on to rule the bloodline. Her younger brother had gained the duty of Venator, and in turn his eldest son, and then Traegard.

The last time he had seen Traegard Montagu, he had been a peaceful young man, with artistic ideals and little interest in fighting.

Seeing him now, watching him kill without mercy, it was like looking at a different person.

Traegard dropped the body of the vampire and flicked the remaining black ribbons from his fingertips. He looked at Kearn, his eyes red with bloodlust. Kearn could feel the exhilaration in him, the excitement, and it bordered on disturbing. He looked away from Traegard, clearing away his curiosity about what had happened to change his cousin, and looked around the room. Only piles of grey ashes remained where the last five Huntingdon vampires had fallen. The blood from the other vampires seeped into it, turning it dark.

Another group of vampires forced their way into the room, spilling through the doors. There were more this time and not all of them had taken Source Blood. The three Venators attacked those who their arms responded to, leaving him and his father to deal with the rest.

Kearn threw himself into the fray, punching any who dared come close to him, and attacking others with his power. His father moved deeper into the group, towards the doors. Kearn tried to keep an eye on him but it was impossible. He had to focus on killing the vampires around him and protecting Amber. He wouldn't let any of them near her.

He used telekinesis to scatter them, tossing two men around his age to his left and thrusting the other three to the right. They barrelled into his father and Kearn turned away. His father would deal with them. He attacked the remaining two, throwing one into the other to knock them back down, and then focusing on his desire for them to die. He curled his fingers into a fist and unleashed his darkest power on them, controlling their blood and their bodies against their will. He snapped arms and broke legs, shattering them from the inside out until they were motionless.

Dead.

His father had dealt with the others in a similar fashion, leaving broken bodies lying at his feet, and the vampires Kearn had left the Venators to deal with were nothing but dust.

It was too easy so far. None of these vampires were any match for a Noble.

Kearn reached deep into his blood, trying to sense Amber and see how she was coping. She was still afraid. Her blood whispered to his, seeking comfort. He sent a message to her, telling her not to fear and that it would be over soon.

Just as he did so, another group of vampires broke through the line of Venators and into the room.

Kearn went to attack them and then stopped.

Kyran was close.

He glanced at his father and before he could say a word, his father rushed into the vampires, tearing them to shreds with his bare hands, and crushing their bones and puncturing their skin with thought alone.

"Fall back," Kearn called to him but his father kept going forwards, towards the doors, and then disappeared through them.

Kearn was halfway to the doors when his father flew backwards into the room and slammed into the far wall. Kearn was on his knees beside him in an instant, helping him into a sitting position.

He swallowed.

Three long lines cut across the chest of his father's black coat. Blood poured from the gashes and he felt his father's strength flowing from him at the same pace, trickling away with each passing second. He had to get him to safety. Kyran would easily kill him in his weakened state.

Kearn placed his father's right arm around his shoulders and carefully stood with him. His father grimaced and placed his arm across his stomach.

"Do not worry about me." His father looked at him with red eyes. "Kyran is too strong. I could not stand against my own son, not even to spare my other child the pain of taking his life."

"Do not speak." Kearn walked with him to the doors of the safe room. He could sense the three Venators watching him. They would have to hold off the vampires without him until he got his father to safety. "It is my duty to carry out the law of the Sovereignty. I am strong enough to do this."

His father growled. Kearn felt his disapproval and knew in his heart that it wasn't about him. He was angry with the Sovereignty too.

Kearn sent another message through his blood, this time to his mother. The gilt doors ahead of them opened a crack and then a wave of distress swept through the room. His mother was at his father's side before Kearn could tell her to remain where she was. She murmured quiet words of love and took his father's other arm, helping him into the room.

Amber waited on the other side of the doors, face pale and eyes enormous. He probably looked terrible by now. His eyes were still red, his fangs still extended, and blood covered him. If she was ever going to think he was a monster, a beast, it would be now.

He set his father down on a chair and went back to the doors. He wanted to go to Amber, his heart telling him to comfort her and to kiss her in case he never saw her again, but he had to return to the fight. He had to end this.

Amber caught his wrist. Her fingers trembled against it and her fear became strong in his blood, bringing out his own.

He looked at the three Venators as they fought the vampires, holding them back. One of them was injured. He could feel his brother getting closer, heralded by a black malevolent wave of power so hideously strong that it turned his insides. Kearn felt weak compared with it, and knew deep inside him that he was no match for his brother. Kyran must have taken more Source Blood in their time apart, boosting his power. The effects of Amber's blood on Kearn were already beginning to fade, and the Sovereignty's power drained his strength too. What chance did they stand when his brother arrived? Kyran had taken his father down without even being close to him.

Kearn placed his hand over Amber's, still facing away from her, and held it. He told her without words that she would be safe with his parents.

A scream pierced the noise of fighting and one of the Venators fell back into the room, his torso and arms cut to ribbons. An injury like that would easily kill him and the severity of it made Kearn's blood run cold. Kyran could only have done it at close quarters.

He was here.

Kearn turned to Amber, his heart beating hard against his chest. He had promised to return to her, but the wave of power sweeping over him was stronger than he had anticipated. Even with her blood, he still wasn't as strong as Kyran. He smiled at her, holding his fear beyond her reach and giving her only his love.

"I will be back soon." He took her hand from his arm, pressed a kiss to her hand and breathed her in, savouring her warm scent. "I love you."

She frowned when he lowered her hand and then released it.

He looked at his mother, and then backed out of the door, his gaze returning to Amber.

It hurt to lie to her, to tell her that he would keep his promise even when he knew he couldn't. He had to do it though. He had to protect her from his brother. He couldn't let her die.

"I love you," she whispered and he sensed the rest of what she wanted to say. She wanted to tell him to come back to her. She knew what was happening.

Stay with me forever.

Her blood said it with such intensity that he had to turn away, had to break the connection between them, couldn't bear to feel her need and her love for him when he was only going to hurt her.

His smile faded. He wanted nothing more than to be with her forever.

Kyran stepped into the room.

But destiny had other plans.

CHAPTER 32

Kearn was a terrible liar.

Amber's chest hurt at the thought of losing him. She didn't want to become a vampire in a world where he didn't exist.

The double doors closed and her attention shifted to Kearn's mother. She was doing something with a panel beside the doors. Amber's eyes widened when she heard a mechanism kick into life and a sheet of metal started to slide down over the doors.

No. She couldn't let Kearn fight alone. She wouldn't live forever without him. She could help him. She didn't know how yet, but she was sure there was something she could do.

Amber glanced at Kearn's mother, and then his father, and then ran at the doors. His mother called out to her but she didn't stop. She shoved the door open, dived through, and slammed it behind her.

It was a warzone on the other side. Her heart stammered in her chest and then began at a rapid pace, sending her blood rushing through her ears. Kearn was fighting Kyran with the assistance of another Venator. He was badly injured and there was no sign of the other two Venators. Kyran wasn't without injury either. A thick red gash darted across his cheek, stark against his pale skin, and another cut into his dark hair above his left temple. He looked at her, his red eyes melting back to blue, and smiled.

Kearn glanced over his shoulder, anger in his red eyes. She had only seen him a moment ago but he already looked worse, his face covered with scratches and bruises, and his lower lip cut. He held his hand out and she obeyed his silent command to keep back even though she wanted to help him.

Kyran grinned and raised his hand. Kearn and the other Venator flew across the room, clearing the path between her and Kyran. Kearn's gun dropped from the holster around his thigh and bounced off the floor. She flinched, afraid it would go off, and then backed away when Kyran stalked towards her.

"Leave her alone!" Kearn threw himself at Kyran. They hit the parquet hard and she sidestepped away from them.

Her gaze strayed to the gun on the other side of the room beyond the remains of the two gold couches. If she could reach it, she could help Kearn.

Pain tore through her and she grimaced against it. The moment it eased, she checked herself over, afraid that she had been caught in the fight. There wasn't a scratch on her. She looked at Kearn. He was clutching his arm and glaring at his brother. It was his pain. The connection between them had reopened. She could feel his weariness and hurt, and the pain that fighting his brother caused him deep in his heart. She wished she could take that away and end this for him, so he didn't have to be the one to kill his brother. She knew he would never forgive himself or the Sovereignty for it.

"Traegard, the door," Kearn said and the other Venator nodded and went out into the gallery. The sound of fighting there increased. He was defending the room so Kearn could fight one on one with Kyran.

No. Not one on one. She was here to fight too.

Amber edged towards the right corner of the room, trying not to draw attention to herself.

Kearn's fight against his brother was vicious and fast, so quick that it was only a blur of punches whenever they clashed. Kyran flew across the room like a ragdoll, slamming into the wall near the fireplace and landing hard on the destroyed couch there. Before he could stand, Kearn was on him, grasping the back of his torn black shirt and hauling him off the ground. He growled and threw Kyran across the other side of the room, away from her.

Amber slunk back against the wall behind her.

Kearn turned to face her with a frown. "I wanted you safe."

She laughed. "Safe... so you can get yourself killed out here alone?"

His expression darkened.

"You're a crappy liar," she muttered and then her eyes shot wide when Kyran got to his feet. She pointed. "Go... I have a plan."

Kearn didn't stick around to ask about it. Amber was thankful. He would have laughed had she said that she intended to shoot his brother for him, pump him full of lead until he couldn't move and Kearn could kill him. She had never fired a gun before. She wasn't even sure if she could. Kearn needed her help though and it wasn't the time to be weak and worry about the consequences. She couldn't kill Kyran with a gun. It would just be flesh wounds to slow him down.

That didn't make her feel better at all. She was still proposing to pull the trigger on someone she knew. The thought alone chilled her blood.

But she kept moving towards the gun, slowly easing her way around the room to where it lay on the other side of the fireplace.

Kearn kicked Kyran across the head but he blocked it by grabbing Kearn's ankle and slamming him into the ground. Amber flinched against the pain that shot through her, numbing her senses. Kearn didn't seem to notice it himself. He brought his other leg up like a rocket, catching Kyran under the jaw with the heel of his boot and sending him soaring upwards. He hit the ceiling and dropped, landing on his knees. Kearn raised his hand and curled his fingers up, and Kyran howled in agony.

Amber didn't like that sound. It was wrong somehow. It sounded like a beast baying for blood. She continued and was close to her target when the world suddenly swept past her. She hit the floor, collapsing onto her shoulder, and struggled to breathe.

What had happened?

"Touch her again and I will—"

"What?" Kyran interjected, cutting Kearn off.

Amber's vision swam when she tried to look at them. Her head felt fuzzy.

"We could always make this a more interesting game." Kyran grinned at Kearn and then turned his smile on her. "Come, Lover."

She had forgotten one very important thing in the midst of her desire to protect Kearn.

Kyran had her blood. He could control her.

Amber shook her head, fighting the effect of Kyran's command. She wouldn't go to him. She didn't want to hurt Kearn again, not as she had at the ball. She wouldn't do it.

He crooked a finger and she was on her feet without thinking and walking towards him, her thoughts of resisting him drifting away. They didn't matter. She wanted to do as Kyran asked.

"Go back, Amber," Kearn said and the connection to Kyran severed.

Amber shrank back again, scowling at Kyran. She had to end this before Kyran managed to gain control over her again. She wouldn't hurt Kearn.

Kyran motioned to her again but this time nothing happened. He turned his steely gaze on Kearn. Kearn's right hand glowed bright blue, lighting the air around him and reflecting off the buckles on his scuffed and dusty black leather boots. He raised it towards Kyran and sparks broke from the surface of his skin, leaping through the tears in his black military-style jacket. Kyran dodged the bolt of white-blue light that shot towards him. Amber didn't waste her chance. She ran for the gun.

She was scrambling over the broken furniture when the floor dropped away again and she was flying. This time she braced for impact. It didn't help. Pain shot through every bone in her body when she smashed into the wall. Her head was a riot of pain, spinning so much that she didn't want to open her eyes. Someone growled. Her blood said it was Kearn, and he was growing angrier by the second, but weaker too. She could feel the strength draining from him.

Carefully, she tried to sense Kyran. His blood flowed strong with hers and his power was incredible. She broke the connection before he noticed and opened her eyes. Her head pounded. Kearn was fighting hard but it wouldn't be enough. They had both taken blood from her in an almost equal quantity, but Kyran was stronger than he was. Why?

A noise from the gallery drew her attention. The other Venator was there, fighting the vampires that were trying to get through. The blue glow of his arm highlighted his weary expression.

Amber looked back at Kearn, remembering the fight at the warehouse. He had been tired after that.

Did the power in his arm drain his energy?

He looked at her as she thought that, his red eyes boring into hers. Just as she felt the answer in her blood, Kyran threw him hard onto the floor, splintering the wooden boards. Kearn grunted on impact, his eyes closing and arms splaying out. The light from his arm flickered and died, leaving only the silver markings behind.

It did drain him. It was making him weak.

Kyran went to attack Kearn, but Kearn grabbed him and managed to get his feet against Kyran's stomach. He launched Kyran into the ceiling and was on his feet before he fell. The moment he did, Kearn spun around and kicked him in the stomach again, sending him shooting across the room. Kyran hit the wall, shaking the room, and the windows exploded out into the night.

The other Venator was on him in a heartbeat, pummelling him with his fists, his eyes vivid red and narrowed.

Kyran threw him away. He landed in amongst the vampires in the gallery but they didn't have a chance to attack him. He struck first, pressing his hand against one vampire's chest. The man unleashed a scream that made her cover her ears and strange black things crept out of the Venator's hand and into the man.

Amber looked away and her gaze fell on the gun only a few feet away.

Kyran had thrown her exactly where she had wanted to go. She smiled, reached for it, and dragged it towards her. She pushed herself onto her knees and lifted the gun. It was heavier than she remembered. Her limbs trembled with pain and her fingers felt so weak she feared she was going to drop the weapon and alert Kyran to her presence again.

He didn't seem to notice her. He was stalking towards Kearn with murder in his red eyes and plaster chalk covering the back of his ruined black shirt and trousers.

Kearn was ready for him but she could still feel his fatigue and see it in his face. He was breathing hard and his desire to sleep ran deep in her veins. He couldn't last much longer against Kyran, and Kyran showed no sign of getting weaker.

Amber raised the gun, using both hands to hold it just as she had seen in the movies, and pointed it at Kyran. It shook all over the place. She wasn't sure that she wanted to do this, wasn't sure if she would be able to live with herself, and wasn't even sure what help it would be.

Kearn had told her that he used the gun to slow the vampires down and that it was his arm that killed them. She had to slow Kyran down for him.

With her heart in her mouth, she yanked the trigger.

It clicked but nothing happened.

Kyran's head snapped around to face her. He grinned.

Crap. The safety. She fumbled with it, trying to figure out how to get it off. Kyran changed course, coming towards her. The switch moved and she raised the gun again, closed her eyes and pulled the trigger.

Her ears rang from the loud cracking noise and she fell backwards from the recoil, landing on her bottom with her legs bent at her side and her back against the wall behind her. She opened her eyes, her heart rushing in her throat, and looked at Kyran.

He stood with his right hand in front of him, staring at it.

Blood covered it.

There was a wet patch on his left shoulder.

She had shot him.

The desire to be sick was overwhelming but Amber held it together. She felt weak but strong too, able to help the man she loved.

Kearn attacked Kyran, shoving his left shoulder so Kyran cried out, and taking him down to the ground. Amber swallowed her heart back down and readied herself in case she would have to shoot Kyran again. He landed on top, pinning Kearn to the ground and punching him hard across the face.

"Why?" Kearn said and Kyran's fist stopped short of his face.

Kyran's expression turned ugly, his frown darkening his eyes, and Amber could feel the anger in him. She didn't want to be able to sense him through her blood. She wanted him out of it.

She raised the gun again. It shook so violently that she couldn't aim straight and her hands felt numb where they gripped it.

"You know why." Kyran's voice was low and hollow. He hit Kearn again but Kearn didn't fight back.

His hand began to glow blue.

Amber could feel his distress, the pain over having to fight Kyran and having hurt him, and the reluctance to carry out the order of the Sovereignty.

"I never chose this life," Kearn whispered, his brow furrowing and his eyes becoming green. Kyran hit him again, his growing frustration clear on his face. Kearn growled. "It chose me!"

"Chose you?" Kyran grabbed Kearn's shoulders, lifted them off the ground and then slammed him back down, so Kearn's head bounced off the wooden floor. Pain speared Amber in the back of her head and she flinched.

Kearn growled, his left hand shot up, and he wrapped it around Kyran's throat.

"You chose your life." Kearn's bitterness ran through her. He hated his life. She had never really suspected his feelings ran this deep. Was there nothing good about the way it had turned out for him? Wasn't she worth what he had gone through? Kearn's gaze slid to her and she felt his answer in his blood. She had made it worthwhile for him. He was grateful for her. He looked back at Kyran and choked him. "You committed sin and broke the law!"

Kearn's hand slipped from his neck and Kyran breathed deeply. A moment later, he was hitting Kearn, his face a mask of pure hatred.

"Fight me then." He punched Kearn.

Kearn didn't respond. He stared at Kyran, taking it all. It broke Amber's heart to feel his sadness and pain, and the sense of responsibility and guilt. It wasn't Kearn's fault that it had turned out like this. It was Kyran's. He had to see that. He was right and Kyran had chosen his path.

When Kyran went to punch him again, Kearn caught his hand with his right one. Kyran snatched his hand back, fear lacing his blood for a moment. He was afraid of Kearn's power. Could Kearn kill him by touching Kyran with his marked hand, just as the other Venator had killed the vampire?

If he could end it so easily, then she would give him the chance he needed.

"I do not want to kill you." Kearn clenched his fists. Amber didn't like the resignation in his voice. He was going to fight his brother whether he liked it or not, or she was going to get the other Venator in to do it for him. He would never forgive her, but it was better than watching him give up and die.

Kyran grinned.

"I do," Amber said and the smile fell off his face.

He didn't have a chance to stop her. Before he could even turn to face her, Amber had pulled the trigger. Kyran fell sideways and hit the floor. She wasn't sure where she had hit him but she didn't care. She got to her feet and aimed again.

Just as the gun was about to fire, she raised it to the ceiling. She couldn't believe she had done such a thing.

"Interfering bitch," Kyran growled and got to his feet. Blood covered his right thigh. She had shot him in the leg? She could have hit Kearn.

Kyran kicked Kearn in the side, causing him to double up, and then raised his hand. Amber dropped the gun even when she told herself not to. She wanted to pick it back up but couldn't move. Kearn groaned. Her gaze strayed to him. The connection between them was weak. Was he losing consciousness? He couldn't be. If he did that, then Kyran would win.

She gasped when she hit the wall, pinned two feet off the floor with her arms and legs spread. Kyran grinned at her, revealing his fangs.

"You are turning out to be more pain than you're worth, Lover. We shall have to see about keeping you under better control."

Her heart missed a beat. She could sense his intent. He was going to drink from her again. If he did that, he would grow stronger and Kearn wouldn't stand a chance.

Kyran's gaze stopped on her throat. He frowned.

"Dirty little bitch," he whispered. "I never thought you would go along with his desire. No matter. Your blood may be weaker now, but it will still empower me. I shall just have to take a little more than before."

Amber shook her head. If he took more than last time, she would die.

She looked past Kyran to Kearn.

She couldn't move but she couldn't let Kyran have her blood. Kearn had to get up, and he had to save her. He had promised he would keep her safe and protect her. He had to get up.

Kearn stirred, frowned, and pushed himself onto his knees and then stood.

She looked back at Kyran. His red gaze bore into her throat. She reached out to him through her blood, telling him that he wanted nothing more than to bite her and that was all that mattered now. He needed her blood. She was his for the taking.

Amber tilted her chin up, luring him in. He grinned again and stepped closer.

The moment he did, Kearn was behind him, his arm coming around and his glowing right hand pressing into Kyran's chest.

Kyran looked shocked to see it there, and then glared at her.

Amber screamed when pain burst through every cell in her body and dropped to the floor, curling up into a ball on her side. It hurt. She clenched her teeth and held herself, tears running down her temple and over her nose. It hurt so much.

The connection between her and Kyran severed and the pain eased.

Kyran cried out instead. Amber managed to open her eyes and look across at him. Kearn had him pinned to the ground, his right palm flat against his chest. There were black snake-like ribbons coming out of his arm and going into Kyran.

She flinched when the pain inside her renewed and she felt the connection to Kyran reopening.

Kyran looked at her, reaching his left hand across the rubble strewn wooden floor to her, his fingers twitching. She stared into his blue eyes, her head heavy and fuzzy, and started to reach back to him. She wanted to ease his pain by going with him into the eternal darkness. Then he wouldn't be alone.

"Leave her out of this," Kearn snarled and her head felt lighter, clearer. She took her hand back and Kyran screamed again when the black things wrapped themselves around his throat. Kearn's voice was soft as she stared into Kyran's blue eyes. "Do not let him take you... I need you."

Amber nodded and curled into a tighter ball, doing her best to fight her desire to go with Kyran. She didn't want to. Kearn had fought for her and it would be over soon. She couldn't fail him and allow him to be alone again. He needed her.

She focused on him instead, trying to open the connection between their blood. It was strong this time and comforting, and she held on to it, using it to keep her link to Kyran closed. She didn't want to go with him. She wanted to stay with Kearn forever.

Kearn's struggle filled her, his physical and emotional pain beating in her body and her heart, and she reinforced the connection between them, feeding him positive feelings to counteract the negative ones that were rampant in his blood. She knew that this was hurting him, and he didn't want to do it, but Kyran had chosen his path in life, and it had led him to this point. She didn't want Kearn to have to kill him, but he needed to in order to protect the things that he loved. She was here with him. She would be with him forever.

Her gaze flickered between Kearn and Kyran, fear crawling over her skin whenever she saw the black twisted ribbons burrowing into Kyran. He was fighting the power of the Sovereignty. She could feel it in her blood. He was reaching out to her both physically and through his blood, and she could sense that he didn't want to die, that he was afraid, and part of her desired to comfort him. His skin greyed and his eyes dulled, and tears filled her eyes as she watched him slip away. His hand fell, fingers resting limply on the floor, still reaching for her.

Her blood suddenly felt empty.

The air in the room grew colder until it was freezing and then the heat of the fire came back again, warming her chilled toes.

The connection to Kearn returned, but she couldn't feel Kyran anymore.

She stared at the grey ash form of him on the floor as it collapsed.

With a weary sigh, Kearn stood and came over to her. His pale face and the dullness in his eyes worried her as much as the pain that beat deep in his blood. She held her hand out to him and he pulled her to her feet. Her knees wobbled and she collapsed, taking Kearn down with her and landing with her back against the wall. Kearn leaned against her, holding her close, his arms tight around her. Amber rested her head on his shoulder.

"Is it over?" she whispered and stroked his silver hair, trying to soothe him.

His fatigue and distress flowed in her blood, bringing tears to her eyes. What he had done tonight would stay with him forever and she knew that he would never be able to forgive himself, even when his brother had left him no choice. She held him close to her, silently telling him through their connection that she was there to help him bear the pain and to ease his suffering, and would stay with him forever so he would never be alone. They could carry this burden together. He had done it for her, to protect her, and she loved him so much for feeling deeply enough for her to do such a thing.

Kearn murmured what she presumed was a yes. He was heavy against her and his desire for sleep ran so deep in her veins that she ached for a soft bed and warm covers. She continued to stroke his hair, smoothing away his pain and comforting him. His feelings lightened a little with each soft kiss she pressed against his hair and each whispered word of love that left her lips.

Amber's gaze fell to his arm. It was no longer glowing. The silver marks were pale against his skin, glimmering in the firelight. Kearn leaned his head against her shoulder and his weight pushed her back at an angle. His head dropped to her breasts and he murmured again. This time it sounded like approval.

Her cheeks blazed when the other Venator returned, battered and bloodied, and raised an eyebrow at her and Kearn.

"The Huntingdons have retreated, Venator Savernake," he said in a deep voice that held a note of disappointment. Had he wanted the fight to continue?

Kearn murmured again.

The other Venator's eyebrow rose higher. The doors to the grand reception room opened. Amber pushed Kearn up so he was no longer using her breasts as pillows. He frowned and then he looked at the place where he had killed Kyran and sorrow filled his green eyes. His parents entered the room and walked towards them. The other Venator saluted Kearn's father, placing a bloodied right hand against the breast of his ripped black jacket.

Kearn went to stand.

"Rest." His father sounded as weary as Kearn felt. Kearn's mother supported him, his arm around her slender shoulders. Amber could see white through his long black coat. Kearn's mother must have sealed the wounds and bandaged them.

Amber glanced at her neck and the new marks there. Kearn's mother had fed his father. Amber wanted to do the same for Kearn, restoring his strength through her blood. She touched the twin puncture marks on her throat. Would he take it if she offered? He was so tired and she had to do something to look after him.

"Father... mother..." Kearn stared at them both and then at the floor again. "I have—"

"We know." His father stopped near them. "Kyran chose his path. You have done your duty and for that we are grateful. You have protected us this night and saved our family and that of Pendragon, and even the Sovereignty. You have done well, and I am proud of you. Rest now."

Kearn nodded. Amber could feel that his father's words had meant a lot to him, but that it wasn't enough to heal the hurt in his heart. He had loved Kyran. She only hoped in time that he could come to forgive himself as his parents had forgiven him.

She stood on stronger legs this time and helped Kearn to his feet.

His parents led the way from the room and Amber took care of Kearn, holding his arm around her shoulders. She walked slowly at a pace he could maintain without weakening himself further. The gallery was quiet now but it was a mess. Glass from the smashed windows littered the hallway, deep grooves marked the walls, and blood mixed with ash on the floor. There were long streaks in it, as though someone had been dragging something. The bodies? She had noticed that only some of the vampires had turned to ash. The surviving vampires must have started clearing up the house.

She looked at the empty places where the family portraits had hung before tonight. Would Kearn's be among them again when they were restored to their places?

Would Kyran's be gone?

Even after everything he had done, there was still a part of her that wanted his painting to remain on the wall. He had been Kearn's family, and they had shared happy times before Kyran had begun to lust for power. She was sure of it.

Her gaze lingered on the wall, her head turning as she walked with Kearn, and she noticed that the other Venator was bringing up the rear. She looked at him and his green eyes met hers. They were colder than glaciers, making Kearn's look positively warm in comparison, even when she had first met him. He stared at her and then nodded, as though acknowledging her in some way. Why? Because she was Kearn's woman?

She smiled.

His look darkened and he dropped his gaze, studying the floor instead.

"Is something wrong?" Kearn whispered beside her and Amber looked back at him, and felt the other Venator's eyes on her. No, not her. On Kearn. She was feeling things through him again. "I am not sure what happened to my cousin, Traegard, but he was once a kind man."

The sense of being watched disappeared. Amber glanced back at the man in question and saw he was staring out of the windows, a distant look in his green eyes. He must have heard Kearn. She studied him, searching for the kindness Kearn had mentioned, but unable to find it. The dark aura around him chilled her and made her want to keep away from him.

Traegard touched his split lip and glanced at her, his eyes deep crimson.

Kearn stopped, turned and stared at him, his own eyes scarlet now. They stared at each other for a long minute and then Traegard's eyes faded to green and he walked past them with his head bowed.

Amber held her smile inside. Even when he was injured and tired, Kearn was still defending her. She rewarded him with a soft kiss even though the way Traegard had looked at her hadn't bothered her. She was growing used to vampires giving her hungry looks and it was far less frightening when it was one man rather than an entire ballroom.

Kearn gave her one of his own when she pulled back, his gaze lingering on her throat and the marks there. She touched them and smiled, relaying through her blood that he could drink from her again if he wanted to. A hint of a smile curved his lips and he pressed a brief kiss to her throat before walking with her again.

They stopped beneath the chandelier in the rubble strewn and blood soaked entrance hall.

Kearn's father spoke to the vampires grouped there. Many of them were badly injured and she couldn't help wondering whether they would survive, and how many the Savernake bloodline had lost tonight.

She looked at Kearn. It was difficult to see him covered in blood and with so many cuts marking his skin. She moved closer, needing to be near him and to have him know that she was with him. His beautiful green eyes slid to her and the barest hint of a smile touched his lips. He didn't need to smile for her if it hurt to do it. She could sense his relief as though it was her own.

Kearn's mother and father ascended the stairs. Amber followed with Kearn, supporting him still. Kearn stopped at the split in the stairs. He looked at his parents where they stood on the left set watching him. Amber waited, giving him time because his blood said that he needed it. He didn't need to speak. He needed to see his parents and see the love back in their eyes, and feel welcome again in his home. It was important to him.

His mother smiled and it seemed to be all that Kearn needed to see. He relaxed against Amber and she turned with him, going up the opposite staircase to his parents.

The solemn air in the house began to drift away as they walked along the gallery on the first floor and then through to the bedroom where they had been together earlier. By the time they had reached the expansive black room, Kearn was walking by himself and no longer felt as drained. She closed the door, took his hand and led him to the black double bed. He sat on the end of it and looked up at her.

"You had me scared for a moment there." She swept her fingers across his bloodied brow, brushing the hair from his eyes. They were full of love, beautiful in the way they shone with it. She smiled and stroked his cheek. "I thought I was going to lose you."

He smiled and then grimaced, and rubbed his jaw. It was bothering him. His irritation disappeared from her blood when their eyes met again.

"I should be the one saying that. What in the Devil's name compelled you to do such a thing? I told you to stay where it was safe," he said.

Amber's smile widened. She ran the backs of her fingers down his cheek and stepped closer to him, so their knees touched.

"I'm always safe with you." She pressed a kiss to his silver hair. "Someone had to stop you from being a hero."

He leaned back, evading her, and frowned.

Amber went to the bathroom, wet a black flannel, and looked at it. If they were going to live together forever, they were going to have to decorate their home more cheerily than his family's mansion. His clean white apartment, bright and spacious, had been perfect for her. Perhaps they could live there.

Having seen the mess on the walls in the reception room downstairs though, she no longer needed to guess at why he had made her close her eyes when leaving his apartment. The clean white walls were probably stark red now.

Kearn was still frowning when she walked back to him. She cleaned the blood from his face with the cloth, careful not to disturb any of the cuts in case they bled again. By the time she had finished, his frown was gone.

"Why did you leave the safe room?" His eyes searched hers.

She cleaned the blood from his neck. "I told you. I had to stop you from being a hero."

"Now tell me the real reason," he whispered and she smiled inside. She wasn't going to give him what he wanted, not even when he said it in a voice that made her quiver.

"I didn't want you to fight alone."

His frown came back. He caught her wrist, kissed her hand and then each of her fingers.

"Tell me." There was more insistence in his tone this time.

He wasn't going to get anywhere by ordering her. She would give him what he wanted, when she wanted. He kissed up her arm, luring her down at the same time. A shiver of anticipation chased ahead of him and the marks on her neck tingled at the thought of him biting her again.

"You're hurt," she said and he stopped by her shoulder. "And you're tired. I... bite me... take my blood."

He looked at her out of the corner of his eye. The edges of his irises turned red and then his eyes changed completely when his gaze moved to her neck.

"I want nothing more... and nothing less..." Kearn pulled her arm and she lost her balance and fell into him.

Before she could ask whether he was alright, she was pinned beneath him on the bed, her legs falling over the end of it with his. Kearn placed his hands on either side of her head.

"Are you afraid of me now?"

That question surprised her. He had been violent during the fight, but she knew that he would never harm her. He had only fought to protect her and she was thankful for it. She shook her head.

"I'll never be afraid of you... I only fear losing you." Her voice shook with nerves. They melted away when he smiled. She reached up and stroked his cheek before sliding her hand around the back of his neck. "I was scared that you were going to leave me."

The sorrow in his blood didn't touch his eyes but she felt it. He hadn't wanted to leave her either.

"I would have gone with you. I didn't want you to be alone." Tears filled her eyes at the thought of him dying, and of following him. "Stupid, right?"

He shook his head. "Beautiful. Exactly what I would expect from my Amber."

"I love you."

"I love you too," Kearn whispered against her lips, lowered himself and kissed her slowly.

He tasted metallic but she didn't mention it. The love and affection in his blood, and in the kiss, warmed her heart until the tears slipped down her temples and into her hair. She had been so afraid of losing him, and now she was so relieved. Her feelings were so muddled that she wasn't sure if she was coming or going yet, but there was one thing she was certain of.

And it was the one thing she knew he wanted to hear.

Kearn kissed over her jaw and down to the marks on her throat. Amber tilted her head to one side and bit her lip when his fangs penetrated her. She wrapped her arms around him, holding him close so he would never leave her and would know she didn't want to be apart from him. She opened her heart to him, held him to her throat, and sent the message through her blood to him, so he would feel it as well as hear it this time.

"Stay with me forever."

Kearn licked her throat, kissed it, and pulled her into his arms. He held her so tightly that it hurt but she smiled through the pain, lost in the depth of his love and his need for her.

Duke Montagu had been right.

She had tamed her Noble and won his heart.

In exchange, she had given hers, and stepped into a strange new world without fear, because she knew that she would always be safe with Kearn. He would never let anything happen to her. He would always love her. And she would always love him.

Kearn pulled back and smiled, causing a blush to burn her cheeks.

Amber said goodbye to her old life.

And embraced her new one, looping her arms around his neck.

She wasn't afraid of the future.

No matter what happened, it would be worth it.

Because Kearn was in it.

And he would stay with her forever.

The End

ABOUT THE AUTHOR

Felicity Heaton is a romance author writing as both Felicity Heaton and F E Heaton. She is passionate about penning paranormal tales full of vampires, witches, werewolves, angels and shape-shifters, and has been interested in all things preternatural and fantastical since she was just a child. Her other passion is science-fiction and she likes nothing more than to immerse herself in a whole new universe and the amazing species therein. She used to while away days at school and college dreaming of vampires, werewolves and witches, or being lost in space, and used to while away evenings watching movies about them or reading gothic horror stories, science-fiction and romances.

Having tried her hand at various romance genres, it was only natural for her to turn her focus back to the paranormal, fantasy and science-fiction worlds she enjoys so much. She loves to write seductive, sexy and strong vampires, werewolves, witches, angels and alien species. The worlds she often dreams up for them are vicious, dark and dangerous, reflecting aspects of the heroines and heroes, but her characters also love deeply, laugh, cry and feel every emotion as keenly as anyone does. She makes no excuses for the darkness surrounding them, especially the paranormal creatures, and says that this is their world. She's just honoured to write down their adventures.

To see her other novels, visit: http://www.felicityheaton.co.uk

To read more about the Vampires Realm series, visit the official website: http://www.vampiresrealm.com

If you have enjoyed this story, please take a moment to contact the author at author@felicityheaton.co.uk or to post a review of the book online

Follow the author on:
Her blog – http://www.indieparanormalromancebooks.com
Twitter – http://twitter.com/felicityheaton
Facebook – http://www.facebook.com/feheaton

12409718R00156